PRAISE FOR WENDY JAMES

"Australia's queen of the domestic thriller . . ."

—Angela Savage, *Books and Writing*, ABC Radio

"A master of suburban suspense."

—Cameron Woodhead, *The Age*

An Accusation

"Both gripping and timely, *An Accusation*'s sharp narrative will demand your attention from page one. Wendy James spins a web of mystery that will leave you feeling upside down, in the very best way. Highly recommend!"

—Liz Fenton and Lisa Steinke, authors of *The Two Lila Bennetts*

"*An Accusation* will grip you from page one . . . Intelligent, suspenseful, and masterfully paced, with a killer twist in the tail, *An Accusation* is domestic noir at its best, perfect for fans of Adele Parks, Caroline Overington, and Liane Moriarty."

—*Better Reading*

"James brilliantly takes this historical true crime and updates it for the internet age."

—*Sydney Morning Herald*

The Golden Child

"James invites the reader to consider a set of close relationships in all their intricacy as those involved hurtle towards an inevitable disaster. This is domestic no⋯ ⋯ intelligent and sharp."

—Su⋯ ⋯ / / *Melbourne Age*

"It takes forty-eight hours to pulse through Wendy James's roller-coaster twenty-first-century story about parenting, which begins with navigating the trick-or-treating dilemma—to accompany or not?—but climaxes with the question, What age is my child legally responsible for criminal actions? . . . A chilling novel of our time, with a truly shocking twist."

—*Australian Women's Weekly*

"This book is utterly brilliant. I just don't know where to even start with a review—it was compelling, it was tragic, it was clever, it was frightening, it was heartbreaking, it was shocking, and it gave me shivers, and it made me question myself as a parent."

—Nicola Moriarty, author, Goodreads

"An engaging and intimate read th will appeal to fans of Liane Moriarty and Jodi Picoult, with nods ionel Shriver and Christos Tsiolkas's *The Slap* . . ."

—*Australian Books + Publishing* (4 stars)

"*The Golden Child* is a gripping novel that transports the reader into the insidious world of cyberbullying and poses confronting questions about parenting."

—*Weekly Times*

"Why we love it: it's a hot topic right now—teenage girls, bullying, and the perils of social media—a topic nailed by Aussie author Wendy James in her latest novel. *The Golden Child* is a disturbing yet funny look at the age-old problem of teenage girls and the very modern problem of cyberbullying."

—Better Reading Book of the Week

The Lost Girls

"A wonderful, unputdownable story by a great Australian author."
—Liane Moriarty, *Australian Women's Weekly*

"The novel is nothing less than compelling . . . *The Lost Girls* grabs hold of you and doesn't let go—the sort of book you find yourself still reading long after you intended to put it down. In short, everything you want a novel of this kind to be."
—*Weekend Australian*

"Wendy James has again demonstrated her flair for suspenseful diversion, buttressed by her not inconsiderable literary talent."
—*Australian Book Review*

The Mistake

"*The Mistake* is a moving book that relentlessly hits the mark."
—Sue Turnbull, *Sydney Morning Herald*

"James . . . won the Ned Kelly award for first crime fiction six years ago—and she tells not just a tense and involving story, but also raises important questions about the role of the media, as the missing baby story becomes a runaway train. *The Mistake*, credible and accomplished, also asks what happens when family members begin to doubt each other, to wonder how well they know each other."
—*The Australian*

"Compelling, well paced, and suspenseful to the end."
—*Courier Mail*

"James is masterful at seamlessly ratcheting up the tension . . . Unputdownable."

—*Good Reading* magazine

"With strong characterisation and a whack of psychological suspense, it is the kind of novel that will have you second-guessing your own reactions and skillfully exposes the troubling expectations we resort to in the absence of hard evidence."

—*The Age*

"James's pacing of her plot is masterly. From less than halfway through the novel the reader has to fight an overwhelming urge to flick to the end, to take a quick test of their intuition and to assuage the escalating suspense. Resist the temptation: the end has its poignant surprises, and James knows exactly where and how to reveal them."

—*Adelaide Advertiser*

"*The Mistake* is a knockout read . . . with a plot that will haunt you long after the final pages."

—Angela Savage, broadcaster

"*The Mistake* is an expertly written, compulsively readable novel that repays the reading with rich reflection. There are no easy answers here and the multiple 'truths' of the novel are continually called into question. Everyone is culpable. There are plenty of parallels between Jodie Garrow's life and those of other real-life women who have been caught up in a media frenzy and judged based on appearance. Nevertheless, the psychological implications go beyond a political statement. This is a powerful book with broad appeal."

—Maggie Ball, *Seattle PI*

"Within its suspenseful narrative, *The Mistake* has important things to say about how we think about motherhood, how the media views women, and how, when it comes to 'the natural relationship between mother and daughter,' few can be neutral."

—Linda Funnell, *Newtown Review of Books*

"As in the public narratives we devour with tea and toast in the morning, there is nothing to convict Jodie upon except our own judgment of her character; we relish or condemn her according to our sense of moral distance from her. We take part as armchair jurors, comfortable in our own safety, never suspecting that buried secrets of our own may one day be uncovered."

—*Canberra Times*

"An amazing book that had me hooked from start to finish . . ."

—Great Aussie Reads

"Brilliant, haunting, and disturbing, with a twist that will leave you gasping, this is both a subtle and closely observed portrayal of a family under stress, and a gripping thriller that leaves you guessing to the very end."

—Sophie Masson, author

"It's sneakily challenging, disconcerting, compelling, car-crash fascinating, and probably one of the best fictional reminders I've had in a while that public and media opinion should never be mistaken for the justice system, regardless of the ultimate outcome."

—AustCrimeFiction.org

"It's hands down one of the best endings I've read in a book, possibly ever."

—*1girl2manybooks*

Where Have You Been?

"*Where Have You Been?* is a novel you'll not want to put down."
—*Australian Bookseller & Publisher*

"The narrative's power and cumulative suspense call to mind Alfred Hitchcock's *Vertigo*."
—Sara Dowse, *Sydney Morning Herald*

"Wendy James's third novel is structured like a symphony . . . Skillful structuring, fine, flexible writing, and suspense that comes to a satisfying, if not limitingly cut-and-dried, conclusion, make this social-realist novel as hard to put down as any thriller."
—Katharine England, *Adelaide Advertiser*

Why She Loves Him

"Emotionally astute, vivid, and eloquent, underpinned by eroticism, James's fiction traces the contours of her characters' lives as they grapple with responsibility, freedom, and love, propelled by multifarious desires. These fresh, sensuous stories are by turns witty, perceptive, and coruscating, many with a delicious wry twist."
—Felicity Plunkett, critic

"Absolutely amazing . . . There is something for everyone in this fantastic book."
—*Australian Bookseller & Publisher*

A
LITTLE
BIRD

ALSO BY WENDY JAMES

A

LITTLE

BIRD

A NOVEL

WENDY JAMES

LAKE UNION
PUBLISHING

Published by Lake Union Publishing, Seattle

www.apub.com

Amazon, the Amazon logo, and Lake Union Publishing are trademarks of Amazon.com, Inc., or its affiliates.

33614082961466

ISBN-13: 9781542026482
ISBN-10: 1542026482

Cover design by Faceout Studio, Lindy Martin

Printed in the United States of America

To Mark and Marie—always transcendent.

For a bird of the air shall carry the voice, and that which hath wings shall tell the matter.

—*Ecclesiastes 10:20*

PART ONE

PART ONE

PROLOGUE

Arthurville, 1994

My mother took the Mini—a '74 model with squeaky brakes, balding tyres, and 120,000 miles on the odometer. Our "good" car, a fifteen-year-old Falcon station wagon, was out of action. The lights had been left on overnight, the battery was dead, and there was no spare cash to replace it. Dad was on an out-of-town shift and didn't like to leave Mum without a car, so he'd cycled to the station on his dodgy old bike.

I left for school just before eight thirty. I was running late (I was always running late) and was glad to escape the noise and the mess and my mother's irritability. Amy was crying (Amy was always crying), she needed feeding (she always needed feeding), and my mother's goodbye had been perfunctory (as her interactions always were since Amy had arrived): a distracted wave, *See you later, have a nice day*.

According to the initial police report, Bev Ryan, who lived across the road, was walking into town for a cut and colour at nine thirty, and had passed by just in time to see Mum close the front door, carry the car seat to the rear of the little pale-blue car, and clip it in. Bev had said hello, peered at the sleeping baby through the window—*What a sweet little thing, all that gorgeous hair*—and walked on.

Lionel Perkins, who had the garage on the corner, had seen her drive past not long after. He'd admired her profile—she was still a looker, despite the two kids—as well as her smooth gear change. You could always tell a farm girl.

She'd waved to Val Darrow, who was sweeping the pavement outside Martin's Newsagency. Val had seen the greeting but ignored it, for reasons that even she couldn't fathom. Ray Yee, stacking apples out the front of Yee's Olde Fruit Shoppe, had seen her turn left onto the main road, heading towards the highway. He'd waved, but too late for her to wave back.

She'd stopped at the BP on the outskirts of town, where Mervyn Ebsworth filled the tank for her. He'd offered to check the oil, the tyres, but she'd already checked them herself. Mervyn, a shy man, especially when it came to women, hadn't said much, but he'd noticed the baby, still rosily asleep in her capsule, and told her that he and his wife had just had their fourth, about the same age, a boy, Timothy. She'd asked him to pass on her regards to Shirley.

She'd passed Errol Simmons and his wife, Wendy, on the highway. They were coming in from Haringey to take Wendy's mother to the hospital. It was the fourth emergency trip they'd made in the last two months. The other three had turned out to be indigestion, but better safe than sorry. Errol recognised the Mini immediately: he'd sold it to my father five years before for a bit too much—it had been his kids' runaround, was well past its use-by date—and had always felt vaguely guilty about it.

Phil Coombes, local stock and station agent, had been heading to town on the back road from Dalhunty. He'd seen Mum waiting at the intersection when he'd turned back onto the highway. He'd flashed his lights, grinned—he'd known her since they were kids, had worked as a jackaroo for her old man—but she hadn't returned his smile, just lifted two fingers off the steering wheel in acknowledgement. He'd watched in his rearview mirror as she put the little car into gear and turned left onto Oxley Road. She was heading east, following the path of the river back towards its source.

How was Phil to know that he would be the last person to see her that day? That he would be the last person to see her at all before she became a headline?

There'd been no signs, no portents.

Or none that any of us had seen, at least—not even me, not even in retrospect.

CHAPTER ONE

A LITTLE BIRD

The community New Year celebrations were a great success—with hundreds of happy Arthurvilleans attending the big BBQ and stalls held at the showground yesterday. The nine-o'clock fireworks were spectacular, but the pony rides provided unexpected entertainment. ~~Especially when Mayor Bob Swalwell went arse over tit on some poor little pony that he should never have been allowed to ride and landed right where he belonged, in six inches of horseshit.~~ The vision of a certain well-known local personage (a high-ranking public official, no less) flying over the top of one reluctant pony's head straight into six inches of mud provided the crowd with some unexpected entertainment.

A Little Bird, *Arthurville Chronicle*, 1992

Jo

Arthurville, 2018

The sky outside the car changes just as I get to the Wellesley Road turnoff—lowering and darkening as if an enormous cloud has settled overhead—and I wind the window down to smell the air. According to the weather report, there is no chance of rain, not for months, but perhaps miracles are still possible.

Or maybe not. The blast of air that hits me is so hot, so cruelly dry, that it is almost impossible to breathe. I close the window fast and turn the air-con up a notch.

No rain.

No rain no rain no rain no rain.

I watched that old Woodstock video at least a dozen times with my father. When I say I watched it with him, I mean we were there together in the room. On every occasion, he was at least half-pissed, barely aware of me curled up on the lounge beside him, trying to be companionable, hoping for a crumb of affection. A crumb that was never offered.

I think about that guy in the documentary now—the one with the microphone. His optimism came straight from the pages of Peter Pan: *Hey, if you think really hard, maybe we can stop this rain?* And the crowd responded with appropriately childlike enthusiasm.

No rain no rain no rain no rain.

The chant worked its magic back then: the rain cleared, the show went on.

The landscape on either side of the red-dirt verge—low grey scrub, yellowing paddocks—bears no resemblance to that muddy New York field. Here, there's been no rain for months. If only the spell could be reversed. Perhaps the desperate chanting of half a million stoned and half-naked young bodies would do the trick, but there's no chance of that happening out here.

It will be a good omen if my return to Arthurville coincides with a downpour, if my arrival heralds the end of the drought. God knows I need something—some sign—to show that I've made the right decision, that I'm not just slinking back, tail between my legs, with nothing to show for all my time in the city—if not a failure, no great success either.

And maybe, just maybe, if I bring the rain with me, the magic will transfer to my own life too.

By the time I pull up in the driveway, it's dark—the sky that deep purple-blue that you only ever see west of the Great Dividing Range. The air is perfectly clear, the innumerable stars close and bright. Maybe I imagined those clouds.

I turn off the ignition and sit in the car for a long moment, enjoying the last of the cool air.

Nothing has changed since I was home last. In fact, nothing has changed since my childhood either. A cracked concrete path neatly dissects the front yard, which is now completely bereft of any vegetation, including grass; the west-facing verandah still displays the cast-iron Italianate three-piece setting Dad inherited from my grandmother, and that no one, as far as I know, has ever used. The blinds are down and the front porch light is off. Well, why would it be any different? I didn't tell him I was coming. I haven't told anyone. What am I doing here?

Welcome home, Jo. I try saying the words brightly, and without irony. As if I mean them.

~

Alligator rushes to greet me as I start up the path. He gives two sharp barks and then falls silent, crouching down on his front paws, whining softly, his tail thumping, not taking his eyes off me as I kneel down to pet him. I push my face into his short bristles, gone from blue to grey now, and breathe in his familiar doggy smell. I stand up slowly. Okay, Gator. Time to face the music.

The front door is unlocked. I trace my fingers along the velvety wallpaper as I creep down the hall, the dog padding silently behind me. Dad is sitting in the lounge room. Other than the light from the television—a new flat-screen, the sound muted—the room is dark. There's a bottle of whiskey on the table beside him, a tall glass—almost empty—a half-full ashtray, and a packet of Winfield reds. The old window Breezair is chugging away desperately, but the air is thick and stale.

I take a deep breath. "Dad?" It comes out too quietly. I try again. This time it's too loud. "Dad?"

He looks up, clearly surprised.

"Jo?"

"The one and only."

His smile is bitten back almost as soon as it appears, but it's more than I expect. I breathe out.

"What're you sitting in the dark for?"

"Waiting for someone to change the bulb."

"Anyone in particular?"

"You'll do."

~

"So what are you doing here?"

I've carted in my luggage, changed the light bulb, and poured myself a drink. Dad is back in his recliner, a cigarette burning between his lips, his whiskey glass topped up. Alligator is lying on the carpet, his head on his paws, his rheumy eyes shifting back and forth between the two of us, following the conversation.

"I've got a job. On the *Chronicle*."

"You're shitting me? The last I heard they were closing it down. Didn't think anyone read it anymore."

"It's being run by a community board now. It's . . . like a nonprofit, I suppose. Just community news."

He snorts. "Right. Drought, drug busts, and bankruptcies?"

"Well, no. I think they're more interested in the good news."

"What—half a page a month then. Not much good news out here."

"Probably not. Anyway—it's a paying job."

"Lost yours, did you?" He shakes his head, doesn't wait for my answer. "I was wondering how long it'd last." Then, as if it's only just occurred to him: "And what happened to your fella? William, was it?"

"Harry. It ended."

"Did he run off with your best mate? Your savings? Did he hit you?"

"Jesus, Dad. No. Do you really have to— It's just . . . it was complicated."

He snorts again. "Complicated, eh? And what does *complicated* mean when it's at home?"

I shrug, gulp down a mouthful of whiskey. It burns my throat, stings my eyes.

"Well, I hope it was worth not speaking to your old man for two bloody years." He glares.

"As I recall, you weren't speaking to me either, Dad." I mutter the words, reduced to my sullen fifteen-year-old self in almost record time.

He looks at me for a long moment, then shakes his head. "Your taste in men is in your arse, Jojo."

I take a deep breath in. Count to five. Breathe out slowly. "I wonder why?" My smile is saccharine.

He changes the subject, as I knew he would.

"You hungry?"

"A bit."

"Enough of this BS then." He pries the glass from my hand. "We better go sort you a feed before you start shouting at me."

~

My father is right. I am shit at choosing men. And *complicated* is a highly euphemistic description of my breakup with Harry.

My father met him only once, during a rare visit to Sydney when we were first going out, but he saw through Harry right away. Dad immediately recognised him as the self-serving, if well-dressed, scoundrel that he is, but it took me longer—two years longer, in fact—to see what lay beneath Harry's good looks, glib charm, and quick wit. What initially appealed to me as an attractive certainty about what he wanted and where he was going had gradually revealed itself as nothing more than a self-serving egotism that wasn't compatible with any sort of long-term relationship.

My father had travelled down to Sydney to see an old mate, and we'd met him for drinks at a city bar that Harry and the rest of his financier friends frequented. I should have realised that the venue was all wrong, that my father would feel like a fish out of water. Dad, who was wearing jeans and a flannelette shirt and a pair of old work boots, stuck out like the proverbial dunny in the desert. Harry, who could be charming, did his best hail-fellow-well-met routine, but Dad wasn't charmed. It hadn't been obvious: he'd accepted Harry's proffered schooner of expensive artisanal beer, taken a few bites of the bar food, and had seemed relaxed enough that I relaxed too. The conversation between the two men had been stilted at times, but Dad had laughed at Harry's jokes, listened to his stories, engaging with him in a way that surprised me. He didn't even say anything inappropriate or speak too loudly. He even managed to tone down his sometimes deliberately hokey drawl. Despite my initial misgivings, I assumed that it was all going well. But when Harry left to get another round, my father put his glass down and looked hard at me. "Josephine, you know I don't like to interfere; it's your life."

"What's wrong?" My father's lack of interference had in fact been a bone of contention between us since my teenage years—sometimes it felt like neglect. Dad's interest in my doings was rare—restricted to moments of bad or dangerous risky behaviour—and inevitably meant some sort of negative judgement was coming my way.

"This bloke, Harry. He's bad news."

"You've only just met him."

"He's a wanker. He's arrogant, and he's trouble."

"For fuck's sake, Dad. You think that anyone who wears a suit to work is a wanker."

"No, love. I just have an unerring sense of bullshittery—and believe me, that fella is full of it." Dad shook his head. "You've got your head up your arse if you can't see it, Jo."

I tried hard to contain it, but the resentment, never far away when it came to my father, quickly surfaced.

"That's crap, Dad. Your so-called bullshit detector is just a garden-variety chip on your shoulder. Talk about having your head up your arse: this isn't about Harry or me—it's about you."

The conversation had gone further downhill from there. And rapidly. By the time Harry came back with the tray of drinks, my father had gone, his parting words as angry as mine. I can't remember all we'd said—though I do recall that I'd told him that I wanted nothing to do with him if he was going to continue being nothing but a negative influence in my life, and Dad rejoining that I wasn't to bring that cockhead if I did deign to visit: he wouldn't have him in the house. In fact, he'd added, I shouldn't even bother coming home until I woke up to myself.

In a way it was nothing new—we'd fought as viciously a thousand times since I hit adolescence—but his final words had hit a nerve. And there'd been no apology. No retraction. I haven't been in contact with him for almost two years.

But here I am, home.

For reasons that go beyond my father, and that cockhead.

Reasons that I'm not willing to advertise to anyone, especially not my father. Reasons that I'm barely willing to admit, even to myself.

I'd visited the medium just after I'd ended things with Harry. The visit had been made on an impulse, and with no particular expectations. One of my workmates had told me that she'd found it helpful after her marriage broke down, better than a psychologist. "I really wasn't interested in hearing about what was wrong with me—I wanted to know where to go next, if you know what I mean. How to move on."

That was what I needed—some guidance as to where I needed to go next, what I should focus on. Even though our relationship had ultimately become toxic, without the structures that scaffolded even a bad relationship, I was drifting, floundering. I thought perhaps a medium would be able to give me a clue. It was worth a try, anyway.

The medium's website had featured angels' wings and signs of the moon, and mentions of spirit guides and psychic healing—but the little blonde lady in a neat brick suburban house wasn't what I was expecting when I made the appointment. The woman was brisk but friendly. She had a tidy bob, was wearing tights and a T-shirt—a fringed satin housecoat her only concession to anything even vaguely bohemian. She invited me in and led me up a carpeted hallway, calling out as we passed through a lounge room, where a couple of teenagers sat playing Fortnite. "I've got a customer, boys. So if you need anything, you'll have to get it yourselves." One of the boys grunted something unintelligible; neither of them looked up. She gave a resigned sigh. "School holidays. That's all they do. I wish they'd go outside and—I don't know—ride their bikes or something."

She led me into a cosy sunroom—the walls painted a pale blue— with a small sofa and two pale lounge chairs, pretty floral cushions. It was so bright and cheery that I wondered momentarily whether I'd come to the wrong place—perhaps I'd gotten the address wrong and inadvertently turned up at a psychologist's rooms, or an accountant's— or perhaps a hairdresser's. There was no sink, no shampoo, no cutting implements, but where were the crystal balls, the tarot cards, the signs that she could commune with the dead?

"Take a seat, love."

I sat on the sofa, and she took the seat across from me.

"Now, what can I do for you?"

I had to ask.

"You are Aura, aren't you? I am in the right place?"

She laughed. "You are. Actually, my real name is Deb-*orah*." She emphasised the final syllables. "But Aura sounds better for a psychic, don't you think? More what people expect."

"I suppose. But—well, you're not—it's not what I was expecting, to be honest. I mean, I've never been to a psychic before, but I was expecting something, I don't know, a bit different."

She wrinkled her nose. "I know. But what can I do? I'm not interested in being all woo-woo—and as you can see, I'm not exactly exciting or glamorous or exotic myself. I'm basically your stock standard soccer mum. Maybe with a few extra pounds.

"The thing is"—she put her chin on her hand, looked at me seriously—"life and death happen the same to everyone, don't they? Soccer mums, and people who work at supermarkets or who do office jobs, they aren't somehow immune to tragedy. It's not like it's reserved for special, smart, interesting people. And so I figure there's no reason someone like me shouldn't have this gift. It's chosen me, if you know what I mean."

I nodded, impressed by the woman's unexpected eloquence.

"And that also means I don't get to choose who I share it with. I mean, I do, in a sense, because I generally only offer my services for money—anyone who's willing to cross my palm with silver. I'm a medium, not a breatharian. And teenage boys cost a bit to keep."

She took a breath, smiled. "Anyway. What is it you're here for—and no, I can't tell." She rolled her eyes theatrically.

"I've just broken up with my partner, and . . ." Suddenly I was at a loss for words. What, exactly, did I want?

The woman gave a sympathetic smile. "And you want to know whether there's any hope?"

"Oh, God, no. It's over. I don't want him back."

"So is there someone else . . . ?"

"No, it's nothing like that. There's no one else." I laughed, embarrassed. "To be honest, I don't really know what it is I want."

"Perhaps that's why you're here?"

"Actually . . ." Maybe there *was* something I wanted, perhaps more than future directions. A message from the past. I cleared my throat. "There is something. I'm worried about someone, someone I haven't heard from for a long time. Years and years. But I'm pretty sure they're alive, to be honest. I mean, I hope they are."

Aura frowned. "If it's something criminal, I don't do that sort of thing. You should go to the police."

"Oh, no. It's not a crime. It's my mum—she left us years ago. When I was eight. With my sister. She left a letter—but that was it. We've never heard from her since. Maybe you could give me some idea of where she is. Maybe that's what I need to focus on now."

I gave a nervous laugh, knowing how silly it sounded. But the woman wasn't laughing.

"Oh, you poor thing. Your mum and your sister. I can't imagine. All this time not hearing from them. That must be so hard."

I tried to smile. "You get used to it. I was very young."

Aura was looking thoughtful. "It's not something I usually do. There *are* people—psychic detectives, they call them. They work with police sometimes. Frankly, I think it's rubbish. They're never ever right as far as I can see."

"Really? Never? I'm sure I've read things where they've found—"

"Occasionally they'll find a . . . resting place. Which makes sense—but half the time they claim to be communing with spirits, the people are just as likely to be alive, if you see what I mean."

16

"So you can't communicate with . . . live people? Your website says you do psychic guidance."

"That's a bit different—that's more like an intuition. That's why I asked if it was about a man. You ask me whether your boyfriend, say, is cheating on you—and I might be able to pick up a sense of what's going on. Or whether there's some hope for the future. But there needs to be some sort of a connection—emotional and physical—through you. But you haven't seen your mother for so long—so the connection might not be there anymore."

"Oh, I see." It was hard to keep the disappointment out of my voice.

The look the woman gave me was full of sympathy. She bit her lip. "Well, I suppose I can try. But don't expect too much."

"I don't have anything of hers, I'm afraid."

The woman laughed again. "I'm a medium, sweetheart, not a beagle. But maybe . . . I don't suppose you have a photo?"

I kept a photo of the two of them, taken a few months after Amy's birth, in my wallet. Mum is sitting on a park swing, clutching a smiling Amy in her lap. The colours had faded and the photograph was worn. I handed it over to Aura, who looked at it for a long moment. "They look lovely. Your mother's so beautiful. You must miss her. You must miss them both."

I nodded.

She closed her eyes for a few seconds, opened them again. "Maybe if you . . . Can you tell me a bit about your mum?"

Where to begin? "Well, you can see she was blonde, small. Beautiful. Nothing like me. She had me when she'd just finished high school, and her family threw her out. She grew up on a farm . . . her family are rich, snobby, and Mum, well, she didn't do what was expected, I guess. She could be very spontaneous. And funny. She had a bad temper, sometimes. She . . ." I faltered, running out of things to say. As always, it was impossible to get a fix on her. To find anything tangible. She was a set of stories, not even real memories anymore. And not all the stories were even my own. What was the point? There was nothing solid about my mother, nothing real. Not anymore. I had no idea whom I was looking for.

Aura's eyes had closed again. She was swaying back and forth gently; her breath had deepened. I watched, feeling strangely uncomfortable.

Her breathing quietened, softened. The swaying stopped. She opened her eyes and blinked. It took her a long time to focus. Eventually she handed back the photograph. She gazed down, pressed her hands against the table. When she finally looked up, she was smiling, but she didn't quite meet my eyes.

"So? Did you . . . feel anything?"

"I did. But to be honest, I don't know quite what it was."

"But can you tell where she is? Whether she's okay?"

The woman frowned. "Yes. No. I don't know. There's something wrong—some terrible sadness. Some pain. But there would be, wouldn't there?" The idea seemed to be a relief. "Of course, that's what it is. She must miss you terribly." She brightened. "And I had a sense of someone else, close to her. A child. Your sister, I expect."

"And could you tell where they were? Were there any clues?" It was impossible to keep the eagerness out of my voice. I didn't believe a word of it, not really. But what if she had seen something—some sign?

"It was odd. The picture was very . . . muddy. It felt submerged, and rippling—it had a watery feel somehow. It's hard to explain." She sat up straight, her voice brisk, now. "Maybe she lives on the coast? It was murky. And deep. A river, or a lake, maybe."

"Oh." It was all so vague.

"I know. I'm sorry it's not clearer."

"Was there anything else?"

"Well, there's something. But I don't know that it's really all that helpful. It's a feeling I'm getting about you."

"About me?"

"Yes. I don't quite understand it myself." She looked doubtful.

"What is it?"

"I'm not sure it's something you really want to hear, darling."

"What do you mean?"

"You didn't grow up in the city, did you?"

"No. I'm from a small town out west. Arthurville. Nowheresville."

"The thing is, I'm getting a strong feeling that you need to go home. That the answers are there."

I'd tried to laugh it off. It was the last thing I'd expected to hear. And the last thing I'd wanted.

Merry

Arthurville, 1985

Merry was a childhood nickname—her older brother Roland's tangled version of Miranda—one that stuck despite, or perhaps because of, the distance between the name and the reality.

Truth was she was far from being merry, even as a child. She wasn't melancholy, exactly—she rarely cried or complained—but you wouldn't call her cheerful. She didn't bring sunshine and laughter into a room, the way a name like that might suggest. She was watchful. She was determined. And she was brave. She hadn't needed any sort of comforter as a baby—dummies were spat out, blankets ignored, teddy bears were flung from the cot. Even as a very small child, she'd take a tumble from a horse and clamber back up without a murmur, grim faced, resolute. Skin her knee and she'd refuse a Band-Aid. She was never aggressive herself, but no one ever bullied her in the schoolyard. She received the ruler once or twice for some nastiness or other—stood in front of the teacher and took a thwack on the hand without flinching.

She stood up to her parents, too, against any perceived unfairness or occasional ill treatment. Her parents weren't abusive; they weren't even especially bad parents, if you took the context of the times and the peculiarities of their class into account, but they were remote—and they could be hard. They were the sort of parents who expected compliance, conformity, and a reasonable level of success from their progeny. Along with hard work and loyalty. Encouragement and approval were never overtly expressed—they were the Beauforts of Pembroke, and nothing more needed to be said. It was a little like being royalty—you were part of a line, not an ordinary family—and that meant doing what was necessary, what was required, what was best for the collective, not the individual—the alternative was unthinkable.

For most of her early life, what was necessary and what Merry wanted more or less aligned, so compliance was easy. Her parents' benign neglect suited her. She wasn't particularly needy, she was smart, she liked to be physically active—a day rambling about the property on her pony suited her well enough, and if she was asked to pitch in during the shearing season or distribute feed in winter, she didn't complain.

The two children were sent to the local Arthurville primary school—more than an hour each way on the rattly school bus. The school wasn't really ideal—the area was impoverished, the teachers generally young and inexperienced. According to their father, most of the other pupils were simpletons, but there was no point spending money on a private tutor when they only needed to learn the basics. Anyway, Merry was bright enough academically—a consistently A-grade student without too much effort.

They made friends with the local kids but never got too close, their parents disinclined to drive them into town for birthday parties or sporting events or after-school activities. Not that there were that many of those on offer, not in Arthurville in the seventies and eighties. There was usually work to do at home on the weekends anyway—fun wasn't a priority. And if socialising was on the agenda, the townsfolk weren't the first port of call—there were people of their own class to invite for tennis matches and dinner parties and barbecues.

Their father died just as Merry hit adolescence. He'd been an older father—already in his fifties when he married her mother, a distant cousin—and he'd been a remote, distracted parent. Roly was devastated, but her father's absence made very little impact on Merry. Her mother had taken over the running of the property with a single-minded devotion that meant that the needs and desires of the children were of even less consequence—although her brother, as putative heir, enjoyed certain privileges. Once they reached high school, the two children were sent away to board at the same Sydney private schools that their parents and grandparents had attended, and from there on in, Merry's narrative should have followed a predictable trajectory—university, respectable work, a suitable marriage, children—this was the life she'd been brought up to expect, the life that her social position, and even her mother, in her offhand way, had mapped out for her. And if she was honest, it was the life she'd imagined herself.

But then she met Mick.

And that was when a lifetime of expectations and Merry's own desires parted company. Where one story ended and another began.

Jo

Arthurville, 2018

Dad's virtual silence after my mother's disappearance meant that I'd grown up knowing very little about her. The fragments I'd learned—what she had been like, what she was good at, what her interests were, her talents—had only ever been given grudgingly. I knew not to ask too much, knew that to pester him about Mum would lead to a swift closing down or, worse, anger. I'd learnt not to ask too much—or only ever tangentially. I'd ask other people whenever I got the opportunity—Nan and Pop, Kirsty, other friends' parents—everyone was kind, but no one seemed to know her well. There was my other grandmother, her mother, and her brother, but even though they lived in the area, contact was impossible, for reasons I never properly understood.

Initially, I'd had my memories of my mother—what she looked like, how she sounded, how she smelled—but all this had gradually disappeared—replaced eventually by what were more like untethered moments, images, fragments. Anything solid—like my memory of my final goodbye—became more like memories of memories. I had no recollection of her working at the paper, for instance, no real concept of her working at all—though surely that had been something that I'd known when she left, that everyone had known. I must have spent time in that office with her, called in on odd occasions. But I couldn't remember any of it.

I had an album of pictures that my grandmother had put together for me in the year after she left. There weren't that many—some blurry snaps of her and Dad when they were first together—at the river, at a party, out at the dam waterskiing with friends. There were a few of her and Dad from their wedding, which had been held when Mum was obviously pregnant, both of them still looking ridiculously adolescent. And then photos of Mum with me, as a newborn—Mum looking a little shell-shocked, and bizarrely young, still no more than a child herself. In all these early photos, my father looks deliriously happy—grinning from ear to ear, his arms around Mum or holding me, obviously proud of his beautiful wife and his little daughter. A father I don't remember. In most of the shots, Mum is smiling, but the smile seems a little half-hearted, put on—maybe it's just the awkward smile of a girl who's uncomfortable with being the centre of attention. Maybe she was sad, suddenly missing her own family, or perhaps she was regretting the whole thing: Dad, the wedding, her future. Me. Or maybe I'm just imagining it. I'd asked Nan once whether Mum had been happy on her wedding day, and she'd laughed and said that no bride was ever really happy. Weddings were full of anxiety; something always went wrong: a broken zipper, a missing ring, a drunken bridegroom, embarrassing speeches, not enough food. So many of my questions about my mother were deflected like this or answered only in the vaguest and most general terms—Nan never told me anything solid, anything meaningful. It took me years to realise that this was only because my grandmother hadn't known what to tell me. In all the important ways, she'd barely known my mother.

The remainder of the photos were of me and Mum—most were just ordinary scenes of everyday family life, candid shots. Me as a baby, clinging on to my absurdly young mother, like a little koala. Mum bathing me in the old laundry tub, pushing me on my trike. Me sitting on Mum's lap while she read to me, holding her hand on my first day of school. Snaps taken around the Christmas tree or at the beach during one of our rare seaside holidays. Others were more formal—taken at school events—the Easter-hat parade, awards nights, the end-of-year play.

I had nothing that had belonged to her. She'd taken a small suitcase of belongings with her when she left, and Dad got rid of the rest of her possessions when it was clear she wasn't coming back. The album was all I had.

From as far back as I could remember, I'd constructed fantasies of her life, of Amy's life—the two of them living in an apartment in New York, Mum an artist, or maybe a writer; or the two of them living in a coastal town, up north, Mum running a little restaurant. Or Mum, somehow retrained as a doctor, working in a hospital, delivering babies, remarried, living in a big house in the suburbs, with her doctor husband. She would have a pool, a family room, air-conditioning, a caravan and a holiday house, trips overseas. I would try not to think about the fact that wherever she was, she'd gone without me. I kept waiting for a call, a letter—for her return. Because despite the fact that my memories of her had almost faded away, there was one thing I was certain of—my mother had loved me.

~

Unlike so many other "true crime" cold cases, there are no websites dedicated to the story of my mother and sister's vanishing, no mentions, as far as I can find, in any books about unsolved disappearances, no theorising about their fate by curious strangers on any dark corner of the web. It seems the kind of story that's ripe for such sensationalised speculations, but no journalist has ever revisited the case, looked into whether my mother had returned to her kith and kin, whether she'd been located, whether there'd been any sort of happy ending.

Once the two letters appeared, the case had been closed—and not just closed but forgotten. It had been left to those of us involved, those of us who knew Mum, to wonder just where she'd gone—and more important—when she'd come back.

~

When I was fifteen, I'd wanted desperately to find out about, and secretly perhaps even find, my mother. I'd gone to the Arthurville library and asked one of the librarians what I needed to do to find old newspaper articles. I'd already searched the internet, but this was early days, long before the true-crime craze, and there were no mentions of my mother. Her disappearance, which was, in the end, found to be completely voluntary, simply wasn't interesting enough. The newspapers I wanted—going back to the 1980s—weren't available online, simultaneously too far back and not far back enough to be available in archives.

Back then, the librarian, who was an Arthurville local who had known my mother, looked at me with concern—she knew exactly what I was after and why. She didn't ask questions, though, had kindly explained how to use the microfilm reader and supplied me with microfilm for every newspaper the library stocked, from the *Chronicle* to the big-city tabloids, and ranging from the week she went missing to the date the investigation was closed.

Eventually I found what I was looking for. I read through the newspaper articles about her disappearance, the reports on the search, the initial suspicions surrounding my father—and then the end of the investigation, when Mum's note to Dad was discovered and her letter to my grandmother arrived. After checking handwriting and typing, the police concluded that Mum had gone of her own free will, and the investigation was called off. I discovered nothing that I didn't already know: Dad, and the wider community, hadn't kept anything from me. It turned out I knew as much as anyone else. The only thing I learned was that Mum taking Amy was considered a custody issue—something I had never heard mentioned.

WOMAN AND CHILD MISSING

Western district police are appealing for urgent public assistance to help find a missing woman and her infant daughter, missing since they left their Arthurville home on Wednesday morning. Miranda Sharpe, 28, and her daughter Amy, six months, were last seen leaving their home on Piercy Street, Arthurville, at around 9:30 a.m. Police hold concerns for the pair's well-being.

Mrs. Sharpe is five foot two, slightly built, with fair shoulder-length hair and blue eyes. At the time of her disappearance, she was wearing a green knitted jumper, black jeans and a black beret with a white flower brooch. Amy has hazel eyes and curly red/brown hair. When last seen, she was wearing a white Bonds wondersuit.

Mrs. Sharpe was seen by neighbours leaving her home with her daughter in a pale-blue 1974 Mini, number plate MKY 505. She was reported missing later that day.

Anyone with any information about the pair's whereabouts should contact Sergeant Les Anderson of the Western district police on (02) 4532 2220.

SEARCH CONTINUES FOR ARTHURVILLE WOMAN AND CHILD

Police again call for witnesses to come forward as search for missing Arthurville mother and child intensifies.

Twenty-eight-year-old Miranda Sharpe and her infant daughter, Amy, have not been seen since last Wednesday. According to witnesses, Mrs. Sharpe left her home with her baby daughter at 9:30 a.m. on July 24 in a pale-blue Mini, number plate MKY 505. She was last sighted heading south on Dalhunty Road, near the corner of Dalhunty Road and Oxley Road at 9:40 a.m.

Police hold grave fears for the pair's safety. Anyone with any information should contact Inspector Dan Smythe of NSW Missing Persons Bureau, 02 9222 2634 . . .

MAN QUESTIONED BY POLICE AFTER WIFE AND IN-FANT DAUGHTER GO MISSING

An Arthurville man has been released after being questioned by the police over the disappearance of his wife and daughter. According to a police source, Mr. Michael Sharpe, 29, "is no longer a suspect" in the disappearance of his wife, Miranda "Merry" Sharpe (28), and their six-month-old daughter, Amy. The mother and infant have not been seen since they left their Arthurville house on July 24. Mrs. Sharpe was driving a pale-blue '70s model Mini—number plate MKY 505.

NEW EVIDENCE IN ARTHURVILLE MISSING MUM AND CHILD CASE

Two letters have led to the investigation into the disappearance of a missing Arthurville woman being called off.

Police sources have revealed that a farewell letter, written by Miranda Sharpe, who disappeared with her infant daughter, Amy, in July this year, has been discovered in her family home. A second letter, sent from a Gold Coast postcode, has also been received by her mother. While neither of the letters has been made public, handwriting and type experts have confirmed that both letters were written by Mrs. Sharpe.

While efforts to contact the woman have not been successful, police say the letters have satisfied them that the woman's disappearance is entirely voluntary, and that there is no evidence of foul play. Despite taking their daughter without the permission of her husband, detectives say Mrs. Sharpe will not face charges of kidnapping. Detective Inspector Dan Smith from the state Missing Persons Bureau said, "Of course people do have the right to leave and make their own lives wherever they wish, whatever the sadness involved. However, because the custody and safety of a minor is involved, we would encourage Mrs. Sharpe to make contact with family and friends or the authorities as soon as she can." When questioned by reporters, Mr. Michael Sharpe, the woman's husband and father of the missing infant, refused to comment.

Over the years, I'd continued to search her name—and every variation I could think of: Miranda Sharpe, Miranda Ruth Sharpe, Miranda Beaufort, Merry Sharpe, Merry Beaufort, Merry Beau, Miranda Fort. I'd spent time looking for Amy, too, had searched for both names together. A search for both names had once linked to a story about a mother and child in South Australia, a woman who'd been interviewed for some story about Adelaide private schools—they'd seemed like the right age, a possibility. But further searches had linked to photographs of a woman and child who were most definitely not my mother and sister. I'd extended my searches globally, but there'd been nothing. No matter where I looked, I found nothing but circuitous byways leading to dead ends.

But hope doesn't rely on possibilities or probabilities or proof—all it needs is a ready heart, an open mind.

CHAPTER TWO

A LITTLE BIRD

Preparations are already underway for this year's Arthurville Agricultural Show. The Miss Showgirl competition has had record entries—almost as many as the past three years combined. This may have something to do with the fact that for the first time the event has been open to girls aged 16 to 25—previously only 16- to 18-year-olds have been able to enter—and the introduction of a "Talent Test"—candidates must now prepare either a speech or a musical item—and not just provide a pretty face. Some residents have expressed considerable disappointment that the bikini girl parade has been mothballed. ~~As one prominent Arthurville citizen griped—I only go for the boobs.~~

A Little Bird, *Arthurville Chronicle*, 1993

Jo

Arthurville, 2018

The job found me. Out of the blue, I'd received an email from the Committee of the Arthurville Community Taskforce, asking if I'd like to interview for the position of journalist on the newly reconstituted *Arthurville Chronicle*. It had come at the perfect time, and I'd replied in the affirmative. The phone interview had been conducted the very next day.

The voice on the other end of the phone wasn't one I recognised.

"Hello, Jo."

"Hello."

"You don't remember me, do you?"

"I'm sorry." The voice was reedy, old. Maybe female, but I couldn't be certain.

"It's Mrs. Darling, love. Eileen Darling."

Mrs. Darling, or Aunty Eileen, as she was known, was a local icon—she'd been one of the first Wiradjuri students to do teacher training, had eventually come back to teach in Arthurville, and had later become the primary school principal. She'd been my kindy teacher, and her voice brought back the sour-milk smell of the kindergarten room and memories of hot afternoons that never seemed to end, of trying and failing to fall asleep on squeaky blue vinyl mats during nap time, of embarrassing Vegemite smears on my red-checked uniform.

"Oh, Mrs. Darling. Of course I remember you. I just didn't realise you'd be interviewing me."

"You were such a clever child. I'll always remember that story you told about the carved kookaburras on the chairs coming to life. Such a talented girl."

"Oh, really? I don't re—"

"And I've followed your career ever since you left. I've actually got a Google alert with your name on it. You know, I think I've read nearly every story you've written."

"Oh, wow. That's amazing." I thought of my earliest efforts, and winced.

"It makes me so proud, you know, seeing our Arthurville kids doing so well . . ."

"Not so well, really. I've never worked on any of the—"

"It's just so sad—all the newspapers closing. I never thought I'd see the day."

"Yes, it's a bit fright—"

She interrupted again. "I particularly liked those local community stories you wrote for the *Northern Weekender* a few years back—they were just so . . . heartwarming."

"I'm so glad you—"

"And they're exactly the sort of thing we're after."

My heart sank, but I mustered up as much enthusiasm as I could. "Well, I think I'm pretty well placed to do that."

"I know you are." She sighed. "Which is why we sent you an invitation to apply."

"That was kind—"

"And just between you and me"—she lowered her voice—"there aren't going to be any other interviews."

"Oh, well, that's, um, that's wonderful."

She must have heard the uncertainty in my voice, because her own was suddenly firm, and very official. "I'll send you the contract in the mail, or via email—and if you wouldn't mind scanning and sending back immediately."

I suddenly remembered the steel behind the sweetness, Mrs. Darling's implacability about matters she considered important—even when it came to her kindergartners. "Of course, yes. But there are a few things I should ask."

"Our major donors—who wish to remain anonymous—have been very generous—and are willing to pay whatever it was you were earning at your last position. Just send us your last pay advice."

"Of course, but I'm actually wondering—"

"And we'd like you to start as soon as possible, dear. Next week, in fact. Can you do that?"

I had no idea whether it was possible or why it was necessary, but what the hell. It was a sign. "Absolutely," I said. "No problem. I'll be there."

~

"This isn't going to be anything like what you're used to. This isn't some flashy city newspaper office." I don't disagree. There's nothing flashy about my new boss either. Barb Cummings, the *Chronicle*'s putative editor, is in her late sixties. She's dressed in exercise tights, a stained Violent Femmes T-shirt, and worn joggers; her lank grey hair, in defiance of numerous clips and combs, falls greasily about her face; she smells of onions and patchouli underarm deodorant, with a strong base note of cigarette smoke.

In fact the tiny office is permeated by *eau de cigarette*, though there are no ashtrays in sight. It's no doubt a consequence of generations of heavy-smoking journalists confined in a small space. The office, which looks as if it hasn't been painted since 1936 (the year the *Chronicle* moved in to the now much-reduced premises, according to a brass plaque on the exterior wall), is a single small, square, unpartitioned room with one south-facing window, heavily barred, that looks out onto a small car park. Twenty years ago, this space had been the admin office where the secretarial, personnel, and advertising staff were stationed, just one section of a busy and thriving country newspaper. Now it accommodates three ageing laminate desks, a rusting metal stationery cupboard, and a two-door sink cabinet. The walls are off-white and—other than a corkboard pinned with a fat pile of faded notices and a few takeaway menus—bare. The bathroom is shared with two other businesses that rent the premises. The only light comes from a flickering fluorescent tube that barely manages to break the gloom. There's no air-con, no fan, no anything that isn't strictly necessary. There are computers on all three of the desks, but they're a far cry from the latest-model Macs I'm used to working on—and I wouldn't be surprised if they use dial-up.

"Yeah, well. Beggars can't be choosers." Whatever her style short-comings, Barb is apparently no slouch when it comes to mind reading.

"Didn't they leave anything?"

She snorts. "I doubt they left a bloody paper clip. They came in on a Saturday morning, and the place had been cleared out by lunchtime. Every pen, every notebook. Every roll of fucking toilet paper. They even took our portrait of the queen. Anything they could sell, I guess. They left some boxes of crap that I haven't got around to clearing out: some old notes and clippings, broken staplers, blunt pencils, that sort of thing. Actually, if you've got a spare half hour, you might want to have a throw out."

"What about old copies of the newspaper?"

"They took them all. Anything before 1960 or so is available in the National Library database—they've digitised them. From about 2000 we can access online, but if you want to read anything from the years in between, you'll have to do a microfilm search at the library."

I shake my head. "It's so sad. All that history."

"They owned everything but the name, honey. We're just lucky there was some legal loophole that meant they couldn't take that too."

She gestures to the desk in the southern corner of the room. "So that one's all yours."

"Great." I sling my bag over the back of the chair, which sways alarmingly.

"Did Eileen tell you much about the job?"

"Eileen? Oh. Mrs. Darling. She didn't say much, to be honest. I just assumed it was a regular local paper job?"

"The *Chronicle* is now a community-run paper, funded by donations. It's probably a bit different to the . . . er . . . model you're used to."

"In what way?"

"Well, after Rural News closed the paper down last year, we managed to get subscriptions from the local community as well as some big
donations from a few of the wealthier families to run the paper. It's not
a lot—just enough to pay for one journalist, the printing, the rent, and
a website. So the paper itself is pretty basic."

"How basic?"

"We're just talking six pages on a Friday—twelve back and front,
all local community news. We don't do any national or wider regional
stuff—that's covered elsewhere. But people want to see their own lives
in the paper. Their own town."

"Fair enough."

"The thing is"—she pauses—"we're only featuring positive news."

"But surely that's not po—"

"Look. Most of the stories about Arthurville are going to be negative,
as I'm sure you know. There's enough crime here, enough tragedy, to fill
twenty newspapers. You name it, we've got it—probably worse than most
places. Drugs, delinquency, domestics. Death. Unemployment. Suicide.
Crime. Family breakdown. But there's no place for that in the *Chronicle*."

"No place? But isn't that what we're here for? To tell the truth about
what's happening—whatever that truth is?"

She pushes her hair back behind her ear, impatient, dismissive.
"Truth, shmooth. That paradigm is dead. And that's not why the newspaper was set up. Bad news might be real life, but believe me, no one
wants to hear about it anymore."

"Okay." I take a deep breath. "So what am I allowed to write about?"

"Well"—her long face lightens—"there's more than you might
imagine. Fetes, birthday parties, spring events, school plays, farming
reports, creative arts, sport, that sort of thing. We have a tiny section—
no more than a paragraph, for the weekly police report. They'll send

it to you on Wednesday afternoon. If there's more than a paragraph worth of crime, you have to cut." She looks at me hard. Takes a breath. "So, the *Chronicle's* not exciting—but the work it does is important. Crucial, in fact."

I don't quite know what to say, put all the enthusiasm I'm not feeling into a half-arsed smile. Change the subject. "And who's the third desk for?"

"Oh, that's Edith's. She came last year to do an internship—and stayed on part-time. She'll do your photos."

"You can afford a photographer?" From what she's told me about the budget and the job itself, I've assumed I'll be doing everything.

"No, they definitely *can't* afford me. This is one hundred percent a love job." A woman I assume must be Edith stands in the doorway, carrying a tray of takeaway coffee. She is in her early twenties, tall, thin, and impossibly beautiful. Her black hair has been pulled back and coiled behind her head; her eyes are a startling blue.

Barb snorts. "Love job, my arse."

Edith walks into the room, passes us each a cup. "So I'm guessing you're the famous Jo Sharpe. Good to meet you at last. Hope you like your coffee weak as piss." Her voice is soft, with what sounds like a South African twang.

"I'm Jo. Not sure about the famous bit."

"Oh, I've heard some things." Her grin is mischievous.

The boss takes a sip of coffee, grimaces. "Okay. Enough chitchat. I've got a big day." She digs in her back pocket, pulls out a folded sheet of lined paper that looks as if it's been torn out of a school exercise book. "There's not all that much on the horizon yet, but things'll come up during the week. People will call you. And keep in touch with the council, the cops, just in case something of interest happens. You should probably go up to the station and introduce yourself. You might want to call the schools, too, just to check in. I think Grandparents' Day or something is coming up at the primary school, and there's a bloke out near Mount Wellesley who thinks he may have grown the world's biggest tomato. Some old dear's poodle went missing when she was visiting her daughter in Dalhunty three weeks ago, and it's just arrived home. Bit footsore and dusty, but right as rain. Everyone seems to be talking about that young fella who's doing that stuff with the kids. That priest? You should talk to him." She pauses for breath. "Oh, and lest I forget—Roland Beaufort is expecting you out at Pembroke today. He wants to talk about regenerative agriculture, apparently. I suspect he wants to explain to the plebs why the Beauforts are still making money in the middle of this bloody drought.

"Okay. That's me done for the day." She hands me her notes. "I've got a lounge and a Netflix series waiting for me at home."

I'm bewildered. "But don't you have to give me some more . . . directions? I mean, what's the procedure? Do you need me to file the stories each day?"

"Nah. Just have them done by Thursday afternoon or early evening at the latest. We go to print on Friday afternoon, these days, but I don't like to be rushed. You've got the list. Edith will tell you what's what. Anything else of interest comes up—it's up to you. The car keys are on the hook. Pay for petrol and keep the receipts. Do the interviews, write the stories. There's petty cash in the tin. I only top it up every fortnight, so don't go mad with the Tim Tams. Turn the fan off when you go home. Key to the bathroom's in the kitchen drawer—side lane, first right."

"But—"

"It's not rocket science, Ms. Sharpe. I'll see you Friday."

She gives an offhand wave, hurries to the door, slams it shut behind her. I turn to Edith, who's leaning against her desk, sipping her coffee. "What the . . . ?"

Edith shrugs, laughs. "That's our Barb."

"I thought she was the editor? Like, a proper trained, experienced newspaper editor. Hasn't she been doing it for years?"

"She was. But she's retired. Now she's just doing the editing part as a volunteer. There's seriously no money to pay an editor. She's been doing the whole paper since Rural left, but she really doesn't have the energy. Time for new blood." That grin. "You."

"And what about you? Where do you come in?"

"Barb has been using me to take pictures a few days a week for the last couple of months, or whenever I'm needed. I'm not a professional photographer, but I know enough. I'm actually doing a PhD. They pay me fifty bucks a shot for my trouble, and I get to use the office space. I hate working at home. Oh, and they let me use the Wi-Fi."

I'm relieved to hear that there's Wi-Fi, at least.

"So am I meant to put the whole thing together? No one said I'd be editing too."

"Barb comes in on Fridays. You give her the copy, and I give her the images. She does the layout—she's got some amazing software. There's not really a lot to do, to be honest. It's usually only a couple hours work for me. You're the only one who gets paid properly."

"I don't get it. I don't understand how this is going to work. How am I meant to write an entire newspaper myself?"

The grin. "Have you actually seen a copy of the paper?"

I haven't.

"There must be one around here."

She fishes in her desk drawer, pulls out a handful of battered pages. "Here it is."

The newspaper, dated three weeks ago, is thin: only twelve pages back to front. The images are oversize—as is the font. And the headlines. The front-page headline reads: ST. MARTHA'S STUDENT TOPS WESTERN REGION MATHS COMP. A colour image of the grinning student, displaying a medal—one Alyx Bridges, year five—takes up a third of the front page, and the story—which is mainly quotes from the student as well as parents and teachers and friends—takes up the final third. On the second page there's yet another large image—this time of a well-dressed elderly lady standing in front of a table covered in empty jars. GLASS JARS NEEDED FOR LOCAL JAM MAKERS, the headline screams. I don't bother to read this one. On the following page, there's more of the same: NEW SWINGS FOR MULGA STREET PARK. The centre spread is called ABOUT TOWN and features a variety of colour images with a line of explanatory text, something between social pages and Instagram snaps: a thirtieth birthday held at a local café, a close-up picture of a camellia flower blooming in Wellington Park, a picture of the town taken from the top of Mount Wellesley just as the morning mist begins to clear. A small column on the next page is devoted to a "police report" that's really nothing more than a list: three people were charged with driving under the influence, eight with possession of drugs. Six break and enters. Four assaults. No details are given: no mention of locations, victims, or alleged perpetrators. The last three pages are devoted to sporting events, both school and town, the lead headline: ARTHURVILLE HIGH SCHOOL VOLLEYBALL TEAM LOSES BELL CUP FOR THIRD YEAR RUNNING.

I look up at Edith, who is watching me closely, her lips compressed.

Now I get it.

Merry

Arthurville, 1985

There was nothing—no years of rebellion, or of pent-up frustration, no real animus between Merry and her mother, no particular feelings of oppression, or resentment, or any repressed desire to break out of the mould. Later, even she would wonder at her own recklessness, her courage, her stubborn, unthinking, dumb defiance.

She'd done her final high school exams, had studied hard enough, but not too hard; she would do well enough but not too well. It was late October, and she was home for the holidays, that four-month gap between the end of secondary school and her new university life. She knew that mostly she'd be stuck at home with nothing much to do, but to be honest, Merry didn't really mind. She had her licence, the use of one of the old cars, and she was happy to mooch around the place. Her mother was likely to be a pain about certain things—she knew that—but Ruth was always so busy, and it was easy enough to avoid any sort of confrontation. As long as Merry kept out of her way, she'd leave her alone.

Merry had come into Arthurville for no particular reason—she'd felt like a drive, wanted to get away before her mother or Roly (who'd somehow metamorphosed into his mother's horribly officious deputy since he left school) suggested she do something like roll the tennis court or whitewash the stables. She had some money left over from her birthday and could do with some new jeans, a few T-shirts, some perfume, maybe a couple of records.

She'd driven in with her foot hard on the accelerator—way over the limit—the radio blaring, singing along to her latest favourite mixtape, given to her by a boy she'd met in a joint drama production at the end of the year. They'd engaged in a mild flirtation throughout the play's short season and ended up in a drunken clinch at the last-night party. The tape, which had been accompanied by a slightly crumpled postcard featuring some obscure German band on the front and a declaration of his undying love on the back, was crammed with songs she'd never heard, by musicians she'd never heard of. The boy, who had disapproved of what he called her bourgeois taste in music, had provided a painstakingly detailed handwritten guide, relating the history of each of the songs and the artists, and though she'd tossed the postcard into the bin, she'd surprised herself by falling in love with much of the music almost instantly. She had played the tape endlessly over the past month, learnt every song by heart.

She'd driven down the main street a little too fast, spotted a vacant parking space across from Richo's Records, and pulled up abruptly, reversed the pickup into a ridiculously tight park, pulled on the hand brake with a satisfying crunk, and sat for a minute as the song—"Sugar Mountain"—ended, enjoying the slight breeze through the window, the feeling of freedom, of escape. She leaned her head back against the seat and closed her eyes, singing along with the final chorus. It was only when she slid out of the car and squeezed herself into the space between the cars that she noticed the boy in the passenger seat of the truck parked alongside her. He was watching her through his open window, grinning widely. "That was an impressive park. Nice use of the hand brake," he'd said. "Can't say the same about the singing."

She'd felt her face redden, but her comeback was fast. "Better than that crap you're listening to." She could hear something that sounded like country music blaring from his car radio. He laughed. "Actually, that's Neil Young too. A later album. But I guess you knew that." He grinned again, taking the sting out of his words. "You don't remember me, do you?"

She looked at him hard. He was around her age, tall and thickset, with a mop of dark curly hair cut short around the sides and long at the back. He had a strong, slightly hooked nose and sported a three-day growth. He wasn't good-looking, exactly, but he wasn't bad. He wasn't even faintly familiar.

"Michael Sharpe. Mick. I think I sat next to you in sixth grade. Davo's class—Mr. Davidson. You're Miranda Beaufort, right?"

Mick. She did remember him now—distinctly recalled the sinking feeling when she'd been sat next to him at the beginning of the year because Mr. Davidson had insisted that boys and girls should occupy alternate desks. She would have preferred someone else—Adam Barnes, whose parents were friends with hers, maybe, or Fergus O'Callaghan, who was the school captain, or David Phillips, who was cute and popular, a star soccer player already—but she didn't really know Michael. At least he was reasonably clean, and wasn't one of the rowdy boys whom this classroom arrangement was designed to quell. But he had turned out to be a good desk mate—quietly funny, willing to share rulers and pencils and the occasional maths solution. In the middle of that year, Merry had been sent to boarding school, and she hadn't seen or even thought about him since.

She smiled. "Of course I remember you. Wow. Mr. Davidson. That feels like forever ago. So what are you doing with yourself these days?" His truck looked vaguely official, and he was wearing a plaid shirt, rolled up just above a tanned and well-muscled forearm.

"I've got a railway job. Track work."

"Do you like it?"

He nodded. "It's pretty cool. We get to travel a bit. What about you?"

"Oh, nothing right now. I'll head to Sydney next year."

"You got a job lined up?"

"Uni." Her tone was slightly apologetic.

"Of course."

Merry cleared her throat. "Anyway, I better get going. I've got a few things to do."

"Sure." He gave a wry grin, as if acknowledging the awkwardness of the encounter. His smile was attractive, a little lopsided, his teeth white, the front one slightly chipped, his eyes crinkling up at the corners.

"It was nice seeing you." Merry waved, nodded, stepped towards the road.

"Hey, Merry." He leaned out the window. "What are you doing tonight?"

She responded honestly. "Nothing."

"There's this band, playing at Tatts—an Angels cover band. They're up from Melbourne. It'll be a good night. You should come in and catch up with the gang. A bunch of us are going. Jacko, Tonks, Hildy, Soc, Dorro. Oh, and Jenny Dooley and Angie Simmons. You remember them, don't you?"

"Oh, I'm not sure I . . ." Merry had no idea what Angel covers were, and the only members of the gang that she actually recalled were the two girls—who had never been particular friends.

He persisted. "I think you'll like the music too."

She hesitated. "I really don't know—"

"Yeah you do. Come on." The look he gave her was half-admiring, half-challenging. She looked down at his arm again, at the coarse hairs glinting in the sun, then back at his crooked grin.

"Why not."

Jo

Arthurville, 2018

"Have you been out to Pembroke before?" Edith is driving the *Chronicle*'s company car—a cute little ten-year-old Volvo c30—so I can do some rapid Google research on "regenerative agriculture." I don't want to look like a complete ignoramus at my first interview.

"A long time ago, maybe."

"They're crazy rich, the Beauforts, apparently."

"So I've heard."

"I guess it's good that they're doing something environmentally useful." She sounds doubtful. "But it seems a bit weird. The son, Roland, is meant to be a bit dodgy. He doesn't exactly look like your environmentalist type."

I don't ask why he's meant to be dodgy, although I'm burning with curiosity. Instead I ask her to turn left.

"But that's the wrong way."

"I thought we could do a bit of a . . . tour of the town first. I haven't really had a chance since I got here. Just for nostalgia's sake, you know."

"No wuckin' furries, mate," Edith says in a broad Aussie accent, and turns left.

We do a circuit of the northern end of town. Almost every street holds some memory from my childhood, some half-forgotten, others still close to the surface: the primary school in Church Street, Mrs. Maxie's Corner Shop, with the best selection of mixed lollies in town. We drive up the hill and do a slow lap of leafy Wellington Boulevard with its stone fences and long driveways, past my childhood frenemy Ally Armstrong's house—scene of the never-to-be-forgiven-nor-forgotten great Barbie decapitation. We drive right out to the frayed edges of town, to my Nan and Pop's old place. A commission home, their place had always been well maintained and welcoming when I was a kid. Now it's difficult to tell whether it is even inhabited. The front yard has been reduced to red dirt; the garden is long gone. The house looks as though it hasn't been painted since Nan died.

We turn across to the high school, with its less innocent memories—the weather sheds at the far end of the oval that had provided the perfect cover for generations of surreptitious smokers, the bushy area down the side of the school where we'd scared the shit out of the occasional snake, and where I'd experienced my first kiss after a "blue light" disco in year eight. The front steps where we toasted our legs in the hopes of an admiring glance from the senior boys or the hot young phys ed intern.

We turn down Brougham Street, pass a house that I remember vaguely—a small nineteenth-century brick cottage, with a green-painted wrought iron verandah. There's a pile of rotting papers and advertising catalogues around the mailbox, and the house looks abandoned—though it's difficult to tell in a street where all the front lawns have turned to red dust. I feel like I know the place, but I have no memory of why.

We drive across the river, and though I'm expecting it, it's still a shock—the water is brown, muddy, sluggish. And lower than I've ever seen it.

My sigh is deep, involuntary.

"It's depressing, isn't it?" Edith keeps her eyes on the road. "I don't get how people stay in a place like this. I think it'd drive me to drugs. It's already driven me to drink. Not that I need much of an excuse."

"Oh, come on. You've only been here for five minutes. It's got its good points." Edith's obvious scorn has set my latent parochial hackles rising, a surprise even to me.

"Really?" She turns, gives me a cool stare. "It's not like you hung around, is it? From what I've heard, you got out of town as soon as you could."

What she says is true.

"Anyway"—she flicks the blinker on, turns back towards the highway—"we'd better get going." She puts on a plummy accent. "The Beauforts are expecting us."

I sigh again, pull out my iPhone, and get googling.

Pembroke is just over an hour's drive from Arthurville. Most of the way the roads are sealed, but the final stretch is rough red clay that clearly makes Edith nervous. After ten judderingly painful minutes during which we seem to have progressed only half a kilometre, I take over the wheel.

"I don't know how people live so far from civilisation."

I'm cautious for the first few kilometres, but once I get the feel of the car, which handles well and has more power than I expected, I put my foot down. I have some fun, testing the car's capacity along with my own muscle memory—it's been a long time since I've driven on dirt. It's not so much fun for poor Edith. She yelps and grips her seat as I slide around a tight corner; her face goes white and then green as I let the car get a little too close to a fence before righting it with a gentle tug of the hand brake. *Faaark,* she breathes as I slow down to cross a cattle grate, red dust billowing around us. "You might've warned me. Where the hell did you learn to drive?"

"My dad did some rally car racing when he was younger. He taught me a little, and what he didn't I worked out myself. This road's a bit boring—too flat, too straight. It's way more fun if there are a few bends, some hills. I'll take you up Mount Wellesley sometime."

"That's okay," she says through gritted teeth. "No hurry."

In contrast to the surrounding countryside, Pembroke is an oasis of green. The surrounding paddocks, although not as verdant as the countryside around here can be during good years, are still reasonably grassed—a stark contrast to most of the farms hereabouts.

I drive up a poplar-lined carriageway and onto a circular driveway. The house is set in a luxuriant parklike garden—a spreading jacaranda, flowering rosebushes, neatly clipped hedges, an immaculately tended lawn. A small stone fountain stands empty—the only apparent concession to the drought. The Federation mansion is grand and imposing—an ivy-clad blue-brick front, a gabled second story with mullioned windows, faux Tudor moulding, shingled turrets. A shiny red Jag—an XJS—parked at a wild angle out the front, adds to the air of opulence. A battered Land Cruiser and a newer Mercedes SUV, both covered in red dust, are parked more sedately in a gravelled area. I pull in beside them.

"OMG." Edith looks around, clearly astounded. She has managed to prise her fingers from the seat, and her colour is almost back to normal. "Who knew there was this sort of money out here?"

"Bizarre, isn't it?"

"How come it's so green? Is this what regenerative agriculture is all about?"

"I don't think so. Pretty sure it's not about lawns and gardens."

"Do they have water trucked in or something?"

"It's possible. They've probably got bore water too."

"But aren't there restrictions on that too?"

"Who knows? Money, eh?"

I climb out of the car, push the door closed quietly, not wanting to advertise our arrival.

I shouldn't have bothered. Edith fails to follow my example, slamming her door hard just as a mob of kelpies descend on us, barking noisily.

"Merry!" Edith opens the car door and is about to dive back in, but there is a sharp whistle, and the dogs stop immediately; another whistle and they sit, tails wagging, panting laboriously.

A man appears from behind the house and follows the path of the dogs, crunching over the gravel towards us.

He is in his early fifties, tall and slender, his face lined and weathered. His flat-brimmed Akubra perches on the back of his head, faded blue eyes narrowed against the glare. "G'day, ladies. What can I do for you?" He has a broad old-school Aussie drawl that goes with the look—a voice that conjures up visions of shrimps on barbies and a laid-back friendliness, which seems odd for someone who I know spent years in an exclusive boarding school.

"We're here from the *Chronicle*. For the interview."

"Ah. The interview. Of course." He holds out his hand. "Roland Beaufort." He shows no signs of recognising me.

"I'm Jo"—I grip his hand firmly, try for a breezy smile—"and this is Edith, who'll be taking photos."

He looks at Edith curiously. "I've met you somewhere before, haven't I?"

"I think maybe . . . at the pub? Tattersalls?"

"Ah. That's right. The Seth Efrican." He smirks.

"I'm from Kenya, actually."

He shrugs. "You're a mate of our resident delinquent whisperer, aren't you?"

"That I am."

"You're doing the thesis on, er, what is it? Juvenile justice?" He rolls his eyes. "I guess a hundred thousand words by another bleeding heart is exactly what the country needs?"

Edith looks as if she'd like to kick him in the groin, but she manages a tight smile. "That's me. Miss Bleeding Heart 2018."

He snorts. "Righto then. Shall we go to the office?"

I'm about to suggest that we conduct the interview outside, in the areas that are currently being farmed, but he turns and heads back to the main house before I can speak. The dogs walk sedately by his side, turning occasionally as if to check that we're following.

The office is in a newly constructed detached building behind the main house. It's a comfortable room, fitted out in a tasteful but somehow uninviting manner. Roland waves for us to sit down, then opens a cupboard and pulls out a bottle of whiskey.

"Too early for you girls?"

I give a rueful smile. "Just a little." Edith looks disappointed.

He pours himself a shot, gulps down the liquor, pours another, and sits down. He sighs, stretching out long legs, and leans back in his chair, smiling for no apparent reason. I take out my notebook, hold up my phone.

"Do you mind if I record this?"

"No problem. What would you like to know?"

"Whatever you can tell us about how you're working the land these days, what new techniques you're using—from what I've heard, and what we've seen already, they're clearly working. And if we could take some . . . er . . . location shots?"

"Roland?"

An elderly woman stands in the doorway. She is striking: tall and straight backed, slender enough to still look good in jeans and riding boots, a white linen shirt ironed and tucked in, thick silvery hair pulled into a tight bun. She exudes money, authority—and an implacable and perhaps malign will.

Roland stands up. "Ah. Here's my mother. Mum, these girls are from the *Arthurville Chronicle*. They've come to talk to us about the . . . er, new farming techniques. They're doing an article."

"They are? I don't recall you telling me anything about an interview, dear." The *dear* is clearly loaded, and Roland looks vaguely uncomfortable.

"It was arranged a few weeks ago, it . . . er . . . must've slipped my mind."

"I see. Well, perhaps you can introduce me to these young ladies, and we can continue the conversation." She steps into the room, and

47

both Edith and I get to our feet. She pauses in front of Edith first, holds out her hand. "Ruth Beaufort."

"Edith Nyangira. I'm the photographer. Good to meet you." Edith's smile is warm and open, a contrast to the older woman's rather cool gaze.

She turns to me, and I see her eyes widen as I take her hand. She doesn't need to hear my name.

"Josephine?"

"Hello, Ruth." It's hard to know what to call her.

"Do you two know each other?" Roland looks between the two of us.

"Josephine is Miranda's daughter. Your niece. My granddaughter." Her voice is steady, but she hasn't taken her eyes off me, is still clasping my hand tightly.

Pembroke, 1993

We were going to visit the Wicked Witch of the West, and I wasn't to tell Dad. I wasn't to tell anyone.

It was a school day. I'd woken with a slight sniffle, and Mum had told me I could stay home. I hadn't even had to ask—it had been her idea. "I don't think we'll send you today, Jojo. Don't want to give anyone else your germs." She wasn't usually this concerned for the health of others. In fact, a day off school for a cold was unheard of, but I accepted the offer without question. I hadn't done my times tables practice the night before, and there was a test first thing, so I was glad to avoid what would no doubt be a shameful exposure of my laziness. I'd hoped that a day off school would mean a day of lounging around in my pyjamas, watching TV, eating vegemite toast, but Mum had told me to get dressed.

When I'd asked why, she just said we were going out, and not to bother her with questions—I would find out soon enough. She was in a strange mood—not one I could put my finger on. She wasn't exactly cheerful, but she wasn't sad, either, or angry. She was distracted, focused on something else, almost as if I weren't there. I was wary—things could change in an instant, but this was a mood I wasn't familiar with. I kept quiet and assumed there was a furnace bubbling beneath that could erupt at any moment. Lately there'd been frequent such eruptions—she always seemed to be cross and tired, even though she went to bed early, woke up late. I'd heard her vomiting a couple of times early in the morning, but when I asked if she was sick, she'd simply looked at me blankly and told me not to be silly.

"And don't put any old thing on," she said now. "Wear that dress—the pretty blue one—that one you got for Christmas from Nan and Pop. And decent shoes. Sandals, not thongs."

It was the first time I'd worn the Christmas dress. It was the prettiest dress imaginable, pale blue with white polka dots, an elegant skirt that whirled out when I turned, and it had been my third-best Christmas present after my bike and the science kit that Santa had brought me. Mum had been less impressed. "It's going to need ironing once I wash it, so I wouldn't get too excited if I were you. What on earth was the woman thinking?" It wasn't hard to work out—Mum was famous for not ironing, and Nan was famously disapproving.

My feet seemed to have outgrown my only pair of decent sandals. Other than that, there were only joggers and an old pair of thongs. And my school shoes.

Mum sighed when I told her. "Oh Jesus, Josephine. Truly?" She took the school shoes, which were scuffed and worn, into the kitchen, wiped them with the dishcloth, handed them back. "They'll have to do."

When I was dressed, she wiped my face and hands with the same cloth, and then wrested my hair into an eye-watering ponytail.

Mum was dressed up too. She was wearing a denim skirt that she despised as being too old ladyish and never even wore to work—another gift from Nan—and a floral button-up shirt. She'd pushed her feet into a pair of shiny red court shoes that I'd never seen her wear. She brushed her own hair into a loose bun, applied eyeliner, lipstick. She smiled at me as I watched her in the mirror. "What do you reckon? Worth a million dollars?"

I nodded, approving. "You look perfectly perfect!" For once—not in her usual jeans and boots—she looked just like all the other mothers.

I waited until we were well out of town before asking again. Mum was driving too fast on a bumpy dirt road, the wheel clenched tight. She had the window down and the radio was blaring.

"Where are we going?"

"We're off to see the Wicked Witch of the West, Dorothy."

"I'm not Dorothy." I hated it when she talked in riddles like this. I could sense her pent-up excitement, her suppressed anxiety.

"It's okay—she's not a real witch. At least I don't think she is."

"But where?" I could hear the whine in my voice. Maybe I really was sick. I peered out the window, trying to get my bearings. It was a sunny winter morning, the frost already burnt off. Out the car window, everything was strangely illuminated: the green fields, blue sky, white woolly sheep, the red dirt of the road, the grey-blue slopes of Mount Wellesley in the distance. The colours were as intense here as in the Land of Oz, and the landscape just as unfamiliar. I looked up into the air nervously, expecting to see something magical, flying monkeys, a wicked witch, a broomstick, at the very least a tornado, heading our way.

I asked one more time, my voice quavering, "Where are we going?"

She didn't turn her head. "That's for me to know and you to find out."

~

The house bore no resemblance to any of the buildings in *The Wizard of Oz*. It bore no resemblance to any house I'd ever been in. In fact it was more like a castle than a house, with balconies and turrets and a garden that was far grander even than Wellington Park—an expanse of green lawn, with borders and hedges and rose beds and one giant tree and others shaped into cones and spheres. There was even a small fountain, with water tinkling prettily from a carved figure in the centre. I had been surprised by my mother's clear lack of respect for these awe-inspiring surroundings—she hadn't parked the car in the obvious parking space, but followed the circular driveway all the way to the front entry, pulling on the hand brake too early so that she'd skidded a little in the gravel.

"Oops." She'd grinned mischievously, winked.

She looked at herself briefly in the mirror, screwed up her nose, took a deep breath. "Here goes nothing." She opened the car door and slid out, slamming it shut without a backwards glance. I wasn't sure whether I was meant to stay in the car or follow, but got out and followed her across the gravelled drive, my steps slowing to match hers as she approached the imposing entry. Before she reached the front steps, the door opened, and a woman walked out onto the wide front verandah. The woman was tall and slender, dressed in jeans and a white shirt, riding boots. Her face was obscured by shadows, but even so I could tell she wasn't a witch. She stood on the verandah, watching, her hands on her hips.

My mother paused at the bottom of the stairs, looked up. "Hello, Mother." Her voice was uncharacteristically formal, and she sounded slightly breathless.

"Miranda." The woman's voice was dark and deep. There was no softness, no give in this voice.

"You must be Josephine?"

It took me a moment to realise she was talking to me—no one ever called me that. My voice stuck in my throat, but Mum was there before me.

"Yep. This is Jojo."

"I suppose you'd better come in then." The woman turned around abruptly and headed back through the front door. The screen door swung closed behind her.

I had expected Mum to wait for me, to take my hand, but she drew up her shoulders and marched across the wide timber verandah. I took the stairs two at a time, trying to catch up, but it was too late; she'd pushed through the door and let it swing closed.

The two women had disappeared into the house. I followed the sound of their footsteps down the hallway. The hall was dim, and wide, and appeared to go on forever. There were paintings—landscapes, mostly, but the occasional portrait—on the walls, an ornately carved hall stand, a huge mirror in a frame painted with flowers. All the doors along the corridor—huge dark timber constructions—were firmly closed. I felt more like Alice than Dorothy—dizzy and shrunk to half my size. The brass doorknobs were too big for my hands, and too high up to reach. Eventually I came to the end of the hallway, to an open door, on the other side a kitchen. My mother and the woman were in there—my mother's voice high, fast, loud, and clearly angry, the other woman—her mother, my grandmother, I understood now—was low and calm—but there was anger there too. I could recognise it—a steely, cold, bottled-up sound like I'd sometimes hear from my father. So different to my mother's anger, which boiled up and overflowed like a saucepan without a lid, but frightening nonetheless.

I paused outside the doorway, too scared to go in. I could see a big timber table, surrounded by chairs decorated with carved kookaburras. They were the most beautiful chairs I'd ever seen.

"I'm not asking for much—just enough so that we can add on a room—or maybe move somewhere bigger before this baby comes. Buy a few things."

"Miranda, it's not possible. I can't just give you money—"

"Don't give me that. Look at this place."

"It's not that simple."

"What have I ever asked for? This is the first time I've asked for anything since I left—"

"Miranda. You haven't spoken to me for, what, seven years? I've never even met my own granddaughter. You've sent back my mail, refused every request I've made to see you. And now—now you come to me for money?"

"It'd be different if it was Roly asking—"

"Your brother doesn't ask."

"He doesn't need to, does he? He's still living here. Still sucking on Mummy's teat—"

"That's enough, Miranda."

"Why would I get in contact?" My mother's voice was getting higher and higher—a danger sign. "Why *would* I let you have anything to do with my child—my life—when you won't—"

I must have made a sound. I heard the woman's indrawn breath, her footsteps coming towards me.

"Josephine?"

The woman towered above me. She was far taller than my mother. She smelt like flowers, and something earthy, animal, like horses or cows. I thought of what Mum had said about her being a witch and couldn't look up.

"You must stop this, Miranda," she spoke quietly. "The poor child is terrified."

"She's fine." Mum pushed past the older woman, grabbed me around the wrist, and pulled me to her.

"Look, why don't you bring her into the kitchen. We can have a cup of tea. I've got some biscuits. Cake. We can talk about what we might be able to do—"

My mother's fingers tightened. "I don't need your help. It's not too late for an abortion. We can probably afford *that*."

She started up the hall, walking briskly, pulling me along after her.

"You don't have to do that. Don't be ridiculous, Miranda." The woman walked through the door, but didn't follow us down the hallway.

"How is that ridiculous?" Mum turned and hissed. "Isn't that what you told me to do last time? That time it was Jo, the granddaughter you've only just met."

I twisted back to look. The witch stood in the doorway. She had shrunk back to normal proportions. Now everything about her was drooping, her neck, her shoulders, her mouth. It was as if she were melting, just like the Wicked Witch of the West. Now it was my mother who was the frightening one, dragging me down the stairs of the house and stamping across the gravel in her bright red shoes. She pushed me into the car and slammed the door hard.

My little sister was born seven months later.

Arthurville, 2018

I watch them in the side mirror until the trees obscure my view: mother and son standing side by side, surrounded by their kelpie pack, sentinels guarding their keep. Edith, who hurried to beat me to the driver's seat, makes her way sedately down the driveway. She slows down even more once we're over the cattle grate and back on the dirt, and doesn't speak until we're back on the highway.

"Well, that was awkward."

"It wasn't that bad."

Once Roly registered his surprise, the interview had continued predictably. I asked the questions I'd formulated about their seemingly successful experiment with sustainable farming techniques, and Ruth, who was clearly the mastermind of the enterprise, had answered them clearly, and concisely, with Roly adding the occasional scientific detail. It was dry stuff, really, and my article would be brief—as per the newspaper's mission. We'd taken a few photographs of the two of them, the green paddocks and well-fed cattle in the background, the dogs cavorting, and these would be the focus of the article. Nothing more was said about our relationship—by either party—but a multitude of unvoiced questions had rippled beneath every statement, every quickly dropped gaze.

"You might have told me. Before we got there."

"What?"

"That they're your family."

"They may be related to me, but they're not family." I turn my head to look out the window. "There's a difference."

I drop Edith home on my way back to the office. She lives on Grace Street with her dentist girlfriend, Felicity—Fizz—in a familiar old weatherboard house diagonally opposite the Anglican church. I laugh. "My friend Fran lived here when she was a kid. Her mum, Nancy, called herself a white witch, which I always thought was funny because she's Wiradjuri. She was a history teacher—she still is—but she did tarot readings as a side gig. And palms too. Star signs. It was kind of a joke, but kind of not."

"Ah. That would explain the astrology charts in the pantry."

"Is there still a drop dunny out the back?"

Edith makes a face. "Yeah, but there's a lovely plumbed toilet indoors, so we don't use it."

"I wouldn't. She once told me that it was a thin place."

"What's that?"

"Maybe a portal to another dimension?"

"Like in *Outlander*?"

"Uh-huh. But you'd have to wade through a hundred years' worth of shit to get there. That is so not appealing." We both snigger.

"Not even if Jamie Fraser was at the other end?"

"Not even."

That night, over dinner—a barbecue chicken and supermarket coleslaw—I tell Dad about my trip out to Pembroke.

"So you met the old battle-ax, did you? How did she behave?"

"Ruth? It was . . . odd. She seemed almost pleased to see me, actually. But the whole thing was very awkward. We didn't discuss anything personal." It's hard to describe the meeting with my grandmother, the strange sense of expectation that lay beneath the surface formality.

"Mum took me out there once, when I was a kid."

"Really?" Dad looks surprised. "I didn't know."

"She and Ruth had a big row—that's all I really remember."

"I only met her the once too. And that wasn't a success either." He gives a snort. "Merry didn't see eye to eye with her mother—but if you ask me, her brother was worse. I'd see him around town occasionally, after Merry left, and he'd deliberately turn his back, the prick—wouldn't even acknowledge me."

"He did look a bit shocked when he realised who I was."

"Probably pissing himself in case Mummy wants to change her will."

"What?"

"Now that you're back. He was always a two-faced prick. Always scamming something. There were stories floating about that Pembroke was going under, not long before your Mum left—they'd had some bad years, overcapitalised. Typical bloody graziers. And then, somehow, they managed to come back from it—like magic."

"Do you think he did something illegal?"

"Well—you hear stuff. I'd sooner trust a brown snake, to be honest. He's not a nice man."

"It sounds like they're not a nice family."

He sighs.

"The only time I ever saw Merry really upset about it all was when she got a letter from her mother, just after you were born. She was hoping it was something . . . friendly, I guess—but it was just some legal document. After that she never spoke about them again."

He chews his food slowly. "I've never understood what they wanted from her, but I do know what they didn't want."

"What?"

He laughs, though without any mirth. "Someone like me in her life. And maybe they were right."

CHAPTER THREE

A LITTLE BIRD

During last week's submission of mayoral candidates, when for the first time in history more than a quarter of the candidates were women, a prominent member of the Arthurville council was heard to say that if the women got in, it would be a disaster. "There'll be no more port and cigars—it'll be cups of tea and doilies." The local CWA has commenced a crocheting drive in an effort to ensure that every candidate has a personal doily before the beginning of next month's session. Rumour has it that if the ladies win, port and cigars (and beer and cigarettes) are to be banned in the meeting rooms; however, cream sherry and scones will be served, followed by after-dinner mints to freshen the breath as well as the conversation.

A Little Bird, *Arthurville Chronicle*, 1994

Jo

Arthurville, 2018

My days quickly take on a familiar, and not entirely unpleasant, rhythm. I've set the bar low, though—assuming that I'm going to feel the same way I did when I was seventeen and desperate to escape the suffocating smallness of country-town life. Back then, life, real life, was somewhere else, and some days it felt as if I would die, literally, if, by some horrific circumstance, I was forced to stay in Arthurville indefinitely.

Home life is pretty much just as I've expected. My father is grouchy and uncompromising. Almost everything I do irritates him, especially when it comes to cooking. If I say I'll make dinner, he doesn't like what I suggest. If he cooks, he's resentful about having to cook for two. If I cook for myself, he's pissed off that I've made a mess, or gotten in his way, or that I'm stuffing his fridge and pantry (empty apart from Gator's dry food when I arrived) with things he can't pronounce, let alone eat. It pisses him off when I get up early for work, pisses him off when I arrive home late. He complains when I use the washing machine (*Can you just leave it on the normal setting, for fuck's sake?*) or park my car (*it's leaking oil*) in the driveway. Still, he takes without comment the two fifties I give him for board and seems happy enough when I quietly sort his overdue bills.

At least he hasn't questioned me any further about the reasons for my return—there've been no more snide comments about Harry, or about the complicated death of our relationship. If he lacks curiosity about my life, he's been as tight-lipped as ever about his own. I've asked him (casually) about the pathology and the imaging request forms he keeps pinned to the old corkboard, and when he tells me (just as casually) that they're nothing, just routine tests, I don't push it. He'll tell me when he's ready. Or not.

I called Fran when I first arrived, asked her whether I should say something, make a point of it, but she said to leave it, that she'd call him if he still hadn't done anything in the next few weeks. "I probably shouldn't have told you, anyway," she said. "It was completely unethical."

It might have been unethical, but I'm glad she told me. Fran, who is one of the only schoolmates I've kept in contact with, is now a GP at old Dr. Cooligan's practice. Doc Cooligan, who delivered me, along with most Arthurvilleans under the age of forty, died only a few years ago, and Fran is now Dad's GP. We met for dinner in Chinatown a few months ago, and she unwittingly let the info drop. "Your dad's looking pretty well," she said, "considering."

I pounced on that final word. "Considering what?"

"Considering the chemo." Even as she spoke the words, Fran realised that she was telling me something I didn't know, that she'd spoken out of turn. It took me precisely three seconds to get her to tell me everything she knew—I promised that I wouldn't say anything to my father, or to anyone else, for that matter. "Come on, Fran. You'd expect me to tell you something . . . I mean, what if it was your kid, and she was taking drugs and I knew about it and didn't tell you." Fran is the mother of two-year-old twin girls, and the analogy was ludicrous, but she got the point.

It turned out my father has prostate cancer. This on top of a back injury that put him out of work ten years ago, chronic depression, and a problem with alcohol. He'd already had one round of treatment for the cancer and had improved—thus far all his indicators have been good—and was due to start another in a few months. He was, surprise, a difficult patient—had refused to give up cigarettes or booze (he had a point), and had a habit of missing appointments, ignoring tests.

"I'm pretty sure it's not going to be fatal. I think we've caught it in time. But he really should make more of an effort to live healthily. And if he wants a reasonable quality of life, he'll have to. At least we know what's going on. Half the time blokes his age don't come to the doctors until it's too late to do anything." Fran's sigh spoke volumes.

I half made the decision to come home then, but the split with Harry solidified it. The job coming up at the *Chronicle* had been the icing on the cake. My boss had done his best to talk me out of leaving. There were other ways to get around the situation, easier ways, he'd said. It was ridiculous for me to leave a position on a real paper and take a bullshit job in Nowheresville. Especially in the current climate. Sick fathers could be looked after by others—there were community carers, weren't there? I could make trips out every couple of weekends. Simple for some. I wasn't planning on staying there forever, I told him. Just until things were sorted out. I'd be back.

His laugh was sour. "You might come back, Jo, but don't assume we'll still be here."

I didn't tell him there were other reasons for my going home. I barely let myself think about them.

Despite my misgivings, work itself is far more satisfying than I'd imagined. I might not be writing the cutting-edge stories I'd planned when I'd been a young reporter, but I'm doing my best to fulfil the paper's mission. In a short space of time, I've learned more than I'd known in eighteen years of living here about Arthurville's numerous volunteer groups, civic organisations, schools, and sporting, musical, and cultural events. I'd worried that I'd run out of things to write about, but instead it seems there are more stories than I can hope to cover. Edith, who's in the office every day even though she's officially on the job only a dozen hours a week, is good company, easy to be around, funny.

I'm expecting my social life here will be pretty much nonexistent. Like me, most of my friends left town once school finished, and headed off to the city for uni or work. Of all my close girlfriends, only Fran came back for good—the rest of us returned for visits that rarely corresponded the older we got. The few kids who'd stayed behind had made their lives here, and were unlikely, or so I imagined, to welcome back prodigals like me.

Arthurville had been a good place to grow up. Despite my personal troubles, I'd been secure, known in a way that's possible only in a place where your family has lived for generations. At some point, though, when I hit sixteen or seventeen, that feeling of being known became unbearably claustrophobic. In Arthurville, I would always be the daughter of, the granddaughter of—that was the same for most of us—but for me there was an additional burden: I would always be Merry's daughter, Amy's sister. It was a burden that was either shame or tragedy—opinions varied. Even for me it could swing one way one day and do a wild reversal the next. In the city, I was nobody. In the city, I could be anybody.

~

So many faces are familiar. Teachers and admin staff at the schools know exactly who I am, even if I don't recognise them, and welcome me home. The bowling club is run by a bloke I recall vaguely from school. One of the mums who looked after me in those first terrible months works behind the deli counter at the supermarket. She gives me a po-faced once-over. "Thought you'd managed to escape." Her words are blunt, but her smile is warm; her eyes twinkle. When I go to introduce myself to the local cops, the sergeant on duty is Phil Deacon, who'd failed me the first time I went for my licence, after I'd deliberately skidded around Martyrs Corner.

At the end of my first week home, Dad and I order Chinese takeaway from the local Chinese—Jan's Café, an Arthurville institution that dates its origins back to the gold rush—and I'm surprised when another old schoolmate, Max Jan, delivers it. "Thought I'd come and say g'day," he says, handing me the plastic bag. "I heard you were home."

Max, who trained as a lawyer and worked for a big Sydney firm for
ten years, tells me that he moved back to help his mother after his dad
died, and then decided to stay. That was five years ago. "I'm married
now," he says. "Two kids and another on the way." He gives a shy smile.
"It's good you're back. Never thought I'd ever move back, but it's not so
bad. A house with no mortgage, lots of space."

I carry the order into the kitchen. Share the food between two
plates and carry them into the lounge room, the only bearable space in
the house. Dad is lying back on his chair with his eyes closed. He grunts
when I put the food down. "Ta, love."

"You Can't Always Get What You Want" is playing softly in the
background. I think about Max, his very obvious contentment. I wonder what it is that I want and where I can get it. Sometimes it feels as
though I don't even know where to begin looking.

~

I've just finished work at the beginning of my second week.

It's been a busy day. I've interviewed last year's top high school
students about their plans, spoken to two local artists about an impending exhibition, and talked with a young couple who've just moved to
town and are hoping to start an organic fruit and vegetable cooperative.
Their enthusiasm in the face of all the difficulties they've encountered—
from the bad weather to unhelpful locals—has made me feel slightly
depressed. I take my time going home—call into the new Woolworths
to pick up a few essentials. Oxley Road—the town's broad main street—
has changed so much since my childhood that it's almost unrecognisable. A wide, treed thoroughfare, with a park that runs along two
blocks on one side, it had been a lively town centre in my childhood.
There'd been all the regular shops—a grocery store, greengrocer, a news
agency, boutiques, a couple of milk bars, hardware stores, a bookshop.
There were solicitors, accountants, hairdressers. There'd even been a

small department store, Ambrose's Emporium, that had been established at the beginning of the century and sold everything from clothing to cutlery.

Anytime you had business in the main street, you were guaranteed to meet at least a dozen people you knew well, and everyone else you'd know by sight. As a small child, I'd loved the sense that wherever I went I was known, that I was recognised, that it was almost impossible to get lost. But by the time I was a teenager, I'd hated that feeling, had found it oppressive. I'd have enjoyed being lost, to not have some nosy acquaintance ask why I wasn't at school, or why I was mysteriously unsteady on my feet in the late afternoon, or hanging out with some unsavoury boy or other, or driving too fast.

But now there's barely anyone around to recognise me.

The butchers, bakers, and candlestick makers are all gone. Half the shops are boarded up, windows are smashed, and walls are sprayed with graffiti. There's a solitary café, a pawnshop, an opportunity shop, and a dingy government office in a strip that was once bustling with people. The beautiful miniature arcade that once housed Ambrose's has been abandoned—shutters down, FOR LEASE signs nailed up—and a windowless behemoth that accommodates a Woolworths, a bottle-o, a dollar shop, and a pharmacy has replaced it as the town's commercial hub.

I'm heading for the centre's underground parking lot and have overtaken a couple—an older woman, talking animatedly, and a younger man, pushing a trolley piled high with groceries. I'd have walked on without a second thought but turn around almost involuntarily at the sound of the woman's voice.

"Kirsty?"

The woman pauses, looks over at me. Her eyes widen. "Oh my God. Jo Sharpe."

She steps forward and hugs me. I hug her back, hard, overcome by the familiarity of her perfume, her sinewy strength. If anyone had acted as a proxy mother in the year or so after my own had disappeared, it was

Kirsty McLeod, but it was later, in my final few months of high school, when her son Lachlan and I had been an item, that I'd really gotten to know her. She'd encouraged the relationship, always welcoming me, inviting me to stay for dinner, letting me stay the night every now and then—in a room far from Lachlan's, but distant enough from the marital suite for us to creep back and forth in the middle of the night. She hadn't expected me to confide in her or been one of those people who are creepy about making friends with their kid's girlfriends, but she'd been a warm maternal presence, nonetheless. There had been a few teary evenings when I'd told her about my seemingly endless rows with my father—his drinking, his intransigence about what seemed to me to be certain unreasonable rules, his meanness with money—and she'd been patient and understanding, had made me feel better without completely undermining Dad. She'd been unobtrusively kind about helping me with the end-of-school formal—offering to lend me money, driving me to Dalhunty when she took Lachlan up to get his suit fitted, helping me choose a dress.

Lachie and I broke up early in the following year. We had moved to separate cities and knew—because doesn't everyone?—that long-distance relationships were doomed. Lachlan had begun life at an exclusive residential college at Melbourne University; I'd moved to Sydney to do whatever I could—working in bars, mostly—to earn enough money to pay for whatever squalid share accommodation I could find. We called and emailed enthusiastically at first, then sporadically, until gradually it all petered out more or less painlessly, though not without some residual regret on my side. A regret that was no doubt coloured rosily: my life in Arthurville might have been dull, and our relationship had been as much for appearances' sake as anything—as teenage romances sometimes are—but after six months of no friends, no family, and no one to talk to bar the couple I lived with—both nurses—who worked permanent night shifts and never seemed to come out of their bedrooms when I was around, I'd been crazy with loneliness. I'd begun to pine for a mythical version of Lachlan, a Lachlan who was better looking, smarter, and more interested in me than he had actually ever been—a Lachlan I felt more for than the reality. I'd stalked him online for a few months, trawled through websites and blogs and Myspace accounts for pictures of him and his new friends, doing all the things rich and privileged kids did at college: formal dinners, tennis matches, rowing regattas, rugby. The boys with their cut jaws and Hugh Grant hair; the girls with their flowing locks and expertly made-up faces, figure-hugging dresses, spiky heels. Girls as unlike me as it was possible to be and far from anything I'd ever aspired to. Lachlan's metamorphosis had been rapid: his hair somehow achieved that signature flop, his skin cleared up, his fashion sense improved. It was a world I half despised as the child of a chippy working-class father, but even so the envy seeped into my heart. And anger, too—at my parents, both of them—for abandoning me in their different, but equally soul-numbing, ways.

I had recovered quickly, of course. I was young and smart and not the type to brood. I'd begun uni the following year, made friends, saved enough to travel overseas, and found a job that suited me, but still—for years I experienced a slight pang whenever I caught sight of him on social media, felt that sense of being excluded, of a life that might have been.

Now Kirsty is holding me at arm's length, looking at me admiringly. "You look wonderful," she says. "I'd heard you were moving back up, but I didn't know when. I barely recognised you. If it wasn't for those amazing Sharpe eyelashes, I'd never have known you. You look so . . . well, so grown up."

Kirsty herself has barely changed. She is older, her hair a silvery bob rather than the cascading blonde I remember. She's slim and upright, her legs still shapely, evenly tanned, dressed stylishly in a smart button-down dress, high-heeled black sandals.

"And Mum's still got the same habit of blurting out the first thing that comes into her head." I register with a slight shock that the man accompanying her is Lachlan. There is no sign of either the rather reserved and studious boy I'd known at school or the more confident college boy he'd become in those heady postschool days. Now tall and slightly gaunt, his hair shaved, dressed in standard office wear, he looks almost middle aged—and despite his playful greeting, his expression is rather grim, his face lined with worry.

He holds out his hand, his smile warm. "Jo. I heard you were back. I've been meaning to get in touch. I've been a little bit . . . distracted."

He gestures ruefully at the well-stacked trolley, and for the first time I notice the contents include a vast number of baby items—disposable nappies, tins of formula, baby wipes, and the like. It is unmistakably the shopping of a family man.

"Oh, wow. Looks like there are some congratulations due. I had no idea."

"Thanks." His smile is slightly strained.

"So, a girl? A boy?"

"A boy, Jeremy. Jem."

"And who's the lucky woman. I didn't even know you were married."

"I . . . well, actually—my wife, Annie. She, ah, she died." He looks almost apologetic.

"Oh, God. Lachlan. I had no idea. I'm so sorry." He goes to say something more, but falters, turns away.

"It's been dreadful, but little Jem is our main focus now. And he's doing beautifully, isn't he, Lachlan?" Kirsty's brisk words seem to help Lachlan regain his composure. He takes a breath, turns back, gives a shaky smile. "He's a pretty cool little dude." He fishes his phone out of his pocket. "I can show you some pictures."

He clicks away, gazes tenderly at the screen, holds out the phone for me to see: as far as I can tell, his Jem is indistinguishable from most six-month-old babies—plump, cross-eyed, a wisp of dark hair on an otherwise bald head—but something in me aches—for the poor motherless babe or for myself, I can't be sure. He's sitting propped up on cushions, dressed in a slightly grimy pastel onesie.

"Oh, he's gorgeous. You're lucky."

"I am." Lachlan smiles proudly. "I've got one of him crawling . . ." He takes the phone back, starts scrolling.

His mother interrupts, rolling her eyes. "No, Lachlan. I'm one hundred percent certain that Jo doesn't want to look at your baby photos right now."

Lachlan grimaces. "I guess not." He puts the phone back in his pocket.

"Not everyone thinks babies are all that interesting, darling. I'm sure there's nothing further from your mind, Jo?"

I shrug, feel myself redden, change the subject. "So where is he now—your Jem?"

"He's at day care two days a week. I work from home once a week, and Mum has him the other two. We moved in with Mum after Annie . . ." He breaks off, looking miserable again.

We stand awkwardly for a moment, conversation at a standstill. Kirsty, ever the diplomat, breaks the silence. "Well, we'd better get on. We need to get Jem before six thirty. It's a long day for such a littlie."

"Of course. And I'd better get going. Dad's waiting for his dinner. It was great seeing you both. And it'd be lovely to meet your little boy sometime."

"I'll organise something soon. A Friday night, maybe." Kirsty smiles. "Anyway, you don't want to keep that cranky bastard waiting." She gives me a hug. "Now, don't be a stranger, will you? We've missed you, you know. Both of us."

~

There's a romantic idea about what life might be like as an only child raised by a single father. I'd encountered it endlessly, especially from my classmates' mothers—who saw my dad as a tragic figure—a young man, younger than most of the other parents, left to raise a child on his own. Perhaps they imagined us a cosy twosome—Dad doing his best to make up for what I'd lost when Mum went, making sure the damage was limited, making sure I felt loved, that I didn't feel abandoned. But that's not really how it was. Not by any stretch of the imagination.

In reality, after Mum left, it felt as if I had been abandoned by both of my parents. Dad provided a roof over my head—food, clothes, a sense of physical security—but very little in the way of outward affection. In company—say at his parents for our weekly dinner, or on the rare occasion he was around other parents—he would ruffle my hair and manage to discuss some aspect of my clothing or my schooling or my health with interest, to show some fatherly concern. At these times, I felt like a flower opening to drink in the warmth of the sun—the slightest attention and I unfurled, desperate for more. But there was very little of even that most basic sort of attention in our day-to-day life. My father's grief—looking back I'm sure that's what it was, but back then, I had no idea—was expressed as anger. It was all encompassing, all consuming—and utterly isolating. Even if that anger wasn't directed at me, what I experienced was, at most, a sort of disinterested, almost managerial kindness. After Mum left, I really was, in a profound sense, on my own.

I have only two clear images of my father in the days after my mother disappeared. The first is of me crying when it first became clear that she wasn't coming back, those desperate heaving sobs that only children are capable of—and Dad picking me up and hugging me hard, his own eyes filling, whispering some words of comfort.

The other is arriving home from school, dropped off at the front gate by one of the revolving cast of helpful mothers during that first terrible year—to find him there already, sprawled on the lounge—drunk, angry, ranting. When he saw me standing at the door, shocked and frightened, he yelled at me to get out, to go to my room, to not come out until he told me.

It was then that I discovered books. The lounge room—where Dad spent his evenings with his bottle, or bottles, where he listened to the same songs, watched the same music DVDs—*Woodstock*, *The Last Waltz*, *Monterey Pop*—over and over again, was somewhere I wasn't welcome, somewhere I didn't want to be. Instead, I'd try to lie low, to disturb him as little as possible—which meant staying in my bedroom, from the time I got home till dinnertime, reading books I'd brought home from school, initially, and then as I got older and was allowed to walk home by myself, from the town library. I would keep reading as the room darkened, lost in someone else's story, and more often than not, eating my dinner, if there was any, in my bedroom. My favourite novels—*Matilda*, *The Secret Garden*, *Harry Potter*, *Great Expectations*, *Jane Eyre*, *Persuasion*—most often featured orphaned children searching for love and a home.

It sometimes feels like I stayed there, alone in that bedroom, like Rapunzel, for the next ten years. But my hair never seemed to grow past my shoulders, and the handsome prince was nowhere in sight.

~

In some ways, our relationship improved as I grew older. Despite everything, I wasn't unpopular at school. I had friends and wanted to do the usual teenage things. So then there were all the usual confrontations—Dad was emotionally neglectful, sure, but he was still reasonably strict: for the most part there was no getting away with truanting, late nights, lies about whom I was with, where I was staying. At least the arguments meant he was forced to engage, after a manner. He took some interest in the music I listened to—mostly telling me to turn it off or turn it down, but occasionally he would comment on what I was listening to, and the comments weren't always negative. Although he would never admit it, I think I introduced him to as much music as he me. Amy Winehouse, the Strokes, Ben Harper, D'Angelo.

Driving was the other area where we were forced to spend some time together. I got my driver's permit as soon as I turned sixteen, despite assuming that it was pointless, that he'd never give me the fifty-odd hours of instruction that were required to get a licence in those days. I had a part-time job at the local fruit market—earning around sixty dollars a week, and more in the holidays—and had decided that I would have to spend virtually all that money on weekly driving lessons. But when I came home with my learner's permit, Dad was surprisingly enthusiastic. His own father had been mad about cars, and as a teenager Dad had been a rally car enthusiast—travelling about the place to watch the races—and had even raced a friend's car, once or twice. He had decided it was important to train me to drive properly—and not like a girl, as he put it. So, unlikely as it was, he'd taken me out to a mate's property every Sunday for six weeks, and taught me to drive on the most difficult surfaces, and under the most extreme circumstances. At first, I'd been terrified, but eventually I'd understood that the worst I could do out here was to roll the car—there was literally nothing to hit—and soon enough I was getting out of skids, doing doughnuts, creating dust clouds. I could drive a whole lot better than any girl I knew, and most of the boys too.

Once I got my licence, we weren't exactly best mates—but at last I'd captured his interest, gained his respect. It turned out I wasn't just my mother's daughter—excelling academically, interested in reading, writing, art—which somehow never failed to insult him, showing signs of my upper-class heritage. If I hadn't already been indisputably his child—something that was obvious to anyone who'd ever seen the two of us together—in some far more important way, I'd finally aligned myself with my father. I was, at long last, approved—unmistakably a chip off the old block.

Now, home again, it seems that not that much has changed. But I'm older, braver, and there are questions that I need to ask him, questions that need answering.

Dad and I sit in the lounge room with the windows opened wide, the lights dimmed, the fan blasting, trying and failing to get the inside temperature down. Dad is on his third whiskey, has his recliner cranked back to fully horizontal. I am lying on the old vinyl lounge—which is simultaneously sticky and slippery with sweat. Alligator lies between the two of us, completely listless, not even wagging his tail when I scratch between his ears.

Dad is watching *The Last Waltz* for the umpteenth time. I say *watching*, but he has his eyes closed, only opening them briefly to pick up his glass. I've been scrolling through Instagram—have somehow found myself on Harry's latest girlfriend's feed (public, naturally) and have been going through her last two years' posts. It has been quite an education to meet one of Harry's conquests this way—to see her in various complex and sexually alluring yoga poses, quaffing glasses of champagne with her equally alluring mates on beaches, yachts, holiday houses in the mountains, with her perfect skin, her perfect hair, her perfect outfits—always #Livingherbestlife. Once I would have been jealous, but now I feel vaguely sorry for her. I wonder whether I should tell her that her #soulmate is a self-obsessed arse who'll dump her when the next cute thing catches his roving eye—but decide that it isn't worth it. In fact, it looks like they're probably a match made in heaven. And anyway, it'd only sound like #sourgrapes. I sigh, impatient with my pettiness—I'm well and truly over him, after all—and close down the app. I have more important things to do. I tuck the iPhone down the side of the lounge.

I gird my loins and ask the question I've been wanting to ask since I arrived.

"Do you still have Mum's letter, Dad?"

Dad doesn't answer or even acknowledge the question, so I ask him again, more loudly, and this time he responds.

"I heard you the first time, Josephine."

"And?"

"And what?"

"Oh, come on, Dad. Stop it. Do you still have Mum's letter?"

"Which one?"

"You know which one—that one I found after she left."

"I do."

"Can I see it?"

There is another lengthy pause.

"Dad?"

"Why? What do you want it for?"

"What do I want it for? I just want to . . . I just want to read it again."

He opens his eyes, turns his head to look at me.

"You don't need to read it again. You can remember it as well as I do."

"No, Dad. I can't remember it. Not word for word."

"You know the gist, though. Surely, that's enough."

I can feel the colour flaring in my cheeks, that old feeling of frustrated rage that he provokes. "I just want to see the letter for myself. It's not asking that much. If you have it, why can't I see it?"

"Well, mostly because I can't be stuffed getting it."

I know that his tone, laconic, amused, is intentional. *Just stirring,* he'd say, deadpan, if I called him on it. *Don't be so sensitive, Jojo.*

"Why don't you just tell me where it is, and I'll get it myself. You don't have to move a muscle."

"I'll get it. But tell me, why do you want it?"

"I don't know, exactly. I just want . . . to see it. Read it again. There's no real reason."

"If you're thinking of getting it tested, that's all been done. It was written by your mother; there's absolutely no doubt that it was her, even if I didn't know that already."

"I know that." I can't really explain to myself why it seems important that I see the letter itself. "I just want to see . . . if the letter really does say what we've always assumed it said? I mean—she didn't say that she was leaving forever, did she? That she'd never come back."

"Of course it bloody means what it's saying. It couldn't be clearer."

"But did she actually say outright that she was leaving? What if—" I hesitate. I don't know where I'm going with this.

Dad pulls the lever of the recliner, sitting upright with a noisy jolt. "Jesus Christ."

He gets out of his chair, walks slowly over to the veneer wall unit, and reaches into a drawer under the television. He scrabbles about, then takes out a small yellow envelope. Passes it to me.

I begin to prise out the letter within, but Dad's hand flashes out and grabs mine, holds it hard.

"Take the bloody thing away. I don't want to see it. And I'm not interested in your speculations. Your mother left, Jo. She didn't want any of us in her life: not me, not her family. Not you. And I'm sorry about that. More sorry than you can imagine. But I can't change it. And I don't want to go back there." His voice, so quiet I can barely hear it above the TV, is a warning. "If you want to find her, that's your business—I've told you that before. But don't bring me into it. Don't even discuss it with me. I've no doubt your mother is alive somewhere—but she's been dead to me for nigh on twenty-five years—and I don't need her in my head."

He releases my hand, sinks back onto his chair, and closes his eyes, clearly exhausted.

"I'm going to sleep out here tonight. Only fucking place cool enough. Leave the fan on when you go."

It's a clear dismissal. I go.

~

Arthurville, 1994

On that particular day I was meant to go home with Ally Armstrong, but I had lied and told her that Dad had the afternoon off, that he'd told me I could walk home on my own.

The walk from school wasn't difficult or even long. It was about a kilometre and a half, with no main roads to cross. I'd walked the route with the neighbouring older kids a few times but had never done it on my own. I half ran the entire way, my backpack bumping painfully, side and legs burning, to make sure I got ahead of the crowd, so that there was no one to stop or question me. My father was going to be furious if he found out what I'd done, but I had a plan. When he got home, I would tell him that Ally's mum had dropped me off on her way to the shops, just a few minutes before he was due home, to save him the trouble of picking me up. There were numerous holes in my plan, but I was a confused eight-year-old, not a logistical genius.

I reached home with a stitch in my side, soaked with sweat, breathless. I bypassed the front gate, went straight down the driveway, through the side gate to the back—the door onto the back verandah was usually left ajar, and even if it happened to be locked, I could climb through my open bedroom window with the help of a chair. I'd had to do it often enough when Mum had forgotten her key. But the back door was unlocked, and I'd let myself in, gone straight to the pantry, hoping that somehow, miraculously, some exciting snacks (chocolate, biscuits, cake, chips) might have materialised. Dad was not one to buy anything more than was required for dinner or school lunches, and there was only the usual: a box of Weet-Bix, another of Nutri-Grain, a loaf of white bread, peanut butter, and Vegemite, a few assorted tinned meals—soups, stews, beans—condiments. I shook the box of Nutri-Grain—it was still half-full—and took it over to the bench. If the teetering pile of dirty dishes on the sink was anything to go by, I was unlikely to find a clean bowl, so I went to the dresser, where the "good" dishes were kept. The good dishes had been a wedding gift from Dad's parents, a pretty gold-rimmed china set that was never used, and that Mum had told me was made from ground-up bones. I reached right to the back to get a small dessert bowl, and found instead an envelope—slightly bent, worn and scrappy—which must have slid from the back of the drawer into the cupboard, as happened occasionally when the drawer got too full. I pulled out the envelope, which had my father's name scrawled across it, and put it on the kitchen table, completely incurious. I poured my cereal and went into the lounge, turned the TV up as loud as I could.

Dad arrived a few hours later. He'd called at the Armstrongs' to pick me up before coming home—an inevitability I'd somehow failed to take into account—and had rushed straight home, angry with me, but even angrier that Ally's mother could have been so stupid. The anger didn't last long, though. Within moments, he saw the envelope on the dresser.

"What's this?"

"I don't know. I found it in the bottom cupboard."

I watched him as he tore open the envelope and read the letter it held. His face paled. I knew even before he'd said anything that it was from my mother.

~

Dear Mick,
You're right about everything, and I'm sorry. So sorry.
I'm going to try and sort it all out.
I never meant to hurt you or Jo.
Merry xx

~

Arthurville, 2018

I am far too wired for sleep, and far too hot. There's a fan in my bedroom, but it barely moves the thick, soupy air. There are so many things that bother me about my mother's letter. Why hadn't she left it somewhere more prominent? Why didn't she contact the police when the search was underway—just to reassure everyone? And why, why has she never been in contact since? There are so many things I need to think about. Or talk through with someone who knows how to listen.

It's only nine thirty, and Tatts will still be open—maybe I'll even recognise someone there. I don't usually like going to pubs on my own, but suddenly I need the company—and the air-conditioning won't go astray. I pull on my jeans, a clean T-shirt, joggers—and creep out the back door, closing it gently behind me. I think about driving, but that would disturb Dad, and anyway it's only a ten-minute walk.

The outside air is stifling and completely still. The stars are brilliant in the dark and infinitely cloudless sky. The ten-minute walk feels like twenty—it's like wading through treacle—and by the time I arrive, my face is streaming, my shirt stuck to my body.

At first, I can't see anyone I know. I stand in the doorway, considering my options. Half a dozen middle-aged blokes, Dad's vintage, are clustered around the bar, in a kind of companionable solitariness. Four youngish men are playing pool, all looking as if they've just come in off the farm—wearing regulation flannies and jeans, despite the heat. There are two other blokes standing at the bar, too, chatting, one of them in a checked shirt and jeans, the other, younger, wearing all black. This one I recognise.

"Shep?"

It's been more than a decade, but I'd know that dark curly hair, those broad shoulders, the solid neck anywhere. When he turns, frowning, a schooner of beer in each hand, I'm forced to second-guess my vision: he's wearing black pants and a black shirt with a stiff white collar.

"Sharpe." The frown turns to a smile—cautiously friendly. "I heard you were back."

"Good news travels so fast. I had no idea *you* were here, though. So what's all this?" I gesture at his costume. "Have you been to a costume party?"

He gives a short laugh. "I guess you could call it a party. Nah. It's actually my uniform. I'm on the job."

"The job? You've joined the cops?"

"What? No. I'm a minister."

I look at him blankly. "Of what?"

"Of religion. A priest."

"But . . . last I heard, you were in the army."

"I did my seven years. I've been out for a long time."

"Oh God. We're officially old."

"We are."

"But how are you a priest? You definitely weren't religious when we were kids."

He raises his eyebrows. "That's news to me."

"Well, you never said anything."

"What should I have said?"

"And you didn't act any different to the rest of us. I mean, it's not like it stopped you . . ." I pause, not wanting to go any further down that route.

He notices my discomfort, laughs. "No. I guess it didn't."

"But isn't that . . . like, a major sin."

He shrugs. "Yeah. But then so is lying."

I don't seem able to change the subject. "But don't priests have to be, like, virgins?"

"Just celibate—at least until they get married."

"You can get married?"

He laughs. "I'm Anglican, not Catholic. Anglican priests have been allowed to marry since, *like*, forever. They can even be female."

"Oh. So, um, are you?"

"Am I what? Female?"

"Married."

"Married? No? Where'd you get that idea?"

"Nowhere." I can feel myself blush, change the subject quickly. "Where do you work?"

"Here. At Saint John's. I've been back just over six months."

"And what do I call you? Vicar? Reverend? Your holiness?"

"Shep'll do."

"Right." I look at him for a long moment, taking it in. "It's just so . . . unexpected. You a priest. I would never . . . it's not how I thought of you."

"That's the good thing about getting away and growing up. You don't have to be who everyone else thought you were."

"No. And you know what else is really weird?"

"What?"

"The fact that we've both ended up back here." I look around the pub, at the old blokes who could have been drinking here when we were teenagers, the posters on the wall that haven't been changed since the nineteen eighties, the carpet that should have been replaced fifty years ago.

"God help us."

For the first time I register his drinking companion, who is leaning back against the bar, observing us with interest. It's my uncle Roly.

"Josephine." His smile is surprisingly friendly.

"Roland." I think about what Dad has told me, keep my expression cool.

"Haven't seen you once in what, more than thirty years, and now twice in one week. Here's to our newly flourishing relationship." He raises his glass, tips back his head, and downs the beer in one go. "I don't want to be a party pooper, but I'd better be getting home. Don't want the constabulary locking me up for drink driving, eh, Father?"

He claps Shep on the shoulder, nods at me, and saunters out the door.

"What a dickhead."

Shep is watching my face. "I forgot he was your uncle. He's your mum's brother, right?"

"Yeah."

"You really haven't seen him for years?"

"I'm not sure that I ever met him before I came back. Not that I can remember, anyway. How do you know him? He seems an unlikely drinking companion."

"I just bumped into him at the bar—we were just discussing business. He lets me use the property for a few projects . . ." Shep doesn't seem keen to elaborate. "Actually, I'm here with a friend." He gestures to a corner table at the back of the room. "I think you might know her." It's Edith. She's on her phone, head down, frowning and intent. She hasn't seen me. "You go over and say g'day, and I'll bring the beers."

Edith isn't in the least surprised to see me. She puts the phone away with a sigh. "Oh God." She sighs, shakes her head ruefully. "I need an intervention."

"Instagram?"

"Worse. Twitter. So many idiots out there. Anyway, fancy meeting you here."

"I'm glad you're here. I just came on spec. I had to get out."

"Same. Too fucking hot at our place. What is it with rentals and no air-con? It ought to be written into the Geneva convention or whatever it is. Like a human right. Fizz wouldn't come out—it's too late for her—but I couldn't stand it. Lucky for me, the good rev is always up for an impromptu late-night brew. I take it you're old mates?" Shep is heading back towards us, drink tray in hand.

Out of the office, Edith is almost unrecognisably glamorous. She's wearing skintight jeans, a midriff top; her hair, released from the severe bun she wears at work, is a mass of long ringlets, her only makeup a slash of scarlet lipstick. Shep passes out the beers, settles in the chair beside her. They're both tall and outrageously good-looking. They make a striking couple. I feel a tiny, and totally unreasonable, pang.

I shake my head. "Of course you two know each other. Why am I not surprised?"

She turns to Shep. "I dunno, do we know each other?" She puckers up expectantly. Shep grins and pats her on the shoulder.

"Too well to fall for that."

Edith grins. "I think your sweet Lucy wouldn't approve."

"Your Lucy?"

He shakes his head. "She's not *my* Lucy. She's just . . . a work colleague."

"I'm not sure that Lucy would agree. Anyway, you know you've got something when even I can't resist your charms."

"What can I say?"

Edith turns to me. "Hey, d'you reckon the good father here is portal-worthy?"

"Portal-worthy?" Shep looks confused.

Edith laughs. "Don't worry about it, Rev. We're discussing matters you don't need to know about. Sex. Sin. I wouldn't want to sully your holy ears."

"What are you talking about? That's kinda my job description. I'm all about the sinners."

Edith raises her glass. "Here's to sinners then. Where would we be without 'em?"

"So what's going on out at Pembroke?"

Edith looks at Shep. "The rev is setting up a cult."

He rolls his eyes. "Hardly."

"You heard your charming uncle mention the delinquent whisperer when we were out there this morning?"

"Vaguely." To be honest, I'd been so struck with just being there, at Pembroke, meeting Ruth, that I'd hardly taken in anything that Roland had said.

"When that wanker—sorry, your charming uncle—was talking about the boys getting into trouble this morning, that's what he was talking about."

"I'm still lost."

"David runs the Second Chance initiative. You must have heard of it—it's been all over the news. The Second Chance boys?" The voice comes from behind me; the speaker is an ethereally beautiful blonde, small and slight and perfectly proportioned, who's wearing what looks like a Regency-era floral sundress—the sort of dress that would look ridiculous on me—and on most people. She is the kind of woman who makes me feel awkward and overweight and decidedly unfeminine.

"You must be Jo." She holds out a pale, long-fingered hand. "I'm Lucy Cavendish. David's curate." Her voice is at odds with her delicate looks—precise and clipped and schoolmarmy, and ever-so-slightly English.

My own intonation deepens, and my accent broadens in reaction to her plummy tones.

"His curate? Isn't that for rashes?"

Lucy isn't amused. "I'm kind of a priest in training. Working under David."

"Oh. Right. Wow. That sounds interesting."

She nods, gives a beatific smile. "You know, Jo, I'm actually a distant cousin of yours."

"You are?"

"My granny and yours were cousins."

"I didn't know Nan had any cousins. She didn't really have any family as far as I knew. I mean, wasn't she adopted?"

"Oh, not the Sharpes." She's quick to correct me. "I'm related to your *other* grandmother. Your Beaufort grandmother."

81

"Oh, Ruth. Right." I should have known—there's no way someone so blatantly well-to-do could have any connection to my father's family. "So did you grow up here? Sorry to be so dim, but we didn't really have anything to do with my mum's family."

"I'm aware of that." Her smile is irritatingly knowing. "I'm from Sydney, originally. Wahroonga? But I've just got the job out here. It's been great to have the family connection. Ruth is lovely."

I blink and nod. I'm not sure what I'm meant to say.

"Okay—who wants another round?" Shep, who has been waiting patiently, intervenes. "Edith's shout."

~

It turns out that Shep's main work is running Saint John's newly established youth ministry. He started a local program, inspired by a bloke up north, which involves him helping boys who've been in trouble with the authorities, by teaching them various practical skills.

It had begun with a couple of the kids he'd picked up when he was running the church's night bus. "We'd been talking about dogs, and I'd told a few stories about how clever farm dogs were, how farmers trained them to work with the animals—some of them didn't have a clue. I told them I'd take them out to see them in action if they turned up on Saturday morning—sober—and two of them actually did. I called Roly—he's got a couple of champions—and he said yes, so I took them out to Pembroke. When they met the dogs, and watched what they were doing, they wanted to have a go themselves. And it's just gone from there, really."

"So what—you teach them farming skills?"

"Not farming, exactly. Rural life skills, you might call it."

"And it's making a difference?"

"A couple of my older lads—those two first boys, actually—are working as stockmen for Roland—and so far it's working out. I'm talking to him now about letting us fit out one of his shepherd's huts up near the Queensland border so I can take a bunch of them out camping for a longer period. A kind of outback intensive."

I'm impressed, but slightly confused. "But how does God come into this? Shouldn't you be telling them Jesus loves them? And what about Sunday school—all that stuff?"

"I think they'll be more likely to believe they're loved when they've got skills, and jobs, to be honest."

"What Mr. Humility isn't telling you is that it's working magic." Edith's smile was as proud as any mother's. "Most of these kids come from such bad places—their families are fucked, they've been inside, or they're heading there. But for some of them, a couple of months spent learning some skills with Father Shep here and they're turning it around. Taking responsibility for their lives, getting jobs, helping their mates. It's some sort of miracle—you can ask anyone. About a dozen kids have done it—just locals so far—and there's already a waiting list."

My doubt must have been obvious. "Why don't you come out with us some time?" Shep says. "You can meet a few of the kids. Check it out."

"To Pembroke?" I made a face.

"Not necessarily. Anyway, I'm sure Roly won't care."

"But what about your boys? Won't I . . . cramp their style?"

"I'll just tell 'em you're me mate. It'll be right. They trust me. And anyway, you've got a few skills that might be worth transferring."

Merry

Arthurville, 1986

She'd only meant it to be a brief and casual interlude before she headed off to uni. In the beginning it was mostly because she was bored, a little bit lonely. She'd known most of these kids as a child—but not well.

Her family had lived out at Pembroke—only sixty or so miles from Arthurville—for over a hundred years. The Beauforts had employed locals as labourers, shearers, jackaroos, boundary riders, domestics— with wages always at the lower end of what they should be—equal opportunity exploitation for all genders, races, and creeds. The family had stumped up money on occasion for halls, park rotundas, civic awards—and retained some inexplicable aura, but they weren't locals, not in any real sense.

Of course, none of this history seemed to matter, not when school was out, and summer meant long days spent floating down the river on air beds, or out at the dam waterskiing, or stretched out like lizards on the scorching cement at the public baths. Nights were for the pub, or partying—drinking and bonging, talking crap, listening to music—and no one cared where you came from or who your parents were. Merry had thrown herself into this new scene enthusiastically, driving into town most weekends when she wasn't needed. Her mother appeared to be indifferent to her activities, but she knew, instinctively, to keep quiet about her relationship with Michael Sharpe, which had developed into something unexpectedly intense. There had been no cringe-inducing protestations of undying affection, no half-baked hopes of longevity, but somehow it was more than simply an itch scratched, for both of them. It's not as though they had much in common. Not background or interests. Mick had left school when he was only fifteen, but he was smart in a way that was different from other boys she knew—practical, observant—and had a dry wit that never failed to surprise her. Though he was a talented driver—he'd won a local car-racing championship at seventeen—he had no real aspirations or ambitions.

His background was one of respectable poverty—his mum a part-time cleaner at the hospital, his dad a linesman for the PMG. His parents, who were relatively old—both in their sixties—were friendly and accepting, though she suspected they had their own reservations about the friendship. She was always welcome to stay the night—his parents politely pretending that she stayed alone on the sleep out, ignoring the muffled giggles and groans after Mick's inevitable creep down the hallway. They spent endless hot afternoons and evenings alternating between making out and listening to music on his state-of-the-art boom box. Compared to her own life, there was no pressure, and no expectations. None that she could see, anyway. His parents' affection was easy and uncomplicated—they were proud of him for working hard, for being loyal, for being honest. He didn't have to prove himself to earn their love—they were satisfied with who he was. Oh, they got angry with him now and then—when he drank too much, or slept too late, or didn't mow the lawn when he'd promised, or failed to dry the dishes after a meal. But it was nothing major, and no one seemed to hold a grudge.

The Sharpes were the sort of people that her mother and Roly patronised, and that her school friends would laugh about openly, if they noticed them at all. Shabby, provincial, uneducated, irredeemably working-class. And yet they enjoyed their family life in a way that she'd never experienced. She liked the way Mick genuinely enjoyed his mum's dull dinners, chops and three veg, tinned pears and packet custard for dessert. The way he laughed good-humouredly at his father's crude jokes. The way all three of them argued and teased each other, the way no one took offence.

But however much she liked Mick, however much fun she was having, Merry knew she was slumming it. Nothing that happened this summer was serious; none of it was real. Merry's future was elsewhere: a long way from Mick, from Arthurville, from Pembroke. She was just waiting for this summer to end, and then she'd be on her way.

She hadn't bothered to go to the doctor—had known what it was right away—the slight queasiness, the aching breasts, the tiredness that made her sleep late, that persisted all through the day. She'd kept it to herself for a week or two, and then told Mick, because who else could she tell? Jenny and Angie weren't close friends, not enough that she'd tell them about something like this. And she knew full well that telling them would be like broadcasting it from a TV station—the whole world would know in about half an hour that Merry Beaufort was up the duff. She couldn't confide in her boarding school friends—the thought of their total incomprehension would make her laugh if the situation wasn't so disastrous. And the thought of telling anyone in her own family made her shudder. It was all so unfair. She'd done all the right things: she'd been on the pill since she was sixteen, had arranged it when she was away at school so there would be no questions asked. Her mother had never given her the "talk," and it would have been excruciating had she tried. In fact her mother had never really talked to her seriously about anything—what to do, how to be—nothing positive, anyway. All instruction came in negatives. Everything important that she'd learned had been through her own experience, her own mistakes.

She told Mick, who was shocked, but not quite as appalled as she'd expected. And who, after digesting her news, was mildly ambivalent when it came to what they ought to do next.

They were lying side by side at Sandy Bank Beach—a shady, slow-moving part of the river, where, if you squinted hard and ignored the texture of the grey gravelly sand, you could pretend to be by the seaside. Even at this time of year, the water, which flowed out from the dam, was freezing.

"You don't have to get rid of it, you know," Mick said quietly. If he was trying to be reassuring, he'd missed the mark.

"What do you mean? Of course I have to get rid of it. I'm not even eighteen. I can't have a baby."

"Well, I mean—I wouldn't mind if you did. A baby would be kinda . . . cool."

He looked down and away from her, his face pink.

"Cool? Are you for real?" She'd laughed. "I don't even know if I want kids ever. And I definitely don't want them right now. And how would I do it, anyway—live on the single mothers' pension?"

"You wouldn't have to be a single mum."

"What?"

"We could get married." He spoke tentatively, but she knew he was in earnest. "I'd kind of like that."

Merry's laughter dried up. "You're serious, aren't you?"

"I mean—would it really be that bad? We could rent a house. I've got over six grand saved up." He frowned. "We could even buy a place. If I do a bit of overtime, I'll make enough to support us both for a while. And then when you want to, when the baby's old enough, you can get a job. Mum and Dad would help. I know they would."

"Mick, I—"

"We really dig each other, don't we? And I reckon it would be good to have kids young. You'd get to grow up with them. I don't want to do it when I'm old, like my parents."

It had never occurred to her that life could be that simple. That she could make her own life—have a baby, buy a house, get a job—with none of the pressures of performing, of being part of her own family, her own crowd, of succeeding—of being constantly judged and always found wanting. She shook her head hard, as if to dislodge this strange idea. It was impossible.

"Don't be ridiculous. I'm not having a bloody baby—I'm going to uni. I'm already booked into college. I want to do things, go places. You know, have a proper life." She jumped up. "I'm having an abortion, and I need to get it sorted fast."

Mick sat up slowly. "I don't really, you know, I don't know what I feel about abortion. I mean, aren't you killing a baby?"

"A baby? No way. It's just a blob. Cells. It's nothing."

He nodded slowly, then gave a cheerful smile to show that he understood.

"It's your decision."

"And you can help pay, if I don't have enough? I can't ask Mum."

He swallowed. "Of course."

"And can you take me wherever I need to go? I'm guessing that's going to be Sydney."

"Whatever. But you know, if you change your mind, I'm here for whatever you need." She nodded her thanks, avoided making eye contact. His expression was so serious, so intense.

In the end, Merry hadn't changed her mind voluntarily. Her mother changed it for her.

She'd eventually seen a doctor, not the family GP—who she knew would tell her mother, despite the rules of patient-doctor confidentiality—but instead had made an appointment with a GP in Namba, a few hours away. She didn't have a clue where or how she was meant to get this thing fixed. There was no one she cared to ask, no one who could be guaranteed to keep quiet, and she had banned Mick from discussing it with any of his friends. The doctor—a middle-aged man—had been mildly disapproving, had clearly not believed her when she told him she was on birth control, that she'd had a bout of gastro that might account for it—but he had given her the number of a place in Sydney anyway. As she'd suspected, there was nowhere closer. She had called up and made the arrangements—all in vague euphemistic terms—for her procedure. She had gasped when they'd told her the cost—it was more than she had imagined, and far more than her own meagre savings would cover. Mick hadn't flinched when she'd told him, though he'd looked glum.

She told her mother that she was going to Sydney for the weekend. She would be staying with her friend Claire, then going to a dinner with some other friends, then to a party, and to a lunch in Mosman—and that Mick would be taking her down. "Will that boy be staying at Claire's too?" her mother had asked, with faux concern. "I don't imagine he'll have much in common with any of your ALC friends." She'd been right, of course—what would Mick have to say to any of her friends? She could imagine Claire's and Rebecca's barely contained disdain as much as Mick's discomfort. Could imagine his discomfort turning to awkwardness, and from there to a sullen stupefaction, or worse, defensiveness. Both parties were her friends, but there was no crossover. What would Rebecca, with her Clara Bow haircut, her passion for cinema verité, or Claire, with her Sylvia Plath obsession, her goth chic, make of someone like Mick, with his Levi's and flannelette shirts, his fifty-cent rubber thongs, his mullet, his broad accent. The dinged-up truck, the complete lack of money and connections. They wouldn't see past this to the keen intelligence, the decency, the honesty, the complete lack of pretentiousness. She suspected that they didn't even know that these values existed, that there were things that were worth more than big bank balances and fashionable causes and concerns—after all, nor had Merry.

But she'd said nothing in response to her mother. Just shrugged and said that Mick had other things to do; he was just dropping her off. Her mother had given a smug smile, but left it there.

Merry had packed her bag and was waiting in the hall for Mick to pick her up on the Thursday afternoon. They'd booked a hotel room in Newtown, walking distance from the surgery. It was a day procedure—just a local anaesthetic—and the whole thing would be done and dusted by lunchtime. Just before Mick was due to arrive, her mother called her into the office, and she'd walked in, suspecting nothing.

Her mother was sitting behind the ancient partner's desk, her face cold. She gestured to Merry to sit down across from her. "I've just been on the phone to Claire's mother."

Merry had pulled out the chair, but stayed standing. "Okay." She wasn't aware that her mother even knew Claire's mother.

"She says she had no idea that you were staying this weekend."

"Well, maybe Claire just hasn't told her."

"Claire isn't at home, Miranda. She's in Scotland."

"Oh." What could she say?

Her mother folded her arms.

"Do you want to tell me where you're really going? Why you lied."

"Not really."

"Do you want me to guess?"

"Not really."

"Because I don't actually need to guess, Miranda. I've heard you in the bathroom in the mornings. You've lost weight. It's not that hard to work out." Her mother sounded more amused than angry.

Merry said nothing. Shrugged.

"So you admit that you're pregnant?"

"Maybe."

Her mother looked at her for a long time.

"I wish you'd come to me, of course, but I'm glad you're doing the right thing."

"Am I?"

It was the first time Merry had even questioned it herself. Despite Mick's reluctance, his offer, she had never seriously thought about whether or not she should continue the pregnancy. An abortion seemed the only possibility open to her. But now the smug certainty on her mother's face pushed her into arguing the opposite case.

"What do you mean?"

"Maybe it's the wrong thing to do. Maybe I should have it." She threw the suggestions out almost experimentally.

"Don't be ridiculous. You're too young."

"Maybe I really want it."

"I hope you don't imagine that I would support you."

"I didn't ever imagine that, no." Her voice scornful.

Her mother ignored her tone. "So what's the option? Surely you're not thinking about staying with that boy."

"Why not?" Merry was curious now. She'd gone this far, why not keep on going, let her mother expose herself completely?

"Well, I don't imagine he's the sort of person you imagined spending your life with." Her mother was openly sneering now.

Merry hadn't heard the car arrive in the drive, the quiet footsteps across the hallway. A hand dropped lightly on her shoulder.

"And what sort of person should she be spending her life with, Mrs. Beaufort?"

Her mother looked shocked, but recovered quickly.

"I don't remember asking you in."

"You didn't."

"I could have you arrested for trespassing."

"Oh, don't be ridiculous." Merry had had enough.

"Did you just tell me not to be ridiculous?" Her mother drew herself up. She was a tall woman, and she knew how to make herself look imposing. The lady of the manor.

"Well, you are. I invited him. He has every right to be here."

"I think you may be the one who's being ridiculous, Miranda. This house belongs to me. I get to say who comes and goes. If I say your slaggy boyfriend isn't welcome in this house, then he isn't." Merry knew she was furious, but her voice was cool, her expression unreadable. "You can leave, young man. You may have impregnated my daughter, but she has no further need of you. Miranda, you can walk him to the door." Her mother nodded dismissively. "You're not to see him again. This is the end of the relationship. I'll arrange the termination with a local doctor and take you myself."

"No. We've already made the arrangement. It's already sorted. We're going to Sydney now, today." She didn't want her mother with her for this. Just Mick. She moved closer to him instinctively.

Mick stepped forward, spoke. His voice was low but steady. "I understand you're upset, Mrs. Beaufort. I really do. This is just as much my responsibility as Miranda's. I don't really know if an abortion is the right thing to do, but I think I should be involved. I know this mainly affects Miranda, and I'm really sorry for that, but it's my problem too."

Her mother made no sign that she heard—Mick might be invisible. She turned to Merry. "This has gone far enough. If you leave this house with this . . . this boy, that's it. You can forget all about university and college."

Merry was suddenly overwhelmed by a wave of anger—and unlike her mother, there was nothing cool or controlled about it. It was fierce, scorching, wild. The decision was made in a blaze of righteousness: whatever her mother wanted, she would do the opposite.

"No."

"What do you mean, 'No'?"

"I'm not ending this relationship."

"Really?"

"You can't tell me who I can be friends with. It's absurd. This is the nineteen eighties, not the eighteen eighties. I'm an adult. You're just a . . . a disgusting snob."

Her mother was unperturbed by the insult. "I'm a realist, dear. I know how life works, who gets ahead and how. I know what you need for a decent life. Money, education, social standing. If that means being a snob, then so be it."

"Maybe I don't want any of those things. Maybe they're all just bullshit."

"So what *do* you want, dear?"

"I don't know. But I do know I don't want you telling me how I should live my life. Blackmailing me into becoming who you want me to be."

"*Blackmailing* you?"

"Isn't that what it is?"

"I just thought I was raising you—not committing some criminal act." She sounded amused. "So, tell me, what are you going to do, Miranda? Go to Sydney on your own? How will you get through uni? You'll have to work. Where will you live? I'm guessing you wouldn't last a week."

Mick moved closer to Merry, gripped her hand.

"Or I guess you could just stay in town, move in with Prince Charming, have the baby. Become a teenage mother. I don't think you'd last a week doing that either."

CHAPTER FOUR

A LITTLE BIRD

That cornucopia of performing arts talent, the Arthurville Eisteddfod, began last week, and everyone agrees that the standard is the best for many years. Some highlights include Mary Slater and Julie Mills' (Arthurville High, year 12) resounding piano duet of the ever-popular opening of Eine Kleine Nachtmusik. According to my sources the foot tapping ~~drowned out~~ was almost as loud as the piano. ~~Thank God.~~ Saint Martha's kindergarten's "Dance of the Flowers" was Wednesday night's show stealer, and we are all hoping that someone caught one little sweetie's brief unrehearsed snooze ~~(along with the dozens of parents who slept throughout the entire performance, lucky things)~~ on film.

A Little Bird, *Arthurville Chronicle*, 1994

Jo

Arthurville, 2018

It's eight in the morning and I'm still half-asleep. Last night's drinking session lasted until the wee hours. Lucy went home early, but the rest of us stayed until close—which seemed to extend indefinitely (perhaps illegally) because of the heat and the numbers, and it wasn't until sometime after two that I stumbled into bed, sloshed and vaguely pleased with the way the evening had turned out. It's been a long time since I've had that sort of fun—the sort of fun that doesn't involve any sort of tangled relationship shit, or weird submerged competition, or tamped-down resentments—just a straight drink-too-much, crap-talking scenario—with no dramas and no consequences to worry about. It feels like a long time since I've had a night like this with only a mild headache and no regrets. Maybe not since I left home. But there is a warm residue from the night before—the possibility of old friendships and new.

It's a busy day. First up, Dad has an early appointment with Fran. She's agreed to see him before the practice is officially open so I can get to work on time. My father is clearly nervous. He grumbles about the time, but as he complains that he never sleeps anyway, and is awake by 4:00 a.m. every morning, his argument lacks conviction. He continues to grumble in the car, cursing the stickiness of the leather seats, the jerkiness of my gear changes, the potholes I don't manage to avoid, my going too fast or alternatively too slow, the distance I've parked from the surgery, but he shuts up once we're inside. Fran is looking tired already—she'd been called out to help with an unexpected labour in the middle of the night. "That's the thing about country practices—there might be less people—but when it happens, it happens." She yawns. "Okay, Mr. Sharpe. Mick." She waves him into her room. "Do you want Jo to come too?"

Dad looks uncertain.

"I know Jo's not exactly the nurse type"—Fran laughs—"but I think it won't hurt to have someone else know exactly where you're up to. You never know—she might even be helpful down the track." Fran winks, but Dad doesn't crack a smile.

He looks at me thoughtfully. "You can come in, Josephine, but that doesn't mean I want you interfering."

I take a deep breath. "Got it."

Fran puts Dad out of his misery quickly—it's good news. "The latest test results for the cancer show that the initial treatment has been effective. You don't need to go back for more—or not yet. And your liver—well, it's not perfect, but it's stable." Dad's relief isn't immediately apparent. He sits stiffly, his shoulders hunched around his ears.

"So that's the good news." Fran's voice is solemn. "But you know what I'm going to say, and I know you don't want me to say it, but it'd be remiss of me not to. You really have to give up drinking completely, Mick."

"Not even a whiskey?"

"Not even one. I know that you've eased up—and most of the damage was done when you were younger. But if things get worse and you need a transplant . . . well—to be frank, they won't even consider you if you're not completely dry. You're already getting close to being considered too old."

"Right."

"And the cigarettes. Your lungs aren't in the best shape. The X-ray results show scarring—and some of that would be from pneumonia. But there's something else as well—it looks like you've got the beginnings of emphysema."

Dad's expression doesn't alter. "My old man had it too. Killed him eventually."

"I remember old Mr. Sharpe. He lived at the end of my grandparents' street—and he was always good to us kids. He used to give us those little rainbow lollipops."

"He did. You wouldn't do that now, though—you'd be locked up."

"Oh God, you would. What a depressing thought. I didn't know that he had emphysema, though. He always seemed pretty fit. I can remember him out there mowing the lawn when he was pretty old."

"He wasn't all that old. He just looked it. Three packs a day will do that. He was only in his early seventies when he died." Dad avoids looking at me.

"Well, you won't make it to sixty if you don't start looking after yourself." Her voice is stern, but not unkind.

"Sixty?" He looks shocked.

"I'm serious. And you need to get serious about looking after yourself. You've been given a bit of a reprieve. I'd expected worse, to be honest. So don't waste it."

"Righto." Dad nods. "I'll give it a go, I guess. Don't want to . . . look a gift horse in the mouth."

"The department has some useful guides." Fran rummages in her desk, brings out a pile of leaflets. "And there are things we can do if you need help to stop drinking."

He waves his hand dismissively. "I'm already down to one a night. I can stop."

She smiles. "Good for you. I'll give you a prescription for nicotine patches too."

He nods. "Now, if you'll excuse me, I need the gents." He pushes himself out of his chair. "You can give all that rubbish to Jo."

Dad shuffles across the room and closes the door behind him.

"Well, that wasn't too terrible." I sigh, relieved. I was expecting worse—both results-wise and in terms of my father's behaviour.

"The tests are surprisingly okay. If he can just keep it up. I honestly thought that he really didn't have long when I spoke to you."

"Maybe it's my great cooking."

Fran smiles at me across the desk. "That's unlikely. But you know what—maybe it's just the fact that you're here."

I snort. "That's even more unlikely. He seems irritated by my presence about ninety-nine percent of the time."

She shrugs. "It happens a lot. People recover when they've got a reason to."

"Maybe. But he's had that same reason my whole life, Fran."

"Well, maybe he's only just realised. That happens a lot too."

By the time I drop Dad off and get to the office, it's past nine.

Edith has just arrived with coffee for us both and is surveying the day's schedule gloomily. First up we have a high school cricket gala day—three visiting regional high schools and more than twenty teams. I didn't play cricket as a kid and am even less excited by it as an adult. Next up is Grandparents' Day at the Catholic primary school: there's a barbecue at lunchtime, followed by a tour of the classrooms to check out the grandparent-themed artwork. In the afternoon, there's an interview with members of the Arthurville Agricultural Show Committee who have put together the program for this year's show.

The cricket gala day is just as exciting as I'd expected: somewhere between watching grass grow and paint dry—pick your metaphor and put it in an oven. The kids look as though they'd rather be anywhere else, too—the fielders in their stained whites squint out into the red-hot cosmos, the batters listless at the crease, all conserving what little energy they have. The playing fields are brown, the turf dead, the pitches just strips of red dirt that turn to dust as the batters shuffle back and forth. I'm relieved when Edith, who's been collecting a photographic record of the event, arrives back.

"All done?"

"Yes, thank God."

"Did you get the names?" I've been caught out a few times publishing a group shot without naming all the participants and then having to put up with complaints from parents and school—and now make sure no one's image goes into the *Chronicle* without due recognition. She nods.

Next up it's the Grandparents' Day barbecue. As ever at any of these events, there are half a dozen people I recognise, and a dozen more who recognise me. "Jo Sharpe," says one very tiny elderly lady, who is wearing a long skirt and a button-up top despite the heat. "You never got those scales two hands together, did you?" The high-pitched cackle she gives at my confused look fills me with dread.

"Sister Bernard?"

"The one and the same."

"Aren't you a nun anymore?" Perhaps she's had a late-life romance.

"We don't have to wear habits these days." Her smile is wry. "I wouldn't mind a nice short skirt like yours, but I don't think the bishop would approve." Sister Bernard had provided cheap piano lessons to generations of Arthurville children, regardless of denomination. In the short time I'd attended her classes, I'd been desperately afraid of her—despite her small stature, she had a fierce temper and was always very generous with her firm right hand. But now she looks sweetly harmless.

After lunch we survey the special grandparent-themed art display in the kinder rooms—the grandparent figures made from toilet rolls and featuring Paddle Pop walking sticks and cotton wool hair are cute but hardly representative—all the grandparents I've spoken to thus far are fit and spry and surprisingly young. We take photos of a few of them clutching the tomato-sauce-smeared hands of their kindergartners, and then head over to the Country Women's Association rooms, where the Arthurville Agriculture Show Committee is meeting, detouring via the office to drop Edith off. She has a chapter due and has already done more than she signed up for this week. She refuses to lend me her camera. "Just use your iPhone. It's not like you want an action shot—just the committee ladies and some knitwear—or one of those incredible pavlovas they do out here."

~

The show committee turns out to be Kirsty, Mrs. Darling, and my newfound cousin, Lucy. Kirsty is, as always, dressed to the nines: she's wearing a slightly risqué fitted black dress with red stilettos, a Hermès scarf slung around her neck. Her golden hair is as bouncy and shiny as a Pantene ad.

Mrs. Darling seems to have hardly aged. Her kind face looks no more lined, her outfit—a starchy floral skirt and white shirt ensemble—is entirely familiar, and her hair in its elegantly coiled bun is no greyer than I recall. Kirsty and Mrs. Darling both give me highly unprofessional hugs. Lucy-the-curate is less forthcoming. "Good to see you again, Jo. Hope you're feeling okay." Her prissy enunciation makes my teeth hurt.

I smile back. "I woke with a whopper of a headache, but hair of the dog, a bit of a vom . . ." She winces but manages a tight smile. Today she's in work gear, her vibe more Audrey Hepburn than Vicar of Dibley: a white-collared black shirt teamed with a smart black pencil skirt and kitten heels.

"Oh. I see you've already met our lovely Lucy," Kirsty bursts in, perhaps sensing the tension. "We have David Shepherd back home as our wonderful new minister, of course—and I'm certainly not going to complain about him—but I have to say it's lovely to have a woman in a position of leadership at the church. It makes such a difference—not that I'm a parishioner. Well, not an active one." She bestows her generous, wide-lipped smile on Lucy. "But still, perhaps it'll get numbers up. That's what's important, isn't it? And I have to say it's lovely to have some young blood in this committee as well. It's wonderful, isn't it, Eileen"—this to Mrs. Darling, who is observing proceedings with a placid smile—"to have so many young people coming back to the old town?"

"It is. Although I'm not sure that our young ministry has done much to help numbers at the church—I imagine our average age is still about ninety-nine. And most of us are dropping off the perch at a rapid rate."

"It's not that bad," Lucy says, frowning. "David and I did a rough estimate a couple of weeks ago—the mean age of the parishioners is only sixty-eight."

"Anyway"—Mrs. Darling looks at me, her eyes twinkling—"that might just be another story you can look into for the *Chronicle*, eh, Jo? But let's talk about this year's show—there's plenty of excitement to be had on that subject, let me tell you."

I get the details down quickly—what the featured exhibits will be this year, along with the old favourites: there's to be a fallen-timber whittling display in the arts pavilion, the bush poetry slam will have a special guest from farther west who will be judging and performing in the Banjo recitation, the new gourmet pavilion will feature a pavlova-making comp, with a celebrity chef as compere, and along with the more physical events— the wood chopping, stockwhip cracking, and target shooting—there's to be a speed-knitting tournament. The jewel in the crown—the Miss Showgirl Award—has been renamed (and reguidelined) the Arthurville Showperson of the Year Award. This is Lucy's innovation.

"Well, the old showgirl pageant was pretty misogynistic," Lucy says in answer to my questions. "We certainly won't be featuring women in bikinis or aprons."

"I don't think bikinis have featured for quite some time, dear," says Mrs. Darling mildly. "Or aprons."

"So what are you looking for in the Miss, I mean, the Showperson of the Year?" I ask. "I'm guessing it's not the biggest boobs." Lucy doesn't even crack a smile.

"We've got four categories: style, scholarship, spirit, and social justice."

"And do you think you'll get many blokes entering?"

"There's been . . . some interest." Even Lucy doesn't sound convinced. "An all-female competition is completely regressive. It's demeaning. Contemporary women don't want to be objectified in that way."

Lucy's face has gone quite pink—there is clearly some ongoing conflict between the two women.

Kirsty sighs. "Lucy, I understand your concerns, but the Miss Showgirl competition is an Arthurville institution. It's been going for more than a hundred years. My mother was the winner in 1961. I know that's a long time ago, but sometimes I think change for the sake of change isn't necessarily a good thing. I think what we're going to end up with is the usual crop of glamour girls plus a few brave souls from the gay community."

"Ah, well. I'm afraid I was never a Miss Showgirl. They didn't let us Black girls enter in the olden days. And it's too late now, I suppose. I'm a bit long in the tooth. Not to mention wide in the girth." Mrs. Darling's tone is so mild, her expression so bland, that Lucy misconstrues her intent.

"Actually, Eileen, we've taken the age restriction off, too—and it's absolutely not about looks anymore. Not that you aren't—I mean—"

Mrs. Darling laughs. "I'm just pulling your leg, lovey. The changes are good, and necessary, and they'll liven us all up a bit, maybe even get a crowd in. It couldn't be worse than the last few years. Maybe you can get that handsome boss of yours to throw his hat in. Now he'd be a crowd-pleaser."

"David? I don't think he'd—"

"Or how about one of his young fellas? Now that would be a remarkable thing—seeing some of those little fellas having a go—and it might do wonders for their confidence."

Lucy gives a slightly pained smile. "I'll mention it to him."

"Now"—Mrs. Darling directs her smile at me—"if you've got enough, we should let you get on, dear. I'm sure you've got a busy afternoon ahead of you."

"I'd better get a photo, or I'll be in trouble." I look around the room. There are none of the expected CWA rooms props, no baked goods or kewpie dolls on sticks or crocheted stubbie holders. In fact, the only appropriately handcrafted object in the room—which is bare save a Formica table and a spotty portrait of a remarkably youthful Queen Elizabeth—is the macramé plant holder, circa 1972, that's hanging from a hook in the ceiling, cradling a half-dead Boston fern. "If you could all stand close together beside this and say . . . er . . . cheesecake . . . or . . . pavlova."

Kirsty and Mrs. Darling smile at my joke, while Lucy gazes pensively to the side.

Kirsty walks down the front steps with me, treading gingerly in her high heels along the unevenly tiled footpath. "Now, how about you come over for dinner tonight? Lachlan and little Jem will be there. It'd be lovely to have you—and it'll cheer him up a bit."

I hesitate, but only briefly—a night away from Dad is worth whatever matchmaking schemes Kirsty has in mind. And anyway, it will be good to catch up with Lachlan, see the baby.

"I said I'd do dinner tonight, so I'll need to go home and sort that first."

"How about I run something around for your father—Michael was always fond of my cooking, as I recall. I wouldn't mind having a chat with him, to be honest. I haven't really spoken to him properly for years. Barely at all since you left. That way you don't have to worry about his dinner. You can freshen up and then come right over after work."

I can see her looking me up and down, her unspoken judgement that I'm not quite fresh enough. Whatever. She's probably right.

I go back and type up the morning's stories, send my uninspired images to Edith. I enlarge the photograph I'd taken of the show committee on my computer monitor. None of the three women were exactly my idea of the CWA/Arthurville show type—whom I remember from my childhood visits with Nan as being almost indistinguishable: permed and blue rinsed, wearing hand-knitted cardigans and pleated skirts, flesh-coloured stockings and sensible shoes. Kirsty looks like the real estate agent she is—prosperous and professional. Mrs. Darling is a little closer to the CWA ladies I recall—comfortably plump, smelling of powdery perfume, likely to have a spare handkerchief or a peppermint in their handbags—likely to carry a handbag! But when I was a kid, those ladies had always been white, as far as I could recall. Cousin Lucy seems far too young, and far too beautiful, to be bothering about such prosaic events as a small-town agricultural show. But her interest in the community is laudable, and her instincts about change seem fair, even if her reforming zeal gets up the nose of people like Kirsty.

Despite the fact that she's my cousin, I haven't particularly warmed to Lucy. I enlarge her image on my computer even more, look at it closely. I'm certain I've never met her, but there's something about her that's familiar. It comes to me with a sudden bitterness, like aspirin dissolving on the tongue—Lucy reminds me of my mother. It's not just the obvious things, her colouring, her build, but there's something about her mouth, the way her lips turn down slightly when she smiles, giving her a vaguely dissatisfied air. I'm surprised I didn't notice it when we first met.

I quickly minimise the image, and go back to read through the story again, then press print. I'd got into the habit, working with an older subeditor, of printing out a hard copy of my work for a final proofread. But the printer, an ancient inkjet, has run out of paper. The *Chronicle* is a pretty spartan outfit—most likely I will have to run down office supplies myself and cross my fingers that I'll be reimbursed. But there's an old timber storage cupboard at the back of the room that looks as if it might once have been a stationery cupboard, and I decide to forage before I head out into the hot street. Or—a far more appealing alternative—decide that I won't worry about printing, after all.

As expected, the stationery cupboard is virtually empty. There are no pens or pencils or sticky tape or staples—and, most crucially, no photocopy paper. There's a bundle of aged manilla envelopes that have all but lost their manilla, and a lone foolscap pad, its edges grimed, the lines faded almost to invisibility. There's a row of old paper boxes sitting on the top shelf, all unmarked. I pull them down one by one, ever hopeful, but these must be the cartons of crap that Barb mentioned on my first day. The boxes are full of useless junk—old pencils, pens with no ink, rusted staplers, hole punches, rulers, worn stamps, and dried-up ink pads. I'm slightly hopeful when I get to the last three, which all feel as if they contain something papery. The first box is crammed full of articles featuring the local rugby league team, or so it seems from a cursory sift; the second seems to be a more random assortment of sporting events; but the third is a little heavier. I open it hopefully, but there's nothing here that a printer will accept, either—just a plastic file holder crammed with newspaper cuttings, some clipped together handwritten notes, and two old-fashioned scrapbooks, both with LITTLE BIRD printed on the front in thick black marker, and with a crude but oddly lively line drawing of an inquisitive-looking sparrow sketched underneath. I flick through the top one. The book is filled with notes, scrawled in barely legible handwriting, and crammed with newspaper cuttings and letters and cards from assorted senders. Intrigued, I take this carton back to my desk, my printing problems forgotten for the moment, but am interrupted by the phone. It's Mrs. Henderson, the admin from the primary school, with names to go with the smiling faces from this morning's photo shoot.

It's one call after another then—Barb rings with story tips for tomorrow, then Mrs. Darling to confirm that I've got the show dates right, a local café to tell me about an event they're organising to raise money for local charity, and there's no time to look in the box again until the end of the day. I'm still curious, but I really don't fancy looking through it right now—the office is even more unappealing as the afternoon progresses, the fluorescent tube barely bright enough to light my dark corner of the room as the shadows lengthen. I grab the box from under the desk and shove it in the boot before driving home.

Dad is sitting at the table in the kitchen, listening to the news on his ancient wireless. He is in a sour mood, despite the fact that, as promised, Kirsty has delivered dinner to his door.

"Who does she think she is?" he mutters. "Lady bloody Godiva? Bringing the peasants sustenance?"

"I think you might mean Lady Bountiful."

"Eh?"

"Lady Godiva's the one who rode naked through the streets."

"Did she now?" Dad scratches his beard. "Kirsty'd be better off doing that—she's not bad for an old boiler."

"She's not a bad cook, either, Dad. Did you see what she's brought you?"

I take the containers out of the fridge. There are three courses, no less: pumpkin soup, roast pork, and veges—with a little tub of what looks like homemade gravy—and a generous slice of raspberry cheesecake.

Dad is suitably impressed. "Yeah, well—if she could just deliver the food and not expect me to sit there and gasbag, I wouldn't say no. It looks a bit better than the rubbish you serve up, anyway."

I decide to ignore the barb. "I guess she just wanted to catch up."

"Catch up on what, mate? She and your mother were friendly, but that was a long time ago."

"I went to her place a lot, didn't I? After Mum went?"

"You were there a bit." He gives a defensive shrug. "You had to go somewhere when I was away and Nan was working."

"And she'd call in too? I can remember that."

"They all did. Someone was always dropping in with a casserole or a slice. Checking up on me." He snorts. "They probably had some sort of roster. Bloody busybodies, the lot of 'em."

That they probably had a point doesn't really need to be said, so I hold my tongue.

I put the soup in the microwave.

"Did Kirsty stay long?"

"Half an hour, maybe."

"And what did you talk about?"

"I don't know. Nothing much. The price of eggs. Jesus. What is this? The Spanish Inquisition?"

"I'm just making conversation, Dad. Being interested. Asking about your day. I believe that's what people who live with one another do. I'm happy to not speak, if you'd prefer it."

The microwave pings. I don't bother decanting the soup into the waiting bowl, just dump the plastic container in front of him with a spoon and head back to the microwave with his second course.

"You're right." His voice is gruff. "That was out of order. I haven't"—he waves a spoon in the air—"I'm out of practice. Haven't had anyone else to worry about for a while." He clears his throat. "Ah, so Kirsty and I chatted about you mostly—about how nice it was that you were back here, how you were enjoying your job, whether you plan to stay." He slurps a spoonful of soup. "She wanted to know if you were single. I told her you'd broken up with that dickhead."

"Thanks, Dad. Always so helpful."

"No worries, mate." He slurps again. "This isn't bad."

I wonder briefly whether Kirsty's curiosity about my single status extends to my father. "I guess even busybodies have their good points?"

"Ha, well, Kirsty was probably the best of them." He looks thoughtful. "She might've been a busybody, but she was always good to you—I'll give her that."

The microwave pings again, and I take out his next course and arrange it on a plate. "She was good to you too. This was kind of her, wasn't it?"

He gives in. "You've made your point, mate. Tell her I said thank you. That the meal was delicious. That she's welcome to call anytime with offerings."

"Hmm. Maybe not that last bit."

He laughs, picks up his knife and fork. "Whatever you reckon." I look at my father dispassionately for a moment—he's currently too thin, and a little bit the worse for wear and tear, but like Kirsty, he's not bad for his age, despite his ill health and his sometimes less than agreeable attitude. His hair is liberally sprinkled with grey, but it's still thick; his jaw hasn't lost its definition; his eyes are full of humour. As far as I know, there've been no other women in his life since Mum left, and no doubt he's built up some heavy-duty woman-proof armour, but it's not impossible to imagine a woman like Kirsty enjoying his company, fancying him. Maybe Kirsty wouldn't be the one to break through the barricades—but surely it was time someone tried.

"So is young Lachlan going to be there tonight?" Dad asks the question between mouthfuls, his voice studiedly casual.

"I think so. Why?"

"Just wondering. He's a decent fella."

"He is."

"He's got some hard years ahead of him, poor kid. No one deserves that."

He doesn't expect a response, and for once I don't provide one.

~

By the time Dad is fed and settled comfortably in front of the television, Alligator stretched out happily beside him, I have fifteen minutes to freshen up. The results are far from satisfactory. I've swapped my work uniform—jeans, T-shirt, riding boots—for what passes as my most stylish skirt—a floral boho confection that somehow manages to be too long to be short and too short to be long—and a fresh black T-shirt. I experiment with my one pair of (lowish) high heels but feel immediately awkward—so slip into comfortably worn Birkenstocks. My hair is limp and could do with a wash, but right now the best I can do is to wrestle it into a coil, stick it with a comb, and hope for the best. A slash of bright lipstick—which I instantly rub off on a tissue—and a smudge of unsteady eyeliner, and I'm ready to go. I sigh at my reflection in the full-length mirror—as Harry pointed out numerous times, despite all my positive attributes, I somehow never manage to look put together in the way that other women do. "You have all the right parts," he told me once, "but you just can't make them work." I'm too big, too messy, too much.

Kirsty gives me a hard hug, looks me up and down. "You look glorious," she sighs. "Lucky girl to have those legs." Kirsty has changed out of this morning's outfit, is dressed more casually—in loose-fitting pale-blue linen pants and a white shirt—but still looks seriously smart. She ushers me inside.

"Lachie," she calls, "Jo's here." I follow her across the tiled foyer and down the familiar hallway of the meticulously restored Federation-era home, peering into each open doorway we pass. Nothing seems to have changed since I was last here. Kirsty's showpiece—the oversize, bay-windowed, snootily designated "drawing room"—is still furnished with incredibly uncomfortable, and no doubt incredibly expensive, period furniture. The dining room is just as I recall, too—hung with terrible moss-green wallpaper, and featuring a huge mahogany table. We go all the way down to the back of the house, past the staircase and the study, to a twentieth-century addition—a large north-facing, well-lit kitchen and family room. Here everything is bright, comfortable, and contemporary. The air-conditioning must be turned up to eleven—it's an oasis of cool. Lachlan is sprawled on a leather modular lounge, watching the news on a huge flat-screen with the sound down. A pastel-outfitted infant is propped up on the rug in front of him, gnawing hungrily on a wooden brush handle.

"Lachlan!" Kirsty swoops in and prises the brush out of the baby's hand. "You're meant to be watching him." The almost identical expressions of surprise on Lachlan's and the baby's faces are comical.

"Jo. Hey." He clambers to his feet, clearly embarrassed. "Sorry, Ma. I just got distracted for a moment. I don't even know where he got hold of that."

Kirsty sighs. "You don't have to apologise, darling, it's just . . ." The baby begins to whimper, as if he's only just worked out that his chew toy has gone missing. Kirsty bends over and picks him up, shushing him gently. "How about I give him some dinner—you get Jo a drink." She looks at her son closely, as if startled. "Lachlan, those shorts. I thought you were going to get changed?" The baby's wailing suddenly intensifies, and Kirsty sighs again, gives me a weak smile, and heads into the kitchen, jiggling and cooing.

"As you can see, I'm a bit of a crap father." Lachlan looks weary, defeated, and far older than he'd seemed when we met in the supermarket.

I mutter something trite about how hard it must be.

"Yeah. Well, it's certainly not how I imagined my life." He blinks, takes off his glasses, wipes his eyes. "Anyway, it's great to see you. Now, what do you want to drink? Nothing's changed—it's still a virtual bar. We have beer. Full strength, mid strength, light. Lager, pilsner, stout. Or wine. Red, white, rosé. Champagne. Gin, whiskey, vodka. Brandy. Port. Sherry."

His mother calls out. "I'm afraid there are no liqueurs anymore, Jo. Not after your teenage efforts."

We all laugh. Lachlan and I had done our share of raiding his parents' prodigious supplies of alcoholic beverages when we were going out. We'd finally been caught when our efforts to top up a rapidly dwindling bottle of Cointreau with water had been discovered. "I'll have a beer—you choose."

He heads out to the bar (which is in a discreet corner of the drawing room) to do the honours. I wander over to where Kirsty is spooning some sort of slop into a now far-more-cheerful Jem.

I haven't had much to do with babies since Amy and am not certain that I ever want one of my own. I've experienced no clucky-ness; no biological clock has started its relentless countdown. Babies seem like completely alien creatures—small, smelly, demanding—and just a little bit pointless. The most intense emotion they elicit from me is a mild anxiety—which has rapidly escalated to terror on those few occasions when I've inadvertently been left alone with, or asked to hold, a stray infant. I watch as Kirsty feeds Jem, now strapped securely in his high chair, some unidentifiable orangey-brown sludge. The baby somehow manages to swallow and spit simultaneously, and then proceeds to smear the remnants over his face. "He's so cute," I offer limply.

"Isn't he just *ador*able," his grandmother says, happily not noticing my lack of enthusiasm, "and *so* much like Lachie at that age. You really can't see anything of poor Annie in him." She sighs, then holds the spoon up to the baby's mouth. "Come on, sweetie, just one more."

"What happened to her? To Annie?" I ask quietly. "Was it some sort of complication with the baby?"

"No. Nothing like that." Kirsty checks the doorway, drops her voice. "It was suicide. She had postnatal depression. Poor Lachlan found her. She overdosed."

"Oh. God. That's . . . awful. Had she—was she being treated?"

"That's the thing. Nobody had any idea. Not even Lachlan. Not her parents. She seemed to be coping well. Enjoying motherhood. But clearly she wasn't." She pauses to spoon more sludge into the baby's waiting mouth. "If only we'd realised."

Lachlan walks in, holding two beers. Kirsty smiles brightly. "Why don't you two go and chat until dinner. I'll sort out Baby, won't I, boo-boo?" She blows a raspberry on the baby's dimpled arm. "You should take Jo out into the courtyard—it should be cool enough now. I don't think she's seen it."

I follow Lachlan out through the French doors on the eastern side of the family room. The elegant doors are new, replacing an exit that once led to a small verandah and laundry, and lead to a circular sandstone courtyard, protected by a pergola dripping with fragrant purple wisteria.

I look around, amazed. Pretty lights strung at roof level, in amongst the wisteria, cast a twinkly half-light. It's unexpected, entrancing—like something out of a fairy tale.

The space is decorated with pretty period pieces—marble-topped tables, wrought iron and timber benches, art deco–looking rattan chairs and tables, as well as a larger outdoor dining setting. We settle in the rattan chairs.

"This is awesome, Lachlan."

"Yeah. It is pretty amazing." He takes a deep breath. "Annie did it. That's how we met. She was a landscape designer. An artist. She designed it—and then put it together. The whole thing." He looks around sadly.

"Oh, God. I'm so sorry." Everything I say seems hideously inadequate.

He shrugs, tries to smile. Fails. "It's been better."

"She must've been incredibly talented."

"Yeah, she was."

"Was she based here?" It seems unlikely.

"No. She came up from Melbourne to do the job. It might seem pretty strange, but she fell in love with the place—Arthurville, I mean—as well as me." He clears his throat. "After we got married, we bought an old house. You'll remember it—the Beckett place, out on Boyd Road. We were doing it up."

"My God. She really was brave." The Beckett place, a late-nineteenth-century farmstead, has been abandoned for as long as I can remember. It had once been part of a huge estate, but by the time we were kids, there was only an acre or two left. There were rumours of a ghost—a woman was meant to have murdered her husband and children there sometime back in the 1920s. It was the perfect place for local teenagers to hold surreptitious parties—there'd been at least one every summer when I was a kid. Most nights would end with a police visit and annoyed parents called.

Lachlan's expression lightens. "Annie was incredibly brave. She called it her lifetime project. And it would have been. Should have been." He gulps his beer.

"Are you living out there now?"

"I go out on the weekends. It's not too bad. Liveable, anyway. We'd got the basics sorted—a kitchen and bathroom. Still a lot to do. We bought it for a song, so we could borrow a heap for renos."

"Is there a ghost?" I regret the words even as they leave my mouth, but Lachlan doesn't seem to notice.

"Nah. No ghost. Just pipes that need replacing. And the odd creaky floorboard."

"And will you keep it?"

He shrugs. "I dunno. Right now, I can't think past today, let alone work out what I'm going to do next year. I go to work, come home, try and look after Jem. That's about my limit. Mum thinks I should sell up and move back home permanently." He speaks without enthusiasm.

"It must be tempting. Less lonely for you."

He laughs, but it is a harsh, humourless sound. "It doesn't make much difference, to be honest." He shakes himself. "But being here is better for Jem, I guess. Anyway"—he picks up his beer—"it's good seeing you again, Jo. I've always wondered, you know, how things were for you. What you were doing. Welcome back." His smile is wide and genuine, and I get a glimpse of a different Lachlan—confident, his golden good looks suddenly apparent.

"Thanks. It's a bit surprising, but I'm actually enjoying being back," I murmur. I take a sip of my drink, inexplicably shy.

We eat in the courtyard. Kirsty turns on a sprinkler (fed by a tank, naturally), and the sound and smell of the descending water in the hot night air creates some indefinable nostalgia—childhood memories of long summer evenings spent outside. Kirsty's idea of a simple meal is, of course, nothing of the sort. The meal, like the one she'd provided for my father, involves three full courses of restaurant-level dishes. We speak very little as we eat, then sit, slightly stupefied, with whiskey-laced coffees. Lachlan is quiet, lets his mother do the talking.

"I meant to ask—did your father enjoy his dinner?"

"He did. He said it was a vast improvement on his usual meals, and he'd . . . be happy for you to make it a permanent gig." It's only a slight exaggeration.

"Really?" Kirsty looks pleased. "We did have a nice chat. It's been too long."

"Oh good. I was worried. I know he can be . . . cantankerous."

She laughs, brushing my words aside. "Oh, that's just—what would Mick call it?—piss and wind. He's always made me laugh. You know"— her voice is mischievous—"he was pretty cute when he was young. That wicked tongue. Actually, I had a bit of a crush on him."

"Jeez, Mum." Lachlan looks embarrassed. "Is that really appropriate?"

She glares at him. "Obviously it was nothing serious. We were all married. But the four of us did have some fun times." She sounds slightly wistful.

Lachlan looks sceptical. "Really? I don't remember you and Dad ever having fun. You were both just busy. And when you weren't, you were fighting."

She frowns. "Lachlan. Really? That's how you remember your childhood?"

"I don't mean it was a bad childhood. But you and Dad . . . well, you never seemed that happy. I actually thought you were going to end up divorced."

"Oh, darling, that's a bit sad. It might not have been perfect, but it was a happy enough marriage."

Lachlan looks as if he is going to say more, but I interrupt.

"Maybe we get our parents' marriages all wrong. Our memories are so strange. Sometimes I feel like I'm making things up—like half the things I remember are just figments of my imagination."

"Yeah, I get that," Lachlan says. "All my memories of Grandma and Grandpa McLeod are a bit like that. They were in Surfers, so I guess we only saw them every now and then."

"Well, your grandma and grandpa McLeod certainly weren't figments of the imagination." Kirsty's voice is dry. "Unfortunately, some would say." Lachlan's eyes widen.

"And nor was your mother. In fact, it gave me a little pang," Kirsty says, holding her hand to her heart, "when you interviewed us today. I know you don't believe me, but you so reminded me of your mother. It's not anything obvious. But something in your expression, your gestures."

I can't help smiling. No one ever says I look like my mother. I'm the dead spit of my old man, as I've been told often enough: tall, olive skinned, and muscular—running to fat if I'm not careful. Dark eyes, dark wavy hair, a strong roman nose. Thick eyebrows that are, happily, currently fashionable. I clearly come from good peasant stock. Irish, Celtic, Greek. My mother was the opposite: willowy, blonde, beautiful; a delicate English rose, harking back to some long-forgotten Scandinavian roots. Blue eyed, straight nose, a mouth that didn't strain the bounds of decency. She could be very plain or very beautiful. I doubt that anyone had ever called her "strong looking" or "handsome" as an awkward sort of compliment. And as far as I can recall, she was never sweaty or red faced.

"I remember when she got her job at the paper," Kirsty says. "She was just so excited."

"I don't really remember that. I always thought she considered it a bit of a drag. It was a bit different to what I'm doing, though, wasn't it? Just office work? Not writing."

"Oh, yes, there was that, of course. But then she got that cadetship."

"A journalism cadetship? Mum?"

"It was when she went back—after she had Amy. I think the job was to begin the following year. It was a great opportunity for her."

"I really never knew that. Or maybe I did know and I forgot . . . ?"

"Maybe." Kirsty looks thoughtful. "It's not necessarily something you would remember. Kids don't care about those sorts of details, do they?"

She's right. "And Dad didn't—*doesn't*—like talking about Mum. There's no reason he would have discussed it with me."

"Pity."

"Mum a journo. I wish I'd known."

Kirsty puts her hand on my shoulder. "Just between you and me, I think she was doing a wee bit of writing even before she had Amy."

"Really?"

"I always had my suspicions. There was a gossip column back then—A Little Bird. It had been running for years—I think it started in the fifties, maybe earlier—and it ran until, oh, maybe ten years ago. It was always a huge secret; no one ever knew who wrote it, but I had a feeling that your mum was responsible for it when she was there. She had a very particular sense of humour. I remember going into the office one day—I used to take in the copy for the emporium's advertising— the weekly 'specials' and so forth, once a week, and I can remember your Mum typing away with this big grin on her face. She covered up the machine when I walked in."

"I knew she was a reader—I mean, we've still got all her books, but I really didn't know she had any interest in writing. It's a . . . a lovely thing to discover, actually."

"I'm so surprised you didn't know. I assumed she'd left something— notes, stories, diaries."

"Perhaps she took it all with her?"

"Of course. That makes sense. I expect she kept a journal. Most writers do, don't they? To practice a bit? Chronicle their lives."

I shrug. "Not me."

"No? I probably have a very romantic idea about writing."

I'm barely listening. "There's just so much I don't know about Mum."

"Darling, don't look so glum—most kids don't know much about their mothers even when they're still around, believe me." She looks at her son, gives a mischievous smile. "And to be honest, maybe that's not such a bad thing."

Merry

Arthurville, 1994

Sometimes the entirety of Merry's life since she'd finished school felt like a dream that she couldn't wake up from—a rupture from her old life, her old expectations, that was so profound she couldn't quite believe it. In her fantasies, it was going to be all fun—she would be free to run her own life, to set up her own home; she'd have someone to love her, unconditionally; she'd be creating her own family—but the reality was something different. It certainly wasn't the summer of love scenario she'd naively envisaged. Instead, it was something far more arduous, and far less romantic. The low-key registry office marriage, Merry in her high school formal dress, loosened around the bust and the middle, with no one but Mick's parents and a few of his mates and their girl-friends in attendance; the reception at his parents' house that featured platters of "horses doovers" (toothpick-skewered tricoloured pickled onions, Jatz and french onion dip, mashed potato rolled up inside slices of devon, tinned smoked oysters), cream sherry, shandies, and no speeches or dancing.

Then there was the shock of childbirth—*Why had no one ever said anything?*—and the upside-down, inside-out craziness of new mother-hood. Both the good parts and the bad were equally overwhelming—who knew that rapturous joy and abject terror could coalesce around the one small being? It was as if she'd fallen into another world that no one had told her existed—one that she could never leave.

There was the other side of it—the base material reality that still needed attention, despite the fact that time and space appeared to have been utterly remade. And so much of this was so far from satisfactory, so far from the life she'd imagined for herself, it was almost laughable. Living in a small house in a bad part of town with dank charity-shop furniture, driving an old rust bucket, not having enough money to replace the bald tyres or buy a new pair of jeans, having to squeeze her postpregnancy belly into the ones she'd bought the winter before she finished school, having a husband who was no older, and no more sensible than she was, and with whom she had so little in common. Oh, they still got on well enough: he still made her laugh, and she still admired him in myriad ways, but somehow all their differences—in education, upbringing, expectations—now loomed large.

Merry was lonely in a way she'd never imagined. Oh, she enjoyed Jo, she really did. And somehow, despite (or perhaps because of) her age, her own parenting, and her limited resources, motherhood came naturally. Jo was a good little baby—easygoing and endlessly entertaining. But a baby, however beloved, couldn't be her whole world. She needed other people, and some sort of social life.

Merry had always had a core of friends, people to talk to when she needed them. But marriage and then a baby at eighteen had put her outside her peer group in a way that nothing else could. There had been a couple of disbelieving phone calls and a few stock WELCOME BABY GIRL! cards with stilted messages when Jo arrived. After that, nothing.

Mick's social life seemed barely changed. He still went out for a beer with his mates—it was unfair to feel resentful, although she did. There was nothing to stop Merry from going out—he was happy to do his share with the baby—but she had nowhere to go, and no one to go with. Some weeks her only outings were to do grocery shopping, or taking the baby for a walk in the pram. Her mother-in-law would call in every now and then, bearing gifts for Jo as well as the odd casserole, and most Sunday nights they would head over to the senior Sharpes' house for one of Mrs. Sharpe's enormous baked dinners. On these evenings, relaxing while the delighted grandparents passed the baby between them, cooing and kissing, all the chat revolving around Jo—her sleeping and eating and growth and developmental milestones—she thought of her own mother. It was impossible to imagine Ruth behaving like this, or as any version of a kindly, interested grandmother. In the first months after she'd left and moved in with Mick, a few envelopes had arrived, bearing her mother's unmistakably spiky cursive, the Pembroke stamp on the back. She'd opened the first one vainly hoping that it might contain words of reconciliation or even love—but it had merely been a copy of a legal document about some Beaufort family trust. She'd sent the rest back unopened. Why salt the wound? And a wound it was, though she didn't let herself dwell on it too much. She saw Roly's truck around town every now and then, but his visits to town didn't tend to involve food shopping, so she'd easily managed to avoid bumping into him. At first she also avoided the places where she was likely to bump into the well-to-do graziers who knew her family. No doubt they'd heard the scandal—and she didn't want the awkward conversations, the knowledge of their disapproval or their pity.

Almost desperate, she'd finally struck up a friendship with Kirsty McLeod, whom she'd met at the child health clinic when she'd taken Jo in for her twelve-month shots. Kirsty, whose family owned the town's century-old department store, Ambrose's Emporium, was a few years older than Merry. After college Kirsty had returned to work in the store temporarily—and then married her father's young accountant and right-hand man, Trevor McLeod. Her baby, Lachlan, was just a few months older than Jo, and when they first met up, she'd laughed—*I thought I was young,* she'd said, *but you're a baby.* Kirsty was from one of Arthurville's most well-to-do families, but they were down a rung or two from the Beauforts and didn't mix in the same circles. And

Kirsty certainly seemed completely unworried when it came to her new friend's reduced social status—she either didn't care or didn't notice—Merry didn't quite know. Like Merry, she just seemed eager for a friend with a baby.

Their friendship had developed quickly, and initially the two women tried to nurture a friendship between their husbands. There'd been a few awkward barbecues and dinners out, but Trevor and Mick had nothing in common. They couldn't have been any more differ-ent—from their dress sense (Mick in his Levi's and faded Led Zeppelin T-shirt, his hair shoulder length, a single silver stud glistening in his ear; Trevor in his Lacoste golf shirt, his pressed pants, his preppy hair style, his unscuffed boat shoes), to their interests (Mick liked fast cars, rugby league, rock and heavy metal; Trevor played tennis, watched union, and listened to talkback radio), to their political affiliations—not that these were ever discussed. Mick had found Trevor uptight and humourless, and no doubt Trevor, polite as he was, considered Mick a bogan. But the two women enjoyed one another's company, and continued to meet for coffee and an occasional picnic at the pool or the park.

To Kirsty, respectable, connected, and busy—golf and tennis club, hospital balls, fundraisers, casual barbies with the town's young worthies—Merry's friendship was one amongst many. But in those first few years of motherhood, Kirsty was Merry's lifeline, her only connection to the world she'd left so nonchalantly. A world she missed more than she'd ever admit.

The job with the *Chronicle* had been another lifeline. It had begun as casual office work in the year after Jo was born—usually only half a day or two a week, depending on her mother-in-law's availability. But by the time Jo was ready for preschool, she was offered part-time work as office admin, which basically meant doing all the vaguely annoying jobs no one else in the busy office could be bothered with: odd bits of research, phone calls, sorting out the classified ads, running errands, making sure the coffee and tea and biscuits didn't run out, making endless cups of coffee for the editor. Merry had quickly shown her workmates that she was skilled in other ways, too—and occasionally she was asked to write a paragraph or two that would be published under an actual journalist's byline. She'd put herself through a touch-typing course—practising in her lunch hour and at home on a little portable machine she'd picked up secondhand—and had begun to teach herself shorthand. Her efforts had been noted, and when, after her first year, the paper's budget and workforce were reduced, the editor asked if she'd like to be responsible—anonymously, as had been the *Chronicle*'s tradition for more than thirty years—for the paper's weekly gossip column.

A Little Bird, as the column was titled, was an Arthurville institution, the first thing most readers turned to when they picked up the paper on a Friday morning. It was a single column that ran alongside the newspaper's ordinary social pages—a centre-page spread featuring photographs of Arthurville's citizenry and visitors attending significant social, sporting, and cultural events, as well as enjoying parties, picnics, or nights out at the local pubs and restaurants. Most long-term Arthurvilleans would be featured once or twice in their lifetimes. There was always something in the final paragraph to laugh about, or speculate over—nothing was ever outright slanderous (it was a newspaper column and the laws were clear), but there was always something a little bit fun—some local bigwig caught doing something mildly embarrassing—and sometimes a little bit malicious. Usually it was easy to work out whom was being referred to—sometimes not so.

The Little Bird stories weren't sought by the paper in the usual investigative manner and didn't involve any serious journalism. Stories were occasionally called in—people would leave hurried messages, but mostly they came as scrawled notes and letters, posted or sometimes pushed under the doorway in the dead of night. Many were too scurrilous to use, the tall tales of vengeful ex-wives and -husbands, resentful business partners, or aggrieved neighbours, and the information was both dubious and defamatory. Following the directions of her editor and the historical model, Merry left any real scandals alone. Occasionally she would give a story to the editor to pursue—sometimes letters contained evidence of wrongdoing that was worth investigating, or reporting to the police, but mostly only the light, amusing stories—bordering on the anodyne—could be used.

Merry was astounded by the information that people were happy to share anonymously. So much of it was of a sexual nature: that long-married DB was having an affair with also-married RS, that DV was sleeping with his secretary, that ZR and one of her senior students had been going at it since he turned sixteen. Accusations of stealing, cheating, bigamy, rape, bestiality, horse stealing, child abuse, satanism, sheep stealing, extortion, drug taking, drug selling, drug making—how could there be so much corruption in one small town? It was hard to look at some people she knew without blushing, even when she was certain that what she'd been told was a lie. There was really no way of confirming the truth of some stories, but Merry quickly developed a sense for what might be true and what was a complete fabrication—and though she shredded some of the most outrageous letters, it was impossible to forget them.

Merry discovered that there was a certain power that came with knowing other people's secrets. Her own anonymity was weirdly intoxicating too. No one other than the *Chronicle*'s editor knew or even suspected that she was writing the columns—she was just the secretary, the girl who brought the coffee, the girl who took the money for the advertising. She was virtually invisible.

~

Merry had only been back from maternity leave for just over a month when she was called into the boss's office in the late afternoon. There'd been rumours for months that the paper was about to restructure, a euphemism for putting off more staff, and she'd been terrified that management's sword would fall on her. They desperately needed the money from her job—Mick's pay covered the mortgage and their bills, but not much else. She was already thinking about where else she might get work. She knew there was receptionist work going at one of the hotels, and one of the banks was hiring tellers. But she needed work that she could fit in around school hours, preferably part-time. And she loved her job. She had made her way to Jack's office reluctantly, a lump in her throat, anticipating the worst.

Jack, a man in his sixties who'd moved from Melbourne to run the paper more than twenty years ago, was a good boss. He hadn't blinked when she told him she was pregnant and would need maternity leave, had even sent flowers when Amy was born. He could be tough—she'd heard the grumbling from the journos—but was well respected. He'd worked hard to make the paper a success, tripling the advertising revenue in the time he'd been in charge. Two major investigations during his tenure (one on a row between a local developer and the council, the other a piece on the appalling treatment of Aboriginal women at the local hospital) had won national prizes. But now he looked tired, defeated. There were rumours that one of the three senior journalists had been given her marching orders earlier in the day, and an older compositor had been asked to consider early retirement.

Now Jack asked her to sit down. He took off his glasses, rubbed his eyes. Sighed.

"This has been a bastard of a week, Merry."

She tried to murmur something soothing, but nothing would come. She nodded stupidly.

He sighed again. Then dredged up something that looked like a smile.

"But it's not all bad. It's been very good to have you back."

"Thank you." Cold comfort.

"You're damn good at your job."

Her voice caught; she nodded again.

"In a way I don't want to—I know you like what you do."

"I do." The tears sprang to her eyes. "I really do."

"But I think you have the potential to do a lot more."

She tried to smile. What could she say? His compliment really wasn't comforting at this point.

"As you probably know, we're going to be down two senior writers—but we've got enough to employ one cadet. It's not going to make up for that loss entirely, but . . ."

"Oh." She felt suddenly hopeful.

"You'll be working five days—or maybe we can make it a nine-day fortnight—I know the childcare might be a problem. And to start with the pay probably won't be any better than what you're getting now. But you're a bright girl, Merry, and a good writer. So I'm hoping you'll agree to take the job."

"I . . . oh God, I'd—I'd love to." She could barely breathe for the happiness that was flooding her now.

"You'd have to train the new admin—and I'd like you to keep writing A Little Bird if you don't mind. I get a lot of compliments about that column. People tell me it's the best thing in the paper. Although I have to say there were less compliments when you were away and I had to do it myself." His smile was genuine. "I think everyone thinks that I do it . . . and I don't tell them otherwise.

"I'd like you to think about enrolling in a communications course, distance ed—just part-time. It's a lot to ask, I know—especially when you've got young kids. But it's a good opportunity for you. And once you're trained, you could go anywhere. I don't need an answer now—we'll make an official start in the new year—but if you could tell me in the next few weeks?"

"I don't need to wait." Merry couldn't contain her excitement.

He raised his eyebrows. "Don't you need to discuss things with your husband? It might make all your lives a bit harder."

"Oh, no. He'll agree. And anyway, even if he doesn't, I don't care. I'm doing it."

Jo

Arthurville, 2018

When I get home, Dad is snoring in his chair. I send him off to bed, pour myself a tall glass of cold white wine, and take it out onto the back verandah, where it's marginally cooler. I bring water for Alligator, who puts his two front paws in the bowl while he laps thirstily, and then lies panting at my feet. I sit in the darkness listening to the kids in the house next door, who are out splashing in their pool despite the late hour. I feel that same lick of envy I'd felt back when I was a kid, and different neighbours, kids who were just a little bit older than me, had done just the same thing in the hot summer evenings. How I'd longed to be invited over to swim, to be part of that group. For some reason the splashing in the pool, the childish shrieks, the calm adult voices a quiet counterpoint, prods something, something raw, that I have been vaguely feeling all day. Something to do with Cousin Lucy, with seeing the kids with their grandparents, the parents at the cricket gala day. Spending time with Kirsty and Lachlan. After Mum left, I'd been constantly stricken by similar feelings of envy—although perhaps that's the wrong way to describe what were really random moments of desolation, a terrible hunger that could never be satisfied. Now I try to reason that feeling away. I sip my wine and focus on all the positives in my current situation—and there definitely are some—I'm making new friends, cultivating old friendships, healing the rift with my father. And now I've learned something about my mother, something that changes my picture of who she was, what she might have wanted. I've mostly thought of her as my mum—beloved, sure, but somehow not as someone three dimensional, with her own interests, her own desires.

I wish I'd known earlier that she'd been working as a journalist—that we had this in common, this desire to write, to tell stories, to create a picture of the world we're in.

That reminds me of the box in the back of the car, Kirsty's theory that Mum was writing the gossip column. I creep along the verandah so as not to disturb Dad, close the boot and then the door quietly.

I pour myself another wine. Add three ice cubes and settle into Dad's recliner, the Breezair on full bore. No doubt Dad will complain in the morning—the noise, the cost, the wear and tear—but right now I don't care.

I dump the contents of the box onto my lap. First, I open the scrapbook. Every page features glued-in cutouts of the same newspaper columns that Kirsty mentioned this evening—A Little Bird. The columns are short—a few hundred words at most, surrounded by a selection of black-and-white photographs. The first cutting is dated August 16, 1991, and the last is August 14, 1994, the week before Mum disappeared. I read through the first couple and laugh. It's a little like looking at my own stories, taken back a generation or two. The columns are an odd but endearing mix of community announcements and personal ads: from lists of who's heading off on distant holidays to news of local bigwigs or dignitaries who happen to be visiting. The occasional marriage or anniversary. Births, deaths, funerals. Announcements about the arrival of new headmasters, teachers, bank managers, businesspeople. All the community information, much of it personal—gossip, really—that doesn't count as "real news." At the top of each column is a humorous story—usually featuring an anonymous protagonist—caught in an embarrassing or comic situation. Most were fairly benign, like the story of a middle-aged worthy falling off a horse at the show. But every now and then a story would be overtly malicious, implicating the unknown protagonist in something that was illicit, shameful, or discreditable—the sort of thing that would have far-reaching consequences were the identities not obscured. I'm sure that most of the disguised "well-known community figures" would have been easy to work out by those in the know. Even with a cursory reading, I can guess that the "local land-owner and political aspirant whose racehorse was disqualified during the Arthurville Picnic Races" is my own uncle Roland. And the revered member of the chamber of commerce, who was experiencing "significant staffing difficulties," could only be Gary Johnson, who owned the local hardware store, and whose wife famously ran off with his tool salesman. It's understandable that the columnist's own identity has been carefully disguised—although it's clearly someone local. I have no way of knowing whether the writer was my mother, but the idea is intriguing. I put the scrapbooks aside to go through later and open the exercise book.

This is a journal of sorts, handwritten, with dated entries. The notes are scrawled, almost indecipherable—people to call, odd bits of info about people, places, events. Some seem to be fragments of ideas, perhaps not even legible to the writer. I open random pages and read what I can:

Anon phone call—SL drove into fence fri night, drunk, but not charged!

Check names for cricket presentation photos

JS & LD holidaying in Bali (second hol this year? how can they afford???)

Memorial for Doug Glasson next Wed

Remember to ring LR about next Thurs—h. 432 4711 w. 432 8990

Letters—most handwritten or typed, some made up of pasted letters cut from magazines—have been pushed between the pages; some float free; others have been stapled or pinned into the book. The letters' contents are a revelatory window into the dark and petty soul of the community—both from the perspective of the writers and those written about. Missive after missive contains damning accusations, denunciations, secrets, complaints. Even from this distance—when most of the participants are probably long gone or heading into their twilight years—it's hard not to be shocked by what I'm reading. Every type of wickedness imaginable is exposed, along with a few I've never imagined: it's utterly sordid and completely addictive.

~

I bring out the box at breakfast the next morning and place the scrapbook down in front of Dad.

"Do you recognise this?"

He looks at it blankly. "No. What is it?"

"Take a look."

He flicks through the yellowing pages. "Where'd you find it?"

"It was in the old stationery cupboard at work."

Dad pauses on one of the pages. Gives a yelp of laughter. "Look at this—back when Phil had hair, eh? The Dark Ages." He points to a photo of our former neighbours, Laura and Phil Doolan. The tagline reads, LAURA AND PHIL DOOLAN ENJOY A NIGHT OUT AT JAN'S CAFÉ LAST SATURDAY NIGHT. The couple are standing awkwardly, both holding glasses of wine. Laura's hair is permed and streaked. Phil sports a luxuriant mullet. "I wonder who they paid to get their photo put in? I remember the column. Boring as batshit, really—they shoulda just called it 'wanker news.' But every now and then there'd be something juicy. I remember there was a funny story about my boss—the big boss, Rupert Hays-Smith—he was caught pissing in some old duck's garden, though it was all kept hush-hush." Dad snorted. "I heard he wanted to sue the paper, but it was a bit difficult when no names had been mentioned, so he'd have been outing himself."

"Did you know who wrote it?"

"Can't say I was all that interested. I only ever bought the *Chronicle* for the classifieds. But I'm pretty sure this column ran for years and years—it was running back when I was a kid. A Little Bird. I never even thought about it. I just assumed one of the reporters wrote it."

"What about this?"

I hand over the exercise book.

He takes the book gingerly, leafs through it slowly, his expression neutral.

"This looks like Miranda's writing."

"That's what I thought."

"You found this at work? After all this time."

"It was shoved in a cupboard."

"What do you think these notes are for? Is it some sort of administrative record?"

"It's actually notes for the social columns. And the Little Bird stuff. I've checked the dates on the cuttings and the notes and they seem to line up."

"What do you mean, 'line up'?"

"Look." I turn to a random page. It's dated April 22, 1992. "Look at the notes—deb ball, tennis presentation, RSL Sat night. Then the list of 'gossip': DP fined for drunk driving (woman phoned in anonymously—might be wife?!!); SR arrived home from holiday in Melbourne alone (see anon letter); BD reverses into car, drives off (SC called in and told editor).

"Now look at this." I go back to the scrapbook, find the page for that same week: it features photos from that year's debutante ball—the girls in their white dresses and long gloves, flowers clutched awkwardly to their chests, another of the Anglican bishop and the mayor. There are a couple of photographs of a tennis presentation, with the tournament winners lined up in a smiling row, holding up trophies—one player, Valerie Barden, who had, according to the tagline, played for NSW in her glory days, holding up three. There were snaps of diners at the local RSL—one very bemused young couple, Miss Jenny Falstaff and Mr. Jeremy Higgins, were lucky enough to be visiting from London. The finale of the written column involved a story about a "certain high-ranking public official" who had been caught driving under the influence near a property on Dalhunty Road. He'd told the officers, apparently, that he'd been dining with a "friend," and there'd been a medical emergency, so he had to get home quickly—but the details of this could not be independently verified, and the man was charged.

"See how they're the notes for the page. There's a list of weekly events—I guess these were just arranged with the photographer, and then there's a separate listing of the gossip that comes in each week—she chose one or two each week from a list of possibles. Sometimes if there's a good story, it's pushed forward to the following week."

Dad closes the notebook. "And you think your mother wrote the columns? I don't know. It does look like her handwriting, but she was just working there three days a week before she had Amy, and then after, it was half days. From what she told me, I thought she was just what they used to call a 'girl Friday'—you know, answering the phone, filing, getting lunch, banking, doing a spot of cleaning. She looked after the classifieds and the advertising. But she wasn't doing any writing as far as I know."

He hands the book back to me, his interest waning.

"Maybe she was keeping the notes for the editor, or for the journo who wrote the column. They had a few more on, back then—not just one. There was the editor—what was his name—Jack Myers. He'd been there for years, and there were two or three reporters too. I used to drink with a young bloke who'd come up from Melbourne for the job. He did the weekend sport, mostly the footy, back when it meant something."

Dad sounds vaguely wistful. "He was a top bloke, actually. But he got put off just before your mother left."

"Kirsty told me that Mum had been offered a cadetship. She was meant to start in the new year."

"A cadetship?" Dad looks genuinely surprised. "I never heard anything about that. Are you sure?"

"I don't know why Kirsty would make that up."

"She might have misunderstood."

"It really doesn't seem like the kind of thing you could misunderstand."

"No. Maybe it's true."

"But then why wouldn't Mum tell you?"

He shrugs. "I suspect there's quite a bit Miranda didn't tell me. We weren't communicating much before she left. And whenever we did, it ended in a battle. I reckon if she'd won the bloody lottery, I'd have been the last to know." His voice is dry.

"The dates in the journal go right up to the week she left. Doesn't that seem . . . odd?"

"No odder than her leaving."

He flicks to the final entry, reads through, his face expressionless. "Anyway, this is all old news, Jo." He closes the book with a snap, and hands me both books, then turns very deliberately back to his breakfast, dismissing me. "And none of it makes any difference to anyone now, does it?"

~

We're driving back into town after interviewing a farmer who is convinced there's a Tasmanian tiger living in the bush around his land. The story is implausible and unpublishable, but the farmer, an elderly widower who appears to be in the early stages of dementia, has provided blurry shots of a doglike creature loping past his chicken coop. Between us, Edith and I have somehow managed to convince him to call his son, a schoolteacher who lives in the Blue Mountains, and have him arrange a visit in the near future. Our civic duty done, I've taken the opportunity to drive back to Arthurville along the narrow dirt road that winds around the lower slopes of Mount Wellesley. Edith is sitting with her head back, eyes closed, praying silently.

A small truck is heading up the road towards us. It pulls over and stops, and the driver waves us down. Edith opens her eyes and sighs with relief as I pull up beside it. Shep winds down his window, leans out. Two teenage boys are squeezed into the cabin beside him, their attention entirely on their phones. A bright-eyed sheepdog hangs out the window of the cramped rear cabin.

"Two meetings in one week, Sharpe?"

"Must be divine providence."

"You're catching on. What're you doing out here?"

"Humouring the elderly population."

He raises his eyebrows, but I don't elaborate.

"Anyway, what're you here for? What's with the truck? And the kids?"

"Work."

"Work?" I'm genuinely confused. "You do church services from the back of a truck?"

"It's a fire truck, Sharpe."

The truck is red and yellow, with RURAL FIRE SERVICE emblazoned on the side. There are taps and hoses. Also ladders.

"Oh, right." I'm relieved to see that he is dressed in actual work gear—flannelette shirt, jeans, work boots—rather than the absurd priestly outfit he'd been wearing at the pub.

"I thought journos were meant to be observant."

"You have to remember she's a city girl now," Edith offers helpfully.

"True."

"So you're a firey as well? How does that work? Are you only a part-time priest?"

"I'm a volunteer."

"And what are you doing here? Is there a fire?"

It's the season, and there are fires burning in other parts of the state, but there are no plumes of smoke on the horizon, no smell of burning in the air.

"We're just taking a recce." He points south. "There's a national park just beyond that paddock. There was a big fire out there last summer—I thought I'd show them some of the, er . . . hot spots—and look at a few places we can do a controlled burn next winter."

"Aren't your mates a bit young to be firefighters?"

"They're eighteen. So not that young. The training is part of their community service."

"That's . . . interesting."

"Dunno if *interesting* is the right word, mate. Anyway, they're learning a new skill. That's what counts."

"Oh, but it is interesting. It's the most interesting thing I've heard all week."

Edith, who can clearly hear the cogs whirring in my head, groans.

"No way. I can't do fires. I've got allergies." She sniffs. "And anyway, I've got stuff to do. You're on your own."

"That's fine. I can take some snaps myself."

Edith clears her throat. "Maybe you should check with the subject before you start writing a story?"

"When did a hero of the RFS ever knock back a story? Or a man of the cloth for that matter?"

Edith looks at the truck doubtfully. "Is there enough room?"

Shep gives an evil grin. "We'll squeeze her into the rear cabin. I reckon you and Fred'll be pretty comfy back there."

I wave a clearly happy-to-escape Edith off, then climb up into the cramped back cabin of the truck, temporarily dislodging Fred, Shep's canine companion, until he works out that he can still access the window via my lap. The two boys, Jayden and Zeke, seem positively indifferent to my presence, neither of them looking up when Shep introduces me, their attention remaining focused on their phones.

Shep nudges the boy closest to him in the ribs. "Jayden. The idea is to look up and say hello when you're introduced to someone."

This time the boy looks up at me briefly, nods, and grins. "Yo, Jo." Then he goes back to his phone.

Shep looks at him for a long moment, but there is no further response. "Honestly. I dunno why I bother."

"Because we're chick magnets, Sheppo," Zeke says, his eyes glued to his device. "We make you look pretty good, I reckon. How else you gonna get a woman?"

"Who says I want one?"

Zeke looks up, suddenly alert. "Are you two . . . ?"

"No."

"Not for a long time."

Our emphatic replies come in unison, and Zeke's eyes narrow. He nods his head disbelievingly. "Uh-huh." He sniggers, nudges his mate. "Hey, Jay, looks like Sheppo's got a girl."

Shep sighs. "Yeah, all right. That's enough. You can get back to your phones." He turns the key, crunches the truck into gear, and we head off down the bumpy road.

~

I was seventeen. Shep was a couple of years older than me, had finished school, and was doing what most of the Arthurville boys who hadn't left for the city or university did—hanging about, vainly looking for work in a town with a youth unemployment rate that was out of control.

We'd been friends since we were kids. Maybe not friends in the same way that people who don't grow up in small towns are friends, but in a way that's peculiar to communities like ours, where the connections stretch back generations, sometimes more than a hundred years—and in the case of some of the local Wiradjuri families, I guess it might be thousands. Our affiliation wasn't quite that long: Shep's old man and my old man had been to school together, as had their fathers and grandmothers and grandfathers before them, most likely. Dad's family had been in Arthurville for as far back as they could trace—family mythology had it that the original Sharpe settler had been a convict with a ticket-of-leave—and Shep's family had a similar story, although with a Wiradjuri mother, his connection to the area went back even further. In a place as small as this, I'm pretty sure if I trawled through Ancestry.com, we'd find that Shep and I have some ancestral, if not genetic, connections—great cousins three times removed who married, or a common great-great-great-grandparent. It's not that the gene pool here is limited, but there's definitely still a large component of the population who're descended from those earliest settlers—indigenous and newcomers—convict, European, and Chinese.

Our parents didn't socialise, not exactly—but our fathers would have a yarn if they met at the pub, our mothers would stop and chat in the street: friendly, but not friends. After Mum left, Shep's mum, who worked as a nurse at the town's aged-care centre, Beaux Reves, would make a point of saying hello if she saw me about. Shep and I saw each other in the playground, at school dos, sporting events, out shopping, down the river. Like most of the kids in town, he was just a fairly neutral part of the familiar backdrop of my life.

But then I got to the final years of high school, and the idea of having a proper boyfriend wasn't a distant fantasy, but a requirement. Suddenly the boys who were slightly older than us—once just annoying jerks who flicked our skirts and called us *shorty*, or in my case, *jumbo*—became highly visible. And, to the senior girls, highly desirable. Unlike our awkward peers, the boys who had left school were old enough to go to the pub, to pick us up from school in their cars, take us to parties, buy us drinks, drugs, whatever. They had money and status—and whether or not they had jobs, or a future, didn't really matter. Just being seen with them was enough.

Shep had spent most of his childhood out of town near the river, on a hard-graft property that had finally gone under when he was in his early teens. His family—his parents, Shep, his two older sisters, and three sheepdogs—moved into town, bankrupt, renting a place on the edge of town. His demoralised father had eventually found seasonal work on one of the big grazing properties, and his mother, who had trained as a nurse, took up the slack, becoming the main breadwinner.

He might've been smart, but, like so many Arthurville boys, Shep was a lousy scholar: a bit of a tough guy, a good footballer, fast enough despite being big, a decent guitar player—and when he used it, he had a strangely haunting singing voice. But for me, the main attraction was the fact that he had a licence—and a car—an orange 1977 Holden Monaro V8 that he'd bought for next to nothing. His laps of Arthurville's main street were of great interest to the local police. And though he was never actually charged, he came close enough times to be considered a bit of a hero to the strenuously law-abiding younger kids. And here I was in luck—Shep's house wasn't far away from mine, and if he saw me wandering home after school, he'd always offer me a lift. Scoring a ride in that low-slung, throbbing beast was a great source of street cred despite the fact that I usually had to share the front seat with Rip, Shep's kelpie cross—his constant companion.

In the end, we got together at an eighteenth birthday party held out of town. The attraction had been bubbling away for a few weeks. I'd noticed him noticing me, wondered whether I was imagining it. Like all my friends I'd flirted, but he was older, cooler, and known to be indifferent to the wiles of most girls. I couldn't quite see what the attraction would be: I wasn't by any stretch of the imagination cool; I was too quiet, too reserved. But I was smart, I wasn't horrendous looking, and I could on occasion be funny. I'd had boyfriends before—but they were all basically preadolescent, and the relationships had involved swapping notes and buying gifts and making elaborate plans for "dates" that never eventuated. I'd had crushes all through high school, but only ever on boys who were completely unattainable. But with Shep, suddenly everything was different. This time there was something real, even though it had appeared mysteriously, as if overnight. Something that meant that when we were in the same room, we ended up sitting together as if magnetically compelled. We'd found ourselves laughing at comic moments that seemed to be completely invisible to others. We didn't actually talk all that much, but there were numerous physical incidents—the accidental brushing of fingers across a table, bumping of knees in the car, until whatever it was between us became as loud and tangible as the thrumming of his car's engine. At least I thought it was—it could have been my fevered imagination. Soon Shep was all I could think about, and I spent most of my time, despite the fact that my half-yearly exams were coming up, trying to engineer accidental-on-purpose meetings with him.

Things came to a head at the June long-weekend party out at Parkers Creek. It was a big event, held in a paddock on Joe Clark's— the birthday boy's—property. There were at least fifty kids, a bonfire, pigs on spits, loud music. Adults were on hand for emergencies, and to do the cooking, but they'd made themselves scarce, so as not to spoil the vibe.

Despite my machinations, I'd had no idea that Shep would be there, and when I saw him, chatting, beer in hand, to one of the birthday boy's older brothers, I knew it was a chance that shouldn't be wasted.

As soon as I'd downed enough Cruisers to make me brave, I stepped away from my bevy of schoolmates and made my way over to Shep. He was standing by the fire beside a group of younger boys who were taking turns drinking from the birthday boy's gallon glass. I'd watched him for a while. Every now and then one of the boys would lurch a little too close to the fire, and Shep would casually steer him back away from the flames.

I greeted him shyly, my voice half sticking in my throat.

He turned, eyes wide with surprise. "Hey." He was clearly pleased to see me.

I gestured towards his charges. "Are you their bodyguard? Or a bouncer?"

He raised his eyebrows.

"Bouncer would be good. I'm more like a . . ."

"A sheepdog?"

He laughed. "Yeah. To tell the truth, I'm a bit over it. Maybe I should test out my bouncing skills. Just give me a minute."

He went over to the boys and slowly manoeuvred them across the lawn until they were a safe distance from the fire. Then he gently pushed the rapidly deteriorating birthday boy right down until he was sitting. The rest of them followed suit, as if they'd been hypnotised.

Shep pulled a couple of bottles out of a tub, and headed back over to where I was waiting, grinning and obviously pleased with his new-found skills.

"I'm impressed."

"Me too. Amazing how easy it is to get drunken eighteen-year-olds to do my bidding."

I raised my eyebrows.

"Lucky I'm not drunk then." I gave what I hoped was an alluring smile. "But I'm almost eighteen."

Our romantic involvement had been brief but intense and had lasted just long enough for me to lose my virginity, as well as my heart.

For those six weeks, we met most Saturday afternoons. Usually we'd have lunch in the park after I'd finished my shift at the newsagent's. We'd sit under a tree by the river, and then head out of town in Shep's car, and find somewhere secluded to pull over. We weren't keeping things quiet, but we weren't quite official. This day I'd bought us a couple of cheesy rolls, orange juice, and blueberry muffins from the bakery as I passed by. I sat under the willows near the riverbank and stretched out, stared into the colourless sky for a while, and then closed my eyes. I was itchy with anticipation, as well as hungry. I was still wearing the black T-shirt and jeans that I'd worn to work, but I'd freshened up my eyeliner, my lashes, and run a brush through my hair. I knew that I was looking—if not incredibly glamorous—certainly good enough for what we had planned—a drive, a picnic, some more lying in the spring sunshine—and the promise of something more.

I waited for Shep for more than four hours, checking for calls on my foldout Nokia every thirty seconds. I tried calling him, but it went straight to his voice mail. After a while, I changed position, got to my feet, and wandered over the bridge to the other side of the park and then back again just to make sure I hadn't confused the meeting place. Every now and then someone I knew would wander past, and I'd put my head down, pretend I hadn't seen them. The last thing I wanted to do was get into a conversation, have to say what I was doing there, admit that I'd been stood up.

By five, it was starting to get dark and cold, and it was clear that Shep wasn't coming. I'd eaten my roll, drunk my orange juice, nibbled at the too-sweet muffin. I dumped the remains of our picnic in the nearest bin, along with the CD I'd mixed for the journey. I dug in my pocket for the condom I'd taken from the box that I had hidden in my underwear drawer for eighteen months and threw that away too.

People disappeared from Arthurville every day. They went for all sorts of reasons—some innocent, some not so.

And mostly, once they left, they never came back.

I'd be next.

CHAPTER FIVE

A LITTLE BIRD

A certain famous former Arthurvillean, renowned
for his skills on the football field, is rumoured to
have been at a well-attended 40th birthday cele-
bration held in Arthurville Memorial Hall last week.
According to my sources, the rather glamorous
young woman who accompanied said VIP stayed
close all night and appeared to be wearing a ring
on a certain finger. We look forward to hearing
more.

A Little Bird, *Arthurville Chronicle*, 1993

Jo

Arthurville, 2018

After we drop the boys off, Shep heads back out of town and towards
the river.

"Where are you going now?" I'm hot and sweaty and smell vaguely smokey. The trip to the Montefiores Forest would provide excellent copy for next week's paper. My townie self had been dubious about tramping about the bush in the heat of the day, but Shep's commentary on the course of last year's fire and his knowledge of fire management had been unexpectedly fascinating—he was a natural, spinning fairly dry (ha!) details into a compelling yarn. The boys were clearly entertained by his stories and interested enough in his instructions—but it was the bush itself that really caught their attention. I could see their enthusiasm for what had perhaps been only a duty, involving mostly dull theory and the prospect of hot, dangerous work, suddenly become a far more meaningful physical reality when they could see the destructive effects of last season's fire and the almost miraculous regeneration, simultaneously. By the time Shep asked for their input about how they might mitigate future fires, the two boys were brimming with ideas— not all of them bad. I'd taken photos of all three of them and, ignoring his protestations, and the boys' jokes that I wanted it for a pinup, a few of Shep solo. Another not-bad idea. There's nothing like a hot priest to sell copy. Now it's past five o'clock, and I'm desperate for a bath and a beer.

"Thought I'd call in and say g'day to Uncle Wal."

"Uncle Wal? I don't think I know—" Then I remember. "Oh, you mean Wally River? I didn't know he was your uncle."

"Yeah, he's not my actual uncle, but he's related somehow."

In his late seventies, Wally is a Wiradjuri elder. He is an eccentric, practically a hermit, who lives, it is said, out in a shack by the river. When he was younger, he'd been a bit of a legend around the area, a crack shearer who'd been headhunted by local farmers every season. But there'd been some sort of a tragedy back in the nineties, and he'd had a breakdown, never recovered. According to legend, he'd camped out on the riverbank for a few months and then decided to stay—hence the nickname. He'd built himself some sort of makeshift dwelling, and had lived out there as long as I could remember, surviving on fishing, trading, and the generosity of friends and family. When I was a teenager, he'd come into town every now and then to sell the wooden handicrafts he made. He had a metal detector, too, and sometimes found treasures along the river that were worth selling.

"I'm surprised he's still alive," I say now.

Shep laughs. "I think Wal's just as surprised."

"Is River really his name?"

"No, he's a Whittaker. River suits him, though. Good way to get a surname. Maybe we should all do it. You could be Jo Journo. It's got a nice ring. And I'd be David Priest. Or David Vicar."

"Actually, you'd just get to keep yours, wouldn't you? Isn't Jesus like a good shepherd or something?"

He laughs again. "Ah. So you know the scriptures, eh? I'm impressed."

"Yeah, well, that's about the sum total of my knowledge. Don't get too excited."

~

I'm not sure what I expected Wally's place to be, but not the neat little whitewashed cottage that Shep pulls up beside. It isn't right on the riverbank, either, but in a paddock a good twenty metres south, surrounded by a well-kept garden.

"This is his place?"

"Not what you were expecting?"

"I thought he lived on a riverbank."

"And you thought that was a literal description?"

"And I was imagining—you know, some sort of . . . something more primitive. A shack, I guess. Homemade."

"It's homemade, all right."

"But definitely more of a cottage than a shack. That'll teach me to listen to town gossip."

"I thought that was your job?" he says, his voice dry.

I give him a hard look. "Have you actually read the local newspaper lately?"

"Not exactly. Actually, not at all." He sounds guilty.

"Well, maybe you should. If you did, you'd know that town gossip might be an improvement on what I'm writing."

He looks ahead. "If you're looking for a story"—he gestures towards the house—"Uncle Wal's not short of them."

I sigh. "Seriously, Shep—if he's got anything more controversial to discuss than, I dunno, the next golf-club fundraiser, it's probably not fit for the newspaper."

"What?"

"Well, if you'd read the *Chronicle* lately, you'd understand that I don't write actual news. That could be contentious, and it's not what the board is after. I'm really just here to record the town events. My job is to boost morale—it's really just a PR exercise."

"Well, you can't blame anyone for that. We could all do with some morale boosting."

The inside of Wal's house isn't what I expected either. It's only two rooms—a kitchen bedsit and a long screened-in verandah running along the north and facing the river. It's sparsely furnished, and as clean and organised as any place I've ever been. There's a little divan that clearly doubles as a bed, and a small timber table and chairs fit neatly into a nook in the minimalist kitchen. Everything is cleverly purpose built—like the fittings on a boat. There's no clutter, nothing extraneous. A little like Uncle Wal himself. For someone who's passed seventy, and who by all accounts has had a hard life, he is remarkably sprightly. He isn't wearing the expected "hermit" wear (what had I expected, rags and shoes held on by cloth strips?), but dark-blue jeans, cowboy boots, and an ironed cotton shirt, tucked in and buttoned up. His dark face is deeply lined, and he wears his long grey hair pulled back from his face in a ponytail. If he is surprised to see Shep, he doesn't show it. He shakes my hand, his long-fingered grip powerful.

"You're writing the paper, eh? That's a big job. So what are you doing hanging about with this lazy God-botherer?"

"To be honest, I'm not quite sure."

Shep answers. "We're here for a cuppa, Uncle, if it's not too much trouble."

"You want a cuppa, Reverend Shepherd, there's the kettle." Wal grins and gestures towards the kitchen. "Chop-chop. I'll be happy to sit and chat to your girlfriend while we wait."

"Oh, but we're not—" I start.

Wal winks. "Your secret's safe with me. I won't be telling any of the congregation. Couldn't drag me inside one of those places for love nor money," he says loudly. "And don't think you'll get me when I'm dead either. You know I'm a Catholic, so you lot better leave me alone, or I'll end up down there."

Shep turns to him, clearly startled. "You're Catholic? Since when?"

"Always was. Went to Saint Martha's. Did my reconciliation, Holy Communion. All that jazz. You lot need to get 'em when they're young. I even went to confession a few times—had plenty to confess back then." He looks thoughtful. "Dunno that it'd be real exciting for anyone these days. Put the poor fulla to sleep."

He manoeuvres me over to the little table and bench, pulls out a chair for me, and sits down opposite.

"Where're the tea bags?" Shep is banging cupboard doors.

"None of your tea bag bulldust here. That's what the teapot's for. Tea's in the caddy. Cups are in the cupboard above the sink. And I mean cups, not mugs—mugs are for coffee. And if you open them painted-on eyes, you'll find some Anzac biscuits in a tin above the sink there, Rev."

"You been baking, Uncle Wal?"

"What do you reckon? Lola Fyshwyk brung 'em out for me a coupla weeks ago." Lola, the mother of another old school friend, is Arthurville's current mayor. "Plates are under the sink."

"You're a fussy old bastard, aren't ya? Real tea. Cups. Plates. It'll be silver teaspoons next."

"The silver's in the left-hand drawer. Milk's in the fridge. No point getting old if you can't be a fussy old bastard."

"My aspiration."

I'm enjoying the to and fro. Somehow I'd forgotten the seemingly endless batting of insults back and forth that constitutes a conversation out here. It was a long way from the polite and distant conversations of shared houses, or even of my life with Harry.

Wal turns back to me. "Now. Let me figure you out. Am I right in thinking your grandad was Razor? Worked for the PMG?"

"That's right."

"So your old man's the young bloke who married the Beaufort girl. That caused a bit of a ruckus, if I remember right."

It's a shock to hear from someone who still considers my dad a young bloke, but I'm not going to contradict him. "Yep. That's the one."

"I knew your Beaufort grandfather, too, then." Wal has settled into his reminiscing. "I was his best shearer, you know, back in the old days. I never liked him much, if you don't mind me saying so. He was a hard bastard, 'scuse the French. I've seen him put good blokes off if they looked at him the wrong way. But he was always pretty decent to me. Paid me the same as the whitefellas, I'll give him that. So he should, eh? I did double the sheep in half the time."

"I actually never met him. He died a long time before I was born."

"That's a sad thing. Maybe he'd been able to talk some sense into that grandmother of yours. Mrs. Beaufort isn't exactly what you would call a warmhearted woman, but I never thought she'd disown her own daughter. There's some bad karma right there."

"You know the story?"

"Of course. And I remember your mum. I knew her when she was just a wee thing. She'd be out riding them big horses they had out there. She was tiny, like a little fairy with all that white hair, but she never had no fear. Seen her fall off and get back up, laughing at a bloody knee."

I feel my eyes fill. I've heard so few stories about my mother's childhood. I want him to keep talking.

"I never understood the way she left yous, eh? And taking the baby. It never felt right. Not like her, if you know what I mean. She never seemed that sort of girl. I didn't know her well, but I could tell she wasn't hard like your grandmother." He looked at me solemnly. "And I remember talking to your old man about that. We were drunk, crying in our beer one night. Both of us—useless wrecks. That was a bad time for us, your dad and me—those two girls clearing out like that." He shook his head. "A real bad time. She never come back, did she? Your mum? Like my Sheila. Cleared out and never come back."

"It was no good for you, either, I'm thinking?" He looks at me sadly.

I nod, clear my throat. "No, it was a pretty crappy year all round."

"I heard she sent a letter. But you never heard any more since?"

"No."

"I never even heard from Sheila. Not a letter. Not a phone call. Nothing." His pain is clearly alive and well.

"Sheila was your daughter?"

Shep has brought over a pot, three cups, milk and sugar, a plate of biscuits. He pulls a chair across, sits down quietly.

"She was. Maybe she still is. It's like your mum—I don't know."

"What happened?"

Wal picks up the teapot and fills each of our cups. Pours in milk, adds sugar to his own, and takes a sip. "You know, I only have one good photo of her. Over there."

He points to a framed picture on the opposite wall. It's a school photo with the standard dark-blue background. Sheila is about twelve: thin, tall, gap-toothed. Her hair is long and darkly auburn, her face freckled, her bright-blue eyes wide and laughing. She's wearing the old Arthurville High winter school uniform—a navy box pleat uniform, white shirt and tie.

"She was a pretty girl, eh? Pretty like her mother—she was an O'Sullivan. You know them? Her parents grew wheat. We didn't stay married for long—not once the divorce laws came in. Seventy-seven, I think it was. That was another bad year. She only married me because she was pregnant, said she didn't want to be married to a blackfella— but it was better than having a baby on her own. She shot through as soon as she could—went to Sydney. I brought Sheila up on me own. Her mother saw her once or twice a year, school holidays, that sort of thing. It wasn't perfect, but it wasn't bad. The O'Sullivans never wanted anything to do with her, but Sheil had plenty of family on my side. She left school when she was sixteen—got a job at the Emporium, in the haberdashery section. You know, looking after the sewing stuff, fabrics and that. She loved sewing, all that—she was clever with the needle, knitting, crocheting. She was a clever girl, all right. She made that blanket there." He nodded at a colourful crocheted blanket hanging over the back of the lounge. "She could make 'em faster than you could unravel the wool."

He pauses, closes his eyes for a moment. Takes a breath and goes on.

"It was early in '94. Sheila'd been working at Ambrose's for five years by then. Some money went missing from the till. They were fifty dollars short each night for a week or so. It was only ever Sheila's till. So she got the blame for it."

"Could it have been anyone else?"

"Nah. Not really. They were pretty careful about all that, the Ambroses. They had codes on all the tills, so apart from the bosses, no one but Sheila had access to her money. And it didn't make any sense for any of them to take the money. There was no one else to blame but Sheila. But she'd never been in any sort of trouble—not even at school.

Not for anything. She never talked back, never wagged class, never got into a fight. Nothing. And she swore to me that she didn't touch it." He paused again. "You see, she didn't need to steal. She saved like a bloody banker." He smiled. "She wanted to get a new car. She had this mesh purse she kept all her cash in—she had more than two thousand."

"What happened? Was she charged?"

"They sacked her straight off—and said they would think about laying charges. That old prick—the father—she tried to talk to him, but he told her to clear off. Not to come back. She was brokenhearted. She loved that job." Wal looks down into his teacup, as if it might contain the answers.

"Anyway, the next morning, it was a Friday, Sheila was gone."

"What do you mean, 'gone'?"

"I got up, maybe a bit later than usual. I'd drunk too much the night before. Angry about it all. And when I woke up, she wasn't there. We were meant to be having dinner with my sister and her mob, and I thought Sheil had probably gone straight there. But she hadn't. She wasn't anywhere. We called all her friends, but no one knew anything. Eventually the police come, but they'd heard about what happened at the Emporium, so they thought she'd just done a runner. She hadn't packed anything that I could tell, but she'd taken that purse, all her money. We checked at the railway station, and the coach stop, but no one had seen her. She hadn't called a cab. She didn't turn up all that day, or the next."

"What did they think had happened?"

"The police said she must've hitched a ride."

"Hitched where?"

"No one could say. She wasn't at her mother's. That was the first place we checked. There were a couple girls she went to school with, who'd moved away. We checked with them, but they hadn't heard anything."

"Did she have a boyfriend?"

He sighed. "That's the thing. There were rumours—she said something to one of the women at work. Told her that she'd met someone. The police reckon she probably had some bloke that she hadn't told anyone about—that she'd taken the money, gone to meet him. But Sheila wasn't that sort of a girl."

"What did you think?"

"What did I think? I thought something happened to her—something bad. Still do. But no one ever believed me. Didn't matter what I said, no one believed me."

Uncle Wal's story was one that under different circumstances I'd be begging to write.

"And so that's why I'm here. I went mad for a few years, wandering about the place, looking for her, drinking. I used to sleep out here on the riverbank, under the stars, most nights. It was touch and go there for a while. I got a bit of a reputation, wandering into town and causing trouble. Old Shep—this fella's old man—he got the shits with me eventually. Made me clean up my act. Once I got off the booze, me and him and the boy here built this old place—and then he gave me the deeds for the land. So when he went bung in the nineties, the bank couldn't take it. They tried, believe me. But it was watertight, that document."

I look at Shep, who is looking steadily down at the table.

"I hadn't realised. So this is your old place?"

"It is."

"Did we drive out here that summer?" I can feel my face heat up at the memory.

"Probably. We went pretty much anywhere we could park." Shep doesn't seem to share my self-consciousness.

I turn to Wal, struck by a sudden thought. Maybe I can't write the story that Wal has told me, Sheila's story, but there's still a story here to be written. "Uncle Wal. You know the paper's always looking for angles—interesting community stories. I wonder if you'd mind if I came out and interviewed you one day?"

He looks doubtful. "What for?"

"It'd be something simple. Just about living out here, what you do. We could take some pictures of your carvings, the house, the river. How it's changed in the drought. How you built the house. Something like that. I mean, this place is pretty amazing. It's exactly what I'm after."

"Well, maybe. I'll think about it."

"Thank you."

He looks at Shep. "You know who you oughta be writing about. Not an old bloke like me, but that young fella."

After we finish our tea, he excuses us from the washing up, and leads us to the front door. There's a high-tech-looking metal detector leaning against the verandah wall, earphones, gum boots, a bucket. As a kid, I'd had a friend whose father spent every spare minute searching for gold out at Diggers Bay—where there was an old river port that dated back to the gold rush—certain that he'd find a fortune. All he'd ever seemed to find were five-cent pieces and rusting bottle tops and—most exciting for us kids—the odd bullet shell.

"Had any luck?" Shep asks Uncle Wal, peering into the bucket.

Wal grins. "Not bad, boyo. Got to be some benefits to the drought, eh? There's a lot of empty riverbed out there now. I've found a bit of good stuff up past Sandy Bank where the pontoon used to be, and further up near the channel. The water's as low as I've ever seen it. I found this this morning." Wal delves in the bucket until he comes up with a small flat disc of dull metal, a cross marked in the middle. "I reckon it's a game token," he says. "Made by convicts, maybe."

He hands the disc to Shep, who transfers it from hand to hand as if testing its weight. "Feels like lead. Worth anything?"

"Could be—depends on who wants it."

"No gold?"

"Nah." He delves into the bucket again, pulls up a sandy handful of coins, keys, and broken jewellery and lets it trickle through his fingers back into the bucket. "Nothing worth selling."

"What do you do with it," I ask, "if it's not worth selling? Put it back?"

Uncle Wal points to a row of white-painted shelves up the other end of the sleep out. "Some of it I keep. Mostly I just throw it back in downstream. Let some other bugger find it."

The shelves are crowded with odd pieces of bric-a-brac—worn-out coins, shards of broken pottery, glass stoppers, ancient bottles. There are two Victorian clay pipes, one in almost perfect condition. There are bits and pieces of jewellery, too—rings and earrings, broken chains, charms and amulets, most of them rusty and worn. One of them catches my eye. It's a brooch, shaped like a flower, about the size of a fifty-cent piece. It's water damaged, rusty, discoloured—but I recognise it immediately. It's a pretty piece, with white enamelled petals, radiating out of a gilded centre. A daisy. My mother had had an identical piece—it was her grandmother's originally, 1960s costume jewellery, but expensive, a Georg Jensen designer piece. Mum had loved it so much her gran had given it to her for her sixteenth birthday. In the winter before she left, Mum had worn it on a little knitted beret she'd bought for the season. I can remember tracing the petals—smooth and long with gold embossed edges—and admiring the golden sun in the centre. Perhaps they're common, but I can't remember seeing another one before or since. I pick it up now, turn it over. My breath catches in my throat.

I hold it up. "Wal, where did you find this? When?"

The old man holds out his hand, peers at it closely for a moment. "I've had it for a long time. Maybe ten years. It come up last drought, I reckon. Two thousand and seven, maybe, or eight. Down near Sandy Bank. It's a pretty thing, isn't it?" He hands it back to me. "You can have it if you want."

"No, it's just . . ." I pause, take a breath. "It was my mother's."

"Your mother's? How can you be sure?" Shep sounds dubious.

I turn the brooch over: the name LOUISA MAC is shakily engraved down the centre of the setting, just above the clasp.

"My great-grandmother's name was Louisa Macartney. She gave it to my mother. I couldn't be more certain."

"Man." Shep shakes his head. "That's completely wild. She must've lost it on a picnic or something. Or maybe someone nicked it?"

I look at the two men. "She didn't lose it. She was wearing it that morning. The morning she left."

~

Wal guides us back along the river, about half a kilometre north, to one of the widest sections of the river, known to locals as Sandy Bank Beach.

He walks out a metre or two into the dry riverbed, digs into the dirt with the heel of his boot. "I can't remember exactly, but it woulda been somewhere around here. The drought wasn't nowhere near as bad that time. It wasn't this dry."

When we were kids, this part of the river was a popular picnic spot, an unusually straight section of what was typically a meandering river, shaded by the surrounding bush, a grey sandy area that was reminiscent of a real beach, at least if you were a kid with a bucket and spade. The water here was calm and relatively shallow—and there was usually a vast expanse of water. It's more than fifty metres to the steep bank on the other side of the river. But now, the current is sluggish, the water muddy, a trickle that's barely a metre wide, the surrounding riverbed dry and crazed. You can walk across the river from bank to bank.

"It doesn't make sense. Why would she have come out here in the middle of winter?" Arthurville summers are hot—but winters can be freezing. And the temperature is even lower out near the river.

"Maybe she was meeting someone?"

"But why would she take off her brooch?" It doesn't make any sense.

I look down at the brooch, as if it holds the answers.

"Maybe she didn't take it off. What was she wearing that day?"

In the beginning, when it was assumed she'd disappeared, I'd had to tell the police details of what Mum was wearing, and it came back now without any effort. "She had a pair of black jeans, her Doc Martens, a navy woollen beret—with the brooch attached on the side—and a dark-green turtleneck.

"She was wearing the brooch on her beret—I'm sure of that. In winter, she wore the beret every day."

"She could have taken it off later in the day. Lost it."

"I suppose it's possible." I can hear the doubt in my voice.

"And then someone might've picked it up. Taken the brooch."

"What—and then lost it themselves?" Shep's suggestion is plausible, but I don't believe it.

"You reckon you found this ten years or so ago, Wal?"

"Give or take a couple a years."

"D'you reckon it had been in the water long?"

"No idea. There's been a bit of damage, so coulda been there awhile. Or it might've been damaged before it went in the water.

"I reckon it was caught up under these rocks." He gestures to a rocky section a few metres into the riverbed. It was once submerged, but is now fully exposed, the bed around it bone dry. "You can't see it, but there's a ledge right in the middle there. I reckon the brooch came from further upstream when the current was stronger and got stuck. I've found a few other bits and bobs in there—nothing valuable—some pottery, glass, bottle tops, that sort of thing."

"Further upstream? I don't suppose we can get there now? Is there some sort of track through the bush?"

I look doubtfully at the surrounding bushland—there is no road in sight, and the trees are dense and, so far as I can tell, impenetrable. But it seems urgent, suddenly, to see if it is possible to trace the route of the brooch. I think suddenly of the medium's vision of my mother's whereabouts: somewhere murky, deep; a river or a lake, she'd said. It wasn't clear.

"You don't need a track, mate," Wal says. "You can walk a fair distance back along the riverbed—until we get to the channel, anyway. I haven't actually been back that far for a couple months, but I'm thinking maybe even that'll be low."

Shep looks concerned. "Jo, we're not going to find anything—not after all this time. Even if it was ten years in the water and not twenty-five—it could have come from anywhere."

I know he's right, but I don't care. I march along the edge of the river as fast as I can, dust at my heels. I keep my eyes peeled, although I don't know what it is exactly that I'm searching for. I can hear the men's footsteps behind me, working hard to keep up, but I don't look back.

About five hundred metres upstream, the bank suddenly steepens, and we're forced to scramble up the slope and walk the rest of the way amongst the willows, on the edge of denser bush. Wal is leading us now, and Shep and I follow his sure footsteps through the trees. A sharp bend, and the river changes, narrowing into a steep-banked channel, rumoured to be the deepest section of the entire waterway, thirty metres long and only three metres across. The water runs swiftly here, and when the river is full, it's a notoriously dangerous stretch—with hidden currents and submerged obstacles. Even now, with the river and dam at an all-time low, it's clear that it has managed to maintain some depth, and the water is still running freely, if not fast. There's a rough dirt road in, and a small clearing around the riverbank, with an aged and rusting council sign, warning people of the dangers of swimming or boating here.

I sit down on the bank, hot and tired and sweaty, and suddenly uncertain about what I'm doing, and why I'm doing it. Shep and Wal sit down beside me. Wal shakes his head. "I've never seen it this low, not in my lifetime. Me and the O'Malley boys used to come out here to swim when we were kids." The youngest O'Malley boy—dead now—was a local hero who'd won gold at the 1962 Commonwealth Games.

Wal looks out across the water, his eyes narrowing. He stands up, moves farther down the bank. He points. "Can you see that?"

I peer across to where he's pointing but can only make out something that looks like a large half-submerged branch floating in the water.

Shep is similarly bemused. "What—you mean that log?"

"It's not a log." He sounds excited. "It's metal. Rusty metal."

He's right. As the water moves, the rust-coloured object emerges, rising and then falling in the current. From this distance it looks big—a metre or so across.

"What do you think it is?"

Shep walks as far down the bank as he can without falling in. He stares across the water for a long while, then turns back to me.

"I think it's a car, Jo," he says quietly. "It's the roof of a small car."

PART TWO

CHAPTER SIX

A LITTLE BIRD

Despite the (very welcome) rain, the annual Church of England Deb Ball ~~(hello 1950s!)~~ was a great success. The fourteen debutantes were radiant in their glorious white gowns, and their tuxedoed partners suitably smart. The girls were presented to the Right Reverend Dr. Edward Salter, bishop of Dalhunty, after which they danced the Pride of Erin with their partners. Bell of the Ball was awarded to Miss Jennifer Wyatt, ~~(guess whose mother runs the debut committee?)~~ who was radiant in a full-skirted white satin and tulle gown and a simple coronet of pink sweet peas. The mayor then gave his traditional ~~(interminable, dull, incoherent)~~ speech congratulating the debutantes and thanking the committee ~~(during which time the venerable Bishop, who is clearly way past retirement age, drifted into a very noisy sleep)~~ for their efforts. Attendance was the highest on record—with more than 400 people braving the downpour and enthusiastically dancing the night away.

A Little Bird, *Arthurville Chronicle*, 1993

Jo

Arthurville, 2018

The police, two senior officers from Dalhunty, both men, come to the house the following afternoon. Dad is prepared—I've told him what I've seen, what I suspect, but we are both holding on to a slim chance that the submerged car is just that—a car. With no occupants. That it will have nothing to do with Mum. Nothing to do with us. But the two men, their voices solemn, their words official, immediately dispel that final hope.

From what they can tell from their initial investigation, the car seems to be a Mini, some of it still coloured a pale blue. The visibility is too poor for the divers to ascertain whether there are any human remains in the car. As they can find no other reports of missing blue Minis in the state during the last twenty years, they are assuming that the car is my mother's.

"We understand that the police—and the family—were satisfied that she'd left voluntarily."

"Yes."

"And you haven't heard from her since?"

"No. We . . . initially I expected her to. She'd taken our daughter, Amy. And she'd left Jo, as well as me. It didn't seem right. But when she didn't get in contact, I just assumed that she'd made a decision to cut all ties. Which seemed cruel, but . . ." He gives a resigned shrug.

"You didn't try to find her? Hire a private investigator?"

Dad glares. "With what? And anyway, Merry had a history of cutting people off. She hadn't spoken to her mother for eight years."

"I see."

"People leave, don't they?" Dad sounds almost defensive.

"They do. More often than you imagine."

"So . . . she came back?"

"We really can't be a hundred percent until we get the car out. But it's looking that way, I'm afraid."

Dad closes his eyes for a moment, then takes a deep breath. "Jesus Christ. I don't understand any of this." He turns to me. "Are you okay?" A curt nod is all I can manage.

"So what happens next?"

"We'll have a truck and divers down at the river first thing in the morning, to pull the car out."

"And if . . . if it is them?" Dad's voice seems to be clogged.

The officer's expression is solemn. "We'll cross that bridge when we come to it."

~

I drive us out to the river early, just after sunrise. Dad and I join a small group huddled on the south bank of the channel—mainly uniformed police, but others, too, there for unexplained official reasons. I'd expected there to be television cameras, someone from the *Dalhunty Times*, perhaps, or a stringer for one of the city papers, but as far as I can see, there's no one from the press. Clearly the Dalhunty police run a tight ship—or maybe it's just not newsworthy. Shep, sombre in his priestly garb, joins us. He exchanges a few words and a handshake with Dad, grips my shoulder briefly, then stands silently between us. His presence is immensely comforting, and I have to resist a sudden desire to lean against him.

The car is almost entirely submerged now—bogged in the silty river mud and snagged in weeds, its movement further downstream impeded—but a rusty patch bobs up through the murk occasionally.

Dad watches, his face set, eyes unwavering, as the officers do their grisly work.

Close to the channel the bank is too steep, so they have to pull the car from a hundred metres or so away. They're pulling it against the current, which makes the process more complicated. The heavy chains are tightened and loosened and tightened; the pulling angle is adjusted again and again. Men shout, swear; the truck reverses too far back, then moves too far forward. Tyres spin, gears crash. The tension climbs with the temperature. But finally, finally, the car shudders free.

My father's eyes are hidden behind sunglasses, but his lips form a grim line, his skin is ashen. My own eyes feel as if they've been stuck open with glue. I am desperate to close them, to turn my gaze away from the horror of what's in front of me, but somehow it's become impossible: most of the pale-blue car enamel has rusted—the tyres have rotted—but it's unmistakably my mother's old Mini.

The officer from Dalhunty comes over to give us an update. Divers believe there are two bodies, he tells us, his voice gentle—one an adult, probably female, the other an infant.

Cows, milling about on the other side of the river, lift their heads, dark eyes mildly curious as the car—a river monster, vomiting muddy water, tangled in weed—is cranked in. One gives a mournful bellow just as my father's legs give way and he sinks to the ground, his head bent, shoulders shaking.

~

Despite Dad's assertion that he's fine, Shep insists on driving us both to the hospital. After initial tests, the ER doctor tells us that they're pretty sure it was just the shock, and not a heart attack or a stroke, but they want to keep Dad under observation for a few more hours. At first he's difficult, refusing to lie down on the hospital bed, claiming he's fine, insisting that he'll be better off at home. He only calms down when

Fran arrives on the scene and tells him in no uncertain terms to do as he's told. "And the rest of you can clear out," she says, glaring. "We need to keep him calm, and you certainly shouldn't be worrying him with questions right now." This last is aimed at the two police officers who have just appeared, clearly eager to begin their investigation. They go only reluctantly, leaving a card. "We'll keep him in overnight."

"Do you want me to stay, Dad?"

Dad gives me a pained look. "No thanks. You'll just fuss. If I have to stay in this place, I'd rather stay alone." Then, clearly making an effort to be conciliatory. "And you don't need to pick me up. I'll get myself home."

Shep gets back in the driver's seat. Ordinarily I'd be annoyed by the presumption, but for some reason I don't mind.

"What about your car? Don't we need to go out to the river, pick it up?"

"Lucy's sorting it."

"Lucky man, to have a girl Friday." Shep blinks. Even I'm surprised by the sharp edge to my comment—am not sure what Shep—or Lucy—have done to deserve it.

"She's my curate," he says mildly. "Helping me out is actually her job."

"Sorry. It's just . . ." I shrug. It's just everything.

"So what are you going to do?"

"I don't know."

"Is there someone I can call?"

"There's no one."

"You probably shouldn't be alone."

He's right. I don't want to think about what it is that's just happened. What it all means. At home alone there'll be nothing else to think about.

"Can we just get out of town?"

"Do you want to drive?"

I don't even have to think about it.

I head north, through the hills, then farther west across the plains, following the river back towards its source. I drive fast, crank the music up so that it's too loud for conversation. Shep is the perfect passenger—staying calm even when I go into a corner a little too fast, overcorrect, and end up bumping along on the gravel shoulder. I apologise, but he's clearly unfazed. I turn back only when the sun has gone down, and the stars are shining brightly in the too-clear sky.

I drop Shep outside the old Anglican rectory, which backs onto the church grounds. It seems an odd place for a young man to be living—dark and a little forbidding.

"Do you want to stay for dinner?" he asks. "Lucy's brought the car over, and we've got a bit of paperwork to do, but you can just . . . chill if you like. Watch TV. Have a beer. Whatever you want. You probably should be with someone right now."

I shake my head. It might be better to be with someone, but the thought of spending an evening with Lucy is less appealing than being alone.

He touches me gently on the cheek with the back of his hand. "I'm here if you need me." I resist the urge to grab his hand and cling to it.

"I'll be okay." I force a smile. "But thanks."

The front door opens as he walks up the path, spilling a welcoming yellow light across the garden. Lucy waits in the doorway, an elegant silhouette. They stand talking for a moment, Shep's back to me, Lucy in shadow, before he enters, and the door closes, leaving me in darkness. I feel something twist low in my abdomen, a hot feeling behind my eyes.

My phone pings. I have been deliberately ignoring all notifications, but right now I could do with any sort of distraction. It's Kirsty.

I've just heard. Come over if you want to talk. XX

~

Kirsty holds out her arms.

"Oh God. I'm so sorry, Jo." She hugs me tightly, then pulls me inside. "Come in.

"I'm so sorry I didn't call you earlier," she says, "but I've been stuck here all day with Jem. I've only just heard." Kirsty's easy, familiar warmth is more than I can handle. For the first time since the car was found, I feel my eyes filling, sobs rise to the surface, uncontainable, uncontrolled.

Kirsty turns around, concerned, but I wave her away. "Oh, you poor lamb." She squeezes my shoulder, then walks briskly up the hall and into the kitchen. "What will it be? Wine or tea? It's too late for coffee." I follow her for a few steps, then hover in the dark hallway, taking deep breaths and trying to get myself under control.

"Where are you?" When Kirsty pokes her head around the kitchen door, I'm standing outside the study, gazing into the room and pretending to be fascinated. It's another exquisitely renovated room—timber and glass bookshelves to the ceiling, deep-red carpet, a beautiful cedar partners desk in the middle of the room, a low-hanging brass pendant light casting a golden glow over everything. There are lovely antique pieces placed strategically—office furniture from the Emporium, perhaps—old timber filing cabinets, shaded lamps, a couple of vintage typewriters, a big black rotary telephone, a small chrome-plated cash register.

"It's a beautiful room, isn't it?"

"It's amazing. I love all the antiques."

She gives a self-deprecating smile. "Some people would call it rubbish. I have a bit of a problem throwing things away, I'm afraid. Trevor used to say this place was the only way I could keep my inner hoarder respectable."

"Well, it's a writer's paradise. I wish my office was like this." I wipe my eyes, give what I hope is a normal-ish smile.

"You haven't answered my question? Wine or tea?"

"Oh, wine. Definitely."

I follow her into the family room, and make myself comfortable on the low sofa. Kirsty brings over a large glass of wine, a box of tissues, then goes back to the kitchen and busies herself preparing nibbles. By the time she arrives with her own glass and a tray of cheese and biscuits, I am almost completely composed.

"Sorry. It just hit me. I can't quite take it in . . ."

Kirsty leans forward, takes my hand briefly. "You don't have to apologise. Or explain. I know what grief's like."

"I don't know why—I'd convinced myself I was okay. And it *should* be okay. I mean, it's been more than twenty years. To be honest, I don't really remember her all that well." I shrug, try to smile. "But I guess . . . I didn't expect that she would, that she was—"

Kirsty's voice is gentle. "It's your mother, Jo. There's no way this wasn't going to be terrible. There were questions before, but now . . . I suppose you've always hoped that you'd find her one day. That she'd come back, or contact you. She was just my friend, not my mother, so I can't pretend to feel how you're feeling. But I always imagined she was out there somewhere—living her best life." Kirsty's eyes glisten. "And I always imagined she'd be back. I guess we've all been waiting. And now"—she gestures—"this. It's just shocking."

I close my eyes for a moment. I'm trying to control it, but the urgency spills through. "That's the thing, Kirsty. Her being there, in the river—it doesn't make any sense."

She frowns. "What are you thinking, sweetheart? What particular . . . aspect doesn't make sense? Have they discovered something new?"

"No. It's nothing like that. They haven't told us anything, really. It's just—I don't understand . . . any of it." The ideas—ideas that are only cohering now, as I speak, tumble out. "It's—I mean, why was she even there at the river? Did she leave town and then come back? She must have: that letter from Surfers came what, a couple of weeks after she disappeared. So what did she come back for? And why did she go to the river? It must've been an accident, mustn't it? But how could she accidentally drive into a river? She was a decent driver. It doesn't add up. None of it . . . works. Not as a story." I shake my head, trying to clear it. "The only alternative is suicide. But why would she come all the way back here to kill herself? And why would she do that to Amy?" There's no way to dress it up, make it better. "Killing your own child—that—that's actually murder." I take a breath. "And she wouldn't have done that, Kirsty. She just wouldn't. I don't—I don't understand any of it."

"Jo. Maybe there's another way to think about it all." Kirsty is looking at me intently.

"What do you mean?"

"We didn't know so much about postnatal depression back then. Not really. Not like we do now. And even now. We missed it completely with poor Lachie's wife. We really had no idea—even with all our modern understanding, all the information that's out there. Maybe your mother . . . ?"

"I suppose. I don't know that it's any consolation, though. And if it was suicide, why didn't she . . . leave some sign? The letter she left Dad—it wasn't a suicide note."

Kirsty looks thoughtful. "But there was also that letter to your grandmother. What did she say? *Don't look for me.* Perhaps it wasn't a message about heading off into a new life . . . perhaps *that* was actually a suicide note."

"But why would she drive all the way to Queensland, write a letter asking Ruth not to look for her, and then come back and kill herself? Why would she go to all that trouble?"

"Oh, Jo. These things are never straightforward. Who knows what was going on in her mind right then. Perhaps she thought she would be able to . . . do it elsewhere. And then she changed her mind, decided to come back. And then changed her mind again. You hear so many stories—people trying to decide, going back and forth, not knowing whether or not they want to live or die."

"But what about Amy? How could she murder her own child?" I can barely remember my little sister, but the thought of someone deliberately destroying the life of a baby makes me gasp. If my mother had simply chosen to die by suicide, that was shocking enough. But this—the calculated destruction of a life she'd brought into the world. What mother does that? It's a type of evil that I can't imagine a loving mother—and in my memory, whatever her faults, Mum was loving—committing. The mother I remember was prickly, difficult, impatient sometimes—but I have no memory of either the sort of sadness or the sort of rage that would lead a mother to such an act.

Kirsty's eyes are full of pity. "Perhaps that's something you'll have to try not to dwell on when you think about your mum."

"But it's not going to go away, is it?" I brush angry tears from my cheeks. "They'll be investigating it now. There'll be an autopsy, and then an inquest. It'll be months, maybe years, before it's all over."

"Well, maybe there'll also be some answers, darling. And that will help. Believe me. It might not seem like it now, but these things do bring closure. I know it sounds like trite rubbish. In the meantime, there's nothing you can do. And you have to face the fact that you might never know what really happened. That you may never find out how or why. It all happened such a long time ago."

"I thought that one day . . ." I can't finish the sentence.

Kirsty refills her glass to give me a moment. "And how's your poor father? He must be gutted."

I tell her about Dad's turn at the river, his trip to the hospital, that I'd spoken to Fran before I arrived, and that he'd passed all the tests with flying colours. Fran was trying to persuade him to stay in overnight but didn't like her chances.

"Have you and your father discussed the . . . situation?"

"It's all happened so fast. We haven't really had time. But I don't like my chances there either." I shrug. "You know, we haven't really discussed the fact that she left."

Kirsty frowns. "He must be in terrible pain. He loved her, you know."

"Do you really think so? He's been so angry since she left."

"Oh, Jo. He adored your mother. I think he never really got over the fact that she chose him. He never measured up. You probably can't understand how it was—how different they were—she was. She was landed gentry, basically—although that seems a very old-fashioned concept—and your father, well, he didn't even finish school. I think he never got over the fact that she stayed with him when she got pregnant with you. That she married him. I suspect he always felt he was punching above his weight. And he may act as if he doesn't care—but I know he does."

I wonder whether maybe my father would've been better off staying in his own lane, marrying someone from his own class. Maybe he felt that Mum had improved his life, but from where I am, it looks as if she destroyed it.

"No dinner?" Lachlan comes into the kitchen, a computer bag slung over his shoulder, his tie askew. He looks tired, rumpled.

"Oh, and hello to you, too, Lachlan," Kirsty says frostily. "I know it's a bit late, but Jo needed a shoulder. There's plenty of leftovers from last night if you can't wait. But come and have a drink first." She pats the seat beside her.

Lachlan moves into the light. "Jo. Sorry, I didn't see you." His expression lightens, a smile appears and then just as rapidly falters. "Oh God. I just heard about your mother. I'm so sorry." He comes over and takes the drink his mother offers him, but stays standing. "I'll just check on Jem. What time did he go down?"

"Oh, a few hours ago." She waves her hand airily. "He had a big day—and he missed his afternoon nap. I thought I'd feed him early, get him down early. It appears to have worked. I haven't heard a peep."

"Yeah. Well, who knows? Most likely he'll be awake at midnight, and that'll be it." Lachlan's voice has an irritable edge that I haven't heard before. He heads off down the hall, his mother watching silently.

"Some days it's hard to get it right." She rolls her eyes. "I'm just a granny—not a mum. And I know he thinks I should, but I'm buggered if I'm getting up every night."

"I'm sure he appreciates everything you do."

"Maybe." She doesn't look convinced. "I thought it would be better for him living here during the week."

"It must be . . . very complicated. He's lucky to have you, though."

Kirsty's smile was sad. "Yes, I think he is. Not every mother. But maybe it was a mistake . . ."

"A mistake?"

"It's difficult, having your kids back as adults. And difficult for the children, too—as I'm sure you know." She gives a sunny smile. "But I'm lucky, really—that I'm able to help. Grandmothers—especially when it's a son's child—don't often get the opportunity to be so involved. I'm really very privileged. Blessed, you could say."

Lachie reenters the room, the baby clutching him, face buried in his shoulder, giving little hiccoughing sobs. "He was wide awake, Mum. Just lying there howling. He looks like he's been crying for a while. And he was sopping wet. I had to change everything. The sheets as well. Didn't you put a new nappy on him before you put him down?"

"Of course I did, Lachlan."

"Well, he clearly wasn't ready for sleep."

"Oh dear. But he went down so happily. He was positively gurgling."

"How did you not know? Haven't you got the monitor on?" Lachlan sounds angry, accusatory—and has clearly forgotten that I'm here.

"You know I hate that thing, Lach. They really don't need to be under twenty-four-hour surveillance. It's wrong." Kirsty sips her drink calmly. "And a bit of crying doesn't hurt either. He needs to learn to go to sleep by himself. He was overtired, overstimulated. He needed to sleep. I do know what I'm doing, darling."

Lachie stands looking at his mother for a moment, as if trying to work out how to respond, but before he can say anything, the baby opens his mouth and breaks into loud cries. "Oh Jesus." Lachlan jiggles him up and down, his mouth tight, clearly furious. "Is there a bottle ready to go?" He storms into the kitchen, his muttering audible even above the baby's cries.

Kirsty sits with her eyes downcast, very upright, smooths her dress down over her legs. Eventually she takes a deep breath and looks up, her smile brilliant. "I really don't know how your generation survived with such hopeless parents."

It's time for me to go. I put down my glass and stand up. "Thanks so much for the wine, Kirsty. And the shoulder. I should get back, see if Dad's made it home."

"Oh, Michael'll be okay for a bit longer," Kirsty says. "Have another drink."

I sit back down slowly, slightly reluctant. "I guess one more—after that I can't drive."

Lachie comes back over to the lounge. The baby is quiet now, sucking calmly on his bottle.

"Sorry, Mum. I shouldn't have gone off—it's just—it's been a really long day. And he was up all night."

"I understand."

Kirsty holds out her hands for the baby. "Give him to me, and you and Jo can have a nice chat."

Lachlan looks down at the babe—sucking ferociously now—his face tender. "Poor little bugger. I might actually take him up to his room and feed him there. See if I can get him to nod off." He gives me an apologetic look. "Sorry, Jo, I don't mean to be rude, but . . ."

"Oh God, please don't apologise. I didn't really come to socialise. I just wanted to be around . . . normal people."

He grimaces. "Not sure that you've come to the right place—"

"Speak for yourself, Lachlan." Kirsty smiles, but her words have an edge.

Lachie doesn't notice. He gives a vague wave and walks out of the room, all his attention on the baby.

Kirsty gazes after him, her disapproval clear.

"I know it's difficult doing it on your own, but he's going to spoil that baby. Jem needs to learn how to put himself to sleep. He's making a rod for his own back, that silly boy. And you know"—she turns and smiles—"I really hope—I mean, I know it's early days for him—but I thought perhaps you and Lachie . . ." She laughs, leaves the statement dangling.

"What? Oh God, no." I'm embarrassed. "I mean. I really like Lachie, but I don't think either of us . . . there's so much going on."

"Ah, well." She's undeterred. "Maybe one day—when things settle. You know, I remember hatching plans with your mother when you two were just babies . . . silly girls that we were. And then you were such a sweet young couple, you know. Even Trevor thought so."

"That was so long ago, Kirsty. We were just kids."

"Lachie's brought back a few girls over the years, but you were always my favourite. Even after he met Annie. She was a beautiful girl, a wonderful mother, but I'm not sure that it would have lasted. They were just too . . . different. Different backgrounds, different values. Not like you." She pauses. "And, I know you say you're not interested, Jo, but I think you'd make a lovely mother . . ." She must see the look of shock on my face, breaks off.

"Oh dear, I'm so sorry. I really don't know what's got into me." She laughs, lifts up the bottle. "The wine, I suppose." She refills her glass.

"It's just I do worry about Lachlan. It's going to be so difficult—what Lachlan's facing . . . bringing up a child all alone. And that poor little babe—having to grow up without a mother." She gives me a serious look. "And you know all about that from the other perspective, don't you, darling?"

"It's sad to think that poor little Jem won't grow up knowing his mother."

"Lachlan will have to do something—make an album of photos and stories, ask the people who knew her. Her parents, her friends.

That's important, isn't it? To try and give the full story. Or as much of it that's appropriate, of course. The good bits."

"I think the bad bits are important, too—as you grow up. Some of them, anyway. Otherwise you spend your life making things up."

Kirsty nods. "I suppose so, not that I imagine there were too many bad bits in such a short life."

I take a deep breath. "Actually, I . . . talking about bad bits—I thought maybe you might know something. About what was going on. With Mum and Dad. She told you about the cadetship—maybe she confided other things."

Kirsty moves closer.

"Darling Jo." She looks at me steadily. "I did know your mother. And we were great friends. But she was a very private person." She speaks softly. "And you know, I actually didn't have a clue until Mick told me. About the baby. Amy. Merry didn't even hint at the truth."

I have no idea what she is talking about, but I don't like to interrupt.

"I dropped you home one afternoon late—it was after a school excursion, I think. A year or so after she left. You and Lachie went outside to play, and I stayed and did a bit of a cleanup. You remember how it was. Your dad was so drunk he could barely move off the lounge, let alone be responsible for a small child. I was angry, and had a few words with him . . . anyway—it came out. He probably doesn't even remember telling me. He was so terribly hurt by it."

She pauses, looks at me sadly. "It had an awful effect on him. I think he couldn't get past that fact. And I think it stopped him from . . . caring that she'd gone. Missing her. His anger was just . . . completely over-whelming. It blotted everything out. It was a terrible thing for a man to find out. A terrible thing for her to have done. And apparently she'd only told him the night before. They'd had a huge fight about it, as you would. And that was the last time your father saw her. He always assumed that that's why she left." She looks thoughtful. "Oh dear, I hope none of that's going to come out now they've found her. It'd be devastating."

She's clearly slightly drunk, rambling.

"Kirsty. I don't have any idea what you're talking about. What would be devastating? What was he so angry about? Do you mean about her taking Amy? Leaving me?"

Kirsty's eyes widen. "Oh God. You don't know. I didn't realise."

"I don't know what? What did he tell you?"

"Oh no. I can't." She shakes her head, clamps her lips together theatrically. "You'll have to ask him yourself. It's not my story to tell."

~

My father is in bed asleep, snoring loudly, when I get home. The hospital must have discharged him—or else he's gone AWOL. His medications appear to have been taken, and there's no sign that he's been drinking or smoking. There are no empty bottles, no full ashtray. The light on his answering machine is flashing, but I ignore it. The news will be out by now; people will want to know what's going on, to discuss the gory details. To know what happens next.

I'm half tempted to shake him awake. To make him tell me what Kirsty has hinted at.

But maybe there are some things I don't need to know.

~

My memory of the day my mother disappeared feels a little too real, a little too definite, all bright colours and sharp edges, like a scene from a film. It's more like a memory that's been reconstructed, a memory of a memory, perhaps, or a memory ossified by multiple retellings. What I remember is basically just the everyday chaos of our family life: me getting up late, reluctantly; Mum scolding me for standing in front of the TV when I should have been eating breakfast, for not getting dressed, for not being able to find my uniform, my shoes, my socks, for not emptying out my lunch box the previous Friday. Amy awake, whining, hungry. Mum annoyed because everything needed washing—her clothes, her bedding, her hair. Time running out, no lunch made, and instead Mum giving me a hastily scribbled brown paper bag lunch order and a dollar to spend on recess, then shooing me out the door, her farewell relieved, distracted, when Sarah and Jasmine—older girls from next door who walked me to school most days—called by to pick me up.

Other memories from around that time aren't as clear—they're fuzzy round the edges, sepia toned—but perhaps somehow all the more real for not being shared.

I can remember being outside in the late winter sunshine, lying on a rug with Mum, drowsy, content, safe. Amy must've been asleep, Dad at work, maybe. I was lying with my head on her chest, listening to her heartbeat. Booboom booboom booboom. Mum was stroking my hair, humming under her breath. "Beautiful soft hair, Jojo," she'd said drowsily. "Beautiful girl."

I can remember being at the supermarket, Amy in the trolley baby seat, me hanging off the back, Mum in a mischievous mood, whizzing us up and down the aisle, spinning the trolley around fast when the coast was clear, holding back giggles when she knocked over an end display of toilet paper, and helping her to quickly restack it into a dangerously leaning pile, and then moving on sedately, continuing our shopping.

I remember seeing my mother's face in repose on the night before she left. At least I think it was the night before she left. I have a feeling that we were sitting at the table, eating dinner, but I don't know for sure, or what it was we ate that night, or whether Dad was there, or Amy. None of those details belong to that memory. But what I do recall is looking up to see Mum looking at me, her face desperately sad, in a way that I'd never seen it before. I remember gazing back at her for a moment, then looking away quickly, a little frightened by the intensity of her regard.

And there's another memory from that same evening—of that I'm certain. It's a memory of words, rather than anything visual. I was standing outside my parents' room, on my way from the kitchen to my bedroom. Their door wasn't quite closed, a crescent of light illuminating the darkness of the hallway. I could hear only my father's voice clearly, and not my mother's, urgent but low. Dad's voice was full of anger and something else I'd never heard before, something deeper and darker, more like the howls of a wounded animal, that instinctively frightened me. None of the words made sense, either; they must both have been standing well away from the door, so that only fragments, disconnected, were audible:

. . . expect me to raise . . .

What about Jo?

. . . should go then, if that's what you want. I'm not going to . . .

The only words from my mother that I can remember—her voice sad, and with none of the anger that I'd heard in my father's:

. . . don't know what it is I want. Who does?

But my father's response, harsh, raw:

That's the thing, Merry. No one ever knows what they want. But that doesn't stop most of us doing what's right.

The light changed as one of them walked towards the door, the shadow casting the hall momentarily into darkness again, and I scurried up to my own bedroom, crept under my quilt, and squeezed my eyes shut. A few moments later, I heard footsteps down the hall, and then pausing in front of my room. I peered out. My mother was standing in the doorway, looking over at me. She began to speak, but Amy cried, and she smiled weakly, gave a little wave, and disappeared back into the darkness.

~

When I wake the next morning, Dad is in the kitchen washing dishes that seem to have been there for days. Maybe years. He looks pretty rough—his eyes bloodshot, his hair unwashed—but for once he doesn't reek of alcohol. I resist asking him how he's feeling, what the prognosis was, knowing that will only irritate him. I can ring Fran later for the details anyway.

174

"Cuppa?"

It's almost the first time my father has offered to make me anything since I got back home. I'm shocked, but I don't make any loud noises or wild gestures, just nod and murmur, swing a chair out, and sit down.

"It's so bloody hot already," I offer blandly.

He grunts an affirmative, plonking a mug containing hot water and a teabag in front of me unceremoniously, the liquid sloshing over the sides.

He pulls out a chair on the other side of the kitchen table and sits down with his cup of strong black instant.

"So. D'you want to talk about it?" His expression is inscrutable—but there's nothing soft about it. No give. Nothing vulnerable. He's not look-ing at me square on, but slightly to the side, as if there's something about me he doesn't want to see. I don't know what he wants, what he needs. I don't know what either of us needs at this point. A psychologist. Or maybe a priest. I chase that particular image away and answer my father.

"I don't really think I do, no. Do you?"

"Fuck no."

He lifts his cup, pauses before it reaches his mouth. "Milk's in the fridge," he says. "We're out of sugar."

I don't worry about either—welcome the burn, the bitterness of the tannin.

"What're you doing today?"

"Thought I'd go back to bed. Wait for the police to call. What about you?"

I speak honestly. "I actually don't know what I'm meant to do, Dad. I don't know what I'm meant to feel. I just . . ." I end on something between a sob and a hiccough, try to swallow down my tears and fail. "I just don't know anything anymore." I wipe my eyes on the bottom of my shirt.

Dad puts down his cup, reaches across the table, and takes my hand.

"Jojo." He looks at me steadily. "I haven't had a clue what to do for the past twenty-five years, and I still don't. You've probably worked that out by now. So maybe my advice isn't going to be worth all that much."

He pauses as if waiting for a response, and I half shrug, half nod. I'm not sure where this is heading, but it's not time to interrupt.

He keeps his fingers tight around mine, eyes never wavering. "I know I've never told you this"—he clears his throat—"but I want you to know that you're the best thing in my life, and the only thing that's kept me going—in whatever limited capacity I've managed. For what it's worth, my advice, darlin', is to find something you care about, focus on that, and just keep going." He loosens his grip and pats my hand. "So wipe your nose, eat your breakfast, get dressed, go to work. And try and keep your shit together."

~

Keeping my shit together is difficult. I sit in front of my computer, flicking through the photos Edith took earlier in the week, and wonder why I'm composing feel-good stories about such cutting-edge issues as the girls' cricket semifinals when I'm in a town where half the population under twenty-five can't find a job, where addicts aren't someone else's sad story, but everybody's problem, where families with fathers barely exist, where the rivers are dry and the water supply is running dangerously low, where farmers are dragging their dead cattle into stinking, fly-ridden piles for burning. Where every second shop front in the once-bustling main street is boarded up. Where my dead mother and sister have just been pulled out of their watery grave after being "missing" for almost twenty-five years. It's one thing to give the town a positive spin—to see the glass half-full—but today it seems like wilful blindness.

There are stories that are not being told here and voices that aren't being heard.

In less than two weeks, I feel as if I've been exposed to more sadness than I'd experience in a year in Sydney.

In the city, whenever my job involved chronicling other people's sadness, it was easy to stay in my protected bubble. To go home, turn on Netflix, pretend that bad things only happened elsewhere. But not here. Here there's no way to pretend. Nowhere to hide from it. Back here it's clear that no one ever escapes.

Perhaps the glass is entirely empty.

I do what I've been itching to do all morning. I close my documents, open Google, and go straight to the local television news website. The story is a long way down: "Bodies pulled from submerged car in the Apsley River believed to be a mother and infant who went missing from Arthurville in 1994." There's a photograph of the car being pulled from the river, the small crowd gathered around. My stomach lurches. I minimise the page and open my cricketing story. I write two lines, delete them and start again, write two words, then close the page. I can't think. And I can't not think.

I stand up and pace around the room. I open empty cupboards and stare into the shelves as if they might contain the answers. I fill the kettle and make myself a cup of instant coffee. The smell makes my stomach churn. I tip it down the sink and go back to my desk. I'm waiting for something, but I don't have any idea what that something is—it's as if I'm a child again in that time of uncertainty. But this time there's only certainty. This is the moment I've been waiting for for twenty-five years, but it's not what I thought it would be.

~

I'm now officially the daughter of a dead woman, a suicide. And—unbearable thought—I'm the sister of a murder victim. I have always imagined that certainty would offer some solace, but instead it feels as if the ground has fallen away beneath me, and there's no safety net.

However slim, there'd always been the possibility of a reunion—and now there's none. But paradoxically I feel, too, as if the fact of her, their, death is something I've always known.

My phone rings. It's an unknown number, not the police, so I don't bother picking it up. I ignore the second call. Pick it up on the third.

"I've got another story for you." It's Shep.

"What sort of story?"

"I'll pick you up in half an hour. Bring a camera."

I take a deep breath, let it out slowly, my anxiety levels considerably lower. What Dad didn't say is maybe it's easier to keep your shit together when someone else is looking out for you.

"Where are we going?"

~

This time there's no dog, and I have the bench seat to myself. Shep heads through the centre of town and then back to the other side of the railway bridge—until we're on the northern outskirts of town. It's an area I haven't driven through since I've been home, a part of town that was just flat scrubby no-man's-land when I was a kid. The homes are less than ten years old, but they're untended and unloved and already look run-down. The remains of the old Watson Mission, which closed down about thirty years ago after a devastating fire, lie just across the river.

"I've got some people I'd like you to meet."

"What kind of people?"

"Kids."

I glance over at his stern profile, the white collar. "More kids? Is this your Sunday school class? I don't know that I can handle any feel-good bullshit today."

He's watching the road, but a blink-and-you'll-miss-it grin flickers over his face. "Not quite."

He pulls up between two of the houses and blasts the horn. Moments later two teenage boys slam through the front screen door of one house, shout something, slam the screen shut again, and jog towards us. They're dressed in name-brand sportswear, caps pulled low over dark sunnies.

Shep blasts the horn again, this time for longer, just as the boys wrench open the back door of the truck and scramble in. Close up the boys are clearly identical twins—all awkward long legs and arms, brilliant white smiles, dark curly hair escaping from under their caps. They're full of an energy that can barely be contained.

"This is Bill and Ben," says Shep, by way of introduction. "Their surname is Potts, but no one's ever explained the joke to them." I'm a little slow on the uptake, and it takes me a moment to work out that he's talking about the old *Flower Pot Men* TV show—featuring Bill and Ben—from our childhood. "Boys," he says, "this is Jo—or Sharpe as we used to call her before she left for the city and got too big for her boots.

"Now, say hello, fellas. Be polite." I'm not sure if he's talking to me or to them, but before any of us can respond, another boy—younger, or maybe just smaller, with red hair and freckles, a cracked front tooth—flings the door open and clambers in noisily. He's red faced, hot, flustered. "Fuck me, Sheppo," he says, "did you have to do that? I was on the bog." He sees me in the front, and his face goes a darker red. "Sorry." He doesn't look at me. "Didn't know there was anyone else here."

"Nice one. Jo, this is Grug. Grug, my mate Jo."

The boy mutters something that might be a greeting in the direction of his collarbone.

"Grug?" I'm still not sure whether I've heard the name right. "Is that the New Zealand version of Greg?"

They all laugh. "Nah—it's just a nickname. It was some book we read at school. About this bloke who looks like a haystack."

"Seat belts," Shep barks. The boys sigh, but comply, and he puts the car into gear and does a U-turn, heads back the way we came, down through the main street, turns left on the highway. There's the occasional spurt of laughter from the back, but they're talking too quietly for me to hear. Shep turns on the radio—it sounds like Willie Nelson singing "Amazing Grace." *Through many dangers, toils and snares . . .* Shep randomly breaks into a deliberately painful off-key harmony. The three boys protest, then groan in unison when he turns up the volume and sings even louder. We're heading south along the highway now. I have no idea where we're going, and for once, I am content to relax and accept the mystery, and the distraction. I put my head back and close my eyes.

'Twas grace hath brought
Us safe thus far
And grace will lead us home . . .

~

When I open my eyes, the radio has been turned off, and we're jolting along a dirt road, going a little too fast, the boys hooting as Shep slides into a wide curve, churning up the dirt in the verge. It takes me a moment to familiarise myself.

"Are we at Pembroke?"

"We are."

"What are we doing here?"

"Driving lessons."

"What?"

"Your grandmother lets me come out here with the boys—there's an old horse-training track a few kilometres from the house. We do laps for a while and then eventually the boys progress onto doughnuts, skids, that sort of thing."

"You're kidding. You're giving driving lessons? Why?"

"One hundred and twenty hours."

"What?"

Shep gestures towards the back of the car.

"It's what you need to get your licence now: a hundred and twenty hours of driving practice."

"Yikes." It had only been fifty when we were kids. "And?"

"So how do you think these kids are going to get their hundred and twenty hours?"

"I dunno. Parents? Lessons?" He turns his head briefly, eyebrows raised. I break off, slightly embarrassed.

"This is going to be a little different to my usual story, isn't it?"

Shep takes a corner too wide, and it takes him a moment to correct the steering.

"Could be."

We turn left near a windbreak of oak trees—a right turn would have taken us up to the house in its startling green oasis. A few kilometres further along an even more rugged track, Shep pulls over in an area that initially looks like a vast sea of red dirt. It takes me a moment to work out that we haven't come upon a desert—the area is surrounded by a well-made timber fence, and there's a primitive grandstand set under some tall gums—but a racecourse. Like so much about Pembroke, it's unexpected and slightly bizarre. I shake my head, laugh.

"Is this for real?"

"Well, lucky for us they're not actually maintaining this through the drought."

"What do you mean?"

"Usually the track'd be grass—which is kinder to the horses. We wouldn't be out here driving on that."

"These people . . . they've got so much money."

"They're your people, mate."

Grug leans over from the back seat—the boys are quiet, listening.

"Is this your place?"

He sounds impressed.

"No, but my mother grew up here."

One of the Flower Pot twins speaks. "Mum says her dad used to work out here back in the day, shearing. Some old bi—some old lady owned it."

The boys snigger.

"That'd be my grandmother." I keep my voice light. "She still owns it."

"How come you don't come out here then?" Grug is doing the asking, but all three boys are clearly interested.

Shep intervenes before I can come up with a suitable answer.

"Okay, everyone out. We're not here to sit around chatting. We've got four hours before I have to be back. You're first, Ben. The rest of you can wait at the grandstand. There are sandwiches and lemonade in the cooler. Go your hardest. Did you bring your camera, Jo?"

I hold up my phone. It won't be up to Edith's standard, but it'll have to do.

Shep grins. "If they do well, you can take them out to do some skids. Maybe some three-sixties. Doughnuts."

"How many lessons have you had?"

"This is the first proper lesson, miss," says Ben politely.

"Might be a bit soon for doughnuts then, don't you think?"

"But we've all had a bit of go around. Not legally—but you know . . . I reckon we can all drive okay."

"Yeah—my uncle let me drive his car before I could even see over the wheel. I'm an old hand." Grug gives his disarming grin.

I'm not reassured, but Shep doesn't seem worried.

"Come on. Like they say—they've been driving for years."

"Why are we doing this if they're such experts?"

He grins. "They need official hours. And I thought we could have some fun, teach them something they can't practice elsewhere. It'll make them better drivers in the long run."

"Anyway, how come you've got a woman teaching us tricks, Sheppo?" Grug asks. "Aren't your balls big enough?"

"Believe me, no one's got bigger balls than Jo Sharpe, mate. Not when it comes to cars."

~

Grug and Shep head back to the truck, and I follow the twins over to the trees. The grandstand is only three tiers, an ageing ramshackle timber construction that looks too dangerous to sit on. We find a shady spot under the trees, and the two boys raid the cooler while I keep half an eye on the driving.

Shep's lesson is fairly tame—just endless stops and starts and jerky gear changes and six-point turns that then evolve into tedious loops of the track. Once the twins have satisfied their seemingly limitless appetites, I attempt some conversation—

"So are you guys all still at school?"

"Yep."

"Here?"

"Yep."

"Any plans for after?"

"Nup."

"Lived here all your lives?"

"Yup."

—but eventually give it up as a hopeless effort.

I lie back with my eyes closed, soaking up the heat, swatting away flies, half listening to the low murmurs of the two boys, their occasional laughter, and let myself drift off.

I wake up to a dig in the ribs. "Oi. Sleeping Beauty."

I squint into the sun. Shep is standing above me, grinning. I sit up slowly, reluctantly. It's nothing I can really put my finger on, but I've woken up feeling shaky, apprehensive, as if something heavy and dank has settled over me.

"You okay?" Shep is quick to sense my mood.

"I dunno. A bad dream, maybe."

"The next few months'll be tough, mate. You need to go easy on yourself."

I nod and look away, avoiding his concerned gaze. The three boys are over by the truck, the twins trying to persuade Grug to relinquish his place behind the wheel.

"How's your old man?"

"I saw him briefly this morning. He didn't seem any different, really: just the usual shit on his liver."

"Have you two talked about it?"

"Nope."

"Well, you should."

"Yeah, probably. There are a lot of things we should talk about. That's how we roll."

"What about you? How're you doing?"

"I'm okay. I'll survive."

"You will. But you know, if you need someone to talk to . . ."

"I guess that's your job now, isn't it?"

"It is. But seriously, Jo. If I can help . . ."

"Do you do confession too?"

"Why? Do you need it?"

"Asking for a friend."

He laughs, holds out a hand. "Come on then. Your turn, Fangio."

"What do you mean? Didn't you want to take them all through their paces first?"

"All done." He raises an eyebrow. "You've been out cold for a couple of hours."

"Jesus. Really? Oh, God, sorry. I mean—"

"You have to stop doing that."

"What?"

"Apologising for saying *Jesus*. You're making me self-conscious."

"It's just . . . well, you know." I put my hands together, try to look saintly. "I don't want to offend you, Father."

"Oh, fuck off, Sharpe."

I gasp, open my eyes wide. "Profanity! Isn't that like a mortal sin or something?"

"Venial, if we're getting technical." He nudges me gently with his boot. "Get up, you dill."

I extend my hand and he pulls me up effortlessly. We stand close for what feels like a long moment, fingers curled together. Eventually he lets my hand go. "You're a bloody sight."

"What do you mean?"

"Look at your shirt. And your strides."

"Strides? Who even uses that word anymore?" I look down—my once-grey T-shirt is covered in a fine layer of red silt. As are my jeans.

"You're not getting in my truck like that."

I laugh, dust myself down. "This place. You forget."

"Really?" He looks doubtful.

"Yeah. Maybe you don't."

I take the boys out into the centre of the racecourse one at a time and show them a few basic techniques. Grug and Ben are both too nervous to really enjoy themselves, but Bill is the surprise star. He has a natural affinity—is quick, fearless, calm. He needs only minimal guidance, seems to know instinctively when to accelerate, when to back off—is unfazed when things go a little further than expected. There's one near miss when I'm sure we're about to go careening into the fence, and even as I'm moving to take the wheel, Bill manages to correct—easing back on the accelerator, turning the wheel exactly the right degree. When he pulls up, well clear, we both give a shout—mine is simple relief, but Bill's is as much exhilaration.

As we're all piling back into Shep's truck, the figure of a man appears in the distance, stalking across the heat-hazed earth like a mirage. The boys are eager to be on their way, make complaining noises, but Shep shushes them, and we wait for him to approach. It's my uncle Roland, his hat tilted back, two black-and-white kelpies padding politely behind. He walks across to the driver's side of the truck, gives a curt nod in greeting.

"How'd it go? Have a win?"

"Not bad at all. They're probably not going to be driving at Bathurst this year—but another—what?—hundred or so hours each and we'll get there."

"Another hundred. Bloody hell. A bit of overkill, isn't it? In our day we just sat the test. There was none of this 'hours' crap."

"If you have any long trips and want a second driver, they're your men."

Roly snorts. "I'll keep it in mind." He suddenly sees me, looks startled.

"What's she doing here?"

Shep looks momentarily put out by the rude question, but he responds mildly enough. "We had Jo come out and give the boys some lessons in, er . . . handling. Skids, that sort of thing. Not really my area of expertise. It's good for them to get used to the dirt."

Roly is too busy glaring at me to listen. "We heard about your mother this morning. No one came out to tell us—a friend of Mum's rang with the news that they'd dragged the car out of the river. You'd think someone official would have called us. Or you."

"I didn't . . ."

"Mum's pretty cut up."

"Any mother would be. It's horrifying." Shep's voice is low, sympathetic.

"I was surprised, to be honest. She's had a long time to get used to it, hasn't she?" Roly looks entirely unmoved. He could be discussing a dead sheep.

"She's barely mentioned her in thirty years. But since Jo came back, it's been Merry this, Merry that. A bit late to be regretful. Anyway, if you could give her a call and let her know what's going on—with the body, or the bodies or whatever they find. And the funeral arrangements. Apparently she wants to be involved." His surprise is evident.

"She was your sister, Roland." It's impossible to keep the edge out of my voice. "Aren't you just a little bit upset?"

He takes a moment to respond. "Honestly? It might sound cold, but no. I've barely thought about her since she left. Your mother and I weren't exactly enemies, Jo. I wouldn't go that far. But we were never friends. Not even when we were kids."

"Why?" I can't resist asking.

"I dunno." He shrugs. "We always ended up fighting, whenever we were together. And even that last meet—" He stops, clears his throat. "Anyway," he says, before turning away, "just give Ruth a call, will you?"

~

"That was your mum? That woman they found in the river?" Bill asks the question, but all three of the boys, subdued during the drive home, are waiting for the answer.

Shep intervenes. "Guys, I don't think Jo—"

"No, it's okay." I turn in my seat, give them a brief reassuring smile. "I'm afraid so. And my baby sister."

"I heard they'd been there for a long time."

"Almost twenty-five years. It is a long time."

"Didn't anyone look for her back then?"

"We didn't know we had to. She'd left letters saying she was going."

"So you didn't know she'd decked herself?"

"We had no idea. And we still don't really know for sure. I mean"—I take a deep breath—"maybe it was an accident."

The twins look sceptical, but Grug nods.

"One of my aunties killed herself a couple years ago. She took an overdose. We had to wait too. They had to make sure it wasn't, like, an accident. Or murder." Grug tells the story without any emotion.

"Yeah. There'll be an autopsy first, and I guess they'll get police experts to look at the car as well."

"They'll have rotted away, won't they? After being in the water that long?" Bill quizzes, innocently curious.

"Mate, that's enough." Shep almost shouts the words, and the other two boys are glaring at the stricken boy.

I put my hand briefly on Bill's shoulder. "No. You're right. I don't really expect they'll find much. But you never know. Maybe there'll be something they can tell us."

"It won't really help, though, will it?" Grug says in his calm, mat-ter-of-fact way. "It's not going to bring them back. Not even Sheppo can do that."

We are only a few kilometres from town when there's a loud bang. The rear passenger tyre has blown. Happily, the road is deserted, and the drive home has been very sedate, and though the truck bucks and skids across the road before coming to a shuddering stop a few metres from a barbed wire fence, we're not in any danger.

"Ah. Another lesson. Perfect." Shep's words are more enthusiastic than his tone. "Come on, fellas. Out. Time to learn how to change a tyre." The three boys groan, but acquiesce without further complaint. Perhaps the excitement has made them more curious than tired. I opt to stay in the cabin—lean back and try to change the radio dial from country to rock and fail.

I'm drifting off again, half listening to a country version of "Blowing in the Wind" when I hear a loud clang, a shouted obscenity, and then . . . silence. I can't see anything from the cabin, climb out.

Shep is on his knees, clutching his hand. His face is frighteningly pale. The three boys huddle around him, eyes wide.

"What's happened?"

"He's dropped the jack on his hand." Grug is spokesman. "He swore."

Ben looks worried. "And he was serious."

~

I drop the boys off on Oxley Road, just across from the park—they have business to do before they head home, Grug tells me, his expression slightly shifty. I don't ask what—it seems unlikely that any sort of legal business would happen on the dark and deserted street.

"Thanks for the lesson, miss," says Bill. "You're pretty good. For a girl."

"And lucky you know how to change a tyre." Grug gives his cracked-tooth smile.

"You were pretty good too. For blokes."

They say goodbye to Shep, but he doesn't respond, having drifted off during the trip back.

"Do you think he's okay?" Ben asks, looking down anxiously at his pale face.

"I think he's in a bit of pain, but I'm sure he'll be fine. Just a dislocation, like he said. And he's pushed it back in."

"I did me collarbone once, playing footy," Grug says. "Thought I was gonna die." The boy looks impressed. "He's a tough mother."

"He is."

"Tell him we'll see him Sunday."

"Sunday? At church?"

"Nah, miss." The boys don't bother to disguise their laughter. "As if. We've got to do this theory so we can do RFS training next year. I reckon church would probably be better."

I'm not sure that I believe my own prognosis. Shep is still pale; his mouth turns down, as if in pain. I turn the truck around and head up towards the hospital. He stirs, opens his eyes. "Where are you going?"

"The hospital. I think you should see a doctor. Make sure it's . . . gone back where it should be. Maybe get some pain relief?"

"I'm fine. Just take me home."

"But you look—"

189

"It's nothing. It's happened before. I know what I'm doing. Honestly."

"Really?"

"Really."

~

Lucy comes out of the church when we arrive at the rectory. She is clearly surprised to see me driving the truck, and frowns when she sees Shep struggling to climb down without using his bad hand.

"What on earth's happened?" I can feel the waves of disapproval.

"Nothing." There's a curtness to his voice that I haven't heard before.

Lucy watches him push the door, sees his weakness as he leans up against the car.

"Well, obviously something's happened." She looks at Shep tenderly, then glares in my direction. "Was it one of those boys again?"

"He dropped a—" I begin.

Shep interrupts. "It's just my hand. It'll be right by tomorrow. Please don't fuss, either of you. If you could bring in the cooler, Jo, and park the truck out on Merton Street behind the church, that'd be great." He tries to grin, but can only grimace.

I carry in the cooler, Lucy peppering me with questions that I answer as vaguely and briefly as I can. Inside, she can't resist fussing around Shep, asking whether he wants her to make him a cuppa or wash up the lunch things, and within minutes, Shep has pushed us both out the front door. "I'm going to bed," he says to me. "Can you just leave the key on the table and lock the door when you've finished." Lucy follows me back to the truck, still trying to get me to give her details of the accident.

"I don't know why you're both being so close lipped," she says finally, scowling, just as I'm about to climb into the truck. "Are you hiding something?"

I sigh. "I think he'd rather tell you himself." I try not to sound like I'm reprimanding her, but fail.

"Of course," she says stiffly, her lovely face colouring. "I'll talk to him tomorrow. Do you want me to wait while you park the truck? You can give me the keys."

"Nah," I say lightly, "I know the way. I'll drop them in." I smile, crunch the truck into gear, and move on.

~

I drop the keys on the kitchen table and am tiptoeing back down the slightly musty hall of the old rectory when Shep calls out.

"That you, Sharpe?"

"It is." I follow the hallway to the back of the house.

His bedroom is dimly lit and papered, as is the entire house, in faded floral velvet wallpaper, stained and peeling in places. It smells of talcum powder and stale perfume, with an undertone of ancient damp. It's starkly furnished: an old timber bed frame, a rickety wardrobe, as old as the wallpaper, and a chair. There is a cross on the wall behind the bedhead. An old desk fan buzzes on the bedside table, but barely moves the air. I walk over to the bed. Shep is lying back against the pillows, his face drawn in pain.

"Is it bad?"

"Getting better."

"Really?"

"No."

"Should I call Fran? Couldn't she give you a shot of something. Morphine?"

"Nah. I spew if I have morphine—and then get a week-long hangover. I've had a Panadol. It'll be fine by tomorrow."

"Is there something I can do?"

"Just . . . stay."

"I thought you wanted us to piss off."

"It's Lucy. She . . . fusses. You're different." He breaks off, takes a deep breath.

"Actually, Jo, I've been wanting to talk to you." He sounds serious.

"Yeah?"

"I just wanted to tell you what happened—back when we were kids. I've never had the chance to explain."

"It was a long time ago, Shep. It doesn't really matter."

"But you deserve an explanation. You see, I got this job offer . . ." He has broken out into a sweat; his skin has a green tinge.

I shake my head. "Seriously. No. You don't need to explain anything. It's really not something I've thought about for a while . . ." He looks at me for a long moment, then nods. He sinks back into the pillows.

His face is pale, sweaty. I angle the fan towards his face, turn it up, but it makes no difference. "What if I make an ice pack? Bring in the fan from the kitchen. Will that help?"

"Can't hurt." He closes his eyes.

By the time I drag in the big fan and a chair and create a makeshift ice pack from a couple of packs of frozen vegetables, he's fallen into a light sleep. His mouth is open and he's snoring slightly. I sit beside him. I've never considered myself the nurse type, but here I am. I sit watching his face, pull the sheet up when he twitches, wipe a flannel over his face, and then his neck, his chest. He comes to consciousness for a moment and grabs my fingers with his good hand, holds them against his cheek. He closes his eyes again. "Don't go," he says softly, a strange smile on his face.

"I'm not going anywhere."

CHAPTER SEVEN

A LITTLE BIRD

You'd better watch out, you'd better not shout. Excitement levels are rising in Arthurville homes as families prepare for Santa's visit next Friday. Santa's mailbag—which can be found just inside Martin's Newsagency—is full to overflowing, and is due to be sent off to Mr. Claus tomorrow.

And just who's been naughty and who's been nice—that's the question on everyone's lips. As per tradition, more than a few of our best-known community members were a little bit naughty at the Golf Club annual Christmas dinner and dance. A little bird tells me that one particularly fine golfer, a married man whose name shall not pass my lips, somehow managed to end up under the mistletoe with not one but two of the pretty young waitresses. Another enthusiastic reveller was found curled up asleep at the 12th hole on Sunday morning—a

little the worse for wear and apparently ruining
some poor golfer's chance of a hole in one.

A Little Bird, *Arthurville Chronicle*, 1992

Jo

Arthurville, 2018

When I arrive in the office the following morning, Edith is already
there, hard at work on her thesis.

She gives me a slightly awkward hug.

"I heard the news, Jo. I'm so sorry. I can't imagine how awful . . ."

"Yeah. It's . . . to be honest, I don't know what it is . . ."

"Do you think you should be at work? I mean—I'm sure Barb can
come in."

I laugh. "I haven't heard a peep from her, so I'm not so sure.
Anyway, I think I'm better off being here, doing something. Keeping
busy. The show must go on. Pretty sure there's some earthshaking news
I need to cover today. Aren't the Presbyterians holding a church fete this
weekend? And I've been looking forward to the heifer sale for weeks."
Edith's eyes widen at my slightly hysterical tone.

I take a breath, try to give a reassuring smile. "Honestly, I'm fine.
Dad has to see a specialist at midday in Dalhunty. I just wanted to
come in for an hour or two, make a few phone calls, get a few things
written up."

"Okay. But if there's anything you need, just say the word." She
gives my shoulder a squeeze. "Oh, I almost forgot. A couple of cops
called in earlier. They want you to give them a call. Or go down to the
station. They'll be there for the next hour, apparently."

"Oh, okay."

"They were an . . . interesting pair."

"What do you mean?"

"You know. Typical detectives: shiny suits, aviator glasses. A little bit . . . arrogant maybe."

"Detectives? Not just two uniforms from Dalhunty?"

"Pretty sure they're the big boys. I think they said homicide."

"Homicide?"

I feel my heart sink. Surely not.

~

I try to find out what's going on, but the young constable at the desk isn't forthcoming. "Sorry, ma'am," she says, "All I know is that the crew from Dalhunty requested homicide late last night."

Eventually the duty sergeant, Phil Deacon, comes out and waves me into his office.

There are two suited detectives, strangers, sitting in the room. One, a man in his fifties, silver-haired, lean, is sitting behind the desk, his head down, reading through a pile of documents. The other, clearly younger but completely bald, is leaning, feet apart and arms folded, against the opposite wall, his face expressionless.

"I'm very sorry for your loss," Phil says almost perfunctorily as he closes the door. He can barely meet my eye, is clearly nervous. "This is Detective Sergeant Nakavisut." He gestures to the older man first. "And this is Detective Constable Simons. Homicide. They've been put in charge of the case." The two men nod, their expressions unreadable.

I nod, take the seat that Phil pulls out for me.

"What's going on?" I ignore the detectives, direct my question at Phil. "We haven't heard anything from anyone—not since . . . not since they pulled the car out. Nothing."

"Apparently the Dalhunty officers, ah, tried to call your father yesterday afternoon. Apparently they left messages. But he didn't respond."

"They knew he was in hospital. Why didn't they contact me?"

"I think they tried that too."

"Nobody's called, believe me. Has there even been an autopsy yet? Why is the homicide squad involved?" The two men are watching coolly.

Phil looks uncomfortable. "There's been a—well, an initial examination . . ." He looks over at the older detective anxiously. "Actually, I might let Detective Sergeant Nakavisut here explain the details. He's got all the information. And I've—I've got things to do." He nods and scurries out.

The detective puts his papers down, comes over to my side of the desk. "Hamish Nakavisut. I'm very sorry about your mother. It must be hard—even after all this time." He holds out his hand.

"They're certain it's her then?"

He nods. "And your sister."

Even though I know what's coming, the official confirmation makes my stomach lurch. I close my eyes briefly, wait for it to pass. I take a deep breath, sit up straight, let my journalistic instincts take over. "What's going on? Why send homicide detectives to investigate a twenty-five-year-old suicide?"

"Because it's not."

"What do you mean?"

"It's a murder." The detective speaks clearly, but the words don't make any sense.

"What are you talking about?"

"I'm afraid your mother was murdered. And your sister." I try to formulate an appropriate response, a question, a statement. Anything. My mouth moves but no sound emerges.

"The medical examiner found that your mother had a fractured skull." His voice is gentle. "She couldn't have driven herself into the river, because she was already dead."

I've read that the best place to talk to a teenager, especially teenage boys, is in a car. Apparently, the lack of eye contact can make conversation easier, confidences more likely. My father is long past his youth, but the principle remains the same—and it's sure easier than telling him anywhere else I can imagine.

When I explained that my father is unwell, frail, that the shock of finding Mum has been enough, the detectives agreed that I should be the one to tell him, and that he should be given some time to compose himself before they question him. "He has an appointment with a specialist this afternoon that can't be put off," I told them. "So I'd like to wait until that's over."

"What time will that be?" Sergeant Nakavisut's tone was suddenly, shockingly, completely businesslike. "We need to talk to him. Today."

"We'll be back around four."

He nodded. "Make sure he understands what's going on. We'll be there."

"You do know he wasn't around when my mother left, don't you? He was working out west. There were multiple witnesses. That was all established when Mum first went missing. It should be in the files."

The detective shook his head. "Everything's up in the air now. We don't know exactly when your mother died. And the fact that your father has an alibi for the day your mother was last seen is meaningless. She could have died days later. Weeks even. Maybe months. If the coroner can establish Amy's exact age—it might be possible to work out the date reasonably accurately—we'll have a better idea. But even without it, your father's alibi doesn't mean a thing."

~

I have rehearsed all the ways I might tell Dad, but in the end I give him the facts baldly, without attempting to dress them up: Mum suffered a fatal blow before she hit the water—it was murder, not suicide. She didn't leave us. I explain that the dates are now in question—that obviously she must have returned sometime after she sent the second letter. He says nothing. I turn my head briefly away from the road to look at him—he has his head back, eyes closed. His breathing is shallow and fast.

Eventually he speaks, his eyes still closed. "I guess there was always going to be a big dump of crap icing on this shit cupcake." I don't know whether to laugh or cry.

~

Even though I'm expecting it, the sight of the police car parked outside the house makes my heart race. I look at Dad, but he doesn't comment. The officers, both unsmiling, their eyes hidden behind dark sunglasses, exit the car when I pull into the driveway. They saunter up the driveway and watch impassively as I open the passenger-side door and Dad begins his slow manoeuvring out. They had been kind enough to me, but their shift in attitude is obvious in their body language.

"We'd like a word, if you don't mind, Mr. Sharpe." Detective Nakavisut's voice isn't exactly unfriendly, but there's no warmth either.

"You can see my father isn't well. Can't it wait?" I'm surprised by my own sudden protectiveness.

"Not really, no."

"Can you just wait until we get inside?"

"No problem."

"Actually, why not just talk to me here? There's no reason we have to invite these pricks indoors, is there?"

Nakavisut appears unmoved, but I note the surprise on the younger officer's face, quickly hidden.

"I'm happy to conduct your interview wherever's convenient, Mr. Sharpe. As long as you don't mind an audience." He gestures at the house across the road, where Bev Ryan's figure can be seen stepping back from her window.

Dad laughs. "Why not? Let's make Bev's day." He sits back heavily on the car seat, and swivels his legs around so he's facing them. "The old dear's been waiting for me to get my comeuppance for thirty-odd years. Now, how can I help you fine upstanding members of the constabulary?"

Nakavisut nods at Simons, who clears his throat, clearly uncomfortable in such an exposed situation. "As I expect your daughter has told you, Mr. Sharpe, the, er . . . new evidence . . ." The poor man can't seem to work out where to begin. "The initial medical examination of your wife's, um, remains . . ."

The older man interrupts. "I'm sure your daughter has told you that the initial medical examination shows that your wife suffered a fatal blow before she entered the water. This means that your wife—and your daughter—were murdered." He doesn't try to soften the brutal facts. "We have no way of knowing at what point your wife went into the water, and no evidence, other than the eyewitness accounts of your wife's movements that morning, and the letter your mother-in-law received from Queensland, that lets us establish a timeline. We're going to have to ask a few questions about your movements in the weeks following your wife's, ah, departure."

"The weeks following my wife's departure, eh? That was almost a quarter of a century ago. Even if I hadn't been pissed for the first six months after her . . . departure, I doubt I'd remember anything worth telling you."

"I'm sure there'll be people you can talk to who might be able to jog your memory," Detective Simons chips in helpfully. "Friends, family. Workmates." He gestures across the road. "Neighbours. Any written records would be useful. Maybe you have old work diaries? Phone records?"

"A work diary?" Dad snorts. "I was a labourer on the railways. I didn't have a fucking secretary." There's a pulse beating on his forehead, and his colour has begun to rise.

"Dad."

"There's no need to get upset, Mr. Sharpe. This is all just preliminary information gathering. We expect the medical examiner will request a coronial inquest, but any details you can provide now will be helpful." Nakavisut nods, his expression impossible to gauge. "Anyway, we won't keep you now. Just see what you can remember. Write it down. Maybe you can get your daughter to help you do some research." He gives a curt nod. "We'll call back tomorrow afternoon." He nods and walks back to the police car, his disconsolate-looking partner trailing after him.

~

We eat early—lamb chops that I find in the freezer, and a very basic salad: lettuce, sliced tomatoes, cucumber, a dash of vinegar to dress it. Dad laughs. "Jeez. This is old school. If you'd added pickled onions, I'd worry you'd been talking to my grandmother." I add a jar of cocktail onions to my mental shopping list.

We don't say anything about what has just transpired. Whenever I go to speak, Dad holds up his hand. *Later.* We go our separate ways once we've eaten. Dad to shower, me to sit on the verandah with a tall ice-filled glass of white wine and Alligator for company.

It wasn't until I was in my teens that I had any idea about the rumours that had swirled around town when my mother first disappeared—that I discovered my father had been a suspect. Perhaps the only suspect.

I'd been standing in a queue at the school canteen one recess. I'd already queued to pick up my regular Mondays-in-winter lunch order, a meat pie and sauce, and had rejoined the line when I discovered that my tomato sauce was missing. The two canteen ladies—both mothers of classmates, one a local, the other a more-recent arrival—were gossiping, their voices loud enough to be heard from where I was standing. It took me a moment to realise whom they were discussing.

She seems okay, though, doesn't she? The daughter?

Ellie says she's very quiet. Smart, though, I think. You can't help but wonder what goes on. I mean, I know that Mick, her dad, had an alibi, and then a letter or something arrived—but . . . it always seemed pretty fishy to me. Too convenient.

And the mother's never been back in contact?

Not as far as I know.

It makes you wonder, doesn't it? Did you know her? The mother?

Not well. She wasn't ever what you'd call friendly. But I never heard anything against her—and she seemed pretty normal.

I just can't imagine ever leaving a child of mine. The father—does he seem dangerous? Violent?

Pete reckons he's not a bad bloke. But you can't tell, can you?

You'd think the police, some authority, would do something. Keep an eye on them—make sure he isn't . . . doing something—

The woman saw me, standing patiently at the front of the line. Her face went pale, then bright red.

I had learnt young to hide my emotions. Knew how to fake them when necessary. I smiled, asked for my sauce. Pretended I hadn't heard a thing.

But I had heard every word. And however hard I tried, it was impossible to unhear.

And impossible to keep from wondering.

~

By ten o'clock I give up trying to sleep.

Dad is in the lounge room as per usual. But tonight, both the TV and the air-con are off. He's lying back in his recliner with his eyes shut, breathing deeply. The room is like an oven. Dad is even paler than usual, and a line of sweat glistens beneath his hairline. I stand there, just watching. Wondering.

Eventually he opens his eyes.

"No TV tonight?" I keep my question as casual as possible.

"Nothing worth watching."

"Do you want the air-con on? It's gruesome in here."

"It's right. I'm not hot."

I put the back of my hand to his forehead. Despite the sweat, his skin is cool to the touch, almost clammy.

"Are you going to do what they asked? The cops? Write it all down—where you were when Mum left. What you did afterwards."

"I can tell you what I did. I was either at work, or at the pub, or here. And when I wasn't at work, I was pissed. End of story." He glares. I glare right back.

I'm the first to look away.

"I thought I might go out tonight."

"Take a key this time, if you're going to be out late, will you?"

"I'm not going to be late."

"I'm too old to be woken by my teenage daughter stumbling about pissed in the middle of the night."

"I'm hardly a teenager, Dad."

"Then don't act like one."

"Also, I wasn't pissed. And even if I was, I'm thirty-two years old."

He interrupts. "Apparently thirty is the new twenty—so you're not far off."

"Well, if it is, fifty must be the new forty." But it's too late—his eyes are closed again, my lame rejoinder wasted.

~

Tonight it isn't noticeably cooler inside Tatts, although I can hear the air conditioner straining above the din. My luck is in—I can see Shep,

202

Edith, and a woman I assume is her girlfriend, Fizz, in a booth up the back, along with someone else I can't quite make out. Delicate well-manicured fingers reach for a champagne glass—Lucy. My sigh is entirely involuntary. First things first, though. I head straight to the bar, where a lone barmaid is struggling with the hot and thirsty crowd.

"Shove over." I squeeze in beside Edith and Fizz, opposite Shep and Lucy. When Edith introduces us, Fizz greets me enthusiastically, kissing me on both cheeks. Lucy gives me a lukewarm smile; Shep's welcome is warmer, if typically laconic. He looks at his watch. "Isn't it way past your bedtime, Sharpe?"

"Who can sleep in this heat?" I push tendrils of sweat-soaked hair away from my face and try not to look down at my shirt, which I know has stuck to every part of me. Of the others, only Fizz seems to be affected by the relentless heat. She looks a little like a dejected clown: her heavy eye makeup has melted; her lipstick is smudged; her hair has flattened into sad, slightly greasy-looking curls. Edith is looking as cool and gorgeous as always. Shep is still in his religious garb despite the heat. Lucy is wearing a dress, a sleeveless white gossamery thing, utterly feminine, and utterly impossible for someone like me to pull off. She looks lovely, like a porcelain doll, her skin clear and not even slightly sweaty, hair hanging in golden ringlets. A little silver cross hangs around her neck, just above a cleavage that manages to be simultaneously modest and sexy. Maybe its modesty is what makes it sexy. It seems highly unlikely that we share any DNA. She is sitting as close to Shep as she can without actually touching.

Edith gives me a smug smile. "You're such a sook. This is nothing. Spring weather where I'm from."

"Oh my God." Fizz rolls her eyes. "If you tell me one more time how much hotter it is in Kenya, I swear I'll pour this bloody beer over your head."

"But it's clearly given me an advantage."

"I lived here for nearly twenty years of my life," I say. "Believe me, it doesn't help. I'm still hot."

"Someone's got tickets on themselves." Shep grins.

"Tickets?" Edith looks at Shep, then closely at me, confused.

Lucy perks up. "It's what you say when someone exaggerates their worth."

"What?" Edith still looks blank.

"Jo just said she's still hot—she meant the temperature, but Shep has taken *hot* as meaning she's still good-looking." Which from cousin Lucy's expression is far from apparent. And what does she mean by "still"?

"I get that," says Edith. "I'm not an idiot. But where do the tickets come into it?"

"Jesus. Sorry, Shep." Fizz gives him an apologetic look. "I mean, *fuck*, you're painful, Edith."

"It means she's got a high price on herself—a ticket—and generally somewhat more than she's worth." Lucy is like a schoolmarm without a class.

I smile thinly. "Well, it would be a ticket if that's what I'd actually meant. But as I was talking about heat, it's a moot point, isn't it?"

Edith shakes her head slowly. "I have absolutely no idea what you're all talking about."

Fizz takes her hand, squeezes it. "I'll explain later, sweetie."

"Still, you're not bad for an old boiler," Shep says with a straight face.

"A what?"

"It's another idiom—a boiler is a chicken that's—" Lucy begins eagerly, but Fizz interrupts. "Oh God no. Please don't. I need another drink." She looks around the table, stands up. "I think it's my shout? And don't ask, Edith. Just don't."

"Talking of silly chooks," I say when she's gone, "how's your thumb?"

204

"WTF is this obsession with poultry?" Edith shakes her head.

Shep holds up his left hand, which has been professionally splinted and bandaged. "I can't move it or feel it, but other than that—hunky-dory."

"I take it that chewing on a bit of leather didn't work?"

"He was in a lot of pain this morning," Lucy says before he can answer. "*And* running a temperature. I called the doctor as soon as I got to work, and she came over and splinted it. And gave him some painkillers. He's had X-rays—it wasn't actually a straightforward dislocation; there's some sort of fracture apparently." Lucy drops her hand on Shep's forearm lightly, looks at me. "He really should have gone straight to emergency. And if you'd told me what had happened, I'd've insisted."

"But I—"

"It's all good." Shep raises his glass deliberately, ending the conversation. "My beer arm's still working."

Halfway through my second schooner, Edith asks me if there's been any news about the car, my mother. It's the question I know they've all been wanting to ask but have been carefully avoiding. Another few sips and I'm able to answer.

"You're not serious? A fractured skull?"

"So does that change things?"

"It means she"—I correct myself—"it means *they* were murdered." He doesn't say anything, but the sympathy in Shep's eyes makes my own fill.

"OMG." Fizz's eyes are wide. "This is like a crime novel."

"Felicity." This time Edith glares at Fizz. "This is Jo's mother we're talking about. And her baby sister."

I shake my head. "No. It's okay. The whole thing *is* completely nuts. And it doesn't feel like real life, somehow."

"So is your father a suspect, now?" Lucy asks. "He doesn't have an alibi anymore, does he? Not if she came back."

"You seem to be very well informed, Lucy." I keep my tone light. Lucy's brisk reasoning, while accurate, immediately raises my hackles.

"I've, ah, known your mother's story since I was a child. It was kind of a family story." She gives a strangled cough. "I mean, my dad has always talked about it. He met your mum once or twice when they were kids, you know. And my granny, she's still pretty close to Ruth."

"Oh, right. A family story. How lovely. I'm glad to have provided some live true-crime entertainment." Lucy doesn't look quite as pretty with a pink face.

Shep diverts the conversation smoothly. "What are the police saying? Have they spoken to your father?"

"They've sent detectives up from Sydney. Homicide detectives. They came around this afternoon, and more or less told him he was a suspect. As Lucy said, there's no firm alibi, because they can't be sure when she, when they, died."

"And how did that go down?"

"Have you met my old man?"

He laughs. "I take it he wasn't . . . cooperative."

"So why is your dad a suspect now," Edith asks, "if he wasn't at the time?"

"He was away the day she disappeared, and people saw her that morning. So that cleared him. And then when my grandmother received the letter, they closed the case."

"What letter?" Fizz looks confused.

"Mum sent a letter a few weeks after she left. She said she was fine and not to look for her."

"And that was it? That was enough to shut down the case?"

"Well, they were certain it was Mum, I guess. And some woman in a petrol station near the border said she'd seen a woman who more or less fit Mum's description—she couldn't remember any details, but the woman was rushing because she had a baby in the car."

"Was the letter handwritten?"

206

"No, it was typed. But they could tell it was Mum's typewriter."

"Why would she have sent a typed letter? Would she even have had access to a printer?"

"It wasn't a computer, so she didn't need a printer. She had a portable typewriter. She worked for the newspaper."

"Sometimes I forget there was actually a time before computers." Fizz picks up her drink, slurps the dregs.

"Back in the Dark Ages."

"So what happened to the typewriter?"

"No one knows. The detectives told me there's no sign of it in the car."

"Maybe she left it in Queensland."

Shep, who has been watching me carefully, speaks quietly. "This changes things, doesn't it? For you, I mean?"

Shep is right. The knowledge that my mother's death was murder, not an accident, not suicide, changes things for everyone—for my father, for Mum's friends, for her family, for the community. My own head is full of contradictory emotions: my mother is dead and nothing will ever bring her back, but somehow there's still a strange comfort in the knowledge that my mother didn't leave me. She *was* the mother I've remembered—the mother who loved me, who would never have deliberately, willingly, left me.

"I guess it does." I avoid making eye contact, polish off my beer in one big gulp, and hold up my glass. "Whose shout?"

~

That night I dream that I'm on the road, driving Mum's little blue car, turning east onto Oxley Road, zipping along, faster than I should, but the road is straight, there's barely a tree, and I've been down this road a thousand times before. I make the right turn onto the dirt road that will take me to the river. I pull over near the channel and get out. There's no one else here, save the cows, who gaze longingly across the electric wire to the greener pasture by the river. But then I sense a movement; a figure emerges and walks slowly towards me. They move closer, but their features are blurred, unrecognisable.

I wake up, sweat soaked, my heart pounding. I close my eyes and try to will myself back to sleep, back into the nightmare. However terrifying, I need to go back, to find out what happens next. But sleep won't come, and the dream scatters, dissolves.

CHAPTER EIGHT

A LITTLE BIRD

Little Bird is wondering who is going to replace Mr. Jasper Goodes, town librarian (see photo on page 8), when he retires at the end of the year. Mr. Goodes has single-handedly run the Arthurville Municipal Library for the last thirty years, and can claim credit for encouraging many fine English scholars at the local high school and beyond. Little Bird has also heard a rumour that certain ~~functionally illiterate~~ local councillors are wondering whether hiring a librarian—or even funding the library—is really a necessity as we enter the computer age: "Books are going the way of the dodo," one worthy was heard opining. "I haven't opened one since I left school forty years ago."

Quod erat demonstrandum, as the cool kids say.

A Little Bird, *Arthurville Chronicle*, 1992

Jo

Arthurville, 2018

"You've been ignoring my phone calls."

My grandmother is standing on the front verandah.

"What?" I blink, dazed by the already-too-bright morning sun. It probably isn't the best way to address her, but in my defence, I am still half-asleep. Half-drunk too.

"I need to talk to you, Josephine. I need your help." Ruth is again dressed in jeans and a white shirt, her hair pulled back neatly, but her pale lipstick has escaped the boundaries of her thinning lips, staining her front teeth.

"You do?" I fold my arms—channelling my best adolescent self. She seems taken aback momentarily, is clearly not used to encountering any sort of resistance.

She glares. "Josephine. Your attitude isn't helpful." She sounds as if she's trying to hide her impatience. "I *am* your grandmother."

I glare back. "You might be my grandmother, but I barely know you. And I don't recall a time when you've ever offered to help *me*."

"That's not—" She pauses. Breathes deeply. Starts again. "The fact that we don't know each other isn't entirely my fault, dear."

"Really?"

"This isn't something we need to talk about now, but one day, perhaps, we can have that conversation." She looks old suddenly—weak, and maybe afraid. The fading eyes, crepe-y neck, the vast net of wrinkles around her eyes.

I step back from the doorway. "Do you want to come in, then, and tell me what you want?"

She looks alarmed. "Oh no. I'd rather not. I'll just wait in my car until you're dressed and we can drive and talk."

"I haven't eaten. Can we get breakfast?"

"I really don't want to see anyone . . ."

"I don't either. We can go to the Maccas drive-through. If that's not too much to ask."

She blinks.

"I'll wait then. Can you be quick? I take it you'll want to get changed, but no need to dress up." She turns and marches down the stairs, clearly eager to get away from the house. I watch as she opens the door to her new model Mercedes SUV and slides into the driver's seat.

"What does the old bat want?"

Dad is standing at the kitchen door with his arms folded. He is still in his pyjamas; an unlit cigarette dangles in the corner of his mouth.

"She says she wants to talk to me. I've no idea why."

"Are you going to talk to her?"

"Looks like we're going for a drive."

"Why doesn't she just come in?"

"Worried she'll bump into you, maybe."

He snorts. "Worried I'll grab her by the scruff of her wrinkly old neck and throw her out, more like."

"Would you?"

He considers the prospect seriously. "Depends on how much she weighs."

I dress quickly and run a brush through my hair. I consider the fact that we'll be close together in the car, clean my teeth and gargle. I don't want to knock the old cow out with my whiskey breath.

Dad is sitting at the kitchen table reading the paper—the still-unlit cigarette has now migrated to the lip of an empty ashtray.

He looks up briefly. "Try and come back in one piece."

I slide into the passenger seat.

"Nice car." It is a nice car—sleek, the five-litre engine purring gently, luxurious leather seats, burl walnut trim. State-of-the-art everything. It's probably worth four times my yearly salary. I run my hand over the glossy dash.

"It's an indulgence, a car like this, but I think at my age I've earned a few indulgences."

This time my eyes widen, but I keep my mouth shut.

She gives me a quick look, smiles faintly.

"I've heard on the grapevine that you share your father's interest in cars?"

I ignore her friendly overture. "What is it you want to talk to me about, Ruth?" I mean to sound coolly impatient, but even to my ears I just sound defensive.

"We'll just get that coffee, shall we," she says mildly, "and then talk."

We drive out to a rarely frequented travel stop on the outskirts of town, where picnic tables with oddly angled tin roofs grace an entirely graceless patch of red dirt by the side of the highway. According to what remains of the signage, the tables were donated by the fundraising committee of the Arthurville—or *Arseville*, as some wit has spray-painted over it—Macquarie Club in 1973. Ruth eyes the green-painted table suspiciously, then swipes it with a clean tissue before she puts her food down. I take a big bite of my muffin, suddenly starving. When I look up, she is regarding me thoughtfully.

"You're very like Merry, you know."

"I am?"

"It's nothing obvious," Ruth says. "But she's there in your expression. The way you hold yourself. Your hands. The shape of your face." She pauses for a moment, watches as I take a self-conscious sip of my coffee. "Your beautiful, beautiful mother."

I almost choke.

She takes a breath, pulls herself upright. "I suppose you're wondering why I've brought you here."

"Well, yes."

"Have you . . . have the police spoken to you since . . ." She gulps. "Since they found them . . . ?"

"I spoke to them yesterday."

212

"And they told you . . . they've told you that it wasn't an accident?"

"They told me that someone hit her over the head and then drove her, and Amy, into the water. Is that what you mean?"

She flinches, then looks at me for a long moment, her face sombre. "Yes. That's what they told us. That she was murdered." Her voice is barely audible.

"Did you bring me here to see if I think my father did it? Because I'm not going to discuss that."

"What? No. It's not that, Josephine. I promise. I never even thought of it. It's your uncle. Roland." Her voice is light, breathless with anxiety. Her hands clench on her coffee cup.

"What about him?"

"The police came early this morning and took him in for questioning."

"The police took Roly? What for?"

"They wanted to question him about your mother. I've rang our solicitor, and he's there now, with Roly. But I haven't heard anything."

"Why do they want to talk to Roly?" As far as I know, he and Mum hadn't spoken for years.

"They seemed to think that he was one of the last people to see her. During the initial investigation, someone told the police that they'd seen his truck outside her, your, house the morning she disappeared. Early that morning."

"Outside our place?" This is something I've never heard.

"Apparently. But then that letter arrived, and they closed the case, and it didn't really matter."

It matters to me, now. "*Was* he there?"

She looks uncomfortable. "He told the police that he wasn't. That he hadn't spoken to her for years. The woman who said she saw his truck—she wasn't a particularly reliable person. And he had an alibi—he'd driven out to Calare that day. He could prove that—there were plenty of witnesses. So the police didn't have any good reason not to believe him."

"And did *you* believe him?"

She turns to look at me, her gaze never wavering, her voice firm.

"At the time, I had no doubt. Now I don't know. I think perhaps he was lying. Why else would they question him?"

"If he saw her, it must have been important. They hadn't seen each other for, what? Eight years or so, had they? Before I was born?"

"I suppose. I don't really know. They were never . . . fond of one another. Even as children." She sounds sad.

"So why would the police want to talk to him now?"

"That's what I don't understand. It's why I've come to you. You're a journalist . . . I thought maybe you could . . . perhaps . . . speak to the detectives. Find out." She looks uncomfortable.

I laugh. "You've just told me that you think your son lied about being one of the last people known to have seen my *murdered* mother—your daughter. And you want me to help him?"

"You're my granddaughter. There is no one else." Her words are plain, her desperation clear, and in that moment she's just a vulnerable old woman, seeking help. But I resist, let the anger, never too far from the surface when it comes to my mother's family, kick in.

"I don't know you. And I don't know Roland. And I don't owe either of you anything."

She flinches, but recovers quickly. Squares her shoulders and turns back to me.

"That's true. Although, as I've said, there are some mitigating factors."

"And as you've said, that's not really what's at issue here."

"No."

"I'm sorry to break it to you, but the police aren't going to tell me anything that will help Roly. If that's all you brought me here for, I'd like to go home. I've got some sleep I need to catch up on. Or is there something else?"

"There's nothing else. And you're right—you don't owe us anything. I'll take you home."

We drive back in silence. When she pulls up outside the house, she turns to me.

"You seem to think that I deserted you—that there were no offers of help after your mother left. But that's not true. I sent letters. Every week, for months. I wanted to see you. I wanted to help."

"That's not what I remember."

"Perhaps you should talk to your father," she says stiffly. "Ask him what happened to the letters. Why he didn't respond."

I don't know what to think. "I'll ask."

She grasps my arm. "And please, if you hear anything . . . please let me know. Whatever else—Roland's your uncle. He's blood. My only remaining child. Please. Can you call me?"

I nod and pull my arm away, although not ungently. "I'll see what I can do."

I push the car door closed, walk through the gate and up to the doorway without turning back.

~

By the afternoon my irritation has been replaced by curiosity.

"Feel like an outing?"

Edith looks up from her computer, gives a moan.

"I shouldn't. I've got so much to do."

"But you will, won't you?"

She looks at her screen, then back at me. "Gah. The world doesn't need another PhD anyway." She pushes back her chair and follows me out into the street without a backward glance. She waits until we're about to get in the car before she asks.

"Can I ask where we're going?"

"Pembroke."

"Right." She swallows. "And, ah, I guess you'll be driving."

"I will."

She opens her mouth to say something, changes her mind. Gives a resigned shrug. "Okay."

Edith gets in without further comment. She buckles up, pulling the strap tight.

I drive through town, cross the North Arthurville Bridge, and turn onto the old Peel Road.

"I thought it was the other way?"

"This takes you in from the other side. It's a big place. It used to be bigger a hundred years ago. It went all the way up to the Queensland border."

Edith looks unimpressed.

"So much red dirt."

"Lovely, isn't it?" I like her attitude. "So much flat red dirt to drive fast on."

We follow the river, winding through the low scrub, heading west. The bitumen changes to dirt about halfway. The extent of the drought is more evident here than further east, where the car was found. The scrub there is still green, the water is running, willows still arch over the banks, but out here even the willows are struggling, the scrub has thinned out, and long sections of the river are completely dry.

I pull up outside a closed gate.

"Edith?"

She looks around dubiously.

"Where are we?"

"This is the bit where the passenger gets out and opens the gate for the driver."

"They do?"

"*You* do."

She climbs out of the car slowly, reluctantly, heads towards the gate as if it were a snake.

I wind down my window. "Hey, Edie."

"What?"

"You need to shut the car door. I have to drive *through* the gate."

"Don't I get back in?"

"Not yet. You have to wait where you are and close the gate after I drive through."

She looks bewildered. "What do you mean? How do I get through once the gate is closed. Are you going to leave me here?"

"You go through while it's still open. Then you close it from the other side and get back in. It's really quite simple."

"Oh, right." She gives an embarrassed laugh. "I'm a city girl. Don't judge me."

This visit, we approach the house from behind. Although the vista isn't quite as impressive as the tree-lined drive, the timber fencing, gravelled road, the sheep grazing on relatively green paddocks, the half acre of bushland that encloses the property, hiding it from view, are from another world. The three dams we pass are almost completely full.

"It's like they just magicked the drought away."

I shake my head. They reckon the past is another country, but so is money.

From behind, the house is far less imposing, its architectural purity marred by timber extensions that have been tacked on at various periods over the last hundred or so years.

We walk around to the front door and haven't even made it up the steps to the verandah when Ruth opens the door. She looks even more dishevelled than she had this morning. Her hair is loose and unkempt; her white shirt has come untucked and is stained in places. Her lipstick has faded into a sickly bluish tone. Once she's recovered from her initial surprise, she seems almost pleased to see us.

"Josephine. I'm glad you've come. And your friend too. Why don't you come in? I was just making tea. Roland's on his way home. He shouldn't be long."

We follow her down that same gloomy hallway I remember so vividly from my childhood. It's still dim, and there's a certain grandeur about it, but now that I'm an adult, it's not quite as overwhelming. And this time I can see how badly in need of repair it is. The old embossed wallpaper is peeling; paintings have been removed and not replaced, leaving large pale patches, isolated nails. The dark mahogany dado is scratched and faded, and the top rail has come loose. The once brightly patterned Turkish hall runner has worn so badly down the middle that the underlay is showing through.

The kitchen itself is dingy, the nineteen eighties timber cabinets grimy, with doors missing, or hanging by a thread. The timber bench tops are scarred and in need of a sand. The sink is far from shiny, and the electric stovetop badly in need of replacing. There's an old wood-fired stove, blackened, but not in use, on one wall and a huge Victorian kauri pine dining table in the middle of the room. It looks big enough to seat a dozen or so—but there are only four chairs—all cheap plastic outdoor seats—the kind you could buy for five dollars at a hardware store. The spindle-backed chairs with the kookaburra carvings that I remember from my childhood visit have gone.

Ruth sees me looking. "You're wondering about those lovely old kookaburra chairs? Turns out they were collectors' items. We sold them a couple of years ago—they paid for most of the new roof."

She gestures for us to sit. She puts the kettle on, spoons instant coffee into mugs with a shaking hand, then comes back to the table and sits down across from me, clearly impatient to hear any news I might bring.

"So were you able to find out anything?"

"That's not why I'm here."

"What do you mean?"

"I want to know if Roly actually saw Mum that morning. And if he did, I want to know why."

She looks thoughtful. "Do you have any theories?"

"Not really . . . although . . ." Seeing the dilapidated nature of the once-grand house up close has given me the glimmering of an idea. "Could it have had something to do with Pembroke?"

"Pembroke? I don't see why."

"What else would Roly have been talking to my mother about? It must have been some sort of family business, surely?"

"But your mother hadn't had anything to do with Pembroke since she left."

"Then what? They weren't friends. It wouldn't have been a visit to welcome the new member of the family."

"I don't know." Ruth wrings her hands. They are hardworking hands, long fingered and elegant once, but gnarled and spotted now.

I sigh. "I think we really need to talk to Roly."

She looks worried. "I suppose you can just wait here. He shouldn't be long."

"I'm here now, Ma. No need to wait." Roland stands in the kitchen doorway.

He looks as if he's aged ten years since the last time I saw him. He's dressed in old grey tracksuit bottoms, his pyjamas, perhaps, an old T-shirt. The way his still-thick hair, unbrushed, falls across his forehead and over one eye reminds me suddenly, unexpectedly, of my mother.

Ruth pushes back her chair and stands up, hands fluttering, her voice suddenly anxious. "Do you want tea, darling? The pot's just boiled. And I can make you something to eat—there's still some of that bacon."

"Oh, for god's sake, don't start fussing." He sounds irritable. "I can do it myself."

Ruth looks stricken. "Of course."

He sighs. "I'm sorry, Mum." He puts his hand on her shoulder, speaks to her gently. "You sit back down. I'm just tired is all."

Roland makes himself a mug of instant coffee. "Is there something you can do to get these detectives off my back?" His voice is brusque again. "They seem to think I'm a suspect. This whole thing's ridiculous."

Edith snorts. "Actually, you've got it back to front, Mr. Beaufort. Jo's not here to help you. She's here to find out what *you* know."

He looks confused.

"But I don't know anything."

"You've been talking to the police for what, six hours now, about nothing?"

"Is there something you haven't told me, Roland? I assume the police don't take people in for questioning for no good reason." Ruth seems to have regained some of her usual assurance.

"It's nothing that concerns any of you. Just a private matter," Roland blusters.

"On the contrary, if it concerns the death of my daughter, Josephine's mother, I'm afraid it can't be a personal matter. What did they want, Roland? There's no point trying to obfuscate, dear. You know I'll find out eventually." She sounds as if she's talking to a recalcitrant teenager, not a man in his fifties. I half expect Roly to give an appropriately sulky rejoinder, so his abruptly honest response comes as a surprise.

"Okay. I did see Merry that morning. Just before she disappeared."

Ruth doesn't look shocked. "But you were in Calare. I remember it coming up before. It was all established at the time, wasn't it? A number of people saw you."

He answers his mother but addresses me. "People saw me there in the afternoon. I went into Arthurville early in the morning, spoke to Merry, then drove the back way so I'd make it in time. I took the old Stuart highway—it's rough, but it's almost an hour faster."

"What did you see her for?"

"I . . . I'd rather not say, to be honest."

His mother drew herself up.

"You don't have a choice, Roland. You will tell us everything. Now."

Merry

Arthurville, 1994

She'd found out about the money in the oddest way—a local legal firm that was looking for a new administrative assistant had placed an ad in the positions-vacant section of the classifieds. This was the second time they'd advertised the position, and the woman who placed the ad, the current admin assistant, was impatient. She had a baby due, but couldn't leave until she trained the new arrival.

"I was meant to get six weeks off before the baby," she huffed down the phone. "And I've only got five to go. We've had one response from someone who's never even worked in an office before. We really need to get someone, or I'll be giving birth behind a typewriter."

"Maybe you could double the money?" Merry suggested, and the woman had laughed. "Well, maybe if some of the lousy arseholes around here paid their bills. Why is it that the wealthiest clients are the slowest to pay? I guess that's why they're rich."

Merry sighed. "Yeah, well. They're probably never as rich as you imagine . . . it's all pretend money."

The woman sounded sceptical. "You reckon? We had one of our clients leave an estate worth almost a million dollars to one of the richest families hereabouts. Her costs were meant to be paid out of the inheritance—and the family is disputing the bill—quibbling about a couple of hours' work."

Merry was alert, immediately interested—maybe there was something here she could use in her column or pass along to the editor.

"Seriously? Which family?"

The woman paused, but only for a moment. Merry wasn't surprised—souls of discretion were few and far between in Arthurville.

"The old lady was Nancy Dawson. You probably don't know her—she was a bit of a recluse, apparently, a widow. She had a place out on Wattle Flat Road. Someone told me she hadn't left the property for more than fifty years. Had everything delivered. Apparently it's a disaster. She was a, you know, one of them hoarders. I heard that one room had a pile of sheep's skulls in the middle that went up to the ceiling."

In fact, Merry knew Nancy Dawson quite well, but she just gave a noncommittal grunt.

"It was a bit of a sad story. Nancy didn't have any kids of her own, so she left her money to her nephew and his family. The nephew was already dead, and her will stipulated that the estate go to his descendants, but the nephew's wife had the kids sign the money over to her."

"Nancy was a Beaufort, wasn't she, before she got married? So the nephew's wife—that would be Ruth Beaufort?"

"Oh. I didn't think anyone around here would know who I was talking about." The woman sounded nervous suddenly. "Um, this isn't public knowledge or anything."

"I don't know them at all, not really," she reassured the woman. "It's just working for the newspaper, you know everyone around here in a way—all the connections."

"Oh, right." She could hear the relief in her voice. "Well, don't you tell anyone I said anything, will you?"

Merry laughed. "Who would I tell? It's not like I can put it in the paper."

It wasn't like she could put it in the paper, but she could make a call.

It was her brother who answered. It was odd—she hadn't spoken to him for almost a decade, but nothing had changed. She'd seen him once or twice over the years. In fact, he'd driven straight past her once, just a few months before, down the main street. She'd seen him in profile, his long forehead, square jaw, eyes hidden behind dark glasses—he'd never given any indication that he'd seen her, and she hadn't waved. Now, the moment she heard that cold, incurious tone, she felt the same mild dislike she'd always felt. He'd never been the big brother who was in her corner—he was that other type of sibling: he resented her birth, wanted her gone, did everything he could to sow seeds of dissension between Merry and her mother—not, as it turned out, that he'd needed to do much in that regard.

She decided not to bother asking for her mother. Roland would know what was going on. She got straight to the point.

"I just heard that old Nancy Dawson died. Six months ago."

The silence was drawn out.

"Who is this?"

"You know who it is, Roland. Don't be a fool."

"Merry?"

"Who else?" She didn't wait for a response. "Tell me, Roland, what happened to Nancy's money?"

"What do you mean? She left it to Dad, and then it automatically went to Mum. It's not really any of your business."

"I don't think that can be right. Nancy wasn't Mum's aunt. She was a Beaufort. I know how people like that work. She would have left it to her direct descendants. Blood. And that's you and me, Roly."

"You got it wrong, sister. She left it to Mum. She wanted her to use it for Pembroke. She grew up there too."

"Oh, come on. She didn't care about Pembroke. When did she ever visit?"

"What would you know?" Roland's voice had flattened even further, a sure sign of rising anger. She could imagine him, determinedly expressionless, his jaw stiff, the pulse beating in his forehead. "It's not like you've had anything to do with this family for the last—what? Almost a decade."

"I'm well aware of that, dear brother. So would you be willing to show me a copy of the will?"

"Why would I want to do that?"

"No, I don't suppose you would. And you know what? You actually don't have to. I believe wills are public documents. I'm pretty sure I can get a copy myself. I know cousin Nancy's lawyers."

She could hear his breath, now, rapid and shallow.

"Jesus Christ, Merry." He sounded defeated. "What do you want?"

"What do you think I want, Rolsy?" She used her childhood nickname for her older brother, but not with any affection. "I want my share."

Jo

Arthurville, 2018

Roly spoke quietly; he looked down, focused on the interior of his coffee cup.

"Merry had phoned me a few weeks before she disappeared, insisting that we meet. She was angry. Demanding."

"Why would she be angry? She'd had nothing to do with you—with either of you—for years."

"She'd found out about . . . something that I'd done."

"And what had you done, Roland?" Ruth's face is pale.

He closes his eyes for a moment. "It was money. I'd . . . I'd taken money that belonged to Merry. And somehow she'd found out about it."

"Money that belonged to Merry? I don't know what you're talking about. She had no money."

"Oh God. Mum. That inheritance from Dad's cousin."

"Nancy Dawson? She left everything to Pembroke."

"No. She didn't."

"What do you mean? Of course she did."

"She didn't leave it to Pembroke. She left it to me and Merry."

Ruth looks bewildered. "I don't understand."

But I am beginning to.

"I signed Merry's share of the estate over to Pembroke. Both our shares. I didn't tell Merry about it. She was still listed as a director of one of our companies—it was just a legal thing; she'd been put on automatically when she turned eighteen, so it wasn't difficult. I forged her signature. No one asked any questions. Why would they? As far as the solicitors were concerned, it was completely aboveboard: Merry was just transferring the proceeds of the inheritance into her own company."

"And what, Mum found out somehow and confronted you?" I know how badly Mum had wanted extra money—a bigger house, a new car—all the things she thought would make her happy.

"Yeah. I still don't know how. She'd called me a few weeks before, and I'd agreed to meet with her that morning."

"And what happened?"

He gave a short laugh. "It didn't go well. She wanted her share—but there was no way I could give it to her. The money was gone. This place—it eats money. Even Nancy's money wasn't enough to get us back in the black. I gave her a few thousand to shut her up and told her there was no way I could ever give her full share back."

"How did she react?"

"How do you think? She was furious."

"What did you say?"

"I—well, at first I tried to come to an arrangement—I thought maybe I could give her small amounts. Pay her in instalments. A few hundred quid a month, maybe. There's no way I could pay the lot back."

"How much did you steal?" Edith likes to call a spade a spade.

Ruth answers for her son, her voice flat. "The combined inheritance was almost a million dollars."

"You'd've been paying her back for a long while."

"Yeah. Well, she wouldn't agree to that, anyway. She wanted larger sums. Ten thousand. Fifty."

"Or?"

"She made threats—she would tell the police, the media, Mum. Expose me. I said I would sort something out. Maybe talk to the bank."

Ruth looks incredulous. "There's no way the bank would've given you anything. We were still only hanging on by the skin of our teeth."

He shrugs. "I know. But I had to agree to something. Merry gave me a month to find a solution. I was going to come home and talk to you—tell you what I'd done. See if we could find a way out . . ."

"Did Mum tell you her plans for the day?"

"It really wasn't that sort of conversation." He gives a bitter little laugh. "I think from memory she told me to fuck off out of there, and I left."

"Oh my good God, Roland. How can you have not told me about this?" Ruth looks down, draws a shuddering breath. "All these years." She presses her hands down on the table to stop them shaking.

"So when Mum disappeared you didn't have to worry anymore, did you? You were off the hook."

He can't quite meet my eye.

"I was relieved. I can't deny it." He swallows. "I'm sorry. But that's the truth."

"I hope you told the police all this?" Ruth glares at her son.

"At first I stuck to my original story—but there was no point. A couple of other people had come forward at the time to say they'd seen my car outside Merry's that morning. And the police also got her phone records back then—her call to me was listed—we'd obviously been in contact. They knew all this, but they didn't bother to investigate further once Merry's letter arrived—it didn't matter that I'd lied once she'd been in contact. There was nothing to investigate." He shrugs. "And as far as I can see, whether or not I lied still doesn't matter, does it? It's not like I was the last person to see her."

"But that's up in the air, isn't it?" I point out. "They don't actually know when she died. And I guess the police figure that if you lied about one thing, you might be lying about others."

Roly's colour deepens; he opens his mouth to respond, but Ruth speaks first.

"Did you harm your sister, Roland?" Her voice trembles, with anger and something else.

He looks at his mother, aghast. "Of course not. How can you ask me that? You know that I wouldn't."

His mother looks at him for a long moment. "I don't know anything anymore." She looks suddenly weary, old, unhappy. "Not about you. Not about anyone."

I know just how she feels.

~

I spend the rest of the afternoon at the office, trying to catch up on the week's stories, but too distracted to get anything done. What I've just learned at my grandmother's has been revealing but not exactly shocking—the more I get to know my uncle, Roland, the less I'm inclined to trust him. He clearly had a motive, but do I really think he killed her? And what about my father? A part of me is certain that he wouldn't, couldn't, do anything to harm my mother. He loved her, of that I'm certain, but Kirsty has hinted that there was some sort of major revelation the night before Mum left. A secret. What is it that my father isn't telling me? It's time for me to find out.

By the time I get home it's late, and Dad is already snoozing. Alligator, who hasn't bothered to greet me at the door tonight, is lying beside him. He thumps his tail back and forth, though he doesn't open his eyes.

I shake Dad gently. He blinks up at me.

"What's up?"

"There's something I need to talk to you about. Actually, there are a few things."

He sits up, clicks the table lamp on. "Do I need a drink?"

I ignore him, launch straight in. "I was at Kirsty's the other night—when you went to the hospital. She told me something."

He makes a face. "She's always been good at that."

"Dad. She told me that you know why Mum left. That it had to do with that fight you had the night before. She said that Mum told you something. Something big. Is it true? Whatever it is, you need to tell me. You owe me that."

At first I think he's not going to respond—he sits there, his shoulders up around his ears, his face deliberately blank. He doesn't meet my eye.

"Dad?"

Eventually he sighs. "I'll tell you, but I don't want you to say anything. I don't want you to comment. I don't want your pity or your

227

commentary. Or your opinions. If you've got any ideas, just fucking keep them to yourself. Do you think you can manage that?"

I swallow. "Sure."

"Your mother and I had a blue. A bad one. We were always fighting— mostly we kept it quiet so you didn't hear. I don't even know how this fight started, but it ended up being about money. Or our lack of it. She wanted things. A bigger house. Decent clothes. Holidays.

"Anyway—we ended up in the same place we always did: our marriage was fucked; it was never going to get better. I had no ambition; all I wanted to do was hang out with my mates, get pissed, watch TV. I didn't even drive anymore. I didn't play sport. I didn't do anything. I was useless, lazy . . ." He pauses. Closes his eyes. "She wasn't wrong, mate—and I guess that's why it made me so angry. Nothing like guilt to make you wild. I always knew that she was more than me, that she deserved something, someone better . . . I was going nowhere, and Merry wanted—she'd always wanted—to go somewhere."

I resist the impulse to reassure him, say that it wasn't true—but it would only anger him. And maybe what he's saying is true, in a way. Not that my mother was better than him—those judgements have always offended me—but that he could have tried harder, been better. Aspired to more. I know from my childhood that there were elements of truth in what she'd said. And he knows that I know.

"I've thought since that things might have been different. Maybe if we'd left town, made our lives elsewhere, it would have been easier. Maybe that's what we should have done. Made a fresh start. But here—I was what I was—just a poor working-class yob, with no expectations. And no aspirations. She could see what she'd lost—every day of the week. She'd grown up in another world. She was a Beaufort of Pembroke—she was one of the private school mob, wearing their Akubras and their R.M. Williams and their big houses and gardens and driving their BMWs and having their tennis nights and trips overseas and boarding school for their kids. And now her reality was an ex–housing commission house on the wrong side of town, a couple of kids, a couple of friends, and me. No overseas trips were on the horizon—maybe a weekend in a caravan park on the coast if we managed to save.

"She was angry. All the time. And nothing I did helped. Nothing. If I stayed home, if I stayed out. If I tried to help with you girls, or if I left her alone. None of it made any difference. It just gave her something else to be angry about. In the end I just kept away as much as I could. And that was wrong too."

"But that night before she left—what happened? What did she tell you?"

Eventually he sighs. "I'd had a few drinks. We both had. Things were simmering. I usually held it together—but this night I went off my rocker—accused her of—well, I accused her of all sorts of shit. Shit that I knew wasn't true. Shit that I didn't really believe. And then it all went pear-shaped."

Merry

Arthurville, 1994

It had begun as a spat about whose turn it was to do the dishes. They were like children this way—both of them resentful of this constant dreary imposition, this incursion into their evening leisure time. And like teenagers, these arguments tended to escalate. There were no parents around to mediate, but the knowledge of their own children—perhaps not yet asleep, or worse, likely to be woken—within hearing distance usually kept them within the bounds of civility—both of them sulking, resentfully attacking the chore, not speaking, or exchanging whispered insults. But tonight the argument turned vicious, marching into the no-man's-land of who had it worse, lurching through the minefield of who owed whom what and then veering into even that most dangerous marital battlefield: sex.

"I just don't want it. I'm tired. I'm up half the night. If you get up and feed her, I'll fuck you. How's that for a deal?"

His laugh was short and scathing. "Oh, piss off, Merry. It wouldn't make any difference. And anyway, don't think I haven't noticed."

"Haven't noticed what?"

"You. Looking."

"What do you mean, you've seen me looking? Looking at what?"

"At men."

"Mick. When do I go anywhere to look at men? I have a six-month-old child. I don't go anywhere but work. And even if I did, the last thing I'd be looking at is another bloke. Jesus. One's bad enough." She'd meant it as a joke, but it wasn't remotely funny.

He stared at her coldly. "We shouldn't have done it, should we?"

"What? Had children? Married?"

"The whole thing."

"Probably not. Never too late to end it, though. I'm willing if you are. It couldn't be worse than this."

"Really?" Her cool matter-of-factness enraged him. "How would you survive?"

She shrugged. "I'd manage."

"I'd like to see it."

"What difference would it make? We might live together, but there's nothing. Nothing between us. There hasn't been . . . for years, has there? Come on, be honest. You don't like me. And I don't like you."

She'd said it. She waited for the response, for a further escalation, but it was as if he hadn't heard her, had started down another track.

"What about the girls?"

"The girls? It's not like you're the greatest father in the world. I mean, what do you actually do to make their lives better?"

She could see the injustice of this last comment, even as she said it. Knew how much it would sting. But she couldn't help pushing. Suddenly she wanted to see how far this could go—and bugger the consequences. She was afraid of where it might all end up, but perhaps even more afraid of continuing to live like this.

"I'm working twelve-hour shifts, six days a week, you ungrateful little bitch. For you. For the extra money you said you wanted. For an extension, a new house—for whatever it is that you think you need."

"But the kids don't see you, do they? Half the time Jo avoids you because you're so tired and shitty. And Amy barely knows you. It'd make no difference to her if she never saw you again. It's not as if there's any bio—" She stopped short.

Mick's eyes narrowed. "What? Not as if there's any what?"

"Nothing. I don't remember what I was going to say."

"Don't give me that crap. You never forget anything. What were you about to say?"

Her face closed up. "Nothing."

"It was about Amy. You said that it'd make no difference if she never saw me again. Why is that, Miranda?"

"I was just . . . it doesn't matter."

"I think it actually does matter. I think it might matter a lot. What were you going to tell me?"

"Nothing."

"I don't care what it is; just fucking tell me."

Now they had reached that place—exactly where she'd wanted to be just a moment ago. But now—now Merry wasn't sure what she wanted. Anything could happen. Everything.

She told him.

Jo

Arthurville, 2018

I'm reeling. "But who was he? Who was Amy's father?"

231

Dad shrugs. "I've no idea. She wouldn't say. He wasn't from here. He was a redhead—that's as much as I know. That's how *she* knew. She'd always told me there were gingers in her family—that Amy was a throwback. But that was complete BS, apparently. There's a shitload of redheaded blokes around town—and I've looked and I've wondered—but I actually believed her when she said he was a blow-in. There was never any gossip. Not a whisper. And believe me, after she left, I asked." He paused. "There's another thing. Your mother didn't tell me this—it's something I found out about later. Amy had a cleft chin—apparently that's almost always inherited from a parent. Neither of us knew that—luckily. And no one ever pointed it out."

"You don't think she was lying? Maybe she didn't want you to know who it was. Not if it was someone local. It would've caused trouble."

"I really don't. And it made sense. I assumed that was why she left the next day—that she'd gone to join him. And why she never came back. I guess I was half expecting it. It was just like Miranda to make a snap decision like that. She didn't stop and think about things—that wasn't her way." He gives a hard little laugh. "That's how we ended up married."

"But Dad, did she actually tell you she was going to leave? Did you tell the police that?"

"We both said a lot of things. I'm pretty sure I said I was going to leave too. I remember your mum went out in the car at some stage, but I don't remember her coming back. She was home the next morning, when I left for work. I didn't tell the cops what we fought about, but I told them that we'd fought. That we'd both said a lot of things . . . things I couldn't remember. I wished I could forget. I was devastated. Finding out about your sister—about Amy. That was a blow. A huge blow. As far as I was concerned, she was my daughter. I've never stopped missing her. I've never forgiven your mother for that. For taking Amy away from me." He looks gaunt, sad, and far older than his years.

"Anyway, when she left, I was sure she'd gone to find him—Amy's father—whoever he was. I thought that telling me had released her. But you know what, Jo, deep down I always expected that we'd hear from her. That she'd be back. For you, if for no other reason."

My eyes fill. I avoid making eye contact with Dad, bend down and scratch between Alligator's ears. Neither of us says anything for a bit, the silence broken only by the whump of the dog's tail, his occasional wheezy breath. Eventually Dad clears his throat. "You said there were a couple of things you wanted to ask."

"Oh." It takes me a moment to gather my thoughts. "It was just something Ruth mentioned. She says after Mum . . . left, she sent letters, offering help, but never got a reply. She told me to ask you about it." It hardly seems important anymore.

"Letters from Ruth? No way. The only letters that came back then woulda been bills, I reckon." He laughs. "Not that I'd've accepted her help anyway. I wouldn't have let that old bitch piss on me if I was on fire."

∼

I leave the office at lunchtime the following day and head to the library, request the *Chronicle* microfilm for 1993. I need to go back nine months before Amy was born. The librarian hands me the box with a wry grin. "The old copies must be better than the current version." His eyes widen as he realises his gaffe. "I mean. Oh blow." He gives up. Clamps his mouth shut and shakes his head. "Sorry."

"It's okay." I can't help laughing. "I know exactly what you mean. But my revenge will be featuring the library in the paper next week." I look around, fix on the latest-releases shelf. "I can see the headlines now: Library buys six new crime novels, and the latest Royal biography." I sigh. It really could be front-page news.

"Actually, there might be a real story." His smile is slightly self-conscious now. "I've just had a novel accepted for publication."

"Really? Sci-fi?" I'd seen his reading matter on the front desk.

"No." He looks even more self-conscious. "It's a Regency romance."

"Wow. That's definitely the sort of story the *Chronicle* needs. It'll be an exciting change from 'year four girl breaks school record in egg and spoon race.'"

I get his mobile number and take my box over to the microfilm machine. After the familiar clunk and whirr, I am deep in the past.

I feed in the film and fast-forward right to the end of the reel. Amy had been born in November '93, and as far as I know, she had arrived right on time—which means that my mother's fling must have been sometime in February. I'm not sure exactly what it is that I'm looking for—all I know is that Mum was working for the *Chronicle* at this time, and maybe, just maybe, the newspaper itself will hold some clue. Viewed from a distance, mid-1990s Arthurville seems far more vital, more energised, more self-consciously and self-confidently community focused than the town I'm living in now. Not only are there many of the same "community" stories that I have been engaged to write—the school fetes, sporting events, and exhibitions—but there are reports of local political scandals, visiting celebrities, politicians, reports of criminal activities, scandalous and banal, articles about the financing of new bridges, new roads, council elections, council meetings, minutes from committees, art exhibitions, amateur theatre productions, musicians playing at the local pubs. And of course there are the social pages—a double-page pullout every Friday, with the familiar Little Bird column down the side. The final four pages are crammed with accounts and images of the town's innumerable sporting activities. It shocks me to see just how many people I recognise, just in this speedy survey—all the people whose lives had once been a part of my own in small but important ways—classmates, teachers, friends' parents, netball coaches, a dance teacher, my doctor, the local vet, the man who ran the servo at the end of our street, the woman at the corner shop. I feel oddly guilty—how easily, how unthinkingly, I'd managed to untangle myself from this web of connections, of community, how I'd sloughed it off without a second thought. It had seemed, when I was eighteen, like something that was nothing but constricting, something that got in the way of the authentic me. All these people who thought they knew me, who seemed to have me summed up before I'd even worked myself out. But now I'm on the outside—it doesn't really seem that much better. I have grown up—learnt about the world, built a career of sorts, developed all the necessary life skills, travelled, had adventures—but coming back has shown me that in all the important ways I'm not really any closer to knowing who I am, or where I'm going. There are still too many unanswered questions.

I slow the machine down when I reach the critical time frame. I don't know what sort of evidence I'm expecting to find. Neither of my parents was the sort to make the social pages regularly. Neither of them played sports or socialised or worked jobs where they were likely to be photographed, but everyone who lives here long enough seems to get a turn at being featured in the *Chronicle* at some point, so it isn't impossible.

I go through the weeks in question carefully, and then go over them again, but there is nothing here that is remotely connected to either Mum or Dad: the biggest news during that time was a massive fire that had broken out in the nearby national park—no lives had been lost, happily, but the fire had taken weeks to put out properly, destroying three farmhouses and threatening an outlying village; two local boys had been contracted to play with Sydney rugby league teams, and the state minister for commerce had visited about some new decentralisation initiative—he'd given a talk to the chamber of commerce, opened a new canning factory that employed twenty locals, and a dinner had been held in his honour. I glance through the story idly. The politician—someone obscure whose name I don't recognise—was a city boy with no experience of the bush. He freely admitted that he'd rarely been west of the Great Dividing Range, and that he was finding the late summer heat difficult. "There's a reason," he'd joked in his speech to the chamber of commerce, "that I'm not the agriculture and lands minister. But if anyone wants to open an air-conditioner factory out here, I'm your man." There are photographs on the front page, and then more in the social pages. He looks surprisingly young for a minister—maybe only in his mid to late thirties—and reasonably good-looking. Even his terrible clothes—shorts with long socks, short-sleeved shirt and tie—can't disguise the decent physique. The photos in the social pages show him dinner suited and looking a little more distinguished, although his wiry hair—a little longer than it should be—looks hard to manage, and gives him a slightly raffish look. He has a rather American-looking face with defined cheekbones, a strong jaw. A cleft chin.

I check his name again: Peter "Ginger" Beggs. So called because of his wild auburn hair.

~

Jo

Namba, 2018

The former minister for commerce lives in Namba, a larger town, well-known for its wineries, northeast of Arthurville. The town itself seems like a rural idyll—well-ordered and prosperous, the main street clearly thriving, with boutiques and cafés, a bookshop, bars, galleries. The streets are buzzing with people—well dressed, busy—tourists as well as locals, I suppose. It's hard to imagine a starker contrast to Arthurville.

Despite the fact that he is no longer an MP, it had taken me only five minutes to find Mr. Beggs's current contact details (thank you, Facebook!), and then another five to send an email asking him for an interview. I'm thinking of doing a series of interviews, I wrote, of notable ex-politicians—a sort of "Where are they now?" theme. Mr. Beggs had come to my interest because of his relative youth, and his very brief tenure. He had written back almost immediately and agreed to meet me the following day.

I drive down early on the Saturday morning—a three-hour trip if I put my foot down—and intend to be back by late afternoon at the latest. I haven't told Dad where I'm going, or why—and don't intend to. I researched Mr. Beggs and his brief parliamentary career before I contacted him: there's nothing much of note, other than the decentralisation program that had occasioned his visit to Arthurville back in the nineties, but his biographical information gave me enough information to begin our conversation, anyway.

His house is in what's obviously the best part of town—a sizable modern concrete-and-glass construction on the crest of a hill, its main feature a long verandah with views of the ranges. He'd moved out here, he tells me, as he makes coffee for us both, after he lost his seat in the 1999 election. "I'd just got married," he says, "and we were having a baby. My wife grew up in Namba and her family were all still here—so it seemed the logical thing to do. I joined her father's law firm. Not the most exciting work in the world, I guess, but it's been a good living, and this was a great place to bring up kids. It was a bit more basic when we first arrived—nothing much for teenagers to do—but it's grown. We ended up with four—no one was more surprised than me. They're almost all grown up now." He looks briefly sad. "Before I moved here I'd hardly been west of Parramatta or north of the Harbour Bridge. Never really saw myself as a country type, but you couldn't drag me away now . . ."

He seems thoroughly comfortable in his persona—his complexion ruddy, his hair faded to grey but still thick and curly, comfortably casual in his shorts and T-shirt, his feet bare. The house is tastefully, if minimally, decorated; a discarded backpack and a low bass rumble evidence that at least one teenager must be around somewhere.

I follow him out onto the verandah and take out my phone. "I hope you don't mind if I record the conversation?"

He nods his assent. "My last interview was definitely premobile. The reporter probably had a big clunky tape recorder." He laughs. "You've probably never even seen one."

"We still had videos when I was a kid, so I have an idea."

"You're a bit older than my lot then. Hard to tell at my age."

"You're what—in your sixties?"

"That's right. Hoping to retire in the next few years. My wife's a bit younger—she's a GP. I'm looking forward to being a kept man." His smile is just this side of smug.

"So when you visited Arthurville in 1993 you'd have been, what, in your midthirties?"

"Arthurville?" He frowns. "I don't—ah, I remember now. I believe I did go there officially once—as part of a decentralisation initiative." He frowns. "But I'm not sure why that's of interest. As far as I recall, nothing of note happened."

"Nothing?"

"I visited some businesses, gave a speech." He frowns. "I don't know what it is you're— What paper did you say you're from?"

"I didn't say. I work for the *Arthurville Chronicle*, but this is research for a . . . private story."

"I still don't see what—"

"You didn't happen to meet a young woman, a young mother, during your visit to Arthurville? Small, blonde. Pretty. In her twenties. She worked for the *Chronicle* too."

He stares at me, eyes wide. Stands up. "You're here under false pretences."

"Did you have a one-night stand with that girl?"

"I think you should leave."

I don't move. "I'm not going anywhere, Mr. Beggs. I don't want anything from you except information. That blonde girl was my mother, Miranda Sharpe. She had a baby nine months after that visit, and the baby, Amy—who wasn't my father's—looked remarkably like you." I pull a picture of my beautiful young mother holding six-month-old Amy—wild haired, smiling gummily, clutching a scrappy fabric doll— out of my bag and slide it across the table. He sits back down, picks up the photo reluctantly, and looks at it for a long moment, then puts it back on the table, facedown.

He runs his fingers through his hair. Swallows. "I remember her. Merry. I didn't ever know her surname. I didn't even know she was married. I thought she was still Miranda Beaufort. We had some friends in common. I'd been to school with her brother—Roland, Roly Beaufort. It was nothing—a drink, a bit of fun. It was just one afternoon. One hot summer night."

Merry

Arthurville, 1993

It was one wild night. No more than that. One wild night of lies and subterfuge and drunken desperate pleasure that changed her life. One wild night of feeling young, of feeling desired, of feeling that life had not passed her by. It was fleeting; there were no strings attached on either side—that was the understanding between them, the bargain they made. No details were sought or given. It didn't matter, neither had any real interest in the other beyond the physical, the here and the now, and even that was transitory. They made no plans and no confidences were shared. When they spoke, it was all present tense.

She regretted it later, of course—oh, not the child; what mother regrets her own flesh and blood? But she regretted her weakness, the hurt she caused, the trail of destruction that this one night of abandon left in its wake.

The editor had asked her to pick up some papers from a state minister who was in town spruiking some new decentralisation plans. She'd called in at the motel, rapped on his door, had barely thought anything of it, her mind already on that week's column, as well as the six thousand things she needed to do this afternoon: dropping off these papers, editing her half-written column, sorting the washing that she'd left in the basket for three days running now, wondering what she could make for dinner tonight that wasn't sausages or spaghetti Bolognese. She barely knew this man's name, had no particular interest in the government of the day—or politics in general—just knew that he was a minister, so was likely to be old, pompous, patronising.

She hadn't expected him to be youngish—older than her, but young enough to be interesting. He wasn't conventionally good-looking—slight but wiry, pale freckled skin, curly auburn hair that looked impossible to manage—but there was something about him. Something that made him more than simply agreeable, something more powerful, electric. It was probably just a politician thing, she would realise later—he was the type of man who made you feel like you were the only person in the room—but at the time, she'd been charmed. He smiled, held out a hand—his sleeves were rolled up, his forearm was smooth and sinewy. "Peter Beggs. Or Ginger Beggs, as the media like to call me," he said. "Good to meet you." His handshake was firm, his voice confident, he looked her right in the eyes. He smelled vaguely of lemons and menthol, reminded her of her boarding school friends' fathers—city men who were quite distinct from the graziers she'd grown up with—powerful men in their own milieus. And different, too, from her husband and his friends, who smelled mainly of sweat and cheap deodorant. Beggs had waved her into the room, apologising. "You'll have to come in for a moment. I told your boss I had the papers ready, but I haven't even unpacked yet." There was nothing suggestive about the invitation, and she had entered the room without a second thought. A bulging briefcase lay open on the bed, surrounded by files. There was an open bottle of wine and a half-filled toothbrush glass on the paperwork-strewn desk. He noticed her glance at the bottle, the glass. "It's probably a little early. But it's been a long day." He ran his fingers through his hair, gave a wry smile. He seemed younger, more vulnerable. And somehow even more attractive.

"It's never too early." Merry kept her voice light.

He lifted up the bottle. "D'you want one?"

She shook her head. "I've got to pick my daughter up from school. Get dinner sorted."

"Seriously? You don't look old enough to have a kid."

It wasn't always meant as a compliment, that particular comment— more often than not it was laced with disapproval—but this time the flattery was clear, the look he gave her warmly appraising.

"Are you sure you don't want a drink? It might take me a bit to find those documents. I'm pretty sure one drink is compatible with parenting—in fact I'm pretty sure it's necessary for survival. I believe there should be another fancy hotel glass here somewhere."

Merry laughed. "Maybe just a small one." She didn't really like wine—had retained her teenage preference for spirits, although they could rarely afford anything but the most basic premix, but right now she didn't care; right now the desire to escape the mundanity of her existence for even five minutes was suddenly overwhelming. She wanted, for just a moment, to be seen as someone more than just a wife and mother. To be seen.

She accepted the glass, which he'd filled with a flourish and an offhand smile. "Take a seat." He pulled out the vinyl chair. She sat down gingerly, taking the proffered glass. "Good on you." He sat down on the edge of the bed. "I'll just finish this, and then I'll sort those documents for you."

He leaned back and loosened his tie, gave a little moan. "God, it's good to sit down. It was a bloody long trip—oh, it's pretty enough once you get out of Sydney, but it's just too far. And it's so bloody hot out here." He sipped his wine, made a face. "Ugh. This needs ice cubes. Sorry."

He looked up at the ceiling fan, whirring busily but doing little to cool the air. "I don't know how you cope without air-conditioning. How you get anything done in this heat."

"You get used to it." Her voice sounded prim, slightly disapproving. She took a quick sip of her wine, embarrassed, hoped he hadn't noticed.

"I guess so." He looked at her thoughtfully. "So you've lived here awhile, then?"

"I went to boarding school in Sydney for a while, but other than that, pretty much around here."

His eyes lit up. "Which school?"

"ALC."

"Ah. An Anglican Lady, eh? I'm an old Saint Paul's boy. I'm probably a bit older than you, but I'll bet we have a few connections. What's your name again?"

"It's Miranda, Merry. Merry . . . Beaufort." She was enjoying herself now—this was something she'd forgotten, a part of her old life she hadn't even known she'd enjoyed until now—knowing people, tracing the myriad connections, sometimes going back generations.

His eyes widened. "I knew a Beaufort at school. Roly."

"He's my brother."

"Oh, right. He was a few years behind me, but we were in the same boardinghouse." The man's lack of enthusiasm was apparent, but she couldn't stop herself from asking.

"And were you friends?"

He looked uncomfortable, his eyes not quite meeting hers. "Not . . . no, I wouldn't say we were friends, exactly."

She burst into laughter. "It's okay. I know my brother's reputation."

He grimaced. "Roly . . . isn't . . . wasn't the easiest person to get on with—not at school, anyway," he amended.

"It's okay, really. My brother isn't easy to get on with anywhere. He's a bit of a prick, really. A snob and a bully."

He laughed. "I take it you're not close, then?"

"Not at all. I've barely spoken to him since I left school."

He looked surprised. "But he lives nearby, surely. Your place—what's it called?"

"Pembroke."

"Yeah, that's it. It's somewhere around here, isn't it?"

"It's about sixty miles northwest. The Beauforts don't really come into town all that often—they'll sometimes go to Dalhunty if they're desperate. Otherwise Sydney—or Melbourne."

"Wow. Do you see your mother?"

"Not for years. She wasn't . . . happy about the baby. And I still haven't been forgiven." Merry didn't mention the fact that she was married. She saw his surreptitious glance at her hand, her bare fourth finger. Her ring had come off in the shower that morning, and she hadn't bothered to put it back on.

He shook his head. "Jesus. That's huge. A bit weird in this day and age."

"You don't know my mother. Once she makes a decision, she doesn't go back on it."

"It's brutal. Almost Victorian. Still, you seem to be doing okay on your own." The look he gave her was warm, admiring. She didn't correct him.

"Oh, yeah. I'm fine. Better off without them, if I'm honest."

"So you're what? A journalist?"

"Uh-huh." She didn't elaborate, or correct him. "Just part-time at the moment."

"You've got a lot on your plate, I imagine."

"A bit."

"So your kid? Girl or a boy?"

"A girl. Josephine. She's seven."

"Cute name."

"After Jo in *Little Women*."

"Not cute then. Another strong writing woman."

"You've read *Little Women*?" Merry was impressed.

"Years ago. Just don't cut off that beautiful hair of yours." He really had read it.

"I don't intend to. By the way, yours isn't too bad either. For a redhead."

He gave a rueful laugh, ran his fingers self-consciously through the messy curls. "It's the bane of my existence—but as some wit in the press gallery pointed out, at least I stand out amongst all the grey suits."

"I like it," she said, feeling unaccountably shy. "And your nickname. It's kinda cool."

The look he gave her was unreadable. "No one, but no one, has called me cool for a very long time."

He held up the wine bottle. "I don't want to be irresponsible—but I'm pretty sure you can have one more and still drive."

She held out her glass without hesitation. "I don't have to drive far, anyway." She wasn't ready to go just yet. The drink, the warmth of the room, his interest—it was all adding up to something. Truth was, she wasn't in any sort of a hurry—school pickup wasn't for another hour, and Jack could wait for his papers.

Right now, in this hotel room with a handsome appreciative stranger, she felt suddenly desirable, in a way that she hadn't since she was a teenager. She was still young, only twenty-four, but lately she'd felt herself transforming into some dull middle-aged version of herself.

She knew that what she was doing was wrong, but just for a little while she wanted to pretend that she still belonged to that world she'd turned her back on so blithely. That world that knew itself to be important, that understood the past, shaped the future; that world where conversation meant something more than sorting out dinner and arguing about whose turn it was to put out the garbage. Surely this was a world that would appreciate Merry—her cleverness, her insight, her beauty.

The politician filled both their glasses, and sat back down on the bed. He sighed and leaned back against the headboard, stretched.

"That seat's not the most comfortable, is it? Plenty of room here." He patted the space beside him.

She moved over to sit beside him, and didn't resist when he put an arm around her, pulled her closer.

Jo

Namba, 2018

Beggs turns the photograph face up again and stares at it for a long time. He gets up slowly, walks across to a table by the window, picks up a framed picture, brings it back and hands it to me. "That's my mother and me." The photograph, taken in the fifties, shows a smiling woman holding an infant—the image is black and white, the outfits dated—but the baby, clearly Beggs, is the image of my sister. That same round face, gummy smile, dimpled chin, that same shock of dark curls. It is hard to imagine that Amy could be anyone's but his.

He cleared his throat. "I didn't know that she was married, but Merry told me that she had a kid. You, I guess. I assumed she was using contraception."

"Looks like she wasn't."

"But what happened? She had the baby and raised it as her husband's— your father's?"

"Yes."

"Then how did you find out about me? Did she tell you?"

"Not exactly."

"Does your father know?"

"He knew some of it . . . that Amy wasn't his. I worked out the rest."

"I really don't know what it is you want from me. Does my—does your sister want to make contact? Is that it?"

"You really don't know?"

"I'm so sorry. I don't know anything. I haven't even thought about your mother since. What happened?"

I recite the facts baldly, without emotion. "My mother and sister drove away from our home in July 1994—when Amy was eight months old. It was a big deal for a few weeks. There was a search. Their photos were in all the papers. TV news. Everywhere."

"Surely you don't think it had anything to do with me?"

"I'm surprised you didn't hear about it."

"I am, too, to be honest. I'm someone who follows the news closely. Even more so back then. If I'd heard the story, I'd have known it was her, surely. There can't be that many Mirandas in Arthurville." He frowns. "Ah. Did you say July 1994? I would have been travelling. There was a trade commission in Asia for a couple of months that year—from July to mid-September. It was before the internet, so we didn't really get much Australian news at all.

"And then when I got back to Australia, I met my wife and I was distracted, to say the least." He seems genuinely shocked and disconcerted, but in no way guilty.

"So what happened—with the investigation? I'm guessing they . . . didn't find her?"

"The investigation ended up being called off after just a few weeks."

"Why?"

"There were letters."

"Letters?"

"There was a note she'd written to my father and me, saying she was sorry, and that she was going to fix things. We always assumed that meant by leaving. And then her mother received a letter from Mum saying she was safe and well. It was enough for the police."

"Did she say where she was going?"

"No. The second one was sent from Queensland, but they were both very vague."

"And there's been nothing since? You've never heard from her?"

"There has been a recent development." I take a breath and tell him about the car, the bodies.

He takes a moment to take it all in. "My God. I'm so sorry. It's . . . it's—it's just unimaginable. Your poor family. I heard about

246

the car being pulled from the river, the bodies . . . but there was no mention of any names."

"It's them. There's no doubt."

"So the police are thinking, what?" He frowns. "That your mother took off to Queensland, and then drove all the way back and . . . had an accident? Or suicide?" He shook his head. "None of it makes sense."

"Actually, the police believe my mother was murdered. That she was dead before she went into the water. There's a head injury."

"Murdered?" He looks bewildered, and then horrified. "And so what, you thought that I—"

"I don't know what I thought, to be honest. I only just found out about Amy—and then I worked out that you were her father. I put two and two together—and I thought—I hoped—that maybe she'd been in contact? That you knew something more—about where she'd been . . . anything."

He shakes his head. "I never heard from her again. It was a lovely—and rare—moment, and there was something between us—but it couldn't mean anything. I wasn't looking for anything permanent. Nor was she. I didn't expect to hear from her again. And I didn't." His smile is sad. "I understand how dreadful it must be, losing your mother and sister like that, but I really don't know that I can help. It's—it's shocking to think I had a child I never knew about. I'm a decent man—and a father. I hope I would have helped her had she ever asked." There is no doubting his sincerity. "I know I only knew your mother for a very short time, and not in any real way, but she seemed to me to be a very smart and lovely young woman. She was very . . . very resourceful. Very certain about herself and what she wanted. And perhaps in other circumstances . . ." He picks up the photo of Amy and Mum, stares at it for another long moment.

"Do you mind if I keep this?"

"Not at all. It's a copy."

"You know, that moment was brief, but it was special . . . and obviously far more magical than I'd known."

Merry

Arthurville, 1993

Her condition announced itself in the usual way—as a cascade of small physical changes, easily ignored or dismissed. There were so many things they could have indicated: mild nausea on waking, tiredness, aching breasts, an unusually long gap between periods, one month, two, more—until the extent of that gap finally dawned on her—and all the small things quickly became a certainty that barely needed the surreptitious visit to a doctor in Dalhunty, the follow-up phone call— congratulatory, because she was a married woman—that confirmed that she was indeed pregnant. Already three months. She knew right away that it was the politician's and not her husband's. The dates matched, and she hadn't had her usual arsenal, just a condom, no cap or spermicide, and there had been a moment—she had forgotten about it almost immediately, when a certain wetness had indicated the possibility of a prophylactic fail. She should have visited the doctor then, seen what, if anything, could be done—two pills taken together, a school friend had told her years ago, would do the trick. But she hadn't thought, hadn't worried. That had always been her major failing, this failure to see into the future, this ability to shrug off the consequences, to wait until it was too late to remedy. That was how she'd ended up pregnant and married in the first place. It was how she ended up pregnant to a man she'd known for only a few days.

It was how she ended up dead.

CHAPTER NINE

A LITTLE BIRD

Little Bird would like to congratulate the local constabulary for their immaculate timing when it comes to matters horticultural. Last Friday evening a senior employee of a state government department, having enjoyed a thirsty night at a local hostelry, decided to answer nature's call in one of Arthurville's finest private gardens. The owners of said garden were pleased to see the flashing blue lights pull up outside their front door, just as they were picking up the phone to make a complaint. The gentleman was caught with his pants down—literally—and a stunning bed of delphiniums have survived to bloom another day.

A Little Bird, *Arthurville Chronicle*, 1994

Jo

Arthurville, 2018

The police are on our doorstep before seven on Sunday morning. Dad is barely awake and is in his usual precoffee state—to say he is irritable would be an understatement—which doesn't augur well for the progress of the interview, or "conversation," as Detective Nakavisut puts it.

"Just a conversation, eh, mate? At seven in the morning? Are you taking the piss? Or is this something you do—coffee and a breakfast chat with random citizens?"

Alligator, sensing the tension, has come into the hallway. He takes up a menacing stance, growls low in his throat.

"You're welcome to call your solicitor if you like, Mr. Sharpe."

"Even if I had my own solicitor, Detective, I don't imagine he'd be up for a chat at this hour either. The billable hours would cost more than the café bill."

The detective shrugs. "It's really up to you. Now, if you wouldn't mind getting rid of the dog and letting us in. Unless you'd prefer that we speak to you out here, of course."

I take Alligator by the collar, push him into the lounge room, and shut the door. He gives a couple of confused barks, scratches on the door before I hear him flopping down with a resigned yap.

Dad moves away from the doorway, ushering them in with a grand gesture that's painfully at odds with his unbrushed hair and the ema-ciated limbs revealed by his pyjama shorts and blue singlet. The scene would be comical if I wasn't so worried.

I follow Dad and the two men into the kitchen. The two detectives acknowledge me silently, with nods, raised eyebrows. Classic detective cool. They sit at the table with their notebooks and devices, and wait expectantly for Dad to take a seat, but he doesn't. Instead he ignores them, makes himself busy at the kitchen counter, filling the jug and preparing his coffee, whistling between his teeth, insouciant, unruffled.

The two men look at each other, then at me. I try to emulate my father: raise an eyebrow. Shrug. I have to work hard to not say something conciliatory. Eventually the older man clears his throat. "Mr. Sharpe, if you wouldn't mind sitting down?"

Dad adds sugar to his cup, one slow teaspoon after another, and then takes a seat at the far end of the table. I glare at him, but he's looking into his coffee cup as he stirs.

Eventually he lifts his head and looks directly across at the two men, his face expressionless.

"Well?"

"Have you managed to do that research, sir—sort out that timeline for us?"

"There you go."

The two detectives watch, bewildered, as Dad pushes an invisible something across the table.

"What's that meant to be?"

"That's your fucking timeline." Dad snorts. "Talk about an exercise in futility, mate. I've got nothing."

It's true. He has nothing. Despite Dad's resistance, we'd spent a few hours the evening before trying to reconstruct his whereabouts in the months after Mum's disappearance. His resistance had, as it turned out, been vindicated.

Now he holds his hands up in a gesture of surrender. "I s'pose you'd better arrest me. I don't have an alibi—and there's no one, save Jo here, who can give me one."

It's true. As far as I can recall, Dad had been pissed every night in the months after Mum had disappeared—he'd spent most nights at the pub when I was staying elsewhere, at Nan's or a friend's—or home alone with me. Days, he'd either been at work or in a drunken stupor.

Sometimes both. There was no way—so many years later—of getting anyone else to confirm his whereabouts.

Detective Nakavisut takes off his glasses, sighs. "I'm getting some very strange vibes here, Mr. Sharpe. This isn't a joke. Your wife and your daughter were murdered. Some evil bastard smashed your wife's skull in, then strapped her back into her car and pushed both of them into the river—"

I interrupt. "This isn't helpful."

"I'm not trying to be helpful. I'm trying to find a killer. I'm sure you know the statistics." He looks at Dad when he speaks—his words harsh, blunt: "Almost forty percent of murdered women are killed by their husbands and intimate partners. It might be difficult to pin this on someone after more than twenty years, but you're my best bet."

The detective pushes the imaginary paper back across the table to Dad. "You might not want to remember where you were for the two months following your wife's death, but believe me, there'll be people in this town who'll remember things. There always are in places like this. Not much happens. I'm sure the lovely lady across the road will be able to help me. I've got State Rail looking into your work roster for the six months after she left." He pushes back his chair with a scrape, his offsider following suit. "Let's hope you didn't make any trips to Queensland during that time, eh?"

"Queensland." My father's laugh is scornful. "That woulda been some sort of miracle. A trip to the shithouse was more than I could manage most nights."

Merry

Arthurville, 1993

The first letter was pushed in under the office doorway late one afternoon. Merry had stayed back. She was having trouble with the week's column—there simply wasn't anything interesting to work with this week—at least nothing that she could legally use. She'd been reduced to detailing the exploits of two slightly tipsy middle-aged men who'd wound up in the police cells overnight after a drunken fall into a meticulously kept garden bed. It was feeble stuff—even with the line about them coming up smelling like roses. She'd been hopeful of a last-minute reprieve when the envelope slid—as if by magic—under the closed front door. She'd slit the envelope eagerly, and quickly skimmed the note. The note was written using letters cut from newspaper and magazine headlines. Such letters appeared occasionally, and she suspected that they were sent by the same writer—the letters were always smudged and never aligned; the spelling was terrible, the nature of the information consistently salacious. She wondered why the elaborate subterfuge was necessary—it seemed ridiculous—she supposed it gave their words an additional sense of drama and intrigue, or added some seriousness to an enterprise that was entirely grubby.

IS Trev MACL BANGING HiS STAF?

Look at LAsT tWo WEEKs SOCAiL GALArY

Despite the appalling spelling, it was easy to work out that the letter writer's current target was Trevor McLeod, Kirsty's husband, who had recently taken over as manager at Ambrose's Emporium. She was surprised. Trevor might not be Merry's cup of tea, but he had always seemed like a decent enough fellow—polite, respectful—if a little bit on the dull side. He was certainly not someone she could imagine cheating on his wife—and even less when that wife was as attractive as Kirsty. But then again, cheating on a spouse, as she knew from experience, wasn't only the prerogative of the obvious social and moral reprobates.

However diverting, it certainly wasn't usable material. She really should get the rosebush column finalised and get home in time to have dinner with Jo. But something about the letter intrigued her. The second line, which hinted at actual evidence, wasn't common—usually such letters contained unsubstantiated accusations, rumours, gossip. Trevor and Kirsty would definitely be classified as being among the town's social movers and shakers. As well as managing the town's only department store, Trevor was a keen Rotarian, and a member of the chamber of commerce. Kirsty was involved in numerous committees and boards. Both played competitive tennis, not brilliantly but well enough to get to the B-grade doubles finals. They had featured in the social pages over the years—photographed at community events, parties, eating out, accepting trophies or handing them out. But Merry couldn't recall having featured them in any of the social pages in the last few weeks—and as she compiled them, she would know.

She pulled out the last two Friday editions and turned to the centre pages. In the first issue, she could see no sign of Trevor in the snaps; there were images from the first night of the AAMS's—Arthurville Amateur Musical Society's—production of *West Side Story*, shots of the rather wild-looking actors, exhilarated after a standing-room-only performance, and of the audience members—locals and visitors who'd come especially to see friends or family perform—during the intermission in various degrees of awkwardness, dressed in their finery, clutching plastic glasses of cask chardonnay or cans of VB. Other than that there were a few shots of racegoers, and a few taken of the happy crowd during Sunday's footy match. Trevor didn't feature in any of them.

At first glance, last Friday's paper showed nothing either. The fundraising ball for the hospital was the main feature—shots of the town's mayor and a local MP and his wife, along with a couple of notable visitors, dominated. There was no mention of Trevor, or anything even vaguely relating to him or the Emporium, in any of the stories either.

Just as she was about to close the paper and give up, a background figure in one of the images caught her eye. Trevor. There he was, a fuzzy silhouette in the background of a photograph of the Lord Mayor and his wife at the fundraiser. The image was blurred, indistinct, easily missed—she'd never have seen him if she hadn't been deliberately on the lookout. He was standing close to a woman, perhaps talking, both of them standing side on, and he had one hand on her shoulder. Merry squinted, trying to make out the woman's features—her face was angled away from the camera, and most of her body obscured by the fore-grounded figures, but there was something familiar in her stance.

She took out the other paper and opened it up to the centre pages again, went through each of the photographs more carefully. She could find nothing in any of the AAMS photographs, and nothing at the races, but in the corner of a photograph of a ten-year-old Aden Porter, dressed in the Arthurville Dingos footy team colours and holding a hot dog triumphantly aloft, gap-toothed tomato-sauce-smeared grin—she found the couple again. They were much farther away from the sub-ject of the photograph in this image, out of focus, grainy—but it was definitely the same couple. Again, they were only recognisable, only visible, because she was looking for them. This time the relationship was unmistakable. Trevor's hand was at the woman's waist; her hand was on his chest, their faces were close together. They were standing in an otherwise deserted spot at the back of the stands, clearly not worried about being observed. Why would they worry? Without their inadvertent capture in the photograph, and the sharp-eyed informant, the clinch would have remained a secret.

The second photo confirmed the girl's identity. Merry didn't know her well, but recognised her just the same. It was Sheila Whittaker, who worked in the fabric section of the Emporium. She was a few years younger than Merry, so a good ten years younger than Trevor, and as unlikely a femme fatale as could be imagined. Her father, a Wiradjuri man, had brought her up on his own after her mother, a Sydney girl, shot through when Sheila was just a baby. Sheila was a natural beauty, with thickly lashed dark-blue eyes, long wavy hair, a sprinkling of freck-les across her nose. She was a remarkably talented seamstress, so gener-ous with her time that she spent every second weekend making wedding dresses—and rarely charging—for family and friends. She was a quiet girl, a bit of a homebody—not the sort of girl who was likely to be having affairs with anyone, let alone her married boss.

Merry snipped the pictures out carefully, and slotted them between the leaves of her notebook. The two images seemed to paint a pretty clear portrait of a tawdry situation, but images out of context weren't always 100 percent reliable as purveyors of truth. Maybe Trevor and Sheila were having an affair, or perhaps the pictures showed something else—an argument, a moment of weakness, a farewell. There was no sense in her jumping to conclusions. And anyway, what business was it of hers? Kirsty was a friend of sorts, but they weren't that close; their conversations, such as they were, were nothing more than superficial, gossip about mutual acquaintances, family, their children, work. Their marriages—their real lives—had never really been up for discussion.

Merry smoothed the clippings, closed the journal, and put it in her drawer.

She went back to the typewriter. She had a story to finish.

Jo

Arthurville, 2018

We stay in the kitchen after the men leave.

"Looks like I'm well fucked, then, eh?"

"It can't be that bad, Dad. There must be someone we can talk to. Someone who'll remember something. If the police can find someone, so can we."

"Like who?"

"You must've have had some . . . friends."

"Any friends I had back then woulda been barflies. Most of them are dead now anyway. And if they're alive—they're not likely to remember what they got up to themselves, let alone what I was doing."

"What about Kirsty?"

"Kirsty?"

"She was around a lot back then—and she seems to . . . well, she seems to remember a lot."

My father looks thoughtful. "Yeah, maybe. But she was your mother's friend, not mine. I didn't have that much to do with her."

"But she looked after me a fair bit," I prod. "She must've had some idea about what you were up to."

"Might be worth asking, I s'pose. But she'll only confirm what we know already—that I was drunk and useless."

I try to stay upbeat. "She has a good memory, Dad. I mean . . . she's told me things about Mum that no one else ever did. Maybe she'll recall some details of what you were doing back then. Or—you never know—maybe *she* kept a work diary."

Dad snorts. "It wouldn't surprise me. She's a bit of a control freak—organising everything and everyone. I always felt a bit sorry for Trev. He was a little . . . under the thumb, I guess you'd call it. And young Lachlan. I'm guessing that poor young wife of Lachlan's copped it too. It wouldn't be easy, being her daughter-in-law . . . Kirsty would've had her nose in every bit of her business."

"Did you ever meet her? Lachlan's wife?"

"I did. I met her at the doctor's once—must have been when they were expecting, but I'd be surprised if she remembered. Although, weird thing is—she actually called me a few days before she died. I missed the call. She left a message. By the time I got round to listening to it, she'd died."

"She called you? You never told me."

"Never told anyone."

"What do you think she wanted?" It seems so unlikely.

"No idea. At first I thought she was one of those salespeople—you know, from overseas. There was a lot of silence. And then she told me who she was and said something about finding some old letters—letters that she shouldn't have."

"That she—that Annie—shouldn't have?"

My father thought for a moment. "No—I'm pretty sure she said 'letters *she* shouldn't have.' But she never said who *she* was. Guess we'll never know now."

I think of all the letters—the letter I found, left by my mother, her farewell letter. The letter she sent her own mother. The letters that my grandmother says she sent us during that first year—letters we never received. And now these mysterious letters, mentioned by a dead woman.

There's something significant here—something not quite tangible, a half memory—like a word that you can't quite remember, that's on the tip of your tongue, a word that only reveals itself later, when you're least expecting it.

∼

Dad goes back to bed—just to rest his eyes, he says—but the interview has clearly exhausted him. At his request, I make him a sugary instant coffee, but when I take it in, he's already deep asleep. Alligator, who has taken up a position at the foot of the bed, opens one eye briefly, gives a contented huff.

I grab Mum's scrapbook and the exercise book, and head into the lounge room, crank the Breezair up full bore, and settle in Dad's chair, tipping it into full recline. I open both books and begin from the beginning. The entries in both books start around three months before my mother's departure (disappearance? death? It's hard to know how to think about it now), which must've been when she went back to work after her maternity leave. I go through the pages carefully, reading everything—all the letters received, all the notes Mum made—cross-referencing every item I can with her Little Bird columns, the social pages.

I still don't know what I'm looking for. Right now, all I have is a faint scratch of memory—I'm not even certain of the questions, let alone the answers.

Merry

Arthurville, 1994

She was driving home late after work on a Thursday evening—there was always too much to do the night before the paper went to print—having just picked up the girls from her mother-in-law. It had been a long day, and there were still so many things to do once she got home—there was washing in the machine from last night that needed to be hung out, a mess in the kitchen from the morning that needed cleaning, the usual bedtime routines to get through—but Doris had been eager to chat. Merry managed to contain her impatience for half an hour, but then made her excuses. She was doing it all on her own at home; Mick was doing long shifts, often travelling hours away, and was unlikely to be home until late. The old lady had suggested that they stay for dinner—she had enough sausages to feed them all, she said—but Merry knew that would make things worse. She'd have to help with the dishes, and then have an even more-tired and fractious baby to deal with when she got home—and still the same mess to clean up. At home she could pour a big glass of wine for herself and open a couple of tins for the kids—baked beans on toast was sounding good—and sit them in front of the television for a half hour of peace before bedtime.

She had taken the shortest route home, skirting the main road and keeping to the quieter parts of town. The streets were almost empty at this time of the evening—everyone safely home, eating dinner, watching television—so she couldn't help but notice the man walking ahead of her, just near the railway lines. It was Trevor McLeod. He had his head down, and was keeping close to the trees, but the headlights illuminated him briefly as he crossed the road ahead of her and turned the corner. It meant travelling in the opposite direction to home, but she followed him, curious, then watched as he ducked down the dunny lane that ran parallel to Brougham Street. She turned the corner again, this time into Brougham Street itself, and pulled up directly across the road from a little weatherboard house with a bull-nosed verandah.

"What are we doing?" Jo asked. "Why are we stopping?"

"Nothing. I just wanted to look at something."

"I'm hungry, Mummy. I want to go home."

Merry ignored her and peered intently out the window, craning her neck to see better.

"What are you looking at?" Jo, curious, got up on her knees to look out the back window, tried to follow her mother's gaze. "There's nothing there. Just a house. Mum?"

"Just shush for a moment, Jo." Now Amy began to whimper, sensing the tension. "Entertain your sister, will you? Here." She passed over the open pack of Jelly Babies she kept in the car for emergencies. "Give her one of these." The two girls quietened immediately.

Merry peered through the window at the house across the road. The cottage was small, but it was on a big block, heavily treed around the side perimeter, isolated from its neighbours. From where she was positioned, she could see right down to the back of the property, to the gate that backed onto the lane. She didn't have to wait more than a few moments before she saw exactly what she was expecting to see—Trevor McLeod, just a silhouette at this distance, and this light, but still recognisable, was coming in through the gate. A second figure, female, advanced down the driveway towards him. The two figures fused into one before disappearing into the shadows. "Poor Kirsty." She barely breathed the words, but of course big ears heard.

"What's wrong with Kirsty?" Jo leaned over the back seat, her face alight with curiosity.

Merry slapped her away. "None of your beeswax. Sit down and put your seat belt back on." The child huffed, but did as she was told.

Merry sat for a moment, thinking, then pulled out, switching the car lights back on only when she was well past the corner.

Jo

Arthurville, 2018

It's late afternoon when I finally put the books down. Dad has been awake for hours. He was surprised to see that I'd taken over his chair but, after some initial grumbling, which I ignored, has somehow managed to contain his curiosity and, no doubt, irritation, settling for the sofa, where he reads the newspaper, making the occasional comment as he completes the sudoku, unravels a crossword. Now he looks at me over his reading glasses.

"How's it going? Have you made a breakthrough?"

"Maybe," I say.

"Anything you want to share?"

"Not yet." It's all so indefinite, so unformed. There is still too much guesswork: vague suppositions, conclusions that seem dubious, accusations that are insubstantial, and anyway impossible to prove. All of it would work in a novel, but in real life they seem impossible, outrageous.

Still.

"Are you up for a drive?" I ask my father. "There's something I want to show you."

He puts down his paper. "May as well. Not like I'm rushed off my feet."

I ignore my father's grumbling about my too-cautious behaviour at stop signs, my rotten cornering, the Volvo's ineffectual air-con, and drive across town sedately, pulling up across the road from the Brougham Street cottage.

Dad looks at me. "So what's going on?"

"Something about this place has been bothering me every time I drive past. And now I've remembered why. I thought you might be able to tell me what it is I've remembered."

"Is it something about your mother?"

"It's very vague. And maybe it's not even anything important. Nothing that explains what happened. It's just that right now everything seems significant."

"What is it?"

"I can remember being in the car. Not the Mini—the old station wagon. Amy was there, so it can't have been that long before Mum—" I have trouble finishing the sentence. "I remember she pulled up over there, on the other side of the road. It must have been late afternoon, maybe dusk? The streetlamps were definitely on."

"She was probably picking you up from Nan's after work. She worked late on Thursdays."

"Mum just sat in the car, watching. I think she'd seen someone she knew. It was odd because she didn't call out or anything. But then she said something to herself—it was something about Kirsty. I remember that—because I asked her what had happened to Kirsty—and she got really angry with me. Maybe that's why I remember it. Does any of this ring a bell?"

Dad shakes his head. "Not a thing." He looks as perplexed as I feel.

"Do you know who lived here back then?"

He thinks for a moment. "You know, I think it was old Wally River's, Wally Whittaker's, place. He lived here with his daughter—before she shot through. Ah, what was her name?"

"Sheila. Sheila Whittaker."

"That's it. Sheila was a nice girl. Pretty, and a real clever dressmaker. Poor old fella never got over it."

"He told me you two had a few . . . sessions after Mum died."

Dad gives a short laugh. "What's the saying? Misery loves company."

I put the car into gear, but keep my foot on the clutch, look at the deserted cottage a little longer. What's that other saying—about the past being another country? And it's a country that won't give up its secrets. Not without a fight.

Merry

Arthurville, 1994

If she hadn't seen the old man that night, she would never have made the connection. It was just plain bad luck—double bad luck, really. The argument with Mick had been, well—it couldn't have been worse. She'd told him—for what reason she had no idea now—some misplaced sense of honour, some foolish idea that if she told him the truth, they could somehow sweep all the past wrongs, all her dirty lies, under the carpet, and start afresh. No, it was stupid. She had told him too much. To learn that your wife has had an affair—that was bad enough. But to be told that the infant daughter you love belongs to another man? Merry didn't know what she'd been thinking.

Now she was driving around and around the town. She'd made a dramatic exit, had said that she'd leave, that she'd stay in a motel for the night. She'd stuffed a few of her clothes into a bag, grabbed her typewriter, and stamped out. "Don't worry," she'd said, "I'll be home before you have to go to work." But the desire to stay elsewhere had evaporated, and she'd ended up driving around the streets aimlessly, waiting for time to pass, trying not to think. If she stayed out long enough, just another hour or so, Mick would have wiped himself out, and she wouldn't have to face him. She prayed that Amy wouldn't wake and need her. If she did, Mick would be worse than useless.

Perhaps the call to Roly that afternoon had precipitated things. The conversation had been short. He wanted to meet, he said, to discuss the matter.

"What's to discuss?" she'd asked. "You just need to get me the money."

"I don't want to talk about this over the phone."

They'd haggled over a time. He wanted to wait until next week—he was busy, he said, but she'd insisted on the following morning. Early.

He could come to her place—there was no point in her dragging Amy out. The timing would be perfect. Mick was heading out west for three days; he'd be leaving at the crack of dawn.

She had told Roly to bring whatever money he could. Maybe it wouldn't be much, but it would be something. She would be able to surprise Mick when he came back. Perhaps the promise of money, the chance to make their lives better, would provide some sort of a balm for what she'd done. She hadn't told him about the cadetship yet, had been waiting to work out how best to spin it into a positive, rather than another drain on their time, their resources—this would be her moment. The promise of extra money would make everything better. Mick could buy the new car he needed. They could renovate the kitchen, the bathroom. Or maybe buy a bigger house in a better part of town. Their lives would improve.

But then in the heat of the moment, in anger—half at him, half at herself—she'd ruined things. She'd confessed the truth to Mick, perhaps hoping that this would somehow scour the unspeakable grubbiness from her soul, and change the way she felt about herself, about what she'd done.

All she had done was to make things worse, immeasurably worse for Mick. And for Amy. And Jo. For all of them.

But there was still a way to fix things up; surely there was time. Tomorrow she would force them—her brother and her mother—into handing over her share of the money. Or if they wouldn't give her the whole lot—a portion, at least. Enough to keep her quiet, to stop her having them investigated for fraud or embezzlement or whatever the hell it was.

Merry had driven farther away from home than she'd meant to, was down near the river, where the street lighting ended, and the blocks were big. Many of the old places were derelict, long deserted. She'd ended up in a cul-de-sac of sorts, and as she'd turned the car, her headlights illuminated the figure of a man, half kneeling, half sprawling, in the gutter. She had driven past slowly, hoping against hope that the man had just bent over to pick something up, that once he gained his feet he would stand up and give her a cheery onward wave, but no such luck. He was still there when she reversed. She pulled over, left the lights on, the engine running, and looked around. There was no one else as far as she could see. The back of her neck tingled. She got out of the car reluctantly, and made her way over to the figure, who was still unmoving. Oh God, she had never seen a dead person—and didn't want to now. Right now she wished she were safe at home in bed. Asleep. Or at home and awake and pissed off because Amy had woken up. That she'd never started whatever it was that she'd started.

She put her hand on the man's shoulder—it was a man, of that she could be certain—and was pleased to find that he was warm, that he was moving and very clearly alive. She shook him gently. "Hey. Are you okay? Do you need a hand?" He muttered drunkenly, his eyes flickering open and then closing again. He smelt like Michael after a heavy night of grog and cigarettes, but nothing worse. It took her a moment to recognise him in the dark. It was Wal Whittaker. She'd known him half her life—he'd worked for her parents out at Pembroke, shearing and doing odd jobs, but their paths hadn't crossed since she'd moved to town. He was a good man, universally respected, and she was surprised to see him in such a state. She shook his shoulder. "Wal. You need to get up. You can't stay here. Are you all right, mate? I can give you a lift, if you want. Or do you need me to get an ambulance." She knew that he wouldn't want this, that the threat would be enough to put some sense into him, and it was.

He sat up, rubbed his head. "Nah. Don't wanna do that, love. I'm just pissed. Nothing major."

"What're you doing out here, Wal?"

"Waiting."

"Waiting? For what?"

"For Sheila."

"For Sheila? What do you mean?"

"My daughter, Sheila. You know Sheila, eh?"

"Of course I know Sheila. But I still don't understand."

"She's gone."

"Where's she gone?"

"That's the thing. I dunno. Nobody knows."

"Do you mean she's gone missing?" It was true that she hadn't noticed Sheila at the Emporium for a while, but there was no real reason she would.

Wal was sitting with his head in his hands now. "I been to the police, but they reckon she just took off from the shame of it."

"The shame of what."

"They reckon she stole money. From Ambrose's."

Merry felt her blood run cold.

"I don't understand."

"You didn't hear about it then? I reckon the whole town knew about it." His voice was bitter. "They sacked her, a few months back."

"But why would they do that? Sheila's amazing. She brings them customers."

"They say she'd been taking money."

"Who says?"

"Old Mr. Ambrose."

"That doesn't sound right."

"It's not. Sheila wouldn't do nothing like that. She'd never take anything from anyone."

"No, I don't think she would."

"They give her the sack, and the next day she was gone. She wouldn't do that to me. To her family. Not Sheila. She was, she *is*—she's a good girl."

Merry knelt down beside him, tried to pull him to his feet, gently. He staggered up, looked around him despairingly. "I come here most nights, bring my beer and talk to God. I think if I pray hard enough, he'll send her back. My beautiful Sheila. It doesn't make sense—that she'd leave."

"Perhaps she was ashamed? Even if she hadn't taken anything. It would be a terrible thing to bear."

He shook his head. "She weren't even that upset, at the end. She said it was going to be okay. That it was a mistake and that he'd sorted everything. That's what she said. And then the next morning, she was gone."

She knew, but asked the question anyway. "Who did she say had sorted everything?"

"That young bloke. McLeod. The son-in-law. Trevor. He come over that night, and they were talking outside for hours. And when she came back in, Sheila—well, Sheila looked as happy as I've ever seen her. She told me not to worry, that Trevor had fixed everything—that he was going to talk to the old man the next day, explain that there'd been some sort of mistake. He told her that she wasn't to worry. So why would she go? Why would she?"

"I don't know."

She couldn't explain it, but there was something there—something that was beginning to make some strange sort of sense.

She helped Wal over to the car. "I'll run you home now," she said. "You get some sleep, sober up. And tomorrow I'll see what I can find out."

Jo

Arthurville, 2018

I try the bell first, then, when there's no answer, bang at the door of the rectory. But the hallway stays dark; there's no one home. The exterior of the church—only ten metres or so away—by contrast, is remarkably well lit. I'd forgotten it was Sunday. Shep is no doubt hard at work tending his flock. I make my way reluctantly back down the path, and head across the lawn to the pretty sandstone building. I hold my breath as I push through the heavy doors, imagining the eyes of an entire congregation turning to look at me, but the pews are empty, the interior gloomy. There's some light coming from a space to the right of the altar, the sound of conversation, laughter. I walk quickly up the aisle, slightly spooked, and breathe a sigh of relief when I see Shep's familiar figure, recognise the laughter as Grug's. Then I remember—it's not Sunday school but the boys' fire training. Half a dozen teenagers and young adults, including a couple of girls, are seated on plastic chairs, notebooks in their laps, pens at the ready, while Shep stands in front of a small portable whiteboard, a marker in his bandaged hand.

"At this point the temperature inside the veh . . ." He looks up as his students register my presence. "Everything okay?"

Even as I reassure him, I'm oddly gratified by his worried expression. "Yeah, all good. Just some ideas I want to run by you."

"You doing some study, too, miss?" Grug looks pointedly at my mother's books, which I'm clutching under one arm.

"I guess I am."

I take a seat in the corner, slightly disconcerted to find myself eye to eye with a giant crucifix. I busy myself flicking through the pages of the scrapbook, but every now and then I look up and watch Shep surreptitiously. He's unsurprisingly good at this—he keeps his students interested and amused, is never patronising, takes even their lamest questions seriously. Every now and then he looks over and catches me watching, and I'm sure I'm not imagining a momentary pause, a light in his eyes, a slight flicker of self-consciousness as he proceeds.

When the class is over, Grug and the twins make a beeline for my quiet corner. "Hey, miss," says Ben, "our uncle told us that your dad did some dirt racing when he was a kid. He won some derby or something?"

"He did." I have to think about it for a moment. "He was the Outback Dirt Derby youth champion. He would've been about your age, maybe." I can remember a big silver trophy in pride of place in my grandparents' lounge room. I've no idea where it is now.

"D'ya reckon *he* would take us out driving?" Bill's question is tentative.

"He hasn't been well," I begin. But why not? Maybe it's exactly what my old man needs. "You know, I might talk to him about it. It's actually a great idea." Bill gives a shy smile.

Shep makes his way over. "All right, you lot. Bugger off home."

Grug gives me a look. "You two got some business, eh? You better watch out, miss, that he doesn't get all *handy*." The three boys laugh uproariously at the terrible joke, then beat a hasty retreat when Shep swats at them with his bandaged hand.

"They're definitely improving, but Lucy is right, they're not exactly angels." I can hear only affection in his voice. "Do you want to talk here, or shall we go back to the rectory? I'm busting for a beer. I mean, I'm assuming you're not here to talk to me about, ah, spiritual matters?"

"Definitely not. But are you sure it's okay? I don't want to start anything."

"Start anything?"

"Oh, you know—gossip. Get you in trouble with your congregation."

"Oh, for . . ." He rolls his eyes, doesn't finish the sentence. "I'd say if anything they're all desperate for me to give them something to gossip about. They've been hinting about me and Lucy since she arrived."

I raise my eyebrows. "And what, nothing to see?"

"Not a thing. Don't get me wrong. She's great—and incredibly beautiful and all that—but she's, ah, I guess she's just not my type. She's too . . ." He breaks off abruptly, turns. "Come on before I die of thirst." I'm suffused with a sudden feeling of warmth, of security, and I don't think it's all to do with my surroundings. The feeling is not exactly spiritual, but it's not entirely physical either.

We take our beers and settle at either end of the slightly lumpy, worn chintz sofa in the rectory sitting room. I take a long thirsty sip and get down to business.

I hand the two books to Shep, explain what they are, tell him what I've discovered.

He reads the notes, looks at the photos, asks a few pertinent questions. He understands what I'm getting at almost immediately, just as I knew he would.

"So you're thinking, what? That your mother might have confronted Trevor? That maybe he . . . ?" He leaves the question dangling.

"It's worth considering, isn't it?" I tell him what I've remembered about Mum parking in front of Uncle Wal's old house. "It's weird, you know—it's such a clear memory. I think Mum must have seen him there—seen Trevor. And then maybe she added it all up, later, after Sheila disappeared. And confronted him."

"But why would she confront Trevor? If she had suspicions, why not go to the police? Surely she'd assume, since Sheila had disappeared, that he might be dangerous."

I think back to the days when I spent time at Kirsty's—when Mum first left and then later, when I was going out with Lachlan. Trevor had been a good ten years older than my father, and he was from a different class—not posh exactly, but very proper, slightly distant, old-fashioned. I remember how disapproving he'd been when Lachlan and I were caught drinking his liqueurs, how disappointed he'd been in both of us. It had seemed laughable at the time—there were so many worse things that kids like us could be doing. And he'd been strict about other things, too, far stricter than Kirsty: Lachlan had to be home by midnight; he had to stand when visitors entered a room; when I was visiting, the door to Lachlan's bedroom had to be kept open. But though he wasn't openly affectionate like his wife, Trevor had always been kind to me. He was quietly spoken, gentle. The type of person who never swore, at least not when ladies were around. A square, in someone like my father's eyes. It was hard enough imagining him in the throes of passion, having an illicit affair, impossible to imagine him committing violence. And perhaps my mother had, stupidly as it turned out, viewed him in just the same way. Gentle, kind, harmless. She was, as Dad always says, never one to think things through.

I say all this to Shep, who looks worried.

"I dunno, Jo. I'm looking at this now, adding two and two and coming up with what really truly might be four, and there's no way *I* would confront him. Even if he did seem as meek as a lamb. I'd go straight to the cops, tell them everything I know. And I'm a bloke. Your mum wasn't silly—she wouldn't put herself in danger unnecessarily. It's not as though she was Trevor's particular friend."

Shep is right. Trevor wasn't my mother's friend. Kirsty was.

~

This time I have requested *Chronicle* microfilm for the three months after Mum left. I read carefully through every story about my mother—from her disappearance to the close of the investigation—and then move on to the social pages. I don't know exactly what it is that I'm looking for, but I feel certain that I'm going to find the answer here. I scroll through each Friday edition slowly, reading through all the Little Bird columns. Without my mother's input, the columns have definitely lost their spark. There are no more cheeky takes on town events or personalities; instead the column offers a rather straight account of the rather dull doings—weddings, parties, babies, holidays, resignations—of various locals and visitors.

Finally, in the issue from the third week after my mother's disappearance, I find something. It's not evidence, not exactly, but it's enough. I press print, the machine clicks and hums, and the past is in my hand.

Merry

Arthurville, 1994

She rings Kirsty early in the morning, after Michael has left, but before the girls are awake. Michael slept on the couch in the sunroom the night before, and had left without saying a word—not even coming into their bedroom to plant a goodbye kiss on Amy's forehead, or to briefly nuzzle into Merry's half-awake warmth.

Merry herself had sat up late into the night—there were so many things running through her head. Things she needed to do. First she sat down and drafted a letter to Michael—the first was pages long, with lengthy capitalised sections, underlinings, crossings out; the tone was emotional, a narrative full of incidents, anecdotes—the last eight years of her life summed up, but incoherently—she had tried and failed to explain all that had led up to her betrayal, how it was about her own feelings of failure, of discontent, that it had nothing to do with the man himself, with Mick—or with Amy. That she would never forgive herself; and that it shouldn't change anything between him and Amy—even if he could never trust Merry again. But on rereading the next morning, the letter shamed her—it was too pat, too queasily self-exculpatory. Too full of rationalisations, justifications. She didn't deserve that. Her husband didn't deserve that. Their circumstances may have been difficult—but Mick had maintained an integrity, a grace that she hadn't managed to achieve. She tore the letter into small pieces, started again. This time a short note—brief and with no extraneous details. And no excuses. She told him she was sorry—that she'd done the wrong thing— that she would work to make it better. For all of them. She didn't know how she would manage that—perhaps they would have to go their separate ways—but she was willing to accept that she had done wrong. That it was all on her. And she was sorry for that. She was sorry for all of them. She wrote the note, put it in an envelope, and pushed it into the dresser drawer. She would give it to Mick when he came home. If he came home.

Next she picked up the phone and dialled Kirsty's number. It was still early—not even seven—but she knew Kirsty would be up. She had bragged about being a light sleeper and an early riser, often enough. She had answered almost immediately, announcing herself in her characteristic brisk, businesslike way. "Kirsty McLeod."

Merry had taken a deep breath, then told her that she needed to talk to her, that she didn't want to do it over the phone, that they needed to meet.

"This all sounds a bit dire." Kirsty sounded surprised—and vaguely amused. "Are you having an affair or something? Do you need my advice?" She laughed. "Although I don't know why you would."

"No. It's nothing to do with me, actually. It's just—look, I really don't want to say more over the phone. Can we meet up today sometime? I've got the day off."

"It's that urgent? How about we meet for lunch? Tatts?"

"No. I don't want to . . ." She couldn't imagine discussing this anywhere public—anywhere either of them would be known, anywhere they could be overheard. "I'd rather go where we can't be heard, to be honest. And I've got Amy. Maybe somewhere outdoors."

"Well, I've got a busy day. We've got a ton of open houses tomorrow. Can we make it early? Say nine thirty?"

"I know," Merry says. "How about Sandy Bank? There's never anyone there at this time of year." It's perfect. The day's cold, but it's supposed to be sunny. She can pack a picnic lunch, and after she's said what she needs to say, she and Amy can spend the morning digging in the sand, playing in the shallows.

Jo

Arthurville, 2018

I make a timeline, fill Shep in, explain what I want to do. What I need to do.

Initially he's dubious. He wants us to take our own advice and go to the police with our suspicions. But I know this would be a mistake—the police will only think I'm trying to divert attention away from various members of my own family—who are, it must be said, currently the only suspects.

It's my mother who died, I tell him, and my father who will live under a cloud if things aren't cleared up. I need to give this my best shot. And I'm going to do it with or without him.

What choice does he have?

~

The column comes out that Friday. Barb doesn't mention it in her weekly email—which confirms my growing suspicion that her position as editor is in name only, and doesn't involve any actual reading, let alone editing. I've prefaced it with a little blurb:

> A Little Bird was a gossip column that ran in the *Arthurville Chronicle* from the 1950s to the late 1990s. The column, which accompanied the newspaper's social pages, was written and sourced anonymously, and featured amusing or scurrilous "gossip" about well-known Arthurville citizens, usually disguised for legal purposes, but often recognisable to readers. For the next few months, the *Chronicle* will feature snippets of the old column, taken from the archives, alongside the current social pages.

Kirsty phones me at the office just before ten thirty on Friday morning. I'm expecting her call.

I get to the river before her. When she arrives, I'm lying back under one of the willows, on the bank just up from the channel, listening to the woosh of the current and the warbling of the magpies, the gentle bellowing of the cows on the other side of the fence.

Kirsty seems surprised that I'm already here. Her smile is perfunctory, doesn't quite reach her eyes.

She is dressed casually—or casually for Kirsty. Shorts, a T-shirt, a pair of sneakers. Her hair is pulled up in a loose ponytail. Somehow she still manages to look glamorous. She's carrying a cane picnic basket that holds a bottle of Bollinger, plastic champagne flutes, a couple of glass food containers. There's a folded copy of today's paper pushed into the side. She sits down beside me, still clutching the basket.

"I'm so glad you could find the time for this. I know you'll have a proper funeral when all the official stuff is done, but I've been wanting to pay my respects ever since they found the car. And now that it sounds like it was . . . that Merry was . . . murdered," she says the word softly, takes a breath, "I felt like it was even more important that I *do* something. Something to acknowledge her. And then this morning, it was such a beautiful day, and I thought, today's the day, and why not ask Jo too." She speaks in a rush, her voice pitched a little higher than usual.

Up close, she smells strangely of woodsmoke, overlaid with something alcoholic. She looks at the dry riverbed, the sluggish water that seems to have gone down another few inches just in the last few days.

"The poor old river. It was so different when I was young. This drought—it's just so terrible. I feel like nothing's ever going to be the same. But I suppose even tragedies have their positive side—it's meant that you were able to get some sort of closure." She sighs. "I just wish, well, I just wish that I'd . . . been able to help her. Whatever was going on."

"I guess we all wish that."

"I suppose the police . . . I mean—is there any new evidence? Are there . . . suspects?" She asks the question hesitantly.

"Just Dad."

"Oh, Jo." Kirsty takes my hand and gives it a sympathetic squeeze, sighs. "But we're here to celebrate your mother's life, regardless. It's the least we can do."

She opens the champagne bottle, fills the glasses, hands me one.

"To Merry."

We clink glasses, and I take a sip. It's the real deal, dry and delicious.

"I've been out in the garden this morning. I know we're not meant to, but I've had the old incinerator going—getting rid of some rubbish—letters, papers. I'm afraid I've got way too much stuff that doesn't pass the Marie Kondo test." She laughs. "So it was a little ironic, really, to open the *Chronicle* this morning and find *your* little blast from the past."

"Oh, you saw my new, well, old really, column? I've been a bit behind on my copy, with everything that's going on. I thought people would enjoy it, and it's a good filler. It's been quite fun," I say, "going through all the old papers. I've discovered some interesting things. I hope you didn't mind being featured like that. I got excited when I saw your holiday mentioned. It felt . . . significant somehow."

"I'm not sure it was significant, but it was wonderful to be reminded." She stretches, relaxed now, her voice low, warm. "That holiday was such a long time ago. You know I'd almost forgotten about that trip. And the column is so quaint and old-fashioned." She unfolds the paper, opens it to the social pages and reads aloud in a prim BBC accent:

"The McLeod family—Trevor, Kirsty, and Lachlan—are heading to Queensland for a much-deserved winter's break. They will be staying with Trevor's parents, John and Sylvia, who have recently moved to Surfers Paradise from Lindfield, Sydney."

She sighs. "It was such an innocent time, looking back. Imagine thinking that some small-town nonentity's holiday plans were newsworthy."

"Maybe not so innocent," I say, my voice flat. "That column was written just a few weeks after Mum . . . went." I sip my champagne.

She looks taken aback. "I'm so sorry, Jo. I didn't mean to be so . . . insensitive. Memory's a funny thing. But thinking back—I know I spent a lot of that trip worrying about your mother."

"And, while you were away, Mum sent that letter to Ruth."

"That's right. Not that the two things are in any way connected, of course." She sounds slightly breathless.

"Are you sure?"

"What do you mean?"

"It just seems odd, a strange coincidence, that Mum would send a letter from the same city where you just happened to be holidaying."

"Oh, I see what you're getting at." Kirsty gives a tinkling laugh. "You think I might've met up with your mother there. That it was all some sort of a conspiracy."

"No. That's not what I think at all."

"Then what?"

"I don't think Mum ever went to Queensland, Kirsty. And I don't think she wrote that letter to her mother. In fact, I don't think she left Arthurville. I think the day she disappeared was the day she died."

Merry

Arthurville, 1994

Kirsty was already there waiting for her. Merry pulled into the make-shift parking area—which was really just a cleared patch of red dirt, in amongst the gums, and parked the Mini in the shadow of Kirsty's shiny new Mercedes. Amy had fallen asleep during the drive, and Merry was loath to wake her. She wound down all the windows, closed the door gently. Kirsty waved to her from a seat on a rock under the willows that arched out across the river, sipping from a takeaway cup. The river was shallow, flowed smoothly here, but narrowed to a fast-running channel just around the bend. It was a beautiful spot, good for swimming in summer—if she and Mick didn't kill one another, if she could find a way to repair things, they should come out here together with the girls. Spend more time together doing family things. There were so many ways she could make their life more pleasant. If it wasn't too late.

"What a morning, eh? Where's that beautiful baby girl?"

"She fell asleep on the way."

"Don't they always? Don't wake her up, whatever you do. My God, I'm glad I'm past all that business."

"I thought we might stay out here for a few hours, have a picnic. It's such a nice day. But if she stays sleeping, I might not worry."

"Absolutely. So what is it that you're so desperate to tell me, Merry? I have to say, I'm intrigued." Kirsty sounded so amused, so lighthearted, so unsuspecting—Merry was tempted to forget the whole thing. She had enough on her own plate, after all. But she thought of Wal, his loss and grief, and it was impossible. A girl was missing—it was far bigger than a betrayal, the end of a marriage. This might be life and death. There was no real way out. She took a deep breath, looked Kirsty in the eye, blurted it out.

"I think Trevor's been having an affair with Sheila Whittaker. I was sent a message about it, at the *Chronicle*—you know how people send gossip to us sometimes. There were photographs. This was months ago—and at first I didn't really think anything more about it—it seemed so trivial. But then I happened to see them together. Well, I saw Trevor going into Wal and Sheila's place one evening. He sort of snuck in, went down the side. I wondered whether I should tell you then, but I thought it was none of my business . . ."

For a moment Kirsty just looked at her, her expression blank, but then she laughed. "Oh, Merry. For such a smart girl, you're such an innocent. Trevor's been having affairs almost since the day we were married. And so have I. It's an open marriage, darling. We don't ask, and don't tell. Those were the terms. I'm shocked, though, that he would, er, poop in the nest so to speak. Work romances never work out well."

There was something bizarre about quiet, well-mannered, and frankly boring Trevor McLeod being some sort of small-town Lothario, but there was no time to worry about the dissonance—why would Kirsty lie? And to be honest, Merry could imagine the glamorous Kirsty living some sort of exciting secret life—perhaps the seemingly mild-mannered Trevor was the biggest secret of all.

"That's not the only thing. It's not the affair itself—it's not all that important."

"Oh dear. What else have you uncovered? I'd always thought you were above village gossip." The look she gave Merry verged on the disdainful.

"I wouldn't have said anything, only . . ."

"Only you did."

"I met Wal, Sheila's father, last night."

"That old drunk."

"He's actually a really decent man, Kirsty. I've known him since I was a kid." Kirsty's expression made her scepticism clear. "Anyway, he told me that Sheila's missing."

"Did he happen to tell you that she's gone missing with over a thousand dollars from my father's till?"

"He said it's completely out of character. That she had money saved. There was no reason for her to steal it. And she loved that job. Everyone knew that."

"Fathers don't always know their daughters, though, do they? She could have told him anything."

"He's worried sick, Kirsty. He hasn't heard from her for months. She isn't with any of her family. She's not with her friends. And the police aren't interested. They think she's just a runaway."

"Why wouldn't she be? It's the most likely answer, surely. Anyway, if every girl that ran away from home was investigated, we'd need to double the police numbers. She's just gone walkabout—probably from the shame. No one likes to be caught stealing." She paused for a moment, frowning. "Anyway, I don't know what that's got to do with Trevor. I mean, I'm shocked to think that someone like Sheila would attract him—and it's dreadful that she was caught stealing. But there's no connection, is there?"

"That's the thing. I'm not sure. Maybe there is. According to Wal, Trevor came over that night, after she'd been sacked. He said he was going to fix things up, that he would look after her."

"So what are you suggesting, Nancy Drew?"

"I don't know. That's why I wanted to talk to you about it, before . . . before I do anything."

"Before you do what?"

"I thought maybe I should go to the police. But . . . I thought—I wanted to warn you first," she said miserably.

"You think my husband, who was having an affair with Sheila, is somehow responsible for her going missing? You think, what—that he's done something to her?"

"I don't know. Perhaps she threatened to tell you, and he lost his temper? I don't know." Now Merry was uncertain; her ideas seemed incoherent, far-fetched. Maybe Sheila *had* been overcome with shame and fear, had run away.

"I see. Forearmed is forewarned, I guess. I suppose I should be grateful." Kirsty's voice was cold, her expression unreadable.

Suddenly Merry was conscious of a sound, a little distant but familiar. At first she thought it was a bird, or perhaps a lamb, calling for its mother, but of course it was the sound of her own abandoned lamb, Amy, waking up, hungry and alone, in the cold car.

"That's Amy. I'll just get her. Won't be a sec."

Kirsty looked at her watch. "I can't stay any longer, anyway. I need to get back to work."

"Oh, but we haven't . . . I still don't know . . ."

Kirsty raised her eyebrows. "I think I'll leave it to you and your conscience, Merry, what you do. I don't want to be involved in any of this. You can take it to the police. I can't stop you—but I'm telling you now, the police will dismiss it—it's nonsensical. Girls like Sheila are a dime a dozen. The fact that some silly old drunk can't believe his daughter would steal money and run away when she's caught doesn't make any of it true."

The two women were standing between the two cars, a little too close for comfort. Merry opened the rear passenger door and bent in to comfort Amy, whose wailing had become more insistent. She was smiling reassuringly at her daughter, stroking her sweaty little face, cooing words that only babies and mothers understand, when the flat river rock hit her hard from behind.

Jo

Arthurville, 2018

"Oh, darling." Kirsty looks at me sadly. "That doesn't make any sense. God knows what was going on with her, but she clearly left and came back. I saw that letter she sent to Ruth—what she wrote. It was Merry all over. It couldn't have been anyone else."

"When did you see the letter? Just out of interest?" I ask the question casually, and her reply is just as offhand.

"Why does it matter?"

"It might. You see, no one apart from Ruth, Dad, the cops, and the writing experts ever saw it. It was a private letter. It was never made public. And the thing is, Kirsty, you weren't even here. We've just established that you were visiting your in-laws when the letter arrived."

"Oh. You're right, of course." Her expression registers mild bemusement. "Perhaps I didn't see it after all. Memory, eh? I guess your father just told me about it."

I'd thought of that, checked with Dad. "He's sure he didn't tell anyone."

"I'm afraid that what Mick has forgotten about those first few months after your mother left is rather more than he remembers, Jo." She lifts up the champagne bottle, offers me another glass. I shake my head, but she ignores me, fills both our glasses. Takes a long sip from her own.

"You know how you wondered whether Mum kept a journal?"

"Uh-huh." Kirsty is taking the lids off the glass containers, seems to be hardly listening as she arranges cheese and crackers, grapes, plates, knives.

"Well, I found one." This gets her attention.

"Heavens. Really? And does it . . . Are there any clues about what might have happened to her?"

"It's not that sort of journal. It's a work journal."

"Oh." She wrinkles her nose. "Not all that exciting then?"

"You'd be surprised. It's full of information—stuff that she used in the Little Bird columns."

Her eyes widen. "So Merry *was* writing that. I always had my suspicions. The notes must be fascinating."

"There's some information in there that concerns you, actually."

"Oh?" Kirsty is poised to bite into a cheese-loaded cracker. "And I suppose it's to do with my husband and his penchant for younger women?"

Her lack of concern is disorienting. "Apparently, he'd had an affair with Sh—"

"Sheila Whittaker." Kirsty rolls her eyes. "Yes, I know. Along with numerous other young things."

"But Sheila disappeared."

"His other . . . *friends* didn't steal money from the till, did they?"

"But she's never come back, Kirsty. Never made contact. She came from a loving family. Where are the phone calls, the letters . . . ? It doesn't make sense."

"Life doesn't make sense, sweetie." Kirsty shrugs. "Anyway, I don't want to talk about Trevor. That's not why we're here. How about we toast your mother?" She fills her glass, raises it.

"Oh, come on, Kirsty. This is bullshit." Suddenly I'm tired of this game we're playing, and I want it to be over. I want the truth to be spoken, the consequences be damned. "I know that column scared you. You don't want to toast Mum's life. You've brought me out here to find out how much I know."

"How much you know about what, dear?"

"About what you did to Mum."

"Are you accusing me of murder, Josephine?" Kirsty sounds mildly amused.

"I know Mum found out about Trevor and Sheila's affair, but what else did she work out? Did you do something to Sheila? Did Mum confront you? Threaten you?"

"Oh, Jo." She's looking at me sadly. "I didn't realise this had all affected you so badly. I think you need to see someone. This is crazy talk."

"She had a fractured skull. You hit her on the back of her head, then strapped her back into the car and pushed her into the water."

I'm so full of my own righteous fury that I don't notice Kirsty swinging the heavy champagne bottle until it hits me hard on the side of my head. I keel forward, dazed, my ears ringing. Kirsty raises the bottle again, and I hunch over, try to prepare myself. But then time slows, stops, and my mind is strangely clear. I can hear the running of the river, the warble of magpies; the light is bright around me. I'm all instinct, reflex. Just as she comes in for another hit, I manage to get hold of her ponytail and yank it hard, pushing her face down into the plate of brie. She tries to wrench herself out of my grasp, but I grab her shoulders, roll my body on top of hers. I pull my arm back deliberately, smash my clenched fist into her lipstick-stained mouth. If it hurts my hand, I don't notice.

"That was for Mum," I whisper. "And this is for Amy."

"Jo. Stop." Shep has come up from behind us. He pulls me back and pinions me, just as I lift my arm. "That's enough."

I glare.

"Where were you? She tried to kill me. You were meant to be listening."

"I was trying, mate. The call cut out. We got here as fast as we could."

Grug and Wal are standing behind him, watching anxiously as Kirsty struggles upright. She is dazed from the blow, spitting blood, moaning. Grug moves quickly, puts a firm hand on her shoulder. "You better stay put, eh?"

Kirsty looks out across the river, speaks dreamily, her voice low.

"It's so beautiful out here, isn't it? Even now, with the water so low." She looks over at me, her eyes sad. "Such a peaceful resting place. You should have left them, Jo. It was safer."

"Safer?"

"I didn't have to think about it."

"Think about what?"

"About any of it. Trevor. That girl. You don't know what it was like, what it did to me. It's hard to explain how much I loved him. I never cared before, not with the others—it never meant anything. He still belonged to me. He was all I ever wanted. But with Sheila, it was different. He fell in love with her. It was real. He was going to leave me."

"What did you do to my girl? Where is she?"

She ignores Wal. "Sheila was so trusting. It was so simple to persuade her to meet that night. She got in the car, thinking it was Trevor. I brought her out here too. But then Merry—I was truly sorry about Merry. We were friends. But what else could I do? She was so close to the truth already. I couldn't let her get any closer." She sighs. "There was nothing else I could do, Jo. You have to see that. Nothing."

Jo

Arthurville, 2018

We all watch as Bill pulls up with the hand brake, spins almost 360 degrees, changes gear, and pulls out again neatly beneath a perfect halo of red dust.

I clap my hands. Shep whistles. Even my father looks impressed.

"Nice to be so young and fearless." He shakes his head admiringly. "Boys."

"What do you mean, 'boys'? Do you know who taught him that? Me. Your daughter."

"Did you now? You were pretty fearless yourself. One decent thing you inherited from your old man."

"And from Mum."

"She wasn't too bad, but she was never as good as she thought she was. She couldn't parallel park for quids. A typical farm girl." Dad sounds more fond than fierce.

"Your mother was never a typical anything," says Ruth, squeezing my shoulder gently. She has driven over to the racetrack with smoko—fresh scones, jam and cream, thermoses of hot coffee and tea. The two boys fall on the scones as if they haven't eaten for weeks, and we have to remind them to save some for Bill.

The funeral for Mum and Amy was held last week. Dad wasn't keen on a church service, but Ruth talked him round. "She was baptised at Saint John's, and if I'd been the mother I should have been, you'd have been married there too." Shep had officiated, and the service had been as beautiful as a funeral could be: short and simple and moving. I had read my own and Ruth's eulogy, and Lucy and Fran did the readings: Psalm 23 and a passage from what I'd discovered was Mum's favourite poem, Kenneth Slessor's "Five Bells." We all sang along to Leonard Cohen's "Hallelujah," led by Edith, who, it turns out, is a first-rate guitarist and has the voice of a two-pack-a-day angel.

I'd been surprised to see the two detectives in the church—they'd both made a very deliberate effort to shake Dad's hand after the service. It was even more surprising to see Peter Beggs standing at the back of the church. He was accompanied by a well-dressed grey-haired woman—his wife, Antonia. "Toni insisted that we come," he said, looking at his wife fondly. "And she's always right." Antonia took my hand, "Thank you for telling Peter about your sister," she said, her eyes glistening. "Even if there was never anything he could do, it's right that it's acknowledged." I wondered briefly whether I should introduce them to Dad, then thought better of it almost immediately. There were some things that were better left unsaid, undone. Lachlan had come, holding a squirming Jem on his lap, but had left the moment the service ended.

We held the wake at Tatts. It was a quiet affair, with only a handful of people, the pub providing sandwiches and drinks. Dad spent the afternoon sitting at the bar talking to Wal. It was a shock to find both of them drinking Diet Coke. Roly had driven Ruth home—she was too tired, too emotional, she said, to be sociable—and had returned and hovered glumly for a period, arguing half-heartedly with Edith about African politics, before joining Wal and Dad at the bar. From what I could hear, the conversation then revolved around football, sheep prices, and the latest odds on the chances of the drought breaking.

Once the olds had departed—Shep drove Dad and Wally home early in the afternoon—and my hostessing role was over, I spent the rest of the afternoon getting quietly blotto. The black dress I'd chosen to wear, the only vaguely funeral-appropriate item in my wardrobe, was made of what felt like recycled plastic bags, and I had to keep my arms down as much as I could (awkward when drinking beer) in order to hide rapidly spreading sweat stains. Lucy, of course, looked impeccable in a demurely sexy dove-grey frock, sleeveless, her itty-bitty silver cross nestled alluringly in her itty-bitty but perfect cleavage. It was a quiet gathering, even Edith and Fizz's endless banter somewhat subdued. Only Lucy seemed her usual learned self, correcting our grammar, making sure we had our facts right. When Edith asked her what next for her career, she gave us a fascinating, if slightly bitter, potted history of female ordi-nation in the Anglican Church, after which Fizz downed a big mouthful of beer, burped, and said that she kinda understood the resistance—maybe there are some things that blokes are better at. To be honest, Fizz said, she would prefer listening to a man blather on about God, but it was a moot point as she really never went to church anyway, apart from weddings, funerals, and the odd christening. Lucy was clearly shocked by Fizz's outburst. She blinked, her mouth went tight, and her itty-bitty nose seemed to twitch: she looked suddenly and rather disarmingly like a small white mouse. A small white mouse on the verge of tears. I grabbed her hand, four swiftly downed beers leaving me entirely unconcerned by my underarm stains, and told her that even though I wasn't all that keen on the whole religion thing, I couldn't wait to hear her sermons, and that she was definitely my favourite second cousin even though she made me look like a heifer and that if she and Shep truly loved one another, I would never stand in their way because that would probably mean I was defying God's will and would be struck dead or dumb or suffer whatever hideous fate was biblically appropriate. What the now extremely pink-complexioned Lucy replied was lost to history, because right at that moment Shep arrived back and made the executive decision to get me the hell out of there. I'm not the praying type, but on the drive home (which was painfully slow, as I insisted he avoid every bump and rise and corner) I sent a desperate request into the ether that Shep had miraculously *sensed* my impending crash and not actually *heard* what I'd said to Lucy. In retrospect I should also have prayed to make it to the bathroom before throwing up—but to rephrase one of my nan's favourite sayings: you throw up in your bed, you lie in it.

Bringing Dad out to the racetrack was Shep's idea. Since the funeral, Dad has been too quiet, too thoughtful, too agreeable—and it's been making me nervous. I'd bumped into Shep at the bottle-o the night before. He had half a dozen cartons of wine stacked in his trolley and was waiting in the long-for-a-Wednesday-afternoon queue. I felt like a teetotaller in comparison, with only a bottle of gin and a six-pack of Guinness to get me through the next few days. "Is that your Communion wine?" I regretted the question even before I finished asking.

Shep rolled his eyes. "It's champagne, Jo."

"Champagne? Isn't it meant to be red? The blood of Christ, all that."

"It's not for church, you nit. It's for a wedding—we . . . er . . . sometimes Lucy and I do a bit of catering. If it's just a small wedding." He looked a little embarrassed.

"Catering? Why?"

"We can both make a few extra bob that way. Lucy's an awesome cook."

Of course she is.

"And what do you do—serve the hors d'oeuvres?" I gave an embarrassingly juvenile giggle.

He glared. "Actually, I help with the cooking and serve the drinks. I pay the boys to do the waiting. They're not that bad." I tried to imagine Grug and Co. wearing aprons and carrying little trays around and failed miserably.

"Come on, mate. A man's gotta make a living." He changed the subject. "Anyway, how are things?"

I shrugged. "Everything's back to normal, really. I had an exciting day today—interviewed the federal communications minister about some grants that are coming up for community projects. It looks like the paper can apply for some additional funding next year. It'd be good to get enough to employ Edith properly, until she finishes her PhD, and maybe we'll be able to afford a cadet."

"Awesome. If you get the money, I might have some decent candidates for you. How's your old man?"

I explained Dad's uncharacteristically good behaviour. How unnerving I found it. "He seems to have turned into a different person. Easier. More thoughtful. I know it sounds stupid, but I'm not sure that I like it. It's like he's trying too hard . . ."

Shep looked thoughtful. "Maybe he needs something to distract him?"

"Like what? He's got nothing to do other than watch TV and listen to his playlists. He needs a hobby, doesn't he? I just wish he had some sort of interest."

"You're saying Mick Sharpe of Outback Dirt Derby fame has no interests?" Shep looked as if he'd just scored a conversion. "I think you may need to rethink that statement."

In the end Dad hadn't taken too much persuading, not in this bizarrely un-Dad-like acquiescent mode.

"You want me to teach these little shits to drive?"

"They're not little shits, Dad. They just need some—"

"They are little shits, actually," Shep said. I tried to interrupt, enraged by the slander, but he took no notice. "But if we can teach them to drive properly, show them how to get on in the world a bit better, they're less likely to grow into *big* shits, aren't they?" I couldn't help admiring his logic. "And if we want this town back to how it was thirty—even twenty—years ago, we're all going to have to put in some effort."

"You know I'm probably not even going to be here to see 'em grow up?"

"You're not dying, Dad. You just need something to do." Dad's tests had once again shown a marked improvement. At our last visit Fran had told him he would need to reconcile himself to living a fairly normal life span if he kept it up. His response had been typical. "So I guess I can cancel that coffin?"

Dad's face gave nothing away. "I'll think about it."

The morning out at the racecourse has been more successful than I'd anticipated. Despite his curmudgeonliness—or perhaps because of it—Dad is something of a hit with the boys. His dirt rally champion status trumps Shep's, whose tours of duty in Iraq and Afghanistan pale into insignificance. Shep takes the three boys through their paces, and Dad watches intently, talks to each of them about what they're doing, what's working, what they need to do better. He hasn't offered to get in a car with any of them yet, but I suspect it won't be long.

I sit down under a tree and watch, happy to be relieved of the responsibility, if I'm honest. And I can sense there'll be a good news story, perhaps multiple stories, down the track.

We manage to avoid talking about the events of the last few weeks until late in the afternoon. It's Grug who brings it up, ever so casually, between hungry mouthfuls of scone.

"So what's going to happen to that old bat who killed your mum and your sister?"

"She's been arrested. There'll be a trial in a few months." After her attack on me out at the river, Kirsty had backtracked from her confession, claiming that she knew nothing about my mother's murder, or Sheila's whereabouts. Despite her protestations, the police were able to charge her with attempted murder, and carry out a search of her house. There they'd found enough incriminating evidence—including my mother's typewriter, and a purse that Wal identified as having belonged to Sheila—to arrest her for murder. They'd also found the charred remains of letters Ruth sent to my father after Mum's death. How she got hold of them is a mystery that might never be solved, although Dad half suspects that he may have given her the key to our post office box along with our house key.

"D'you think she'll get put away?" Ben asks.

"I hope so. There's a lot of evidence, but you can never tell. Anything can happen in court."

"Depends on the cops. If they want to take her down, they'll find a way." Grug licks the cream off his lips, nods wisely. "A proper confession would be better, though, wouldn't it?"

"Of course. But there's not much likelihood of that."

"What if she tells them she went off her rocker and couldn't help it? Won't they send her to the loony bin instead of jail?"

"That's not quite how it works, mate," says Shep. "Let's just hope she gets . . . whatever help she needs."

I think of all the times Kirsty was there giving me the help I so desperately needed as a young girl, and shudder. I think of Lachlan, too, having to come to terms with what his mother has done. Perhaps little Jem will provide some much-needed distraction.

"Her poor son. First his wife and now his mother." It's as if Ruth has read my mind. "He'll have to leave town, won't he? You couldn't stay. Not after something like that."

Shep is watching me carefully. My father is watching Shep watching me. Ruth is watching all of us. I feel myself colour, stand up, and begin cleaning up the remnants of morning tea.

"You know what?" Grug muses, dipping his finger into the jam jar and licking it slowly. "I'll bet she's a serial killer. If she's killed three people, there's probably more. Isn't that how it works?" He looks at me. "Arthurville's first serial killer. I reckon that might be a good story for the *Chronicle*, if you're looking for one."

~

Dad takes it into his head to drive the boys back into town.

"May as well get started with these lessons. I can show 'em a few things while we're out here. Nothing like a badly maintained dirt road for learning how to get out of a scrape," he says, obviously directing the barb at Ruth, who just as obviously ignores him. He makes a few derogatory comments about my Volvo, and Shep takes the hint, offering him his truck, which, though still not ideal, is slightly more to his liking. "I might have to look into upgrading my own car," he says. "Yous'll need to experience something a bit better than these crapmobiles if you're going to learn to drive properly." The boys pile into the car with him, full of excitement at the prospect, despite the fact that they've been out here for hours.

"You go back to the rev's, and I'll pick you up from there." As my father's health improves, his bossiness increases. It occurs to me to argue that it would be just as sensible to drop off "the rev" and go home myself, but I stop myself. Sometimes it's easier to just agree.

There has been talk of storms coming from the east in the next few days, and as we head back to town in the late afternoon, there are cloudlike formations on the horizon. I drive sedately for a change, too tired and hot to make the effort. Even with the Volvo's air-con up full bore, the air feels thick, slightly sticky.

"Do you think it actually might happen?" I ask. Shep, who has barely spoken, is gazing out the passenger window.

"Huh?"

"Do you think it might actually rain? It's definitely humid. And there's a sort of tension in the atmosphere—electricity?—something anyway."

He laughs, but he doesn't seem amused. "Maybe. Although maybe the tension in the atmosphere isn't just the weather."

"Okay." I'm not sure where he's going here. I keep my eyes fixed on the road.

"I know you said it doesn't matter, but I really want to explain. Why I left. I started to tell you before, when I hurt my hand. It's been bothering me."

"But it's so long ago." I give a dismissive wave. "Water under the bridge." But I wonder, even as I say the words, whether I'm being completely honest with him. Or with myself. Sure, it was a long time ago—fifteen years—but isn't it something I avoid thinking about? Doesn't the memory still hurt a little? A lot? And maybe there's some truth to what he's saying—maybe there is some sort of an atmosphere between us, air that needs to be cleared.

He ignores me.

"That day I didn't turn up at the park. I'd got the offer of a job in Brisbane. And a lift up. It happened really quickly—I only had a few hours' notice. It was an opportunity. I'd been out of work for almost a year by then, so I had to take it."

"But why didn't you contact me?"

"My phone had busted, and by the time I got it sorted out a few days later, it was too late. You wouldn't respond."

I remember the texts I'd deleted without reading, the messages I didn't listen to, the calls I didn't pick up.

He looks at me, speaks softly. "The thing is, I didn't actually think you cared."

"You didn't think I cared? But we . . . I . . . How much more obvious could I make it? I'd slept with you. It was—it was a big deal. I thought it meant something."

He looks simultaneously surprised and guilty. Clears his throat.

"I'd been told that you were keen on Lachlan, that I was in the way."

"Lachlan? But that was later. After you went."

"He was pretty keen on you, though. Everyone knew that."

"I mean—maybe? I certainly didn't know anything about it. But who told you that?"

He clears his throat. "So that's the thing. It was Kirsty who told me that you and Lachie were—that there was something between you. That I should stop wasting my time."

"Kirsty told you that? When?"

"It was the night before I went. We'd been at that party out at the old Beckett place. The police turned up and turfed us all out, remember? Kirsty gave us a lift back into town."

"That's right. Lachie spewed in the car and passed out. She was pretty pissed off."

"She dropped you off first, and then we got talking. You know, I honestly thought she was being kind. Trying to stop me getting hurt."

"But why would you get hurt? I mean, we were just kids." I swerve to avoid a pothole.

"Maybe she just didn't approve? I got the sense that she thought you were way out of my league."

I laugh. "Out of your league? But we were barely respectable. Mum was long gone. Dad was a drunk. Everyone knew that. If anything, you were higher up the social scale."

"Depends what scale you're using, doesn't it? I didn't have much going for me at the time, remember, not even a job. I wasn't exactly the catch of the week."

"I thought you were." I deliberately drive over a rough patch to cover up the wistfulness that even I can hear.

293

"You know," I say, "maybe it's less sinister. Maybe Kirsty just wanted me to go out with Lachie. She told me that she and Mum had joked about us getting married when we were babies." Even with all we've discovered, it's hard to reconcile this new version of Kirsty with the Kirsty I'd grown up with, the Kirsty who'd been fond of me, helped me. Maybe loved me in her own way.

Shep's thoughts are, as always, in sync. "Maybe she felt bad about it later. It's just hard to compute. I mean, since I got back, she's done everything she can to help me get things going here. She set up all the connections with juvenile justice, sorted out funding, a hundred things. She wasn't even a member of the congregation." He sighs. "It would be easier, wouldn't it, if she was all bad?"

"Her matchmaking was a complete failure, anyway. To be honest, I think Kirsty was keener than either of us. I always got the feeling that Lachlan liked the idea of me way more than the reality."

Shep snorts. "Me, I like the reality—it's the idea that's a bit of a worry."

"What do you mean?"

"How am I going to explain to my congregation that I fancy a potty-mouthed, hard-driving heathen?"

The atmosphere outside the car has changed dramatically. Dark clouds are scudding across a rapidly darkening sky. There's a flash, then an answering boom, high in the heavens. Somehow, I manage to keep my hands steady on the wheel.

"It can't be any worse than having to explain to my hard-driving, foul-mouthed heathen father that I fancy a poncy Bible-thumping do-gooder."

I turn my head briefly, meet Shep's laughing eyes. A fat drop of water splats onto the windscreen. Then another. I roll the windows down, and welcome in the rain.

EPILOGUE

Kirsty

Arthurville, 2018

It was a pity, really. She'd liked the girl well enough, although she wouldn't necessarily have chosen her, had the decision been hers to make. But what mother gets to choose the wife of her son, the mother of her grandchildren? The grandchild—he was everything that was delightful. And without the inconvenience of a mother—hers to shape, to mould. And perhaps she would be given more of a say next time (because of course there would be a next time) over her son's choice— oh, not directly—he would resist any obvious matchmaking—what man would allow such a thing?—but she could push him, ever so subtly, in the right direction.

She needed someone malleable, or someone without a mother themselves, perhaps, someone who would accept her authority as the matriarch, whose loyalty wasn't divided. This had always been the problem with Annie. Her parents might be distant in a geographical sense, but their influence—so different to her own—could be felt in the way the girl did things. Her rejection of the offer of free childminding had hurt—what mother would do that to a devoted grandmother? Kirsty had made it clear—but in the gentlest way possible—that the girl's decision to give up working, to focus on the child for the first few years, was wrongheaded when they were so clearly in need of the extra income. The girl had been determined, too, to buy that outlandish property. Had persuaded Lachlan to sink too much money—and too much time—into the project. There was little chance of him getting ahead in his career at this crucial time in his life with such a drain on his time and his pocket.

Still—she could have coped with all this, found ways around the girl's decisions, undermining where necessary, learning to live with less-important differences—if it hadn't been for her stupid curiosity, her unexpected meddling.

They'd been getting ready to work on the new patio, had been moving things out of the old laundry, ready to demolish it, when Annie came across the letters. The girl—who had minimalist instincts that Kirsty admired even if she didn't share them—had told her to be ruthless, to throw away everything that didn't serve a purpose, and Kirsty was, on the whole, happy to comply—had already discarded several cartons full of unnecessary household paraphernalia: shoe-cleaning kits that hadn't been used since Trevor died, a box of jars, saved for jam making that had never happened, a stack of old Emporium stationery—envelopes, cards, notepaper—dating back to the nineteen seventies. The letters had been stored in an old shortbread tin—the type that great-aunts and grand-mothers always had on hand at Christmastime—which had been shoved in a corner of an old storage cabinet, crammed with forgotten bits and bobs. She had the tin open before Kirsty, who had gone inside to check on the baby, asleep in a cot set up in Lachlan's old bedroom, even knew that she'd found it. When she stepped back into the chaotic room, the girl held one of the envelopes—yellowing and dusty—up for her to see.

"This is a bit strange," she said.

"Oh? What is it?" Kirsty had known exactly what she was holding up, had known exactly why they were there, had inwardly cursed her own irrepressible collector's instincts.

"There's a bunch of envelopes here—maybe a dozen—all from nineteen ninety-four, all addressed to a Michael Sharpe." She turned the envelope over, frowned. "And they're all from the same person—Mrs. Ruth Beaufort. Pembroke. That's that big property off the Dalhunty Road, isn't it? That Edwardian mansion. I've always wanted to have a look at that. The gardens are meant to be amazing."

"Oh? How very odd. I wonder why they're here." Kirsty managed to keep her voice light, her expression bland. She held out her hand. "Show me."

But the girl was taking the paper from the envelope; she scanned it, then read aloud.

> *Dear Michael,*
>
> *I'm writing once again to request that you get in contact. As I have stated in previous letters, I would very much like to establish some sort of relationship with my granddaughter, and additionally to help you with both finances and family responsibilities, since the departure of my daughter has put you in what I know must be a very difficult position. I feel this would be in Josephine's best interests. However, if there is no response to this letter, I will assume that your answer is in the negative and will discontinue my attempts to communicate with you. I have attached my phone and fax numbers if you would prefer to call.*
>
> *Whatever your decision, I wish you all the best.*
> *Ruth Beaufort*

"Oh my goodness. That's so sad." The girl's eyes had filled with tears. She swiped them away. Gave a shaky laugh. "Oh dear, these bloody hormones. Still, I wonder what they're doing here? We should give them back."

She put the letter back in the tin, pushed the lid down.

Kirsty cleared her throat. "I have no idea . . . maybe something to do with Jo? She was a friend of Lachie's—she was around all the time when they were young."

The girl's eyes widened. "Oh, Jo Sharpe—she was Lachie's high school girlfriend, wasn't she? I wonder why she hid them here?"

"Oh, teenagers. Who knows why they do anything."

But the girl wasn't listening. "Actually, I'm pretty sure I met her dad once. He's Mick, right? We were at the doctor's when I was pregnant. Lachie introduced him. He seemed like a bit of a character. Lachie told me the story about his wife up and leaving them, taking the baby. So sad. I wonder why he didn't reply to the grandmother? It sounds like she genuinely wanted to help."

"Michael would have had his reasons, no doubt." Kirsty kept her voice light. "Anyway, it's all ancient history now, isn't it?"

"It is. I suppose." She chewed on the bottom of her lip, her mind clearly whirring. "We really should get in contact—tell him we've got them—see if he wants them back."

"Oh, I don't think that's necessary. Why reopen old wounds?" She held out her hand again. "I'll put them in the rubbish pile."

But the girl wouldn't relinquish them. "Oh, goodness no. That wouldn't be ethical. It's someone else's property." Her face cleared. "You know what, I might give him a call—see if he wants me to drop them over."

"There's no need for you to do that. I know Michael—I'll let him know."

But the girl was stupidly stubborn. "No, I'd like to. Maybe I can wrangle a visit out to Pembroke too."

There was no way for Kirsty to insist without making things worse. She shrugged, smiled, murmured something vaguely acquiescent. Watched as the girl stood up and took the tin, clutched to her chest like treasure, inside.

Later, as Kirsty counted out the benzos she kept on hand for insomnia, she thought about the conversation she would have with her son about his poor dead wife's difficulties adjusting to motherhood, the insidious and sometimes secret nature of postnatal depression. She thought, although not unkindly, of her husband, Trevor, and wondered at the damage he'd wrought—three young women gone, a baby too; families shattered, generations scarred—because he was weak and deceitful. If only he'd kept his dick in his pants. It was typical, she thought—even Adam, cowering in the garden, let his wife take responsibility for his foolishness. All through history, it was up to women like Kirsty, like Eve, to tidy up, set things straight. To ensure the next generation's survival.

And later still, after the funeral, she wondered whether there was a way to get Jo Sharpe to move back to Arthurville. She'd heard that her father was sick; surely, he needed her. Perhaps all she needed was a nudge, a push in the right direction. Maybe a job—an offer she couldn't refuse. She had always been fond of Jo. She'd make a good wife, a lovely mother, a perfect daughter-in-law.

ACKNOWLEDGEMENTS

As always, huge thanks are owed to the people who helped make *A Little Bird*'s flight into the world possible:

To my agent Alexis Hurley, for getting this fledgling off the ground; my publisher Alicia Clancy for keeping it in the air; and to the team at Lake Union—Danielle Marshall, Melody Kellis, Gabe Dumpit, Emma Reh, James Gallagher, Elizabeth Asborno, and Kellie Osborne—for ensuring a safe landing. To Wiradjuri elder Rod Towney, for his generous advice and support. To my earliest readers, Rebecca James and Shari Kocher, who asked all the right questions, and my daughter, Nell Shepherd, who answered a few.

And last, but not least, to my readers, who make writing meaningful—and remind me that it's fun!

AUTHOR'S NOTE

Arthurville is an imaginary town in central NSW, located somewhere west of Orange and east of Dubbo, and though it bears some slight similarity to the wonderful town of Wellington (where I was lucky enough to spend my formative years—and where much of my family still lives), no character in this book is based on any real person, living or dead.

ABOUT THE AUTHOR

Photo © 2013 EMG Photography

Wendy James is Australia's queen of the domestic thriller. She is the author of nine novels, including *An Accusation*, *The Golden Child*— short-listed for the 2017 Ned Kelly Award—and the bestselling *The Mistake*. Her debut novel, *Out of the Silence*, won the 2006 Ned Kelly Award for first crime novel and was short-listed for the Nita May Dobbie Award for women's writing. Wendy has a PhD from the University of New England, and she works as an editor, teacher, and researcher. She writes some of the sharpest, most topical domestic noir in the country.